Lassoed Love

ELLE MARIAH

Cover Design: Coffin Print Designs

Editing: Indie Proofreading

Formatting: Indie Proofreading

Author's Note

As you embark on the journey through Lassoed Love, I want to offer a gentle reminder and a word of caution. This novel delves into the deep emotional landscapes of anxiety, alcoholism, and the profound impact of Alzheimer's Disease. These themes are portrayed in a realistic and sometimes raw manner, aiming to reflect the complexities faced by those experiencing these challenges and their loved ones. Grief and loss are also central to the story, portraying the pain of losing a loved one and the lingering effects it can have on those left behind.

Remember, that it is okay to pause, to breathe, and to seek support if needed.

Each heart carries its burdens differently, and there is no shame in reaching out for a guiding hand amidst the storm.

If the weight of these words becomes too heavy, know that help is always within reach. I hope you find solace, understanding, and perhaps a bit of healing within these pages.

Thank you for joining me on this emotional journey.

***This book contains mature themes, and is not suitable for**

readers under the age of eighteen years old.*

To those who found the courage to chase their heart's desires,
by overcoming life's challenges; the fighters who rise above pain and
grief,
turning adversity into strength and resilience.
And to the girls who loved to watch 'Farmer Wants a Wife'
and dreamed of living out that fantasy.
This one's for you.

Playlist

THEME SONG:
CHEMICALS - MATT HANSEN

Something In The Orange - Zach Bryan
Burn, Burn, Burn - Zach Bryan
Fences - Melanie Dyer
Cover Me Up - Morgan Wallen
Breakaway - Kelly Clarkson
Everybody Needs Someone - Noah Cyrus, Vance Joy
1, 2, Many - Luke Combs
Hurricane - I Prevail

Hunger - Ross Copperman

Like A Stone - Audioslave

Take Me Back To Eden - Sleep Token

Before He Cheats - Carrie Underwood

Iris - The Goo Goo Dolls

5 Foot 9 - Tyler Hubbard

Work Song - Hozier

You're On Your Own, Kid - Taylor Swift

Just Can't Get Enough - Black Eyed Peas

Decode - Paramore

Breath - Taylor Swift, Colbie Caillat

For The Love Of A Daughter - Demi Lovato

Hanging By A Moment - Lifehouse

Conversations In The Dark - John Legend

Father - Demi Lovato

My Love Won't Let You Down - Little Mix

I Get To Love You - Ruelle

Rock and A Hard Place - Bailey Zimmerman

Tennessee Whiskey (Acoustic) - Amber Leigh Irish, Kevin Simm

Follow You - Bring Me The Horizon

Give You Love - Jessica Mauboy, Jason Derulo

Lasso - Carter Faith

Your Bones (Acoustic) - Chelsea Cutler

Blown Away - Carrie Underwood

I Wouldn't Mind - He Is We

Footprints in the Sand   Leona Lewis

How Do I Say Goodbye - Dean Lewis

In The Stars - Benson Boone

When It Rains It Pours - Luke Combs

Naked - James Arthur

I Don't Wanna Go To Heaven - Nate Smith

Spin You Around - Morgan Wallen

Us - James Bay, Alicia Keys

Prologue

Isla

12 YEARS AGO

High school is a peculiar blend of chaos and routine, full of surprises and kangaroo-sized dramas.

I sling my backpack over one shoulder, trying to navigate the crowded hallways of Springbrook Creek High School. The fluorescent lights overhead flicker, casting a harsh glow on the sea of students.

At fifteen, high school is proving to be a maze of challenges, but none more daunting than the daily trek through these hallways. A ripple of whispers and laughter sweeps through the hallway. I glance up to look ahead of me as I continue to walk and involuntarily lock eyes with him—Xavier Mitchell. The guy every girl dreams about, the star of the touch football team, and the unattainable senior. Tall, athletic, and perpetually surrounded by an aura of popularity, he walks as if he owns the joint. His entourage included Trent Oldman, whose 'charming' smile was the envy of every Year 12 girl, Jake Samuels, Brody Hunt and Kieran—whose last name I don't care enough to know—who is known to have a penchant for teasing and usually the instigator.

I can feel the heat rising to my cheeks as they approach, but I keep my gaze straight ahead. Maybe if I ignore them, they'll disappear. Lies.

"Oi, Isla!" Kieran's voice echoes down the corridor. My heart sinks, somehow just knowing what is coming next.

"Are you auditioning for the role of the school nun with that skirt?" he jeers, the words dripping with sarcasm. The other two join in, their laughter echoing off the lockers.

Girls around here like to roll their skirts up, making them practically non-existent. Bend over, and it's like a free show. The thought repulses me—it's just not my style. I've never been one to follow trends or 'willingly' bring attention to myself. Just when I think it can't get worse, Xavier chimes in with a comment of his own, "At least she's dressed modest," he says with a smirk. It's not as harsh as Kieran's, but it still stings. My face flares up with embarrassment, but no way am I giving those idiots the satisfaction. Sticking the finger up at him, I hustle toward the classroom, completely ignoring their dumb comments. Imogen spotting me from the back of the classroom, shoots me a concerned look, probably noticing my expression, as I slip into my seat next to her.

"What happened?" she whispers.

"Nothing, don't worry," I reply softly, shrugging it off. I glance around the classroom, anxiously checking to see if anyone had heard the comment made whilst walking in, but they seem oblivious. Thank God.

"Don't tell me it was those idiots again?" she whispers.

"It's okay, nothing I can't handle," I say with a smile that doesn't quite meet my eyes.

"One day, those wankers are going to get it, I swear. Karma is nothing but a bad bitch." I just laugh at this, and nod—hoping Imogen's words are true.

I settle myself in, determined to let the embarrassment roll off my back. As I do, my mind, ever the traitorous cow, can't help but drift back to those boys, wondering why they always pick on me—to be fair, they pick on everyone—those stupid pricks. But I wonder why me? Xavier is very easy on the eyes, something I've always noticed about him. I know he's older, but that doesn't stop me from wondering what it would actually be like to be friends with him if he wasn't such a dickwad.

Every girl just froths over him, and his reputation precedes him for messing around with both senior AND junior girls in my grade. Ugh. I just don't understand why.

Lunchtime rolls around at about 1:30pm, and Claire, Imogen, and I snag our usual spot outside in the playground. We're chatting away about the latest whatever when I spot those guys again, lingering near the bathrooms just a bit further down from where we're seated. This time, there are two more boys added to the mix. Seriously, do they live near the bathrooms or something? They always seem to be there. What, like you notice? Shut up.

Imogen's eyes light up with excitement as she suggests, "Hey, we should totally hang out this weekend and watch that new rom-com movie. I heard Maddie talking about it in science. She spent half the lesson going on about how she hooked up with some guy in Year 11, bleh. Anyway, what do you girls think?"

Claire and I exchange glances before she says, "Of course she was. She's become a little ganga lately, aye? I heard she also effed Kieran at Trent's party last weekend. Bleh." She sticks her finger in her mouth and gags, then nods enthusiastically, "But, yes! That sounds fun!" Imogen laughs and then turns to me, waiting for my reply.

"Yeah, sounds fun! I'll just need to check with mum, but I'm in."

Imogen grins. "Alright, mad! It's a plan, then. Movie night this Sat!"

As we continue discussing our weekend plans, I sneak another glance over at the guys near the bathrooms. I can't resist. It's like this weird magnetic pull, something I can't explain. Don't judge; we've all been there. As I glance up, I notice Xavier is now looking straight at me. Shit—what? Panic mode sets in, and I'm trying to act all casual, like I wasn't just caught staring. Smooth, Isla, real smooth.

Imogen elbows me, somehow catching on. "Hey, why is Xavier staring at you?"

"What? No way. He's probably looking at someone behind me or something," I mumble, desperately trying to play it off.

Just then Claire chimes in, "Uh, guys! He's walking over here," as she notices Xavier heading our way. My heart skips a beat. No. No way—now internally freaking out. Why is he coming over here? Did he catch me looking at him? Fucking hell, silently cursing at my curiosity.

Xavier, with his effortless coolness, approaches. "Hi," he says, giving that killer smile—showing a row full of perfectly straight white teeth—that makes my stomach do somersaults, and I hate myself for it.

"Uh, hey," I manage to squeak out, pretending I'm not internally hyperventilating.

Imogen and Claire exchange wide-eyed glances, probably sensing the internal chaos within me.

His green eyes are like laser beams as they lock on to mine, and for a moment, I forget how to breathe. "Uh, did you happen to see a small black Nike bag in Mr. Ferguson's class last period? I was in there this morning, and I think I left it there."

How did he know I was in Mr. Ferguson's classroom last period?

Suddenly I forget how to speak. I somehow miraculously manage to stammer out a response. "Uh, I don't think so. Sorry," I say as I wince. "Maybe go back to the classroom and have another look around. It'll pop up somewhere."

As we talk, I become aware that the guys have now noticed Xavier had left them. Kieran, never one to miss an opportunity to stir the pot, decides to dive in as the others run up towards us.

"Oi, look who's on a mission! Coming to proclaim a 'confession' to the nun, are we?" he chuckles, shooting a wink in my direction.

"Piss off, Kieran. Stop calling her that," she retorts, grateful for her comeback—while I just sit there stunned, averting his gaze.

"Oh, c'mon. Don't you agree she dresses like a nun? She's probably never even hooked up with a bloke!"

The boys erupt in laughter, and Trent, not missing a beat, throws in his two cents. "That's if she can even find one."

Imogen, not about to let them run the show, steps in with a killer comeback. "Anyone who would even dare to kiss either of you are fucking fried. Who knows what diseases all you wankers are carrying?"

Xavier, caught in the middle of this teenage circus, throws his hands up, "Hey, I just came to ask a question."

But Imogen's not having it. "Please, like you're one to talk. Just piss off, all of you."

Xavier, now taking control of the situation, looks at me with almost a hint of apology in his eyes, cutting off any more attempts from the boys to crack jokes. "Right, well, thanks, anyway, Isla," he says, then directs the guys off in another direction.

As they walk away, Kieran turns back around and does the sign of the cross, looking straight at me. "I'm praying for you, Isla."

"Fuck off, Kieran," I spit at him. Smug asshole.

As Xavier and the boys walk away, my eyes linger on them for a few moments, silently seething at those idiots. I fucking hate Kieran. My thoughts race, replaying the encounter in my mind. Xavier, however, approached me not to tease or make fun of me, but to ask a simple question. As I'm stuck in my thoughts, I notice that Xavier has turned back to look at me. What the fuck. What does he want?

I freeze and my heart drops.

My mind returns to my thoughts—for a moment, he stood over me, all tall and bulky from the sports he plays. I couldn't help but admire his physique, the way it seemed to take my breath away, but not in a good way. His hair, cut short, almost like a buzz cut, made his piercing green eyes stand out even more. I quickly shake off these thoughts, the lingering sense of hatred returning. No matter how attractive I find that bastard, I'll never end up with someone like that. They're just pieces of shit, and as Mumma always says, 'Darling, you have a heart of gold and an even better brain. Use it to do great things and don't let anyone ever talk you down.'

I hate them all—feeling nothing but disgust for those boys. And to think, Xavier was actually coming over to talk to me. What a joke. That's all I'll ever be to boys like that.

Just a punchline.

I take a deep breath, pushing aside the conflicting feelings, and re-mind myself of Mumma's words. Hatred won't bring me down—it'll only fuel my determination to prove them wrong.

Isla's always been in the background, a quiet melody amid the chaotic symphony of high school life. I've seen her from a distance, *heard her soft laughter, and watched her disappear into the shadows. But today, something's different. There's a pull—a gravitational force that draws me toward her. How did I know she was in Ferguson's class last period? Well, let's just say I pay more attention than people give me credit for. I knew I had left my bag in the classroom, just to have a lame excuse to go and talk to her. How pathetic am I?*

Then the guys had to come in and ruin everything. Trying to fit in and laugh with them is exhausting. I can't stand them sometimes, especially when they go overboard with their lame jokes and antics. But they're a force of their own, and I'm not about to stop them in front of everyone. Screw it—I'm such an idiot.

During the little showdown, I couldn't help but watch Isla's reaction. She handled it way better than I expected, didn't even bat an eyelid. Maybe there's more to her than meets the eye—she's definitely a little firecracker underneath that shy exterior.

My mind races, replaying the encounter. I approached her to ask a simple question, not to tease her. As we walk away, I can't help but look back. Ah, so I've caught her eye, too. She is watching us, and when she notices I've turned to look, she looks away hurriedly. Interesting.

For a moment, my thoughts drift to her—sitting there, the way her curves challenge the typical high school norms. Her long brown curly hair, her passion for music and art. There's something refreshing about her not following the herd. She's different, and I like it. I'll never admit it to the guys, but she's gorgeous. Not the typical girl that usually makes their presence known around me, but that's what makes her stand out.

As we move farther away, I try to shake off these thoughts. I remind myself I'm not supposed to care about all this. Yet, there's this curiosity, a fascination that lingers. I want her to know she's more than what these idiots make her out to be, but I'm just not sure how to approach that yet.

I turn away, leading my mates in another direction, leaving behind the teenage drama circus. Maybe it's time to find out more about the girl who doesn't fit the mould.

1

Isla

"CONGRATS BITCH! It's not everyday you become an owner of an animal hospital at the age of twenty-seven years old in the span of less than a month," Imogen urges way too excitedly for my liking, her strawberry-blonde hair catching the light as she dances around my living room. "Let's go out and celebrate," she exclaims.

The soft hum of cicadas fill the air from outside the open windows as I stand in my dimly lit living room, clutching the papers that officially declare me the owner of Wattle Creek Veterinary Hospital. How I managed to get to where I am now is beyond me. It feels like just yesterday that I was working in the city of Sydney, and now, here I am, back in Wattle Creek. The weight of the moment is palpable, a mix of pride and nostalgia tugging at my heart. Just a month back in Wattle Creek, and now I hold the culmination of my dreams in my hands.

My apartment, though modest, exudes a comforting familiarity that the city had never quite offered. Still, I stubbornly cling to my independence, refusing to succumb to the allure of the family farm out in the country, where my father lives. My decision to stay in town was met with scepticism on my part, and others, I'm sure, but it was a choice I had made for myself, and I was determined to carve my own path. Tonight, though, was about celebration, an acknowledgment of my achievement. Claire and Imogen, my best friends since *childhood*, were buzzing with excitement as they primped and preened in my living room.

Claire joins in, "Seriously, Isla, you've been living like a recluse since you got back. This is your moment. Own it!"

I sigh, glancing at myself in the small mirror above the vanity.

The tight black halter neck dress clings to me like a second skin, accentuating every dip, bulge, and curve, and the strappy sandals feel alien on my feet. Living out of a suitcase for the past month hasn't exactly done wonders for my wardrobe, but tonight is about breaking free from the routines that have wrapped themselves around me.

"Ugh. Isn't there anything else I can wear?" I exclaim, tugging the dress down as far as it will go. "Why can't I just wear jeans and a top?"

"Are you serious right now? Absolutely not, no. We're going to a bar, Isla, not a hoedown throwdown in a barn," Imogen quips.

"Trust us, you look stunning. I would kill to have your curves, girl," Claire chimes in.

As my friends try to boost my confidence, a swirl of self-doubt weaves its way through my mind. Wearing tight clothing has always been a source of insecurity for me. My curves—bulges, lumps, and dips—have never aligned. The pressure to have a flat stomach and narrow hips is an ever-present weight, and my ample breasts have often been a point of comparison. *And not in a good way.*

I'd spent so many hours, minutes, and days wishing I had thinner hips, smaller boobs, and a skinny waist. Imogen, a part-time hairdresser, had offered to do my hair, and had persuaded me to let her do my makeup. I guess I'm still learning to embrace the body that I was given.

I push these thoughts aside, because after everything my friends have done for me this past month, the least I could do was go out with them for one night. *I'd kept them waiting long enough.*

"Fine, but if I flash someone accidentally, I'm blaming you," I relent, a small smile escaping my lips.

Imogen chuckles, "Trust me, babe, in that dress, you'll be turning heads for all the right reasons."

"Now, let's go!"

"Just one drink," I remind them.

"You say that now, but wait until you're two shots deep and dancing on the bar," Claire teases.

"Isla on the bar? Now, that's a sight I'd pay big bucks to see," Imogen quips, her infectious laughter filling the room, eyes sparkling with mischief.

We'd decided earlier on the Loose Lasso, a rustic pub just on the outskirts of town. *When I say 'we', I mean Claire and Imogen.* With one last glance in the mirror, admiring how well Imogen had painted my face—*it almost looks like I am wearing nothing, if not for the faint liner on my eyes and red lips*—we head out the door.

We catch a taxi into town and it takes us about twenty minutes to get there from my place. As we pull up to the curb, Claire pulls out her wallet at the same time I do. She notices and quickly places her hand on mind to push it away.

"I've got this one, babe," she says and takes out a twenty-dollar note to pay the driver.

The three of us hop out and thank the driver. As we step into the night, the warm breeze carries the scent of eucalyptus and earth. Wattle Creek, bathed in the soft glow of streetlights, feels both familiar, yet different.

Now, standing on the footpath outside the Loose Lasso, I look up to the vibrant sign above us; the light casting a warm flickering glow in the night, and just below it, a weathered lasso hangs proudly, its origins probably shrouded in the enigma of decades gone by. From what Imogen and Claire have told me, it has become quite the popular hangout recently for both the young and elderly locals. If not for the resilient support of these local patrons, this timeworn structure probably would have been shut down by now.

The pub comes alive as we enter through the doors, the low hum of conversations blending with the rhythmic beat of country music playing in the background. The wooden floor of The Loose Lasso embraces our footsteps as we navigate through the lively crowd. The warm, amber glow of the bar casts a welcoming hue on its patrons—a diverse mix of farmers, town locals, and the occasional traveller passing through.

Imogen, always the social butterfly, leads the way, her infectious energy drawing smiles from familiar faces. Claire, the orchestrator of my newfound appearance, walks beside me, her chestnut curls bouncing with every step. The air buzzes with excitement, and I can't help but be swept up in the infectious atmosphere. Imogen guides us towards the bar, signalling the waiter for a round of drinks as we pass by.

Her blue eyes sparkle playfully as she searches the guy's shirt for—a name tag? He must've sensed her intention because he introduces himself right away. "The name's Garrett. What can I get for you, pretty lady?

"Oh, quite the charmer, aren't ya?" She giggles, flipping her hair over her shoulder.

"Three shots of your finest whiskey please, Garrett," she practically purrs, earning a chuckle from the bartender.

Garrett brings out three shot glasses and pours the amber-coloured liquid into each glass, filling them to the brim. Imogen grabs them and hands them out. The sharp scent of whiskey fills the air as we raise our glasses, toasting to the night.

"To new beginnings," Imogen declares.

"And may I never have to deal with another angry cat again."

Claire playfully nudges me. "Oh, come on! Remember Mr. Whiskers? He practically declared war on you. But let's be real, you're a vet. There'll be plenty more"

"I think he's still plotting his revenge," Imogen adds, and I chuckle, clinking our glasses together, and we down the liquid in unison. The warmth spreads from my throat to my chest, leaving behind a fiery trail.

"You know tonight we're not just celebrating the clinic. We're celebrating life, freedom, and the fact that your hair is finally free from that perpetual ponytail!" Imogen declares.

Claire laughs loudly and chimes in. "Come on, girl, you're a vet, not a hermit! It's about time you wore something other than scrubs."

I chuckle, feeling a sense of liberation mingling with the nerves.

"Alright, but we made a deal, remember? One drink, a little dancing, and then I reserve the right to retreat back into my sanctuary," I say as Imogen turns back to the bar to order another round of shots.

So much for one drink.

"Okay, okay! But just one more shot! You never know, you might even find yourself a cowboy for the night." Imogen leans in, her eyes dancing with mischief.

I roll my eyes.

"Trust you to bring up any mention of a cowboy, or any man, for that matter."

"You just wait... A hot cowboy might be exactly what you need. Someone to ride for the night!"

I admonish Imogen for the suggestive joke, "Seriously? I'm not in the market for a cowboy... wait, you know they're not called that around here, right?

She laughs, "Duh, but cowboy sounds a lot better than 'Hot

Farmer? Come on, Isla, live a little. Who knows, you might enjoy the rodeo."

Claire joins in, "Isla, babe, as much as we can have fun together, there are certain things only a man can provide you."

I roll my eyes. "Please spare me the details. I don't need a man to have fun when I've got the two of you."

Claire smirks. "True, but again, we're missing *vital* parts." She mimics her previous statement with a wiggle of her eyebrows.

Imogen hands Claire and I our whiskey shots, and we down them simultaneously. I shake my head, already regretting this night's trajectory.

And with that, Imogen seizes my wrist with her right and Claire's with her left, pulling us toward the dance floor where couples twirl and laugh to the twangy melody. The rhythm of the music envelops us, and for a moment, I allow myself to be carried away. Imogen and Claire, my partners in crime for the night, spin around me with infectious enthusiasm. The constraints of the past weeks melt away, and the familiar strains of a country song blend with the pulse of the vibrant atmosphere.

But just as the night seems to stretch endlessly, a familiar voice cuts through the music.

"Well, well, if it ain't Isla Thompson."

I turn to face the source of the drawling voice, and leaning against a wooden beam with a cocky grin, is Trent Oldman. *Oh, here we go.*

"Wattle Creek just got a whole lot more interesting. What brings you back, Isla? Couldn't handle the city lights?" he drawls, his gaze trailing over me.

The resentment for this guy that has been simmering beneath the surface for years flares up. Trent, always relishing the chance to rile me up, seems to take particular pleasure in my obvious discomfort.

I plaster a fake smile on my face. "Just visiting, Trent. *I lie.* You know, catching up on the thrilling life in our charming town."

He chuckles, the sound grating on my nerves. "Visiting, huh? How long's the city girl planning to grace us with her presence? And why now?"

Imogen, sensing my unease, shoots Trent a glare. "Why don't you fuck off, Trent? Isla doesn't need your interrogations tonight."

Claire, never one to mince words, adds, "Yeah, Trent, go back to your little fan club and leave us in peace," as she points to the table behind him with a few people who went to school with us, but are not important enough to remember their names.

Trent, seemingly unfazed, holds his hands up in surrender with a sly grin on his face, "Woah, woah. Easy there, ladies, wouldn't want you to get your knickers in a knot."

I hate him.

Imogen scoffs. "You must be delusional if you think anyone wants you near their knickers."

Trent smirks. "Well, well, Imogen, still as feisty as ever. Maybe you're the one who needs some company."

Claire chimes in, "Honestly, Trent, fuck off. No cares for your bullshit. It's a pity you haven't changed since high school."

I roll my eyes. "Trent, save your charm for someone who gives a fuck. We're not interested."

Trent, looking somewhat defeated, finally retreats. "Alright, alright, relax. I was just checking if Wattle Creek's very own prodigal daughter had any exciting news for us old timers."

Claire retorts, "Well, she doesn't. Now, again, fuck off!"

"You three always did have the worst foul mouths. Shit." He winks, almost as if to insinuate something dirty. *Disgusting prick.*

With that, Trent finally turns around to saunter off, but just before he can disappear into the crowd, he stops abruptly and then turns back around, leaning in closer to me. His eyes narrow, and he lowers his voice. "Does Xavier know you're back in town, Isla? Or is it a surprise for him, too?"

I freeze on the spot, my eyes widening. A surge of anger courses through me, my fists clenching involuntarily. "Why? It's none of his fucking business, or yours, for that matter."

Trent finds this amusing; he laughs and counters, "Don't worry, he'll find out sooner or later. It's a small town, after all. And I'll thoroughly enjoy seeing the two of you butt heads again." He adds with a smirk, "Maybe you should've stayed back in the city. It's bad enough your dad runs amuck around town. Should be embarrassed, really."

This remark infuriates Claire and Imogen.

They snap at him in unison, "Fuck off!" Their displeasure is evident in their expressions. With that, he does a mock salute, winks, and confidently walks back to his table.

My friends exchange concerned glances, and I force a reassuring smile. But beneath the surface, the unexpected encounter with Trent has now stirred up a tempest of emotions. Tears threaten to spill from my eyes.

Claire shoots a disdainful look in the direction Trent had disappeared.

"That guy is a worthless piece of shit, always has been, since high school. Ignore him, Isla. You're here to have a good time. You've been so wrapped up in the clinic these past four weeks. Let loose for once!"

Imogen adds, "Absolutely! Don't worry about Xavier. That man hardly ever leaves his farm. He's too busy being a full-time farmer—working 24/7. I heard he's become the ultimate recluse. Completely different from his high school days when he was the social butterfly, don't you think?" She smirks, and we share a chuckle at the image of Xavier immersed in farm life, worlds away from his past socialising self.

Imogen continues, "And your dad is doing alright. He's had a few ups and downs, but you know how it is. Dad has been around to check in on him from time to time. But I think *you* should check in with him soon." *Ugh.*

I sigh. "Yeah, I guess I should, aye. I appreciate that. Thanks, Midge." She shoots me a playful glare, clearly not a fan of the nickname. Says it makes her feel like she's pint-sized—and let's be honest, she kinda is.

Imogen grabs my hand, determination in her eyes. "Come on, let's dance. Fuck everyone. We won't let one loser ruin our night." I hesitate, a bit apprehensive, but their words finally sink in. Blinking away the threatening tears, I nod and join my friends in dancing away the troubles of the night.

"Wait!" Claire says as she saunters off quickly heading straight for the bar, and in less than five minutes she's heading back towards us holding three shot glasses—this time of a clear liquid with a twinge of pink through it.

"Wet pussy shot, bitchessss!!!" she exclaims. Imogen and I just look at each other and chuckle.

We down the shots simultaneously, expecting the liquid to burn or taste like shit, but the taste never comes. Instead, it's sweet and tangy. *Wow, that's actually quite nice.* I look over to Imogen, who's cursing and wiping her mouth of the trickles of liquid that had escaped from the shot glass, missing her mouth entirely.

"Fucking hell," she shouts, flicking her hand away, laughing it off.

"Sip happens," I say, slurring my words and joining in on the laughter.

"*Sip?*" Claire looks at me like I've grown two heads and starts pissing out laughing.

"Oh shit, I meant to say *shit,* not sip." But the girls are howling with laughter; Imogen bowls over, holding her stomach.

Fuck, my head is buzzing already—after three shots—and it's not even midnight. *It's going to be one long, hopefully fun, night.*

The dance floor welcomes us back, the beats pulsating through the air. The endless amounts of shots begin to work their magic, adding a buzz to the mix. Imogen twirls with carefree abandon, and Claire matches her enthusiasm move for move.

We laugh, we dance, and for a moment, the weight of the past is forgotten.

2

Xavier

PRESENT

The sun sets over the vast expanse of our family farm, casting long shadows that stretch across the fields. The air is thick with the familiar scent of hay, and a gentle breeze rustles through the grass. I guide the horses back into the barn, Buddy following at my heels.

It'd been a relentless day on the farm today—I am fucking knackered. I'd spent most of my day mowing all the fields closest to our property, which weren't even half of the acres that cover our property. You'd need a whole week to properly mow that shit.

The sheep had been wrangled, with the help of Buddy, moving them with practised efficiency into their enclosed pen for the night.

The rest of the animals had been tended to with meticulous care—my silent companions in this rustic symphony. Honestly, they're the lifeblood of this place, their well-being non-negotiable. Each stallion, mare, and sheep holds a special place in the rhythm of this farm.

As I walk towards our barn, I look to my right, to where my John Deere has been parked for the evening. Its hum has become a constant companion, echoing in my ears long after the engine is silenced. The satisfaction of a well-groomed property, however, is tempered by the persistent ache in my muscles. Fuck, I need a massage *and* a long bath.

This shit doesn't get easier no matter how much experience you have, believe me. Exhaustion starts to settle in, but the day's work is not yet complete. Trotting along behind me is my favourite girl, Duchess—my prized mare.

"Duchess, c'mon girl," I call, a soft whistle escaping my lips. She ambles in, her movements slow and hesitant. *She has been acting off for the past few days.* The fatigue in her gait mirrors my own, and I can't shake the feeling that something's not right. Her usual enthusiasm for the nightly treat is replaced by a subdued reluctance.

"Easy, girl," I murmur, guiding her into the stable with a gentle pat on her back.

The barn door creaks shut behind her, and a sense of foreboding settles over me. As I secure the latch, I can't help but wonder what's been bothering her. Horses, like people, have their moods, but Duchess's recent demeanour is a cause for concern.

Reaching for an apple from the hessian bag hanging off the stable door, I offer it to her. She sniffs, but refuses to take a bite.

"C'mon, girl, you barely ate anything today," I murmur, my brow furrowing.

She whinnies softly and shuffles back, avoiding the treat. Frustration wells up in me as I drop the apple back into the bag. Leaving the barn, I pull the door closed, my mind still on Duchess. Our farmhouse—a converted barn with thick stone walls and oak beams—looms ahead. A beacon of relaxation after a long day spent under the relentless Aussie sun.

As I walk up the cobblestone path towards the house, my phone vibrates in my back pocket. Trent Oldman's name flickers on the screen as I pull it out—*What the fuck?* A blast from the past. Haven't heard from the bloke in months... I raise an eyebrow, contemplating why he'd choose this ungodly hour to shoot me a message.

I unlock the message, my fingers moving across the screen.

Trent: You're not going to believe who is in town...

the message simply reads.

Curiosity piqued, I find myself at a loss. This town's not exactly a bustling metropolis—surprises are a rare commodity here. *Well, this should be interesting.*

I quickly type out a reply to Trent.

Me: Who?

Seconds feel like hours as I wait for his response. When it finally comes, my pulse quickens.

Trent: Isla Thompson. Back in Wattle Creek.

My heart skips a beat. Isla Thompson. The name echoes in my

head, as my mind races with questions and emotions I thought I had long since locked away. What does this mean? Why is she back?

I remember back to high school, when I was infatuated—woah, relax, getting ahead of yourself there, Xav. Let's say, more *interested* in her. She'd had a distinct flair, never quite fitting the mould of Springbrook High School's rep. Regrettably, I never got the chance to know her better, or to apologise for the way I, but mostly my mates, had treated her.

I had heard she'd left this town to study in the city, from a few friends back in the day, but since then, not a thought of her had crossed my mind. Now, one simple text has changed that.

I don't bother to reply. I slip my phone back into my pocket, my mind consumed with thoughts of Isla Thompson and the curiosity of what she's like now, after all these years.

This town just got a whole lot more interesting.

3

Isla

The morning sun pierces through my bedroom window, illuminating the aftermath of last night's shenanigans at The Loose Lasso. Lying sprawled on my stomach, face down in my pillow, I slowly lift my head, groaning at the unwelcome brightness. Battling a hangover—a testament to one too many whiskey shots—I reluctantly open my eyes.

The room spins as I sit up abruptly, a wave of nausea threatening to stage a revolt. Stumbling towards the bathroom, I clutch my mouth, and with an unpleasant lurch, I find myself hunched over the toilet—regretting every decision that led to last night. Trying to recall how many drinks I had, after the three, no wait, *maybe four* shots, I fail miserably. The only bits I can remember are Trent pissing me off, dancing with the girls, and then everything else is blank.

Each retch echoes in the small bathroom, a cacophony of remorse. *Why did I let the girls talk me into drinking so much?* As the waves of nausea subside, I flush the toilet, the gurgling water a half-hearted attempt to erase any evidence from the night before. Collapsing back against the cool tiles, I release a tired sigh, the throbbing headache doing nothing to alleviate the situation.

Standing up slowly, I make my way to the basin, splashing cold water on my face, and brush my teeth to rid my mouth of the lingering taste of various alcohols. Snatching a makeup wipe from the cabinet underneath, I scrub my face vigorously of all the leftover makeup still clinging to my skin.

Tossing the used wipe into the bin, I return to my room to check the time on my phone. 9:43 am.

The realisation hits me like a punch in the gut—I was supposed to be at the clinic by 8:30 am. "Fuck," I curse, leaping towards my tallboy, frantically rummaging through the drawers for my work clothes.

As I rush to get dressed, my legs become entangled in the fabric of my pants, and I nearly trip over. With a string of muttered curses, I manage to wrestle into my clothes, hastily pulling on my scrubs with record speed. I shove my feet into my favourite worn brown steel-cap boots and clip half of my unruly hair up—a desperate attempt to rein in the disarray of both my thoughts and appearance.

Bustling into the kitchen, I snatch a banana from the bowl in the middle of my kitchen island, reducing brekky to a grab-and-go necessity. Not ideal—but I am so fucking late.

I stumble out the door, the gravel driveway crunching beneath my hurried steps. My metallic grey 2008 Volkswagen Golf, parked out front, awaits me as the morning sun beats down relentlessly. I hop into the driver's seat; the engine roars to life as I put the key in ignition and shift the gear stick into drive. My tires crunch on the loose stones as I accelerate, leaving behind a trail of dust in its wake—the chaos of the morning disappearing along with it.

I arrive at the clinic at exactly 10 am, thanking my lucky stars that I don't live too far. The proximity to the clinic was precisely why I chose the apartment in the first place—a decision I am currently praising the universe for. Exiting the car, I tap out a quick text to the girls in our group chat.

> **Me:** I am never letting you two take me out ever again!

Claire responds almost immediately—Imogen follows soon after.

> **Claire:** Good Morning to you too!

> **Me:** It's definitely not a good morning. I am so late for work... This is so unprofessional of me.

> **Claire:** It's not like you do it often, babe. Plus, if it makes you feel any better, I JUST made it to the airport this morning for my flight... only to find out it'd been delayed by two hours!!!! What's a little morning chaos, right?

> **Imogen:** She has a point, and by 'little,' she means EPIC. You're welcome for the memories AND a fun night!

> **Me:** What memories? I can't remember much at all other than Trent pissing me the fuck off, dancing with you two, and then the rest... idk.

Claire: OMG! It was so fun! Dancing all night, who knows how many shots later, girl, you let loose alright.

Imogen: Yeah, you were the life of the party! LOL! Flirting with that guy at the bar, demanding to dance on a chair.

Me: Flirting? Dancing on a chair? Are you sure we were at the same place last night? That sounds more like Midge than me.

Claire: 🤭

Imogen: 😅

Me: No... I did not! Get fucked!

Claire: You did, I swear! It was all in good fun, though. Besides, you really enjoyed yourself!

Imogen: Sip Happens, remember?

Claire: 😂😂

Claire just responds with a shit ton of laughing face emojis. I stifle a laugh.

Yeah, I remember that one.

Imogen: But nah, seriously, chaos and all, we love you, Isla!

Smiling to myself, and probably looking like an idiot doing so, I shove my phone into my pocket and make my way to the clinic's entrance. As I approach the front desk, where Katy, the receptionist, sits, I can't help but feel a twinge of guilt for my tardiness.

"I am so incredibly sorry," I apologise hurriedly, my cheeks flushing with embarrassment. "It's not like me ever to be late."

Katy, a woman in her fifties with dark brown hair styled into a short bob, looks up from her desk, her warm smile instantly putting me at ease. Thinly framed glasses rest on the bridge of her nose, adding a touch of sophistication to her appearance.

I've only worked with Katy for a few weeks now, but there's a sense of comfort around her, one that unexpectedly reminds me of my mother. *I miss her so much.*

"It's all good, Isla, honestly. We've all had those mornings. And besides, the clinic has been surprisingly quiet today, apart from Henry vomiting up his meds this morning. You haven't missed much," she replies.

Henry was our foster Italian Greyhound with Hip Dysplasia in his back legs. He was left outside our clinic about two weeks ago inside a cardboard box, and since then, we've been looking after him. Katy offered to foster him, *bless her,* so she takes him to and from the clinic every now and then.

"Oh, no! Poor fella," I exclaim and glance up at the clock on the wall above the reception desk.

"Let's wait another twenty minutes or so before giving him another dose of Cartophen. That'll settle the discomfort."

Katy nods and turns back to the computer.

"Your coffee is on your desk inside, by the way," she says without looking away from the screen. I sigh with relief, genuinely grateful for her understanding and attentiveness. "It's probably cold by now, though," she adds, to which I just give her an apologetic shrug.

"Thank you so much, Katy. I appreciate you more than you know. I'll make it up to you. My shout tomorrow."

I make my way to my office, the aroma of coffee welcoming me. As I settle into my chair, I pick up the takeaway coffee cup, which is now, in fact, cold, but nevertheless, I take a sip of it, anyway, the bitter taste instantly relieving the stresses overwhelming me.

Placing my coffee down, I dive straight into today's paperwork, familiarising myself with important documents for the clinic.

Twenty minutes pass, and my mind, ever the multitasker, reminds me that Henry needs his tablet. A quick glance at the clock reminds me that Molly, my assistant nurse that I hired recently, would be arriving for her shift at 10:30am. Strategically, I contemplate allowing Molly to deal with the administration of Henry's tablet. *That'll buy me a few more minutes to sort through this bloody paperwork.*

Just as I move to rise from my chair to head to the back, the tranquillity of the clinic is instantly shattered by the sound of screeching of tires outside. A large man hops out of his black ute and hurries in, shouting, "Is there a vet available? My horse..."

His voice trails off as he registers my presence, his hurried steps coming to an abrupt halt. His eyes meet mine in the most intense stare, blue orbs glinting with an emotion I can't quite decipher. Brows furrowed, his gaze pierces into mine, leaving me momentarily breathless.

I pause outside my office, unable to move on the spot. Shock courses through me as I register the familiar face standing before me.

Xavier Mitchell.

Xavier fucking Mitchell—the bane of my high school existence—is now standing right in front of me. Someone I hadn't seen in years, and certainly not someone I expected to encounter so soon. His rugged features hold an unreadable expression, and for a moment, I'm lost in the memory of our shared history.

Maybe he won't recognise me. I mean, it has been what, over twelve years now? The air crackles with tension as our eyes continue to stay locked on each other.

"I-Isla?" His brows furrow, confusion written all over his face as he stammers.

Fuck.

4

Xavier

The air in the clinic seems to crackle with unresolved tension as Isla and I face each other. My eyes bore into hers, the weight of years of animosity hanging heavily between us.

Fuck, she has changed so much. Twelve years have passed since I last saw her. The last time was when I graduated Year 12, and she was finishing grade 10. But there's no mistaking those eyes, that face. There's no way I could forget the face that had been flooding my mind throughout my last few years of high school. And as of this weekend, *now*.

Trent's texts from last night sink in, and realisation dawns on me. *She's a vet?* Here? So, is she back for good? *Fuck.* He hadn't specified this information, and honestly, I didn't bother prying for more.

This is definitely not what I had expected to walk in to on Monday morning.

"What's happened?" She breaks the silence, her tone clinical, attempting to mask the turbulent emotions beneath.

"If I knew that, I wouldn't be here, would I?" I reply, a hint of snarkiness in my voice. The familiarity of old adversaries echoes in the air.

"Still an asshole, I see." She scoffs, looking behind me to where my car has been haphazardly parked. "Where is your horse?" There's caution in her voice, a subtle hint of apprehension.

"Out in the trailer," I respond without taking my eyes off her. Why does she have to be so intense?

She shifts awkwardly. "Okay, well, I'd like to take a closer look at him. Could you bring your ute over to the back?"

"Her," I correct her and head out the door.

As I do, a pang of guilt hits me. I'm being a dick, but I can't quite pinpoint these emotions spiralling in my head. It's been a long time since I last saw her, and things are different. Yet, here I am, acting like an arse.

My ute sits there, the engine purring quietly as I approach. Duchess is in the back trailer, agitated and putting up a fuss. Climbing into the driver's seat, I take a deep breath, trying to shake off the unsettling mix of emotions. Starting the engine, I guide the car to the back as Isla requested.

As I step out, the door slamming behind me, I make my way to the back of the trailer. Isla stands there, prepared to dive into the task at hand. I observe her, wondering if she senses the awkwardness between us. I push those thoughts aside, focusing on the matter at hand—Duchess's well-being.

Rounding the trailer to open the latch holding the door closed, I can sense the distress Duchess is in. The horse whinnies loudly, banging against the sides of the trailer. I drop the ramp down to the ground, and Isla cautiously enters the trailer, making cooing sounds to settle Duchess. She places her hand softly on her mane.

"What symptoms have you observed so far?" she asks, while moving her stethoscope carefully around Duchess's chest.

"Loss of appetite, restlessness, and she ain't been herself lately," I grumble, begrudgingly providing details.

Nodding, Isla asks, "How long has it been going on for?"

"It started a few days ago. She's refusing to eat and acting all skittish. Thought maybe she'd just had a bad day or two, but it's been getting progressively worse," I relay with a hint of concern in my voice.

"This must be a real inconvenience for you. Having a working horse out of commission," Isla comments.

I nod. "You have no idea. Duchess is my best working horse, and with her sick, it's a real pain."

As Isla resumes her inspection, I can feel her eyes on me, her presence overwhelming. I decide to break the silence, "So, uh, how long have you been in town? When did you start working at this place?"

"Um, just a few weeks," she replies shyly. *Hm.*

"I thought this place would have shut down by now. I drove past and was surprised to see it was open."

"It was going to, but then I handed the previous owners an offer and they accepted." She shrugs, annoyance creeping up.

Isla looks at me curiously. "So, uh, you work on a farm now or something?"

I clear my throat. "Uh, yeah, my family farm. I took over after I graduated high school."

She pauses, and recognition forms in her eyes. She responds with a simple, "Oh. Okay."

She's working here, and I had no clue. Why didn't she say something earlier? How would she have told you? That voice in my head snorts. Don't be such a dumb cunt, Xavier. I should probably be more aware of the changes in my own damn town.

"So you own this joint now?"

"Yep," she says matter-of-factly.

Despite the weight of the situation, I can't help but notice Isla's presence. I find myself staring at her, taking her in, observing her now, twelve years later. There is no ounce of that timid girl; she's still shy, but not so sheltered, perhaps. She's wearing green scrubs, with a stethoscope around her neck. Her hair, still long, brown, and curly, has been half clipped up, a few tendrils framing her face. Her face, fuck. She's still as beautiful as I'd remembered her.

She moves to listen to Duchess's heartbeat, pressing her stethoscope just behind her elbow. In doing so, she inadvertently makes a sudden movement which causes Duchess to rear back, hitting the side of the trailer. She drops her stethoscope, and I move quickly, shuffling closer to her side, a look of concern adorning my face.

"Fuck. Woah, easy girl," I attempt to soothe the horse, rubbing the top of her back. Isla just stands there, seemingly unharmed.

"You alright?" I ask, brows furrowed.

She nods. "Peachy," she quips, shooting me a side-eyed glance.

Smartass.

I successfully calm Duchess down while continuing to rub her neck. Isla relays her findings, explaining, "Her heartbeat is a little quick, and her pupils are dilated.

"Colic," she says, her tone clinical despite the underlying tension. "It's likely caused by a sudden increase in fresh spring grass in her diet, altering the pH in her hind-gut. She'll need an injectable pain relief to prevent her stomach from rolling further."

My jaw tightens. A look of recognition forms in my eyes as I absorb the information. I remember my father letting her out the other day; she probably ate too much of the long grass.

"So, what now, Doc?" I ask, my voice gruff.

She turns to me, raising an eyebrow. "Take her home, keep her comfortable, and make sure she stays away from the pasture for a few days to let the injection settle. If symptoms persist, you'll need to bring her in for an emergency stomach tubing."

Before I get a chance to respond, my phone rings from my back pocket. I glance at the screen, and it's Harrison's name flashing. I roll my eyes and silence the phone, choosing to ignore the call. After a few minutes, it vibrates again, persistent as ever. I let out a reluctant sigh, realising I can't avoid the fucker. Apologising to Isla, I pick up the phone and answer it.

"Xav, mate, where the hell are you right now?" Harrison's voice comes through, annoyed.

"Just dealing with something. What's up?" I reply, trying to keep it brief.

"Bruh, I need your help at the garage. We've got a tractor stuck, and we could use your muscle to get it out."

I shoot a glance at Isla, whose attention is on the horse. "Can't you ask Michael?" I ask.

"He's here. The wanker is no help at all!" He groans. I can just make out Michael yell out, *'Fuck off cunt. I'm the one doing all the work here',* and I can't help but smirk. These two knuckleheads are like chalk and cheese. They're brothers, but they couldn't be any more opposite. I catch Isla watching me then, an expression on her face I can't quite make out as she looks me up and down. Is she checking me out? I meet her eyes and smirk, and she looks away quickly, returning her attention back to Duchess, who has seemed to calm down now.

"Look, I'll be there in a bit, alright? Got something I need to handle first."

Harrison grumbles a response, and I end the call, sliding the phone back into my pocket. Turning back to Isla, I maintain my smirk, wanting to stir the pot a little. "Get a good look?" I say with a raised eyebrow.

"Sorry, what?" Isla retorts, her frown evident, avoiding my question as she turns to pat Duchess again. She shifts gears with a feisty tone, attempting to change the subject. "I hope you're more focused on your horse than trying to impress me with your *charming* personality."

Well, well, the feisty Isla is back. I can't help but feel a tug of amusement at her resilience. I decide to play along and rile her up a bit more. Leaning casually against the trailer, I raise an eyebrow and add, "Do you gawk at all your clients that way?"

She lets out an exasperated sigh, clearly unamused by my teasing. "Gawk? Fuck off, I did no such thing. Now, if you're done distracting me, I'd appreciate it."

"Mhm, sure thing, Doc. Still the firecracker, I see."

She rolls her eyes. "And you're still the same pompous ass—anyway," she changes the subject real quick, "So you know what you need to do?" she questions.

I cross my arms, my gruff demeanour returning. "Yep. I've got a sick horse and a list of instructions. Looks like I've got my hands full." My gaze sweeps over Isla momentarily. "Anything else, Doc?"

Isla meets my gaze with a level stare, shifting on the spot uneasily.

"Isla is fine. Thanks," she says, referring to the little nickname. I think I like it, enjoying the way it riles her up. "Just follow the instructions, Mitchell. Your horse will be fine as long as you do," she assures as she shuffles past Duchess and me in the trailer, gracefully walking down the ramp.

"Xavier is fine," I quip, mimicking her previous retort, while ignoring her snarky response. Without looking up at her face, I just know she has that defiant look on that annoyingly beautiful face of hers. Damn it, Xavier, focus. I need to stop getting lost in her features and settle this horse business. Time to get this over with and get out of here.

"Right, well, I'll need to explain costs, so would you—" she begins, but I cut her off with a dismissive tone.

"No need to explain anything. Whatever it costs, I don't care. I'll pay it," I state, determined to settle the matter.

"Sure. Follow me, then."

I lift the ramp and close the trailer door, securing the latch. As we walk into the clinic, my eyes unintentionally trace the curves of her hips and the alluring sway of her movements. Damn it, Xavier, get it together.

But fuck—I find myself captivated by her curvaceous figure, a stark contrast to the girl I used to know. Just when I thought I'd finally rid her from my thoughts, here we are again, back to square one.

Maybe, just maybe, it's time to find out more about the girl who never used to fit the mould, a girl who now very much embodies womanhood. As we step into the clinic, I can't shake the feeling that this unexpected reunion might lead to more than just tending to a sick horse. The thought both infuriates me and intrigues the fuck out of me. I don't need distractions, especially not from someone like her, but in this small town, old flames have a way of reigniting whether you like it or not.

I'm fucked.

5

Isla

Claire and I are comfortably seated across the dining table, cold beers in hand, as we swap stories about our day. The evening is settling, and the atmosphere at my place is filled with laughter and the clinking of beer bottles. I take a casual sip of my beer, eyes fixed on Claire as I drop the bomb.

"So, uh, Xavier Mitchell paid a visit to the clinic today."

Claire, mid-sip, chokes on her beer, spraying it across the table. I can't help but burst into laughter at her dramatic reaction. She recovers, sputtering, "Bitch, warn a girl next time!" Her voice is a higher octave than usual.

Wiping the beer from her face, she demands, "What the fuck! Explain yourself."

I chuckle, unfazed by her outburst. "His horse is suffering from a bout of colic. He stormed in, demanding immediate attention as if he owned the place, throwing out sarcastic remarks."

Claire scoffs, "Oh, what a prick!"

"The expression on his face was priceless, Claire, like a deer caught in headlights when he realised it was me," I share, but internally, I acknowledge my own stunned and awkward reaction in that moment.

For the next twenty minutes or so, I recount to Claire how Xavier, true to his usual pompous self, mirrored my words, throwing snarky remarks in the midst of our conversations. It prompts me to wonder when the last time was that I'd seen him smile. Even back in high school, despite his popularity, he had never been one to express joy easily. A perpetual grump, sauntering through life seemingly carefree. Yet, as my mind dwells on this, I can't ignore the peculiar sensation that today, just for a fleeting moment, his mouth almost betrayed a hint of an upward curve—something I never believed possible on his typically scowling face.

"And... to make matters worse, I was caught ogling him," I continue.

Claire nearly chokes on her beer again. "You were what?"

I nod, deadpan. "Caught. O-g-l-i-n-g. Him."

"Why were you checking him out, Isla?" She questions me with a mischievous look and sly grin. I pick up the discarded bottle cap next to me on the table and launch it at her. "Piss off!"

Claire bursts into laughter. "This is fucking gold! I have to tell Imogen."

I try to hide my amusement. "Nooo, don't. She'll never let me live it down."

Claire grins, mischief in her eyes. "Too late, babe. This is prime material for our entertainment," she says as she hurriedly moves her fingers over the phone screen that has now magically appeared in her hands. *What the fuck... when did she pull her phone out?*

I shake my head. To my right, the chime of multiple messages interrupts the moment. No doubt Imogen is currently freaking out over the phone, fueled by whatever dramatic rendition Claire has shared with her.

Claire leans in, her eyes gleaming with curiosity. "So then, what did he look like? What was he wearing?"

I raise an eyebrow, considering her question. "Rugged and all 'I'm a farmer' vibes. Wearing jeans, a flannel shirt, and a fucking *cowboy* hat." I scoff. Internally, I recall how I couldn't help but notice his hair poking out from underneath his hat, curls and all. *Oh, piss off.* He's infiltrating my thoughts, and it's an unwelcome intrusion. Damn him.

Claire smirks. "Sounds like he hasn't changed much."

Having both abandoned our small-town roots for city dreams—me in pursuit of Veterinary Science and Claire in pursuit of a Marketing degree—she, much like myself, hasn't caught sight of Xavier in years.

"Imogen has said he was 'known' to be a player back in the day, way after school, but has never actually settled down." She uses hand gestures to signal air quotes. "What's he like now?"

I scrunch up my nose. "Trust me, not someone I'd consider dating."

She laughs. "Come on, it's just a speculation. Imogen says he's still single, and you've got to admit, he's not hard on the eyes from what I can remember in high school. I can only imagine what he must look like now as a grown man.

"The man's a mystery. I'm kinda curious."

I shoot her a sceptical look. "Curious about what, exactly?"

Claire grins mischievously. "What he's like now. Who knows, maybe he's turned into a decent bloke."

I roll my eyes, dismissing the idea. "Highly doubt it. Besides, I'm not interested in finding out."

My phone chimes again, and I reluctantly pick it up, my screen lighting up with a thread of messages, all from Imogen.

> **Imogen:** It's been ages since you dated, Isla. You need to move on from Justin. It's been almost two years now! You need to get back out there.

Now, of all places, is the last place I want to be thinking about Justin. *Ugh.* I hadn't thought of him in ages, maybe months, actually. This, while moving back home, really distracted me. Now thoughts of him start to surface. Back then, I was head over heels for him, completely oblivious to the fact that I was falling under his spell. Looking back now, I can't deny how incredibly brainwashed I was by his narcissistic ways and how his antics had me wrapped around his finger. His selfishness had finally reached a point where I had to put an end to our almost four-year relationship. It's funny—I had genuinely believed we were *destined* to be together.

Now and then, I catch myself thinking about his family—his two sisters and mother. I had inevitably formed strong connections with them all, especially with his mother, who had been there for me in times when I had desperately needed a motherly figure. Now, even though they used to reach out occasionally, their messages have become scarce. I had done so much for his family. It's a real pity. *But I know better now.*

I push these thoughts aside and continue reading the rest of Imogen's messages.

Imogen: You NEED DICK! 🔪

I stifle a laugh. *True. But I'll never admit it. Part of me is too proud to do so.*

Imogen: I don't think he is the same boy from high school. You need to get over that now! He's a man now, in his early thirties, single, with a stable job. 😏

Imogen: Pun intended... Get it? 😉

This idiot.

Imogen: Seriously, give it a thought! Maybe Xavier could be a good start to meeting new people? 😉

I'm revolted by the thought and the amount of wink faces Imogen has used in the span of one minute.

Me: I'd rather stick needles in my eyes than date Xavier Mitchell.

Claire chuckles from beside me. "Come on, Isla. It's been years. Imogen might be onto something. He might just surprise you." She winks.

I shake my head, dismissing the idea. "I highly doubt it."

Later that night while I lay awake in bed, the quiet of the night surrounds me. I can't help but replay the encounter in my mind. Annoyance lingers, intensified by today's unexpected interaction. I had gone so long without thinking of him or seeing him, and now there's an inexplicable undercurrent of something else—perhaps a flicker of excitement or anticipation. *Snap out of it, Isla.*

High school days were filled with girls frothing over him, and despite the three-grade gap between us, his antics never seemed to cease. However, age has brought wisdom, and I won't be fooled by his charms or any man's, for that matter.

Ironically, my mind is evidently quite fickle. *Traitorous bitch.*

6

Xavier

The aroma of freshly brewed coffee wafts through the kitchen as I pour myself a cup. Dad sits at the counter, his attention focused on the morning paper and a steaming mug in his hand. Mum is at the table, methodically folding tea towels.

"How'd it go with Duchess?" Dad inquires, glancing up from the paper, his eyes questioning me over the rim of his coffee mug.

"Fine," I grunt.

Mum interjects abruptly, her voice tinged with excitement. "Oh my goodness, that reminds me, did y'all hear? Isla Thompson is back. I overheard Bessie and Karen talking about it at the grocer this morning. Apparently, she's taken over one of the clinics in town. Bought it anonymously, but word travels fast." She looks at me, eyes shining. "Heard anything?"

The mention of Isla's return doesn't sit well with Dad. His expression sours, lines deepening on his weathered face. "Great," he mutters, more to himself than anyone else. "Just what we needed."

"Yep. She's the vet who looked at Duchess yesterday," I deadpan, void of any enthusiasm.

Mum's eyes light up with interest, and she leans in. "Well, be a gentleman and make sure you say thanks. She's got it tough, you know, losing her mum right after high school from that forsaken disease, and now her father—" she trails off. "It's a damn pity, really."

Her father? What's wrong with her father? Fuck, I really need to get out in town more. Let's face it though, that probably won't happen. Dad's face tightens, lines etching deeper as he shuts her down, slamming his paper on the table. "Enough, Grace! I would like to enjoy my morning coffee without having to hear the Thompson name uttered in my house. God rest Cheryl's soul, but enough."

Mum purses her lips, retreating back to folding her tea towels. I suppress a sigh. The mention of Isla Thompson is like adding fuel to a simmering fire. I don't want to think about the way she looked yesterday—the woman that she's now become. It annoys me more than I care to admit. I can't help but ponder on what Mum said. I know her father has been struggling with alcoholism for a while now, but is there something else I don't know? Focusing on my coffee, I push aside these unsettling thoughts.

As I take a sip, Dad clears his throat, a subtle signal that he wants my attention. "Got a few things on the agenda for today, son. Need to mend that broken fence near the southern pasture. Bloody cows've been getting out again."

I grunt in acknowledgement, my focus more on the swirling coffee in my mug than on Dad's words. The list of tasks on the farm seems endless, and I just want to finish my coffee and get out to the fields. Sensing my reluctance, he persists, "And we need to fix the water pump near the barn. Can't have those bloody animals becoming parched."

"Yeah," I mumble, my eyes locked on the weathered floorboards beneath my boots. *Worn-out like my patience.*

The vast expanse of our farm's open fields unfolds before me as I make my way towards the grazing livestock. Buddy trots alongside, tail wagging with anticipation. Nestled in the heart of the field sits my trusty, worn John Deere tractor—a relic that bears witness to decades of hard, unyielding work.

Rounding the tractor to the driver's side, I hop in, the familiar creak of the door echoing through the still morning. Buddy leaps onto the seat beside me, his eager eyes fixed on mine.

"Ready to work, Bud?" Buddy responds with a single bark, a clear sign of readiness.

As I rev the engine, the tractor lurches forward, tires rolling over the uneven terrain. The rhythmic hum of the engine drowns out the surrounding quiet, and I find solace in the comforting routine of farm life. Leaning back in the worn seat, I engage in a one-sided conversation with Buddy, discussing the day's tasks and the peculiarities of our livestock. Buddy barks intermittently, his canine responses punctuating the steady drone of the engine.

In the monotonous rhythm of farm work, my mind involuntarily drifts to the years spent toiling under the sun, shaping this land. It's the only life I've ever known. While Bradley ventured into law enforcement and Liv pursued business studies at university, I remained tethered to the farm—whether out of duty, loyalty, or a simple lack of imagination.

As the tractor navigates the open fields, my thoughts betray me, leading to none other than Isla Thompson. I can't help but wonder about her city life, the path she chose. The realisation hits me like a ton of bricks, and I shake my head in disbelief.

What the fuck. Now well and truly annoyed that thoughts of Isla have involuntarily invaded my mind.

I sigh. "Today is going to be a long fucking day." *Just like every other day.*

The absurdity of it all doesn't escape me, and I continue manoeuvring through the fields, determined to drown out these unwelcome musings with the sounds of the engine and Buddy's barks.

7

Isla

Another week has passed and the following Thursday rolls in—the afternoon sun now streaming through the clinic's windows, casting a warm glow over the stainless steel surfaces and the distinct scent of antiseptic. Molly, my enthusiastic seventeen-year-old assistant, in her final years of high school, and I gather around Nala, who recently underwent surgery for elbow dysplasia.

"Alright, Nala, time for a wash, pretty girl," I say, giving her a reassuring pat. Molly chuckles, nodding in agreement. As the warm water cascades over Nala's fur, I can't help but appreciate the simplicity of the moment. The poor girl's a bit drowsy—but hey, she's giving us the eye like she's the queen of the joint, ready for her royal wash and blow-dry treatment. *She's a sassy girl, this one.*

We go about the process with efficiency, shampooing and rinsing Nala's thick coat. The warm water is soothing, and Nala seems to enjoy the attention. Molly handles the shampooing, and I take over the rinsing duties, ensuring not a single bubble is left behind.

This clinic is practically famous for its pet spa vibes. I've only been working here for almost a month and the clinic has become the talk of the town. I mean, we've got pampering down to an art. The previous owners didn't have pet washing on the menu, but new management, new rules. Post-surgery, we roll out the red carpet—or, in this case, the wet towels. It's like a little thank-you treatment for our fur babies. We're basically the Intercontinental for dogs. And you know what they say, happy dogs, happy owners. It's practically a quote from a canine philosophy book or something—*don't quote me...*

Molly, quickly glancing at me and ever the gossip enthusiast, shoots me a sly smile.

"Sooo... What's the deal with you and the mysterious cowboy?" *What is it with this cowboy term?*

I freeze for a moment, genuinely surprised. "Who told you?" I ask, my eyes narrowing.

Molly simply grins. "Who else?" she replies, a mischievous twinkle in her eyes.

I roll mine. *Katy.* Of course.

"I need all the deets!!" she exclaims while patting Nala dry with a fluffy white towel. I shake my head whilst grabbing the blow dryer, plugged in from underneath us, and turn it on, drawing out Molly as she rambles on, too enthusiastically for my liking. *Where does she find all this energy, man?*

She pouts, clearly hoping for juicier details. "Come on, Isla! There must be something more. What did he say? What did he *LOOK* like?" She enunciates the word 'look' by widening her eyes and wiggling her eyebrows. *Teens these days.*

"It was a professional encounter, not a meet-cute. Shoosh!" I say, a hint of a smile on my face. I halt. *Wha–What the fuck… why am I smiling? Because you find him attractive, you idiot.*

"Oi! I see your smile. You're hiding something, Isla Thompson," she shouts over the blow dryer. I just ignore her, hoping she'll give it up. *She doesn't—who am I kidding—insert the annoyed emoji face.* That would describe my expression right about now.

"Fine, be all secretive. But I'm getting the scoop one way or another!" she quips.

As Molly and I continue our buoyant conversation, my phone buzzes with an incoming FaceTime call from Imogen. Intrigued by the unexpected interruption, I shoot her an apologetic glance and excuse myself from Nala's little pampering session.

"Give me just a minute, Molly. Keep Nala looking fabulous," I instruct, stepping out of the room to answer Imogen's call.

Imogen's face lights up on the screen, her mischievous grin already telling me there's more to this call than meets the eye. "Hi, Gorg!!!" she exclaims, and before I can utter a greeting back, dives straight into the conversation.

"Claire's rolling into town on Saturday! Got herself a big-girl promotion, and she's coming to party with us—I think she'll be flying down tomorrow arvo."

My eyes widen in genuine excitement. Claire's promotion is amazing news, and the prospect of another weekend catch up amplifies the joy. I can't help but smile.

"Oh, beaut! That's amazing, Midge! She can crash at mine. I've got my comfy sofa bed waiting for her."

Imogen nods appreciatively. "That beats my ancient sofa any day, and don't get me started on Dad's epic snore symphony." She chuckles, and I can't help but join in.

Our spontaneous get-togethers are practically stand-up comedy nights, and with Claire's big news, this one is gearing up to be another showstopper. Despite the chaos of last weekend's shenanigans, I genuinely do enjoy a night out with the girls. These don't happen often—when I lived in the city, we were lucky if we managed to get together once a month. I hadn't even managed to see Claire that often, and she didn't live far from me at all. Now that I'm back home, we're making up for lost time. I'd feel bad about standing up the girls this time, especially with Claire flying up. It's not something that would be convenient for her, but it's Claire—always willing to go all out for others. I just can't seem to shake the feeling that this weekend might just spring a few more surprises on us than we bargained for.

With the afternoon sun doing its farewell performance, casting a deep, warm orange glow across the clinic's interior, I'm doing my best to wrap things up. Flicking off the lights one by one, I play janitor for a moment, ensuring every nook and cranny is secure. Another day in the thrilling world of veterinary practice has come and gone. Molly's already halfway home, Katy left an hour ago and

Nala, our star of the day, is back in the arms of her grateful owner, Mirette. Rumour has it, homemade Pavlova is coming my way this week as a token of appreciation. *Pavlova… Well, twist my arm, why don't ya?*

I've locked up the entrance, the clinic now silent, and I'm walking to my car. My trusty Volkswagen, parked like it's on standby for an escape mission. Unlocking the car, I pull out my phone from my back pocket—4:01 pm. Right around Dad's tea time.

Here comes the internal debate. *Should I grace Dad with a surprise visit?* I briefly consider it, imagining his reaction. A hesitant smirk plays on my lips as I wonder if he'd appreciate the spontaneity or if I'm about to unleash chaos. To be polite—or just cautious—I decide to give him a heads up. Dialling the home phone, I listen to the ring tone that seems to stretch for ages. *Is he ignoring me? Maybe he's finally learned how to socialise and is out with the townsfolk.*

Multiple attempts later, only the relentless ringing tone answers me.

With a muttered, "Fuck it," I slide into the driver's seat. The decision's made—I'm heading to Dad's place, surprise or not. Let the unpredictable evening commence.

I pull up to Dad's place, the engine grumbling to a halt. Despite my confident decision to drop by unannounced, nerves decide to make a fashionable entrance.

It's been a while since I stepped foot in this house, the last time being Mum's funeral. A wave of reluctance washes over me, but I squash it down. I'm here for Dad, and maybe, just maybe, I can make this an uneventful visit.

Turning off the ignition, I open the car door, my worn boots meeting the familiar gravel driveway. The air is filled with the scent of fresh-cut timber, and I glance around, recognizing the familiar surroundings. As I step out, closing the car door with more force than necessary, I catch movement from the corner of my eye.

Dad emerges from around the side of the house, a stack of recently cut timber in his arms. His brows furrow in confusion as he spots me. I stand there, rooted in place, caught in the act of spontaneity. He looks at me, timber still in hand, like I'm some sort of mythical creature that's appeared out of thin air. The atmosphere hangs, my intentions suddenly feeling like they need a lot more explanation than I initially thought.

He stops mid-walk and drops the pieces of timber to the ground with a muffled thud. Turning back to look at me, the air thickens with tension and apprehension.

"Bout time you came by," he says, and without waiting for a response, he strides ahead, climbing the steps of the front porch and disappearing inside. The door hangs open, a clear invitation to follow.

I release the breath I hadn't realised I was holding and reluctantly trail behind him. Closing the screen door with a soft creak, I'm hit with a wave of nostalgia. The familiar musty scent of pine, the lingering aroma of tobacco, and oddly enough, a hint of cinnamon fill the air. Glancing to my left into the lounge room, I spot a lit candle on the mantelpiece with a sticker that reads 'cinnamon spice'. *Huh*—that explains that. As I walk further into the house, I notice my dad bustling around the kitchen, turning on the kettle with a clatter.

Breaking the silence, he offers, "Tea? Coffee? I ain't got much—none of those stupid flavours, but I got chamomile?" he mutters.

"Chamomile is fine, thanks," I reply, grateful for the neutral option.

Feeling the weight of awkwardness settle, I shift on the spot, absentmindedly pulling at a frayed strand of yarn on my long cardigan. Dad must sense my apprehension and gruffly tells me to sit, gesturing to the kitchen stools.

I lower myself onto one of them, the creaking echoing through the room. The atmosphere is laden with years of unspoken words and unresolved tension. Dad places a steaming mug of chamomile in front of me and stands across the bench top, nursing his own cup, gaze avoiding mine.

As we sit in the kitchen, Dad's eyes drift to my uniform, and I realise I'm still dressed in my scrubs. He clears his throat, a gruff noise that preludes his clipped words. "Well, that explains why you came back here."

I shift uncomfortably in my seat. "Yeah, it wasn't planned. The clinic in town was shutting down. Imogen mentioned it to me, and I thought it was time for a change, so I bought it."

"You make a lot of money or somethin'?" Dad questions, raising an eyebrow.

"Not really, but I saved a huge load over the years," I counter back.

Dad nods slowly. "Still kept in touch, I see," he says, and I catch the undercurrent of his words, hinting at the mention of Imogen's name, the fact that I hadn't made much effort to stay connected.

The room falls into a tense silence again, and I sip my tea, the warmth providing a slight comfort in the bitterness of our reunion.

I really had genuinely attempted to reach out to him during my time away, but the calls had gone unanswered. Whether deliberate *or* accidental, it's still unclear. *Knowing Dad, it was probably deliberate.*

I remain silent, uncertainty swirling in my mind about how Dad will react to what I say next.

"How have things been?"

"Well, you know, the same old things." *No, I don't know.* "Things have been a bit fuzzy over the last few months, though. Nothins' changed much..." he trails off, rambling. *What does he mean by that?*

"How's things around the house going? Still got any of the live-stock?" I question, but Dad just stares at his mug of tea. *Oo-kay...*

My eyes shift to the antique crystal vase, its delicate charm heightened by the blooming everlasting daisies on the kitchen bench.

In an attempt to break the silent tension, I change the subject. "These are pretty. When did you pick them?" I say quietly. My dad looks at me for a second, brows furrowed, confusion written on his face. Then he glances towards the vase, and I notice his expression change, almost instantly, from confusion to a look of… endearment?

"Oh, just this mornin'. Roses aren't blooming yet, so I picked 'em out just for your mother. I saw 'em this morning, and they reminded me of her, ya know—because of her everlasting love." I turn to look at the bunch of flowers, tears creeping up, taken aback by his admission.

As I turn to look back at my father, he continues quickly, "She'll be home soon actually…" He glances at the clock on the wall above the vase, "She'll be real surprised." Wait… *What the fuck? Surely he's not referring to Mum as in….*

I freeze, realisation hitting me straight to the gut. My intuition, telling me to just go along with what he's saying to see if my assumptions are correct, consumes me.

"Oh, really? Where did she go?" I manage to stammer out, trying to process the moment.

My father responds casually, "Oh, she just ran to the grocery store—ran out of them damn apples that she needs for her home-made apple pie, you know, them green ones, all sour 'n shit," he exclaims with an unexpected burst of animosity, yet a smile adorns his face.

Oh my god. Surely, no. The tears that threatened to spill just before now slowly break the surface. A lone tear slipping down my cheek.

I remember when Mum used to make her homemade apple pies.

Overwhelmed, I abruptly get off the chair, and I force a smile, attempting to conceal the turmoil brewing within me. "Um, you know what, Dad? I just realised I need to run to the grocery store for a few things for dinner. It completely slipped my mind," I say, my voice shaky with the unexpected upheaval of emotions. *Lie.*

I turn to leave, desperately trying to hold back tears and hoping he won't see the distress etched on my face.

"Dinner? You were just about to sit down. What happened?" My father looks puzzled, and at this point, tears are freely falling. I keep my head down, unable to meet his gaze.

"Yeah, I know, but it's last-minute stuff. Can't have dinner without it." I lie, again, my voice shaky with the unexpected surge of emotions.

Desperation for air grips me. "Oh.. well, don't you wanna wait for ya Mum? At least to say hi?" he asks, and I freeze. The mention of Mum in the present tense, as if she's still around, adds another layer of pain.

"No, it's fine. She can catch me later. Just need to grab a few things," I manage to mumble, repeating my words, as I open the door to leave, the weight of the revelation heavy on my shoulders.

I manage a weak, "Thank you for tea, Dad," as I practically run out, the door slamming behind me. Rushing to my car, I'm desperate for air. I can't breathe. My body starts to heave. Anxiety courses through my body, making my hands tremble as I clutch the side of my car for support. I feel the familiar sensation of nausea creeping up my throat, threatening to overwhelm me.

Breathe, Isla. Deep breaths—In, out, in, out, I chant in my head, trying to calm the rising panic.

Hunched over, I try to regain my composure, but the weight of the realisation continues to press down on me, threatening to crush me. Tears well up in my eyes, and I can't hold them back any longer. Eventually, I manage to pull my keys out of my pocket, but my trembling hands make them clatter to the ground.

The sound of the keys clattering to the ground intensifies my breakdown, and I cry out even more as I pick them up. Fiddling with the keys, I manage to open the car door and collapse into the driver's seat. As I turn the key to start the ignition, I look up at the house, and through my blurred vision, I can just make out Dad standing by the screen door, watching. *Oh god.* The weight of his gaze only adds to my anguish, and I start the engine, desperate to escape.

Putting the car in reverse, I drive away, leaving behind a flood of memories and a father who now seems like a stranger.

My heart pounds with the weight of guilt. I've been gone for so long that I had no idea my father has fucking dementia—*Is it dementia? I actually don't fucking know what just happened...*

I've been around enough people, however, in my life to know what signs of early onset dementia look like. My Pop had it, so did Nana, Dad's mother and father. It's hereditary, so it would make sense. *I don't know.*

As the distance between me and the house grows, the weight of my absence over these past years bears down on me. *How long has this been going on for? Does anyone know? If only I had been here, I would have seen signs. I would have noticed the subtle changes in his demeanour.*

The guilt intensifies, and I can't shake the feeling that I've missed out on such crucial moments in his life. He's been all alone. My surge of emotions make it hard to focus on the road, but I keep driving, desperately hoping that somehow, just somehow, I can make up for the lost time.

A nauseating wave of regret settles in the pit of my stomach.

What have I done?

8

Isla

Morning creeps in with a stubborn persistence, and I find myself groggily waking to a reality still stained by yesterday's revelations. The weight of my dad's condition hangs in the air, a heavy fog that refuses to dissipate. Sleep has been elusive, leaving me in a daze as the first light of day sneaks through my window.

With a heavy heart, I decide to take the day off from the clinic. The emotional toll of yesterday's events demands attention, and I just can't bring myself to face the routine of work today. I roll over to my side and reach for my phone on my bedside table. Dialling Katy's number, not the clinic's, I sit up, resting my back up against the headboard.

In less than a minute, Katy's voice fills my ear. "Hello, dear?"

"Hey, Katy. I'm so sorry, but I won't be able to make it to work today." Katy responds with immediate concern.

"Darling, is everything okay? You sound a bit off."

I rub my temples, feeling the exhaustion from a sleepless night. "Just had a rough night, couldn't sleep. Some personal stuff to sort out."

Katy's voice softens, "I'm sorry to hear that, darling. Take all the time you need. Your well-being comes first. I can shuffle appointments around and ask Molly to handle things at the clinic. Don't worry about work today." *Oh my god, bless this woman.*

I express my gratitude, "Thanks, Katy. I appreciate your understanding. I'll keep you posted if anything changes." The unspoken weight of yesterday's events lingers in the air, and I know today is reserved for navigating the storm of emotions within me.

Desperate to shake off the relentless thoughts that have consumed my mind, I hastily rummage through my wardrobe. In a rush, I opt for my favourite pair of Nike React runners, a pair of black bike shorts, an old sports bra with the tag worn off, and throw a loose tee over the top for comfort.

Grabbing my Apple watch from the stand beside my bed, I head into the kitchen and snatch a bottle of water from the fridge with an urgency that matches the chaos in my mind. The cool surface briefly soothes my warm fingertips. Grabbing my AirPods, I make a swift exit, the door closing with a resounding click.

Outside, the merciless sunlight intensifies the urgency within me. Stepping outside my little brick apartment complex, I inhale deeply, attempting to fill my lungs with air. But the oppressive heat outside has transformed the atmosphere into a suffocating blend of warmth and humidity. *Fuuuuck, this heat is a bitch!*

The early morning, usually a time of crispness, offers no reprieve. It's almost 8.30am, and the temperature has already soared to twenty-six degrees, according to the weather app on my phone.

I chide myself for choosing the worst possible time to go on a run, yet the need to clear my mind propels me forward. The small apartment complex I call home is situated about twenty minutes from the town's centre, and as I navigate my surroundings, I find myself engulfed by the bush. The quietude of nature juxtaposes the chaos within, each step echoing my desperate attempt to outrun the thoughts that threaten to overwhelm me.

Pounding along the dirt path, I'm immersed in the earthy scent of wood and eucalyptus. The heat intensifies, making each breath a struggle, and I can practically feel beads of sweat forming on my skin. It's hot as balls out here, and I'm convinced I've sweated out every millilitre of water I consumed today.

My loose shirt is now clinging to me. Ugh, yuck. 'Hurricane' by I Prevail blares through my AirPods—*huh, that's fitting*—adding an extra surge of oppressive energy as I press on.

Minutes turn into hours, and I push through, alternating between a walk and jog so I don't overexert myself in this heat. Despite being gone for seven or so years, I'm still able to recognise and navigate my way around these dirt trails. I used to walk these, when I was younger, with Mum and Dad, sometimes. Back when things were normal, when things were okay.

But things aren't okay now. My dad… I don't even know where to begin. He's stuck in his ways, and I'm stuck, unsure how to work my way around this situation with him. On top of that, Xavier keeps filtering into my thoughts. His image from Monday at the clinic replays in my mind. Fuck me, the man has changed so much, yet still remains the same annoying guy. My mind wanders to his appearance—the way he is just so masculine, so manly—rockin' that cowboy hat and mullet of his, a beard now, which is a distinct change since high school. I can't help but think about how much I loved the sight of it. He's still so incredibly attractive, and I'm embarrassed to say my thoughts as a fifteen-year-old, back then, have still not changed.

Fuck, I shouldn't care. I don't want to care about the way he looks. He shouldn't have an effect on me at all. But damn, he does. Why does he have to look so good? It's infuriating. I need to focus on something else, anything else. But my thoughts still race.

I'd spent the last seven years, while at uni, successfully avoiding any thoughts of high school or of him, and now one stupid fucking encounter is jeopardizing that. My mind keeps replaying our conversation, analysing every word and gesture. Why is he even on my mind? This is ridiculous. I shake my head, trying to clear my thoughts, but his image lingers, stubbornly refusing to fade.

I've been so lost in my thoughts that the music blaring in my ears was lost in the background. As I regain my breathing, I realise the song has now shifted to 'Decode' by Paramore. Thats *two* songs now that ironically match my mood—the universe must be fucking with me. This is just great.

I glance at my Apple Watch, which dutifully informs me that I've trekked five kilometres so far. Despite the oppressive heat, I push through. Shaking off my previous thoughts, I continue running until I reach what appears to be the edge of a property.

Rounding a bend, I continue to observe the fenced property, its boundaries lined by a series of Australian Pine trees. As I trudge along the path, my mind races with a jumble of thoughts and emotions. The rhythmic pounding of my feet against the earth is both soothing and agitating, a physical manifestation of my inner turmoil. I've been lost in my own head for what feels like ages, trying to sort through the mess of my thoughts, but now, with the sudden realisation of where I've ended up, my focus snaps sharply into the present.

About fifteen minutes ago, I passed an archway with a sign labelled 'Mitchell Valley Farm', yet at the time, being so consumed in my thoughts, it hadn't occurred to me that I'd been approaching his farm.

My heart starts to race as anxiety sets in, triggering a flurry of conflicting emotions. Dread, curiosity, and a healthy dose of annoyance all bubble up inside me.

As I slow my pace, a house in the far distance comes into view, yet it remains shrouded in a lack of detail, too distant for my eyes to make out. So, despite my deafening thoughts to stop walking, I trudge forward. Up ahead, I spot a figure standing amidst the swaying grass, a horse at his side. My instinct screams at me to stop, to turn around and hightail it out of there. I freeze. *No, no, no. I should turn back.* But of course, my insatiable curiosity refuses to let me heed that sensible voice. *God, I can be such an idiot sometimes.*

As I draw closer, the realisation hits me like a punch to the gut. *Xavier Mitchell.* Of course it's him. I'd spot that cowboy hat and mullet from a mile away. Out of all the farms in this godforsaken area, fate just had to lead me to his. Typical.

The universe has a twisted sense of humour, that's for sure.

I can feel my heart rate skyrocketing as I debate my next move. Every instinct tells me to flee, to retreat back into the safety of anonymity. But there's a stubborn part of me that wants to stay, to see what happens. Maybe it's morbid curiosity, or maybe I'm just a glutton for punishment.

Either way, I'm stuck between a rock and a hard place. And as Xavier's silhouette looms larger in my vision, I can't help but curse my own damn nosiness. I try to rationalise my predicament, but it's no use. I'm stuck, caught between my desire to leave and the nagging curiosity that brought me here in the first place. *Stupid, stupid girl.*

I mutter to myself, "Shit! What should I do? I've walked too far up now to turn around."

Hastily, I seek refuge behind a nearby tree, using its trunk as a flimsy shield. My mind races as I try to come up with a plan. Running back the way I came seems futile; Xavier would undoubtedly spot me. Could this day get any worse?

In the midst of my racing thoughts, I feel a slight sensation moving up my arm and movement catches my peripheral vision. I turn, only to come face to face with the ugliest bloody spider I've ever seen—on my fucking *shoulder*. I practically jump out of my skin, instantaneously smacking my arm whilst letting out a screech that echoes through the air like a banshee.

Well, *now* I'm fucked.

9

Xavier

In the serene expanse of the field, I find a momentary pause to tend to Blue, my trusted companion, whose saddle and reins are proving a tad unruly. The rhythmic sounds of nature envelop us—birds singing, leaves rustling—creating a soothing melody that is momentarily disrupted by an unexpected screech echoing from the distance, emanating from the nearby trees. Instinctively, my head snaps in the direction of the disturbance.

"Easy, Blue," I mutter, my voice low. I know the importance of keeping him calm to avoid any unnecessary spooking. The horse responds, his intelligent eyes reflecting understanding as I command him to heel. *What the fuck.*

Irritation bubbles beneath the surface as the peaceful ambiance is now shattered. Gripping the reins with a firm resolve, I shift my gaze back towards the source of the disturbance and sure enough, by the nearby trees, I catch sight of a woman flailing around and screaming as if the world is coming to an end. Annoyance now creeps in, marring the peacefulness that once enveloped the moment.

Surely I'm seeing shit?

Without hesitation, I swing myself onto Blue's back, a seamless motion born from years of practice. A subtle nudge to his stomach and a short clicking noise signal our departure, and we canter off towards the growing ruckus. As I saunter closer to the source of the commotion, Blue's hooves crunching on the dry ground, I instinctively pull back on the reins as recognition dawns. *Isla Thompson.* My annoyance at the disturbance is momentarily eclipsed by the sheer surprise of encountering her in such an unexpected place.

What the fuck would she be doing all the way over here? I ponder silently. The desire to tease her, to taunt her, creeps up irresistibly, and I find myself unable to resist.

"You following me, Doc?" I quip, my tone laced with a mocking undertone.

Isla levels me with a glare, scoffing at my suggestion. However, her unsettled demeanour doesn't go unnoticed as she turns in a circle, scanning her surroundings.

"You right? What's all the screeching for?" I inquire, a smirk playing on my lips.

"If you must know, *no*, I am not okay. I was just going about my day, going for my morning jog, when I stumbled onto your fucking property. And on top of that, a fucking spider lands on my shoulder," she admonishes, frustration evident in her voice as her whole body shudders in disgust. A smile threatens to surface, and a chuckle lingers beneath the surface, but I resist letting it break free. She'd be a few kilometres away from town now, assuming that is where she lives.

"Are you fucking smiling at me? Do you think this is funny, Xavier Mitchell?" Isla retorts, her anger palpable.

I don't miss the way my name easily rolls off her tongue. Internally, I berate myself for even thinking about it, reminding myself that Isla Thompson is nothing more than an unexpected, and frankly unwelcome, intrusion on my peaceful morning.

"Oh, it's hilarious, really," I reply in a mockingly sympathetic tone. "Finding yourself out in the bush, which is literally surrounding you, and coming across your friendly neighbourhood huntsman. The horror."

She narrows her eyes, clearly not amused by my remark. "Save the sarcasm for someone who gives a fuck, Xavier. I don't need your commentary this early in the morning, thanks."

I lean back slightly, maintaining a cool demeanour. "Well, well, the fearless vet, scared of a little spider."

She scoffs, crossing her arms defensively. "It's not about the spider, it's about being on your property unexpectedly. I really don't need this right now."

"Doc, there's a lot of things we don't want in life, but life has a funny way of delivering them, anyway." A smirk plays on my lips. "Like, you, on *my* property, for instance," I counter.

"Not cut out for the outdoors, I see." Nodding my head, referring to her little outburst.

She shoots me another glare that could curdle milk. *I think that glare is permanently etched into her face by now.*

"Says the one not cut out for any human interaction," she snaps back. *Ooft. Feisty one.* I'll give her that one, though. *She's right.*

I chuckle lightly at her attempt at a comeback. "Touché, Doc. Now, since you've invaded *my* property and we've shared a moment of genuine *human interaction*, as you say, what's your grand plan now?"

Her eyes narrow further, and I can practically see the gears turning in her head. "I plan to get out of here and continue my run, spider-free and without any unwanted company." She furrows her brows.

"Wait... Did you just... laugh?" she questions, raising her perfectly shaped eyebrow. *Why am I noticing that?*

I ignore her question, just giving her a smirk, noticing the way her cheeks flush. Her gaze wanders toward Blue, my Roan Quarter horse. Unable to resist a tease, I remark, "What, never seen a horse before?" I counter, knowing damn well she'd have encountered horses in her line of work—and most recently Duchess.

"Ha ha," she deadpans. "Just admiring its colour," her tone casual. *Yeah, he's known for that.*

I think to myself, trying to keep a stoic expression. Out loud, I add, "He's a Roan-Blue Quarter horse... bought him a while back. He wasn't cheap, but he's my most agile."

"Yeah, I can imagine. These colours are quite rare in horses," Isla counters.

I find myself momentarily surprised at her apparent horse knowledge. Well, well. She knows a bit about horses. *She's a veterinarian, you dickhead. Of course, she'd know.* I silently chide myself. But outwardly, I maintain my nonchalant demeanour. As her curious stares persist, I suggest, "You can come closer. He doesn't bite. He loves to be pet, actually." Why am I telling her this?

"Could I?" she quips, and for some reason, her excitement makes me feel funny inside. I wasn't expecting her to be so willing.

"Uh, sure. Just hop on through the fence," I say, now subtly enjoying the prospect of her getting closer to Blue—*and me. What the fuck am I doing?*

She does as I suggest, manoeuvring herself easily between the two panels of timber, walking cautiously up to Blue.

Seizing the opportunity, I hop off the horse with a muffled thud as my boots hit the ground. Buddy, my loyal companion, sits on the grass, wagging his tail happily. Isla notices Buddy and can't help but exclaim, "Oh my goodness, you're so cute! Boy or girl?" she asks whilst patting buddy, who has now jumped up onto her thighs, resting his paws there, tongue hanging out of his mouth. *Bastard.*

"Boy. Name's Buddy," I reply with a smirk, realising that even a dog can't escape her charm.

Isla coos at Buddy, "Aren't you just the cutest, Buddy!" while ruffling up his fur and giving him a scratch on his head.

As she does this, I can't help but notice what she is wearing. Jesus. She's got on the tightest black shorts, showing off her curvaceous figure—wide hips, long legs, thick but muscular thighs, a round ass which looks to be more than a handful. The t-shirt she's wearing showcases the silhouette of her ample breasts. I shouldn't be looking. *Why am I looking?*

She's all womanly now, filled out in just the right places, and I can't help but appreciate that, as a man. *Look away, you perv.* I admonish myself internally, subtly readjusting the semi I am now rocking under my jeans. Clearing my throat to shake off these thoughts, I catch Buddy's attention, which prompts him to jump down from Isla's legs.

Isla then looks up to Blue, raising her hand slowly towards his face. Blue, ever the friendly horse, bends towards her hand, allowing Isla to pet him.

"You're gorgeous, aren't you?" she says to Blue. "What's his name?" she asks.

I reply, "Blue."

And she scoffs. "How original."

"Hey," I warn, and point to her. "Watch it; Blue picked out the name, not me," I say, holding up my hands in a mock surrender.

"You're an idiot," she stifles her laugh, but a slight giggle comes out, and for some *odd* reason, I immediately want her to do it again.

Somehow sensing her unvoiced question, I ask, "Wanna ride him?"

She hesitates, "Oh, no, no, I don't want to impose," almost as if finally realising where she actually is and who she's talking to. She retreats backward.

"You're not imposing, plus he loves a ride," I say quickly, and as if on cue, Blue neighs. *Yeah, you and me both, buddy. God knows it's been a while—fuck.*

She looks at me quickly, her eyes moving up and down very subtly, but I catch it.

Isla

"So do you wanna?" he asks again. For a second, I forget what he is asking and my heart races. *The horse, he's asking about the horse, you idiot.*

"Oh, um, y-yeah, sure. I mean, with the horse. Riding. Blue," I stammer, feeling the heat rise to my cheeks.

I shift awkwardly on the spot, trying to conceal the fact that my clothes are sticking to me from all the sweat. I grab my t-shirt and fan it outwards to loosen up the fabric a little and air it out. Why did I choose black in this scorching heat? I catch Xavier's amused gaze as it lingers on me for a moment, and I feel that familiar heat creeping up my neck again, probably painting my face an even deeper shade of red than before. I avert my eyes, focusing on the path ahead, hoping the blush will subside.

"Righto, then. Let's get you up there," he says, walking over to Blue and gesturing for me to follow.

I cautiously approach the horse, feeling a mix of excitement and nerves. I turn to Xavier, "I haven't been on a horse in years," I confess, reaching out to pet Blue's neck.

Xavier smirks. "Don't worry, Blue here is a gentleman. You'll be fine." His signature teasing tone returns.

Xavier starts to position himself behind me, and on instinct, I pivot abruptly to face him. "This is weird, right?... It's weird? I mean... We're not even friends," I blurt out, the words tumbling out of my mouth too fast.

Fuckkkk, I am nervous. Why am I so nervous? *Oh, grow a pair, Isla*. I mentally provide myself with a pep talk. *It's no use. Who am I kidding?*

He looks down at me, his mouth turning upwards. "Why would it be weird?" he says casually, a smirk playing on his lips. "I teach people how to ride all the time, no big deal," he says matter-of-factly. This prompts my mind to involuntarily drift to the thought of him 'teaching' someone how to ride... and I'm not talking about a horse. *NO, no. Stop.*

"We can be acquaintances, right?" he adds, his tone almost teasing. Acquaintances? *Acquaintances?* That's a stretch, considering our complicated history. *Does this dickhead not remember anything?*

I don't really know what to call this dynamic ... dysfunctional? Weird? I had avoided him and his friends like the plague, any chance I could get in high school, and here I am now, seven years later, on his property, engaged in a somewhat decent conversation while riding his horse. *Whaaat?*

I lift my gaze to meet him, momentarily realising how close he actually is to me. I can practically feel his breath fanning across my face. "It's one horse ride, Isla. Turn," he retorts, his tone low and gravelly. The way he accentuates my name rolling his tongue on the 'la' sends a shiver straight down my spine. *Well, fuck me sideways. That voice... he'd always had a deep voice, but now—oh, just kill me now.*

I turn back around, mentally scolding myself for the weird mix of nerves and attraction. *Get it together, Isla.*

As I turn to face the horse, Xavier's hands encircle my waist with a confident grip. "I'm going to lift you up, okay?" he asks, gauging my permission. I simply nod, unable to form words as his hands tighten around me. At the touch of his hands on my waist, I freeze, voicing my concern.

"Wait, there's no way you'll be able to lift me up that way," I ramble quickly, embarrassment creeping up, making my cheeks flush.

His response is instant, a low growl, almost a challenge. "Watch me." With effortless strength, he firmly grips my waist and, without breaking a sweat, hoists me gracefully onto the back of the horse. I instinctively wrap my arms around Blue's withers, smoothly lifting my leg up and around his back, finally settling myself into the saddle.

"Hold the reins like this," he demonstrates, his large, calloused hands guiding mine. *I'm sweating profusely now, and it's not because of the heat.* "Keep a firm but gentle hold. You're leading him, not the other way around." Why does that sound so *dirty*? *Oh, shut up you, horny cow.*

I nod, trying to absorb his guidance while fighting the distraction of his proximity.

"And keep your heels down," he adds. "It helps with balance. You'll get the hang of it."

"Got it," I manage to say, my voice slightly shaky. I can feel the warmth of his body as he leans over to adjust something on the saddle, his chest brushing against my bare thigh.

"Okay, that should do it," he says, pulling back.

"Right, thanks," I reply, trying to focus on the task at hand. *Riding a horse, not getting flustered by a handsome cowboy.*

Looking out into the distance, the vast expanse of the farm overwhelms me. *Where the fuck am I supposed to go?* I glance back at Xavier nervously. "Go on," he urges, and with a soft click of his tongue, Blue starts to move forward. *Well, there's definitely no going back now.*

"Lead the way then, cowboy," I say, attempting to sound light-hearted while inwardly cringing at my awkward attempt at humour.

As I continue my 'walk'—let's not kid ourselves, it's more of a leisurely stroll at this point—in the direction I was originally running, my anxiety prevents me from pushing Blue into anything resembling a trot. Xavier trails behind me, Buddy faithfully following. The relentless chirping of crickets resonates loudly, blending harmoniously with the distant chorus of birds.

Xavier, perhaps sensing my silent struggle, breaks the serenity of the moment. "Just about another kilometre or two up towards the left is our farmhouse," he trails off hesitantly.

"We could stop here, if you like."

To be honest, my ass is on fire, and my thighs are protesting vehemently from the prolonged saddle seat. How people manage to endure these horses for longer periods, I'll never know.

I glance to my right, where a small path continues past the property's fencing, trailing downwards. Lights adorn the tree branches, casting an illuminated yellow glow along the path, although the blaring sunlight somewhat mutes their effect. "What's down there?" I ask, curiosity getting the best of me once again.

Xavier turns to follow my gaze toward the path leading down. "Leads down toward a water bank," he remarks. He seems to ponder on this for a moment before deciding, "I don't usually take the horses down there, but Blue'll be fine. Come, I'll show you."

"Oh, no, no, we don't have to. Seriously, I was just asking. I'm sure you've got a full day's work ahead of you and I should go," I ramble on, desperately trying to find an excuse not to go. *You should have just kept your mouth shut.* I scold myself inwardly.

Ignoring my protests, Xavier gives a gentle pull on the rope attached to Blue's reins, directing us down towards the path. "Today's my easier day. There ain't much to do out here. I just took Blue out for a run earlier to get him moving." His nonchalant demeanour adds to the charm that I find both irritating and strangely appealing.

The path stretches ahead of us, winding through the tranquil landscape, and despite my feeble attempts to resist, I find myself following Xavier down the trail. Blue ambles along obediently, seemingly unperturbed by the deviation from his usual route.

The path gradually descends, and I catch glimpses of the water bank through the trees, its surface glinting in the filtered sunlight. My initial reluctance begins to wane as curiosity takes over.

As we approach the water bank, Xavier guides Blue to a halt, and I do the same. The scenery is breathtaking—the gentle rustle of leaves, the shimmering water, and the occasional ripple as a fish breaks the surface. I can't help but marvel at the serenity of what is in front of me.

The water bank reflects the surrounding greenery like a mirror, and the rustling leaves provide a soothing backdrop. It's a stark contrast to the city life I had now left behind in Sydney. I'd forgotten how to appreciate the simple things—like mother nature..

The city had its own allure, with its towering buildings and a constant hum of activity. Yet, in the heart of this never ending bush, I rediscover the calming embrace of nature. I realise how much I've missed this—being surrounded by lush greenery.

Xavier watches me, his expression unreadable. "So, um, how's Duchess?" I ask, trying to break the awkward silence. The mention of his horse seems to soften his features, a hint of a smile playing at the corners of his lips.

"Duchess is doing much better since Monday," he replies, a note of relief in his voice. "Hasn't chucked up since then and has returned to her usual self."

I nod, a sense of understanding passing between us. It's clear that

Duchess holds a special place in his heart.

"How many horses do you have?"

"Only two now," he answers. "We used to have three, but Dad sold Jazz a few years ago to a local breeder."

"Oh, okay," I reply, not wanting to pry further.

After our brief exchange about the horses, we lapse back into silence. I take the opportunity to take in the scenery around me, the beauty of the bushland soothing my frayed nerves.

Xavier speaks up, breaking the silence. "Quite a change from city life, huh?" he remarks, gesturing to the tranquil surroundings.

I smile softly, the memories of my childhood flooding back. "You forget, I once used to live here."

"Never thought you'd pack up and leave either," he remarks, his tone taking a sombre turn. The entire mood shifts, and a heavy silence settles between us.

Amidst the introspection, a realisation hits me—I'm finding it increasingly challenging to dislike the man. After all these years, maybe, just maybe, he's not the guy I painted him out to be. The infuriating thought intrigues me, and for a moment, I question if Imogen was right. *Damn her.*

The thought of Imogen spurs on a feeling of animosity, but it's quickly overshadowed by the realisation that I've been so enveloped in our conversations and the scenery that I haven't spared a thought for Dad. It's a sudden shift, and the realisation brings a mix of emotions—grief, anger, and an unexpected yearning for closure. A feeling of anxiety creeps its way up my throat, I try my best to swallow the bubble forming in my throat. Deep breaths Isla—take a deep breath.

The weight of realisation rattles me, and I shake my head to clear the thoughts that threaten to consume me. I inhale from my nose and release my breath. Without giving myself a chance to dwell on the sudden surge of emotions, I decide to break away from the serene moment.

"I, uh, I should go," I stammer, avoiding Xavier's gaze. I take a few steps towards the path that led us here.

Glancing nervously at my Apple Watch, the digital display reads 10:04 am. Time had slipped away unnoticed. The last time I checked, it was only 8:30. A message pops up from Claire and panic sets in as I read it.

> **Claire:** Change of plans!!! I'll be flying out earlier than planned. I should be there within the next hour or so 🖤 🖤

Shit.

"What? ...Wait, let me walk you up, at least—" I cut him off, my words coming out in a hurry.

"No, no, it's fine, really. I need to go. Thanks for... Uh, today," I manage to mutter. *Arrgh. Why do I do this to myself?*

As I briskly jog away, I hear Xavier call my name out loudly, in a harsh tone, but I don't look back. The urgency to get back into the comfort of my home propels me to pick up my pace. My heart pounds in my chest, matching the rhythm of my steps.

As I continue my run back home, a peculiar mix of emotions swirl within me.

I can't help but wonder if, in some strange way, he was the unwelcome distraction I needed to clear my mind. His unexpected presence has injected a surge of chaos into the mundane rhythm of my daily routine. A whirlwind of conflicting emotions swirls within me—irritation at the disruption, curiosity about his changed demeanour, and a nagging feeling that perhaps there's more to Xavier now than the high school memories I've clung to.

It's a peculiar mix of annoyance and a tinge of something I'm reluctant to admit.

10

Xavier

Friday night rolls around, and as expected, our family dinner is a lively affair. Mum's in her element, bustling about the kitchen, while Dad pours our drinks. Olivia and Bradley are already seated at the table, and I take my usual seat. I'm so fucking tired, all I want to do, is crash in bed. I don't even have an appetite, but for Mum, I'll sit and eat.

Liv, the youngest of us Mitchell siblings, jumps straight into her latest tales from university in Sydney. Her eyes shine with excitement as she recounts her adventures, and I can't help but roll my eyes at her exaggerated enthusiasm.

"Oh my gosh, you guys won't believe what happened last weekend!" she exclaims, her excitement palpable. "We decided to explore the city, and we ended up getting lost in this maze of alleyways. But then we stumbled upon this hidden café, and let me tell you, the coffee was to die for!"

Mum interjects, placing a dish on the table, "Oh, Liv, you always have the best stories."

Dad takes a moment from his meal to ask, "So, you got any more classes?"

"Nah, I'm all done now for the year. I'm waiting for my final transcript to arrive, and then I'm done. Not sure when the graduation ceremony will be, but I'll let you know," Liv replies.

"That's excellent news, sweetie. Let us know as soon as you find out," Mum says.

"Will do. Sooo, any news round here?"

"Not much. Same old," Dad grunts, while Mum chimes in, "Oh well, the Animal Hospital down near Springbrook Reserve has reopened, and the new owner is Isla Thompson."

Curiosity sparks in my sister's eyes. "Oh. Isla Thompson? That name rings a bell. Who is she?"

Before anyone can answer, I cut in abruptly, "It's not important." Yeah, right. *Keep telling yourself that, Xav.*

Liv raises her hands in mock surrender. "Woah, easy there champ. You don't always have to be so grumpy. That's his job," she says, pointing a playful finger at Brad, who cracks a smirk.

"Ha, ha. You're hilarious," I deadpan.

"So, have you found a girl yet? I'm sick of being the only young female in this family," Liv scoffs.

I glare at her.

"Seriously, you need to get out, and you know, go on dates."

"Coming from a twenty-year-old who still keeps her stuffed animals. Grow up."

"Twenty-three, actually," she quips, her voice laced with attitude. "And hey, I'll never get rid of them. They're sentimental. I'll pass them down to my kids one day."

"At least I have a cuddle buddy. You should try it sometime."

"Yeah sure, no worries." From beside me, I hear Bradley snort.

"Oh leave him alone, Liv. He'll find someone when he's ready. Both of you. I'm not getting any younger, I'd like to have my grand-kids runnin' around while I'm still moving." Mum chides.

I release a heavy exhale. "Yeah, no pressure at all, Mum." I scoff.

"Just saying," she says, raising her hands before wiping them on a napkin.

Rightio, that's enough interaction for me. With a sigh, I push back from the table, my plate in hand. Liv's words echo in my mind, stirring up that familiar frustration about my love life. But dwelling on it only irritates me further.

Isla's image flits through my thoughts briefly. The other day at the clinic keeps replaying in my mind—seeing her in those green scrubs, the first time I've seen her in years since high school. She's back home now, but for what reason? Part of me wants to know why she's back, what made her return after all this time. But another part of me tells me it's none of my business. We've both moved on, or at least, that's what I keep telling myself.

And then today. Today was different, however. Fuck, thoughts of her now flood my mind, the way we actually had a decent conversa-tion, how things seemed to be going alright during the horse ride. I let my guard down, allowed myself to enjoy the moment, but then she took off like all of a sudden the thought of being around me repulsed her. It's left me bewildered, my mind still trying to process everything.

Bloody hell, the thought of her stirs something deep down, a mix of longing and frustration. She's still just as attractive as she was in high school, still rocking those curves that used to drive me crazy. I need to stop this, I tell myself, shaking my head as if to physically shake off the thoughts.

"I'm heading upstairs," I announce, passing by Mum and giving her a kiss on the head. "Thanks for dinner, Ma."

As I trudge upstairs, leaving everyone downstairs, my phone vibrates in my pocket, interrupting my thoughts. It's a message from the group chat with Harrison.

Harrison: Alright, you old fuck, Michael and I and a few other boys are going out tomorrow night for drinks down at the pub. You're coming.

I scoff as I type out a reply.

Me: Am I now?

Harrison: Yes, you are. C'mon man. You never come out. It's just one night. Stay for a few drinks and then you can fuck off.

I stare at the screen, contemplating. Going out has never been my thing, especially now, as an adult, and lately, I've really embraced the whole hermit lifestyle. But maybe a night out, a change of scenery, and a few drinks will help me clear my head. I can't deny that Isla's been on my mind more than usual lately.

Fuck, I might need a drink after all.

Michael: C'mon Xav. It'll shut him up if you say yes.

Me: Fine. But I'm not staying out too late

I type out begrudgingly. Harrison's reply comes swiftly.

Harrison: You beauty! We'll meet around 8?

Michael: Thank fuck.

I just respond with a thumbs up emoji before collapsing onto my bed, face down. With a deep groan, I stretch my arms underneath my pillow, feeling the weight of the evening settling in my mind like a heavy blanket. The thought of socialising for hours already exhausts me, but I've committed now.

I better not regret this decision, I think to myself, my mind already racing with a mix of anticipation and dread.

11

Isla

As Saturday night unfurls, the air is buzzing with anticipation, and Claire and Imogen are stirring with excitement. *Here we go again.* The girls are in the midst of our usual pre-night-out ritual, each armed with their makeup kits and a trove of outfits sprawled across my bed.

Imogen, the resident hairstylist of the trio, is wielding a straightener, transforming my hair into a silky straight do—something different to the waves I usually wear—while Claire is rummaging through her seemingly bottomless bag of cosmetics.

"So, what's the plan tonight?" Imogen chirps.

"We're hitting up Madison's first, right?" Claire pipes in, mascara wand in hand.

Madison's is a popular diner in town. Tonight would be my first time visiting the joint since I'd been back, and to say I was feeling slightly nervous would be an understatement.

"Yeah, I think Madison's is the move," I respond, casting a sidelong glance at the duo.

Amidst the excitement of our pre-night-out rituals, my mind involuntarily slips back to the unsettling conversation with Claire the day before. As Imogen works her hairstyling magic, my thoughts replay our conversation, and the unease planted by my revelation about Dad's condition festers.

On Friday afternoon, I had bared my worries about my father's enigmatic ailment to Claire, and her genuine concern had offered a comforting balm.

"Wait, what?" Claire exclaims, eyes wide with disbelief. "You think your dad has dementia? Like… early onset?" I just nod, a knot of worry tightening in my stomach.

"Yeah, it makes sense. Nan and Pop had it, too," I respond, my voice tinged with a touch of immaturity.

I had also confided in Claire about Imogen's strange silence regarding Dad's health, and Claire, looking as puzzled as I felt, swore up and down that she knew nothing. She hadn't chatted with Imogen about Dad in ages, and the last time she did, his apparent condition hadn't even flickered on the radar.

The strangeness of it lingers, though, casting a shadow over my thoughts. I needed to confront Imogen. Surely she'd know something. I mean, she does live here, after all.

Claire reassures me, "Don't let it stress you out too much. If Imogen knew something, she'd have told you by now. Let's just have some fun tomorrow night while we're together again and see how things go." Who am I kidding? I'm worried and unsure—how can I not stress?

I'd just nodded in agreement, clinging to the hope that a carefree night might just dispel my doubts. Yet, beneath the surface, uncertainty still loomed. I needed to talk to Imogen.

The girls carry on, oblivious to the undercurrent of unease that ripples through my thoughts. Imogen continues to expertly weave her hairstyling magic, while Claire expertly curls her own short bob. The air is filled with a mix of hair products, laughter, and anticipatory excitement.

Imogen breaks the lively chatter with a sly grin. "So, any news with our *cowboy*. Or should I say farmer?" she asks casually, and I feel a slight prickling of nerves. My attempt at nonchalance fails, and I freeze mid-hair straightening.

Claire, ever the perceptive one, picks up on my hesitation. "She does! You better spill now, bitch!" she exclaims, her eyes wide with excitement.

Imogen feigns innocence, "What??"

Claire rolls her eyes. "Oh, come on, didn't you see her freeze? Like a stunned mullet."

I shrug, trying to downplay the situation. "It's nothing, relax." The girls exchange knowing glances, and Claire, unable to contain her curiosity, pounces.

"Come on, Isla, spill the beans. We've got time to kill, and I need some juicy details to spice up tonight."

Imogen joins in, wielding the curling iron like a weapon. "Yeah, c'mon, chop chop! Don't leave us hanging."

I resist for a moment, but their insistence breaks me down. I resist the urge to roll my eyes and sigh.

"Fine, fine." I sigh.

"Yesterday I went for a run and somehow ended up right near his property,"—unbeknownst to me at the time —"and my curiosity got the better of me. I didn't want him to see me, so I literally fucking *hid* behind a tree in hopes that he wouldn't notice anything." And now that I think back on it, what an idiot... Wishful thinking, *I guess.*

"But then, a bloody spider crawled up on my shoulder, and, well, let's just say you could probably hear my screams from kilometres away." I roll my eyes, stifling a laugh.

The room bursts into laughter, led by the infectious mirth of Claire. "You know, for someone who doesn't get out much, you sure find a way to get yourself into the most hilarious situations." I squint my eyes at her and fake a laugh.

Imogen interjects, feigning disbelief, "A spider, Isla? After growing up here, literally running through the bush all day long as kids, with huntsmans, snakes, lizards, and the whole lot—*now*, you're scared of a small spider?"

I counter, with a hint of defensiveness, "*Small!!* When did I say it was small? That fucker was not small, it was gigantic... on my *fucking* shoulder. And, yes, we used to *run* through the bush, not bloody linger long enough for one to hop on our shoulders and say G'day!!"

"You've been gone for too long. It's about damn time you came back. Time to get back into your roots. I call it fate that that hospital was on the brink of closure," she admits, placing her hands on her hips.

I dismiss their amusement with a wave of my hand, declaring, "Yeah, sure... anyway, enough about that." All the while secretly vowing not to admit out loud that maybe Xavier *isn't* the person he used to be.

Pride, after all, is a formidable foe, and I refuse to concede to Imogen being right. *I refuse. She'll just grow a head and never let me live it down.*

Stuffed to the brim from dinner at Madison's diner, I groan, "I am so bloody full, fuck. I need to go for a walk to digest all that food."

Imogen, sharing my sentiment, enthusiastically agrees, "Fucking same, girl!"

Claire, seemingly impervious to the food coma, just laughs. "Fine, let's go walk down there." She points towards a lit-up street adorned with fairy lights, courtesy of some well-meaning locals probably attempting to elevate the town's charm. Claire continues, "And then we'll decide what we wanna do next. It's still early," lifting up her phone to reveal the time, a mere 8:30 pm.

"And if we're gonna truly celebrate, we'll need drinks."

Imogen quips, "OMG, yes! Where to but?"

There's a shared understanding that there's only one place in this small town equipped for such celebrations.

Claire gives her a confirming look, and I just roll my eyes. *The Loose Lasso it is... again.*

Seated at the bar, nursing my *second* whiskey and coke—unusual for me, especially considering we'd only been here for about half an hour since finishing dinner. I look over to Claire, who is aimlessly scrolling on her phone looking at what looks to be an email. I can't help but voice my thoughts. "You've come here to get away from work and celebrate your promotion, and yet you're sitting on your phone checking work emails," I tease Claire.

"I know, I'm sorry," she replies, shutting her phone off and tucking it away into her handbag. Meanwhile, Imogen, standing beside Claire, sways to the rhythm of '1, 2 Many' by Luke Combs, playing softly in the background, creating an upbeat ambiance.

As the night's bartender approaches, his familiar voice catches me off guard. "Isla? Shit, I haven't seen you in years! Where've you been?" he asks, a smirk tilting his mouth upward.

It takes me a moment to register—David Kent, *no way*. A fellow high schooler, who was a year below the girls and I.

"David? Wow, I almost didn't recognise you. You've changed so much," I exclaim, and he laughs. Continuing the conversation, I share, "After school, I moved to the city after Mum died, to study Veterinary Science. I'd just needed a change of scenery."

His expression softens. "Ah... shit, yeah. Sorry about your mum," he offers sympathetically.

"No need to be sorry, it was a long time ago," I reply, though in my mind, it feels like *yesterday*. I muster a smile, but it doesn't quite reach my eyes. Sensing my unease, he quickly changes the subject. "Congrats on your studies, though. So, have you been in town for long?"

Grateful for the subject change, I relax slightly. "About just over a month now, almost two. I own the Animal Hospital down near Springbrook Reserve," I share.

David's eyebrows raise in surprise. "No shit! Wow, so you own that joint now, huh? I thought it'd closed down ages ago."

"Nope, it's still open now," I quip.

"That's good to know, in case I ever need to bring my dog over. The only other nearest vet is about thirty minutes away. This one is more local, much more convenient," he replies.

Curious, I ask, "Oh, what dog do you have?"

"Oh, Bessie's an Old English Sheepdog. She's an old timer, that one," he laughs, a genuine smile playing across his features.

I can't help but notice his looks. He exudes that young, boyish appeal—soft features, little to no facial hair, and his light brown hair is shaved close to his scalp, just a tad too short for my liking and a bit too light for that matter, I think to myself.

I prefer a guy's hair dark, longish, with curls, ideally a tapered cut—like someone in particular, a brooding *farmer* perhaps... No, no. *What the fuck? No, shut up.*

David still carries that baby face he'd sported in high school, just more grown up now. *Well, obviously, Isla.*

"So, you're here for good now, then?" He looks me up and down, and I squirm in my seat, feeling a touch insecure under his gaze. Before I can say anything, Claire chimes in, entirely forgetting that the girls had been next to me this whole time, watching this awkward encounter.

"Yes, she is! And she is very, very single." She winks at David.

"Claire!" I smack her arm, and Imogen giggles from beside her.

"For now, I guess," I counter, quickly shooting her a look, glancing back at David, who is still watching me intently. He just laughs. He has a nice laugh, not the kind that stirs up butterflies, but one that just makes you smile back. Which is what I do.

"Noted! Nice to see you *two*, as well." He nods to the girls. "Still stuck together, I see."

"Yep, like superglue," Imogen says, now standing between us, hugging both Claire and me together, rocking side to side. I can't help but shake my head.

"Well, we should definitely get together one day, Isla, when you're not busy wrangling animals, that is." He winks.

"Yeah, th-that sounds good." He watches me, waiting for me to say something else maybe, but I falter, not quite catching on.

"Do you have a pen and paper so she can give you her number?" Claire says from beside me, always the provocateur.

"Yeah, I do. Hold on," he says, scurrying off to the side to search for the items.

I tsk out loud, "Why'd you say that? Now he's going to message me wanting to go out."

"That's the whole point, dickhead."

David returns with a small sticky notepad and pen in hand, placing them on the bench. "Thanks," Claire says for me, proceeding to write my number on the sticky note and sliding it back over to him. *I hate her.*

"Don't mind her, David. She's just shy, is all. Has been since school." I roll my eyes.

"Haha, all good! The shy ones are usually the most fun," he says to me and winks. I avert his gaze, feeling a surge of embarrassment.

"Here, have a round on me, girls."

"Oh no, please, you don't have to—" he cuts me off.

"Trust me, I insist. On the house," he says, pushing over a round of shots that look to be vodka.

The girls and I say thank you in unison and down the shots on a count of three, simultaneously feeling the familiar burn that doesn't sit well, and I almost gag. *I hate vodka!*

"Congrats again on the promotion, Claire bear!" I say, hugging her close to my side.

"Yes, congrats, boo. It is very well deserved," Imogen joins in.

"Thanks, girls. Love you both soo much."

We share another embrace, but the moment is broken as Claire announces, "Alright, grab your drinks ladies, let's go find us a table," and saunters off. Imogen and I follow closely behind, but before I get too far, I decide to turn back around and thank David for the drinks again. I'm responded back with a wink and nod.

The girls and I have now had one too many drinks and are sitting in a rounded booth in the far corner of the pub, singing along out loud to Carrie Underwood's 'Before He Cheats'.

The volume of the music had been amped up, probably sometime a while ago, now drawing out most of the conversations of the locals all gathered around, both on the dancefloor and the booths.

Have I mentioned that intoxicated Claire can be very touchy? She's an affectionate drunk, and currently snuggling up against me, telling me she loves me again and again, whereas Imogen just loves to stir up shit. *She's an aggressive drunk.*

Just moments ago, a group of three middle-aged men, probably in their 40s, walked past our table cat-calling at us, so, Imogen had just casually stood up and yelled, "Oi, you fucknuts, do that again and I'll cut your dicks off," and they'd just scurried off. Claire and I burst out laughing, almost pissing ourselves in the process.

Me, on the other hand, I don't drink—well, let myself get drunk—enough to know what my other persona is. Well, other than the other night at the Loose Lasso, but apart from that, I'd never drink much, same goes for when I was living in Sydney.

The idea of letting loose and having a few too many drinks is both thrilling and nerve-wracking. I've always been the responsible one, the one who keeps it together. Maybe a few drinks will help me forget about everything that's been weighing on my mind lately. Tonight, I want to be someone else, someone who isn't afraid to take risks and have a little fun. I sip the rest of my drink quickly, placing it back down on the table.

The room spins gently as laughter echoes around me, warmth running up and down my body. Feeling the urge to pee, I turn to

Claire. "I need to pee, come with me?"

"No! You can't break the seal yet. We're only just getting started," Imogen exclaims from across the booth.

"Break the seal? What?"

"Oh, I forgot, you're a recluse. If you go now, you'll have to get up to pee every five minutes."

"That's not even a real thing.. That's just called being hydrated because you're consuming liquids, you idiot."

"Oh, Isla, you naïve girl. Whatever you say."

Imogen was right. I'd gotten up to pee twice in the span of about twenty minutes. No wonder they say to hold out for as long as you can. Going to the loo every few minutes is so fucking inconvenient.

The pub is starting to blur around me, but the laughter and chatter of the crowd remain clear. Imogen, not long ago, ordered us another round of drinks. Despite my usual routine, I accepted the third drink with a smile, because tonight, I just want to forget about everything for a while.

The girls are well and truly tipsy now, each word flowing from them with a carefree abandon. I join in with a smile, letting myself relax and forget, if only for a moment.

Amid the clinking glasses and muffled music, my senses sharpen suddenly, hyper-awareness settling in. A conversation in a nearby booth catches my attention, and as I strain to listen, the words make my spine crawl. I crane my head to the left, and spot a group of men, perhaps locals, who are indeed speaking loudly enough for anyone, or more importantly, *me,* to overhear.

My senses are now heightened. The voices belong to a group of men—local townies perhaps—their drawl thick with accents that carry a distinct small-town flavour.

"... ol' Callum Thompson, poor fella. Word is his noggin's all twisted, seeing ghosts and drowning his sorrows since his little girl took off."

My heart skips a beat, and I try to focus on my drink, suddenly feeling exposed in the midst of this clandestine revelation. Claire and Imogen, in their boozy bliss, seem oblivious to the shift in the conversation.

One of the men, a burly figure with a voice that rumbled like distant thunder, adds, *"Yeah, used to be a proud dad, boasting 'bout his daughter, Isla. Now he's just a sad sack."*

Another, with a weathered face etched with years of hard living, chimes in, *"Heard she hightailed it to the big city, left the ol' man high and dry. Can't blame her, though, dealing with a father gone to the dogs."*

Their words hang in the air, laden with the heavy drawl of locals. My hands tighten around the edge of the bar, nails digging into the wood. Eyes darting around, I become acutely aware that others could be catching snippets of this raw revelation about my father.

The atmosphere shifts abruptly as the girls pick up on my uneasy demeanour, turning their heads toward the men engrossed in their conversation. Claire, perceptive as ever, is the first to utter my name, "Isla..."

Embarrassment and anger intertwines within me, manifesting in a sharp and irritated retort. "What, Claire?" I snap, my voice laden with frustration.

Imogen, sensing the brewing storm, chimes in with a plea for calm, "Woah, calm down, Isla."

A bitter laugh escapes me, my anger simmering just beneath the surface. "Calm down? How can I fucking calm down when I have those wankers bad-mouthing my dad? Like I'm right fucking here."

The gravity of the situation hangs heavy in the air, shrouding our table in a palpable tension that replaces the earlier revelry. Imogen reaches out, her hand on my arm as if trying to anchor me in the storm brewing within. "Isla, they're not worth it. Just a bunch of old townies on the piss," she urges, her eyes imploring me to reconsider.

"No, Imogen, I can't let them talk about my dad like that." Intentions solely fueled by the alcohol coursing through my veins, drown out any sense of reason.

Claire, now more sober-minded, leans over and whispers, "Isla, please, it's not worth it. Let's just finish our drinks and get out of here." She tries to be the voice of reason, but my resolve is unyielding. Had I been sober, such a confrontation would have never crossed my mind.

As I stand up, my gaze locks onto the men in conversation, and one of them has the audacity to make another insulting comment about my father. "Probably better off without a daughter who's abandoned him," he sneers.

That's it. A line has now been crossed. The last shred of restraint snaps, and my resolve solidifies. I pull away from Claire's grip, fueled by an anger that eclipses any ounce of sobriety. The confrontation was inevitable. I storm over to their booth, fueled by hot, molten rage.

Claire and Imogen trail behind me. The men, a group of local townies, look both shocked and unimpressed as I approach.

"Is there a problem here?" I demand, my voice cutting through the air like a blade. Their faces go from nonchalant to surprised at the unexpected confrontation. I can see the shock lacing their expressions as they process me standing in front of them. One of them must recognize me, as he says, "Bloody 'ell, didn't know you'd come back."

One of the men, a burly figure with a thick drawl, chuckles dismissively. "Well, well. Thompson's girl, huh? Your old man's been making quite a spectacle of himself lately." What's it to them? It's none of their fucking business. Oh, how I do not miss the small-town gossip, and how everybody just about knows everybody in this fucking town, I think to myself, frustration bubbling under the surface.

I feel Claire and Imogen tense behind me, but I wasn't about to back down. "Cut the crap. What are you talking about? What's it any of your business?"

The men exchange glances, clearly caught off guard by my direct approach. One, a lanky figure with a cocky demeanour, decides to spill the beans. "We were just talking about how he's gone off the deep end. Imagining his dead wife, drowning his sorrows in booze. Ain't that right, boys?"

This hits a sore spot in me, and my eyes start to blur with unshed tears, but I hold them at bay. The others chuckle in agreement, their faces sneering. The news hit me like a punch to the gut, and a surge of anger and embarrassment courses through me. I glare at each of them in turn, my fists clenching at my sides.

"You've got some nerve talking about my dad like that." I seethe, my voice sharp.

Unbothered by my words, one of the men continues, "He's the town drunk now, living in some delusional world. We're just calling it like we see it."

"Show some fucking respect." I feel my blood boil. "You think it's funny to mock someone clearly struggling with things? You spineless pricks."

The second man chimes in, "Just stating the facts, sweetheart. We all know he's a lost cause."

My frustration boils over, and I take a step closer. "You have no idea what he's been through."

"And what, you do, young lady? Last time I checked, you packed up and left him all by himself to deal with the aftermath. No wonder he's become a looney."

"You have no fucking idea what you're talking about." Those tears that I held back are fighting too hard to fall freely. I swallow hard, my emotions raw and unfiltered.

Claire, sensing the tension escalating, tries to intervene, "Come on, Isla, let's go."

"Oh, everyone knows about it. Quite sad actually, but he did it to himself. All those years of drinking finally caught up to him. Just ask her." He nods up towards the girls behind me. Her? *Imogen.*

I turn to Imogen. "What's he talking about?"

Imogen, visibly shaken, is stunned into silence, slowly shaking her head while stuttering, "I-I swear I didn't know it was this bad. Dad never mentioned anything of the sort, just that he hadn't been himself."

I scoff in disbelief, raising my voice. "And you didn't think that would be worth fucking mentioning to me? Your own best friend?"

Imogen, unsure of what to say, stutters, "I wasn't sure of anything. I thought maybe it was best if you could see him in person—" I cut her off, my anger surfacing, "He's obviously not fucking well, Imogen, and probably hasn't been for a while. You could have fucking told me—I would have come back straight away." *He's no world's No.1 Dad—but he's my fucking father, my blood.*

Imogen, now triggered by my confrontation, starts to raise her voice. "Don't you dare fucking blame me, Isla.... You left—it was your decision. Don't put the blame on me for not noticing something sooner when it's you who hasn't been here to be with your dad in the first place."

My blood boils at her words, and just as I'm about to retort, the same burly man from before butts into the conversation, "Good luck dealing with that. Sounds like a real piece of work. Bet he's a burden, just like he was to your poor mother. You're better off staying away."

My fury reaches its boiling point, and without a second thought, my hand shoots out, delivering a resonant slap across the man's face. The now abrupt silence of the pub amplifies the echo of my action. In that suspended moment, a voice pierces through the stillness, demanding, "What the fuck is going on here?"

My heart skips a beat as I freeze, instantly recognizing the deep drawl from behind me. Goosebumps crawl up my skin.

12

Xavier

The Loose Lasso is pumping tonight, which has become the norm for a Saturday night here in Wattle Creek. The town hasn't always been this lively, especially during the evenings. It's more of a recent thing over the years, a change I still quite haven't gotten used to.

I don't even know what I'm doing here. Yet, somehow, I let my best mate, Harrison, convince me and a couple of other guys, Tom, Jackson—who I've met once or twice before—and Michael, Harrison's younger brother, to come out tonight for a few drinks. The whole idea of socialising in crowded places has never been my scene, but Harrison insisted it would be good for a change.

It'd been a long and hard week, dealing with the influx of stock, needing to send shipments out to our local retailers and outside the town. The responsibilities on the farm are relentless, a never-ending cycle of hard work that keeps me occupied day in and day out.

We aren't that well known by any means, but we are known to produce some fresh produce, and the local townies have been munching off our humble harvest. The farm life has its own rhythm, a quiet and steady existence that I've grown accustomed to.

I hate shit like this. Always have. I'd had my fair share of partying back in the day. When I was in high school, it was all we would do on a Friday or Saturday night. Getting drunk with the boys and usually a few chicks and just running amuck... Those were simpler times, times I've left far behind.

That was years ago. I'm not the same person I was before. Usually, they say people age and change for the better. I, on the other hand, have not. The weight of responsibilities and time has moulded me into a quieter, more contemplative version of myself.

I know what people must think of me, but quite frankly, *I don't give a fuck.*

Keeping to myself these days has kept me out of people's business, and in a small town like ours, there is bullshit left, right, and centre.

So here I am, seated at a booth in one of the corners of the Loose Lasso.

The dim lights cast a warm glow on the worn wooden table, and the low hum of conversations mixes with the distant sound of country music. I'm nursing a single beer, an anomaly in a sea of guys who've already downed a few rounds. Pacing myself, not my usual scene.

Harrison, boisterous as ever, slaps me on the back. "Xav, my man! I'm so glad you came. Thought you might need a breather."

I grunt in response, not much for words, especially in a place like this. The guys around the table share a few laughs, clearly at ease with the noisy camaraderie. Tom's lanky frame leans in, a sly grin playing on his face. "Xav, mate, good to see you out and about. You should ditch the farm more often. Duchess the only female you socialise with or what? Apart from your Ma, of course."

I shoot Tom a sharp glare, my stoic expression saying more than words ever could. Without uttering a sound, I shake my head and take a deliberate sip of my beer, emphasising my disinterest in the conversation.

The guys pick up their banter, the volume rising as the night progresses. Harrison, with a boisterous laugh, nudges me. "Mate, you checking out the ladies tonight?"

I remain silent, my eyes scanning the room. The dim lights cast a flattering glow on the women scattered across the pub. The guys, however, continue with their crass commentary, assessing the women with the subtlety of a freight train.

"Look at that one by the bar, bro," chimes in Michael, a bit too loud. "The blonde one. Legs for days!"

Tom adds with a wolfish grin, "And did you see that other redhead by the pool table? Farrrk me."

I resist the urge to roll my eyes, choosing to focus on the rhythmic clinking of glasses and the distant twang of country music.

My gaze lingers on the group at the bar, and I can't help but notice the details. Long brown hair cascading down, a short red dress—accentuating her never ending curves—paired with brown western boots. My eyes trace her form, taking in the sight before the recognition sets in—Isla Thompson. Unmistakably standing out even in the dim light. Imogen and Claire, the other two from the trio, accompany her.

Well, fuck me.

Curiosity piqued, I take another sip of my beer, not entirely sure why Isla Thompson in a place like this is something that bothers me. As I continue observing, I can't help but notice Isla's animated expressions, her laughter cutting through the ambient noise.

Irritation settles in as I watch Isla at the bar with the girls. She's engrossed in conversation with the bartender, and it's evident that he's flirting with her—no subtlety about it. Bloody wanker. Though I'm not entirely sure why it bothers me as much as it does. Whatever it is, I can't deny the annoyance building up within me as I observe the scene.

Watching Claire scribble something on a paper and hand it back to the bartender adds another layer of curiosity to the mix. I narrow my eyes and squint, as if I have supersonic eyesight that'll allow me to see from all the way over here. *What the hell is going on over there? Why do I care?* Really, Xavier.

I notice Imogen and Claire, Isla's best friends since high school, are with her. *Doesn't Claire live in the city?* I may not get out 'n all, but I do remember her leaving town years ago. Part of me warms at the thought that they've remained friends since high school. Unlike myself and my mates. Not that I give a fuck. I've seen Trent around here and there, but not for a while now. Kieran, fuck who knows where that bloke ended up. He's definitely not in Wattle Creek any-more. Probably for the best.

I guess it's just Harrison, Michael, and I now. We've been friends, more like brothers, since a young age. They didn't go to the same high school, but that didn't deter us.

The guys beside me are still droning on about the women in town, discussing them as if they're commodities up for grabs. Disgusted by the objectification, I catch myself in a moment of self-reflection. The eighteen-year-old version of me, a testosterone-fueled, immature idiot, would have reveled in these conversations. The mere thought of it makes me cringe. The superficial conversations, the lewd comments—they all grate on my nerves, a stark reminder of a version of myself I'd rather forget.

Now, at thirty, the idea of such shallowness makes me hate my younger self even more. *How did I ever find that appealing?*

One of the guys poses a question to me. My attention, however, remains fixed on Isla at the bar, her long, brown hair cascading down her back. She's engrossed in conversation, seemingly unaware of my presence in the pub. I don't register the question thrown my way.

Harrison's booming voice cuts through the banter. "Xav, my man, you've been staring at that one for a while…"

I roll my eyes at the assumption, but before I can respond, Harrison drops the bomb. "Oh shit, that's ol' Callum Thompson's daughter."

Recognition flickers on Tom's face. "Bullshit, no! Shit, she's changed, aye? Bit more on the fuller side now." He chuckles and an unpleasant tension tightens my jaw as I shoot Tom a disapproving glare.

"Well, look who's talking," I fire back, giving a casual wave in the general direction of Tom's towering but less-than-impressive frame. Seriously, the guy's built like a stretched-out scarecrow, and it looks like he hasn't seen a barber since the invention of scissors. Stammering ensues, caught off guard by my unexpected jab.

"Oi, woah. Relax, man, I was just messing around. Didn't realise you were so possessive," Tom protests. *I am not.*

Meanwhile, Harrison and Michael find the teasing so uproarious that they practically pee themselves laughing. My unexpected comeback evidently has them in stitches, doubling over like a pair of hyenas at a stand-up comedy show. *Idiots.*

Tom, not knowing when to quit, *clearly,* continues, "You throwing dibs on that one, are ya?" He tries to play it cool, but I've had enough.

"Fuck off, cunt," I retort, not in the mood for his games. But the wanker just laughs, probably revelling in the fact that he has me all riled up. Am I that obvious? *Shit, I am..*

Harrison chimes in, "It's alright, Xav. You know the fucker just loves to stir some shit."

I shoot the guys a glare, ignoring their attempts at banter. They return to their conversations, and I just drown them out, listening to the blaring music. I turn my attention back to the bar and notice that Isla and the girls are no longer there. *Shit.*

Moments pass, and I wonder where she went off to. I seize the opportunity to finish the last gulp of my now-empty beer. I rise from my seat, leaving the raucous group behind, and saunter off to the bar, desperate for a refill to drown out the residual frustration.

The atmosphere is thick with the usual pub cacophony—laughter, clinking glasses, and country music.

As I approach the bar, a sudden commotion grabs my attention from one of the booths in the far corner. Weary, but intrigued, I squint to make out the unfolding drama, but it doesn't phase me. This is Wattle Creek, after all, where the norm involves local drunks roughin' it out with one another..

I decide to stay put and turn back towards the bar, when a fragment of the argument reaches my ears. "Show some fucking respect..." The words are muffled by the blaring music, but I catch the disdainful tone of a... *woman?* A loud, "You spineless pricks," punctuates the air, and my curiosity intensifies.

The bartender, the same wanker Isla was chatting with earlier, seems to have caught on to the commotion. "Oh, shit! Is–is that Isla?" *What?* My face instantly drops, and I whip back around to locate the source of the disturbance.

My eyes follow his, and there, standing at a table occupied by three burly locals, is Isla. She's towering over them, throwing emphatic hand gestures, seemingly engaged in a heated exchange. *Oh, shit.*

Without a second thought, I storm off towards her, standing at the booth, a growing crowd now gathered around the group. Nosy fucks. Pushing a few people out of the way, I bark out, "What the fuck is going on here?" As I approach, the men stiffen as they realise my presence.

One of them, Richard, catches my eye, and a flicker of recognition crosses my mind. He's the proprietor of the grocery store down the road, the one we regularly supply with our fresh eggs and cow's milk. Isla turns to look at me, her eyes filled with unmistakable grief, tears staining her face. My unexpected appearance seems to have caught her off guard. Claire and Imogen stand behind her, sharing identical expressions, although Imogen's carries an extra layer of displeasure. *Hm.*

Richard speaks up, attempting to downplay the situation. "Nothing to see here, Xavier, mate, just some minors getting all ruffled by a good ol' chinwag, is all."

"Oh, bull-fucking-shit, there's nothing pleasant about any of that, you fuc—" cutting off her words.

"Isla!" I declare. "Settle down." I hold my hand up, trying to diffuse the situation. Her eyes widen for a split second, appalled by my interruption, before shooting daggers at me.

Isla's frustration escalates, her voice gaining volume with noticeable slurring, indicating she's well past the point of sobriety. "No, this is fucking bullshit. These meatheads over here think it's okay to talk fucking shit while I'm standing right fucking here."

Just then, another guy next to Richard decides to toss in his two bobs worth in, muttering under his breath, "No wonder she's a mess with a dad who can't hold his liquor *or* his life together..." further intensifying the tension.

"Watch your fucking mouth before I come over there and shut it for you," I growl, anger resonating in my voice. *Piece of shit.*

But Isla shrugs off Claire's hand, her rage consuming her. "Please, don't fucking touch me," she spits, her words dripping with anger.

"I don't feel like being consoled right now," she adds firmly.

Claire looks shocked by Isla's reaction, her eyes wide with concern. Imogen steps in, coming to Claire's defence. "Hey! Isla, you need to calm down. She's just trying to help," Imogen says firmly, her voice tinged with frustration.

"Calm down?" Isla huffs in disbelief. *Fuck me, this is not getting any better.*

Isla raises her hands in surrender, and mutters, "I'm fucking done," and then wipes at her eyes, forcefully shoving past me and everyone else in the crowd, heading towards the door.

Noticing that people are still gawking, I bark out, "What the fuck are you all looking at? Carry on, move!" My voice reverberates through the pub, and people instantly scatter back to their tables and toward the bar.

I pivot back toward Richard, now red-faced, and the other two lowlifes next to him, glaring at them. "You should fucking know better than to disrespect a young woman like that. Grow the fuck up!" I growl, my voice low for only them to hear.

The girls, Claire and Imogen, still stand by the booth, rooted in place, wearing expressions of disbelief. Now well and truly riled up, I shoot them a glare, raising an eyebrow as I storm off in the direction Isla left.

As I step out of The Loose Lasso, I scan the area, but there's no sign of Isla to my left. I turn to my right, and about fifty metres down the street, there she is, walking away into the distance. *Where the fuck is she going?*

Growing increasingly frustrated, I grit through clenched teeth, "For fuck's sake!" as I stride around to my Tacoma parked on the side. I hop in and accelerate down the road, catching up to Isla.

Pulling up alongside her, I roll down the car window and yell, "Isla, where do you think you're going?"

But she's stubborn, refusing to acknowledge my request. "Go away, Xavier, seriously!" Frustration building, I raise my voice. "I'm not letting you walk home drunk."

"I'm not drunk!" she fires back, her voice defiant.

I persist, frustration evident in my tone, "There ain't no way you're walking home in those boots of yours," nodding toward the small heel she's sporting.

"You don't know where I live; it could well and truly be only a few minutes away." *I couldn't give a fuck.* "Just go, Xavier. I'm not your problem." The back-and-forth continues as our words clash, creating a tension hanging thick in the air.

Her words fuel my frustration even more. I swerve my car in her direction, careful not to get too close, and slam on my brakes. Startled, she stops abruptly on the spot. I get out, slamming my door with a force that echoes my frustration, stepping in front of her.

"Get in the fucking car, Isla, please," I growl, my anger radiating off me in waves. "Don't make me ask again or I'll throw you over my shoulder."

As I stand there, my heart pounding in my chest, I can't help but wonder—*What the hell is wrong with me? Why do I care so much? Why am I dragging this out?* Deep down, I know the answers. I care because... well, I just do.

"Ugh! What the fuck is wrong with you? What do you want from me?" She counters, throwing her hands up in exasperation. "I told you to leave, Xavier. I just need to be alone," her voice cracks on that last statement.

She doesn't want to be alone, I might not know much about women's emotions, but this I'm certain of. Not when her mind is probably running a kilometre a minute. *I don't want her to be alone.*

As Isla continues to resist, her words a mix of frustration and desperation, I reach a breaking point.

That's it.

If she wants to be stubborn, fine. Without hesitating, I step forward, lift her effortlessly, and settle her over my shoulders. Despite her protests, a mixture of anger and defeat, her attempts are futile. She's not really putting up much of a fight. *Maybe my assumptions were correct.* Swiftly, I move around to the passenger door, swing it open, and gently place her in the seat.

Isla, caught between shock and disbelief, scoffs in astonishment. As I settle into the driver's seat, I glance over at Isla. Her arms are crossed tightly over her chest, her expression a mix of defiance and resignation. I start the car, the engine roaring to life, breaking the tense silence between us.

"Isla, I'm not doing this because I enjoy it," I say, my voice softer now, tinged with frustration. "I just... I don't want you to be alone right now." I don't even know what I'm saying.

She doesn't respond, her gaze fixed out the window, lost in her own thoughts. I shift the car into gear and accelerate down the road, the palpable tension between us hanging in the air. I drive in silence, the only sound the hum of the engine and the occasional sniffle from Isla.

13

Isla

The nerve of this fucker. Who does he think he is?

I sit in the passenger seat of Xavier's ute, the silence between us thick, except for the distant hums of country music playing in the background. It's 'The Cowboy in Me' by Tim McGraw—fitting for the surreal situation I have currently found myself in. I can't help but wonder why the fuck he cares so much to go out of his way and take me home…? It's confusing, and I'm grappling with the whirlwind of emotions.

I just wanted to be alone, to sort through my thoughts and feelings in peace. But deep down, right now, I don't want to be alone. This man is infuriating, and I don't even know why. Maybe it's the way he looked at me, like he could see right through me. Or maybe it's the way he stood up for me, even when I was pushing him away.

As we drive, my mind keeps circling back to him. Why did he have to be so damn stubborn? Why couldn't he just leave me alone like I asked? And yet, a small part of me is grateful for his persistence. It's unsettling, this mix of frustration and gratitude.

I glance over at Xavier, his jaw clenched in concentration as he drives. What is it about him that makes me feel this way? Why does his presence affect me so much? I shake my head, trying to clear my thoughts. This is ridiculous. I just need to focus on getting home and putting this whole mess behind me.

As we continue driving down the road, heading farther away from The Loose Lasso, I try to make out the streets around me. There's a hint of recognition slowly forming, but despite being away for quite some time, the streets now blur into each other, creating a disorienting landscape.

Lost in my thoughts, I absentmindedly play with the edge of my dress. In doing so, I momentarily realise it has ridden halfway up my thighs, exposing too much skin for my comfort—no doubt a result of being manhandled by the big brute beside me. Embarrassment creeps up, and I quickly pull the dress down, covering my thighs. The awkward silence between us lingers, accompanied only by the rhythmic hum of the engine and the twang of the country song playing in the background.

Shifting in my seat, my gaze involuntarily lingers on Xavier, and I am overwhelmed by the intrusion of warmth that surges straight down to my core. Seriously, why is his clenched-jaw, veins-showing thing so damn attractive? *Ugh.* I curse inwardly, trying to shake off the inexplicable allure.

I can't help but explore his ruggedly handsome features—his long, thick eyelashes, dark, furrowed brows, and that absurdly good-looking Grecian nose. Why do I find his *nose* attractive? *Isla, are you fucked? Am I really admiring this man's nose? What's wrong with you?*

No, seriously, why do men get those effortlessly perfect lashes while we're stuck fucking around with different mascaras and lash curlers?

A pang of insecurity creeps in as I compare myself to this man-sculpted-like-a-Greek-god specimen. And here I am, feeling like a fat cow next to him. *There's absolutely no way in this world this man could ever find someone like me attractive.* Why do I care?

Ignoring the warmth pooling at my centre, I squirm in my seat awkwardly. Xavier breaks the silence. "Stop staring at me like that, Isla." Fuck.

"Li-like what?" I stutter. *Great.* Way to sound confident, Isla. *You're not, you silly girl. Who are you fooling?*

He turns to look at me slowly, his eyes darting straight to my thighs, like he knows exactly why I'm clenching them. Oh boy. His gaze returns to my face. "Do you even know where you're going?"

"Nope," he deadpans, eyes still on me, one hand gripping the steering wheel.

"Can you look at the road... and stop looking at me?" I say nervously. A hint of a smirk appears on his infuriatingly handsome face. Ugh...

"So it's okay for you to stare at me, but I can't look at you?" He fires back, leaning into a playful banter.

"Yes! Seriously! This is how accidents happen."

"Trust me, sweetheart, I know these roads like the back of my hand." My eyes involuntarily drift to his hands—incredibly huge, veiny, with long fingers. I gulp nervously and clear my throat. "Where are we going?" I sigh. "I could have just caught an Uber. You didn't have to drive me."

I feel a mix of irritation, and something else I can't quite place, as Xavier's demeanour shifts, the half-smirk on his lips disappearing. He glances at me, his expression serious.

"Didn't like the idea of you stumbling home this late at night, especially intoxicated."

I frown. "Well, thanks for the concern, but I could've managed."

"I'm sure you could have," he drawls, and I turn to look over at him as he continues, "I didn't like seeing you upset and shit–don't have a clue why, but... I just did," he says, matter-of-factly, his voice low. *That's... that's not what I was expecting him to say.*

"But why?" I press, my tone softening.

Xavier's gaze lingers on the road ahead, his jaw tightening slightly. "I don't know," he admits, his voice barely above a whisper. "I just... felt like I had to."

I furrow my brows, studying his profile in the dim light of the car. There's a vulnerability in his eyes that I've never seen before, and it catches me off guard. "Had to?" I echo, my voice softening with curiosity.

He nods, his grip on the steering wheel tightening. "Yeah." He glances at me briefly as if to say something more, but he just returns his focus to the road.

His words linger in the air between us, heavy with unspoken

thoughts and emotions. I'm not sure what to say, how to respond to this unexpected display of concern from someone like Xavier. So, I simply sit in silence, the country music playing softly in the background, and let his words sink in.

The nervousness dissipates momentarily as something shifts. The alcohol's effects are wearing off, leaving behind a faint buzz that's still granting me some liquid courage.

In the moment, I can't hold back, and I blurt out, "Is it okay if we just keep driving?" My hand instinctively covers my mouth, and I curse myself in my mind for letting those words escape.

Wait... why did I say that? Do I really want to spend more time with him? Or is it just the alcohol talking? I glance at him, my heart pounding in my chest, and notice his features soften.

"Any particular place you'd like to go?" Nerves dance through me, and butterflies erupt in my stomach.

I freeze. "Uh, I don't know," I mumble, realising I hadn't thought this through before I opened my big mouth. As much as I hate to admit it, I'm actually enjoying Xavier's company.

Reading between the lines, as if he knew I'd say something like this, Xavier uses one hand on the steering wheel and takes a right turn down a narrow road surrounded by bushes.

The night sky unfurls with breathtaking brilliance; stars shimmer above as I gaze out of the window. Our journey takes an unexpected turn, leading us to a dead end, where a fence cradles the cliff's edge, revealing a captivating view of a large valley with a river below.

Xavier slows the car, parking near the fence. Facing the cliff, we peer out at the river meandering beneath the radiant night sky. Despite the probable midnight hour, the stars cast an enchanting glow over the horizon, tricking the eyes into thinking it's still late in the afternoon. The serenity is palpable. Xavier rolls our windows down, inviting in the cool night breeze that instantly soothes my overheating body.

"Wow," I murmur, my voice barely audible above the gentle rustle of the wind, "This is incredible." The view is like something out of a dream.

Xavier smirks, seemingly pleased with my reaction. "Yeah. I come here sometimes, when I need to clear my head."

As I absorb the breathtaking scene, I can't help but agree. It's a welcome escape from the chaos of the night. "Where are we?" I ask, unable to resist the curiosity.

"Just off Wattle Creek's National Park," he points straight ahead, towards a larger expanse of bush and trees, across the valley. "They call this 'Royal Cove Lookout'."

Royal Cove Lookout, I repeat in my mind, making a mental note. A hidden gem tucked away in familiar territory. As we sit there, the stars overhead seem to multiply, casting a spell of tranquillity over the night.

The music now softly hums in the background, and I hadn't even noticed when Xavier turned the volume down. I'd been so engulfed by the view before me. "I never knew this place existed," I confess, my thoughts swirling.

Xavier chuckles softly. "Yeah, not many do." *His laugh. Oh my god.*

I fixate on this, as I haven't heard him laugh much at all. His chuckle is *light*, and I revel in the sound of it. It's just so–so manly, so him.

"It's one of my favourite spots," he adds.

I frown, trying to dissect his words, searching for any hidden meaning. Does he bring all the girls he meets here? Why does that irritate me? *Ugh, get a grip, Isla.*

My mind races with thoughts as I glance at Xavier. The air changes between us, and I sense something… *I don't know what I'm sensing.* But this is the second time now Xavier has been in close proximity to me, and I just can't quite grasp my thoughts.

Even in this large ute, Xavier seems to tower over me, making me feel small, vulnerable. The wind softly blows inside the car, carrying his scent. It's a fusion of citrus and a hint of oud that perfectly complements his presence. It's a scent that evokes confidence, which Xavier Mitchell exudes without having to damn try. I feel a strange, magnetic pull, and I realise it's coming from *him.* Just him.

I cross my thighs, adjusting into my seat, undeniably more relaxed now than I was before. The movement inadvertently hitches my dress upwards. I catch his eyes trailing down my thighs, and the sudden proximity is electrifying. He leans closer, his upper arm brushing against mine, the sensation sending shivers down my spine. He's so close now, if I were to turn my head, our faces would practically be inches apart.

Mere inches away from him, feeling bold, I decide to break the silence. "This place is so serene. Peaceful." My voice barely above a whisper.

His smirk deepens, and I feel a warmth spreading through my entire body. I can practically feel how wet my panties are, and the realisation makes me bite my lower lip.

His deep voice interrupts my wandering thoughts. "Mhm." But he's not even looking out at the cliff's edge, his eyes are locked on *me*. My breath hitches, getting caught in my throat.

I don't really understand what's happening here and how we can go from yelling at each other in one moment to sharing this charged, intimate moment the next.

Without much thought, I blurt out, "You probably bring all the girls you meet here." I scoff and laugh, to mask my nervousness. *Idiot.*

"No, actually. Just you." *Just me?* Yeah right, wishful thinking. He looks back and forth between my eyes, and I'm captivated by the intensity of his blue eyes. My heart skips a beat, and I can feel my cheeks flushing with heat. The magnetic pull between us is undeniable. My mind races with a whirlwind of conflicting emotions. A bold impulse overtakes me as I inch closer to him, closing the gap between us. The anticipation builds, and just before I feel the grazing of our lips together, he pulls back.

My heart sinks, disappointment washing over me. *Why am I even disappointed?* Just moments ago, I was internally freaking out, unsure if I wanted this. Now, the sudden withdrawal leaves me oddly wanting. What am I doing? Is this really happening? My mind is a whirlwind of conflicting emotions, and I'm struggling to make sense of it all.

"Isla," he sighs. "You've had a bit to drink." Sensing my reaction, he adds, "I don't want you doing anything you'll regret, and trust me, when I kiss you, I want you fully aware and sober." *When... not... if...?*

A mix of frustration and embarrassment bubbles within me. I shift back into my seat, creating a little distance. The night air suddenly feels cooler. Was it the alcohol making me bold, or was there something real in that moment?

Xavier starts the engine, breaking the charged atmosphere. "I should get you home. I'll need an address, though," he says.

I sigh, rattling off my address while staring out the window. Goosebumps prickle my skin, and it's not just from the cool breeze. *Ugh.* I can't quite figure him out. And honestly, I can't even figure myself out right now, with all these thoughts running through my head.

The ride back is accompanied by a mix of silence and the soft hum of the engine. Xavier glances over at me every now and then, but I just keep looking ahead of me. The soft glow of streetlights passes in a blur, matching the whirlwind of thoughts in my mind.

The events of tonight have taken unexpected turns, leaving me questioning the boundaries we've just somewhat explored. What does this mean for us now? But... there is no *'us'.* My heart races. I wonder if he feels the same, too. *Obviously not, idiot. He didn't try to kiss you back.*

As we pull up outside my apartment, Xavier parks out front and turns off the engine. He turns to me, removing the key from the ignition. Before he can say anything, I open the car door.

"Th-thank you, for the ride, Xavier," I stutter like an idiot, and step out onto the pavement. The cool night air hits me, and I start walking toward the entrance of the apartment. I hear him open his door and mutter something under his breath, slamming the door. He catches up to me in a few strides.

"You don't have to walk me up. You can go," I say, now slightly irritated, my boot heels clicking against the pavement.

He falls into step beside me, his presence towering. "I'm gonna do it, anyway, just to make sure you get there okay," he replies. My annoyance deepens, but I don't argue. We walk in silence, into the building and up the first flight of stairs to level one, the tension from earlier resurfacing. What's with this man and his persistent protectiveness? Is he genuinely concerned, or is it out of pity for blowing me off earlier?

As we reach my front door, I turn to him. *This is so awkward. Fuck, fuck.*

Xavier's facial expression softens slightly, and he breaks the awkward silence. "I'm sorry about what happened back at the pub. Those men are just a bunch of fuckwits who clearly can't handle their liquor. You shouldn't have to deal with that bullshit."

I shift awkwardly on the spot. "Thanks, but an apology is not necessary. It won't fix what's been said now, will it?"

"No, it won't. But it shouldn't happen again. I made sure of it."

"Well, thanks, I guess... and for walking me up," I say, looking straight into his eyes as he looks down at me. "I'm sorry for my outburst earlier. I'm so embarrassed."

"Apology not necessary," he mimics my earlier statement. I roll my eyes, shaking my head as I put the key into the lock, opening my door.

Xavier reaches out, gently touching my arm. "Hey, don't be embarrassed. We all have our moments. You stood up for yourself, and that's important." His kindness catches me off guard, and I can't help but wish he was still the grumpy guy I first met. At least then I'd have a reason not to like him.

His brow furrows slightly, and he opens his mouth as if to speak, but then he hesitates, his expression shifting to one of uncertainty. After a minute, he clears his throat and takes a half step back, as if reconsidering.

"Right, well, goodnight," he drawls, nodding and walking backward towards the stairs. He lingers for a moment, as if unsure, before turning to leave. Now standing inside my doorway, I'm left pondering his actions. Why did he hesitate? Why did he linger? Why do I feel the need to turn back around and look at him one more time? I don't know, but I do.

I turn back around, just in time to catch Xavier going through a similar internal struggle. Our eyes meet again, and there's a moment of silent communication between us. The intensity in his gaze builds, until finally, he mutters, "Fuck it."

In one... two... three long strides, he storms over to me. Before I have a moment to realise what's happening, he is towering over me, gripping my face with both hands, slamming his mouth to mine.

Fuck. Fuck me.

The kiss is explosive, a sudden surge of heat coursing through my body.

It's as if a dormant spark has ignited into a fiery inferno, leaving me breathless and wanting more. A whimper echoes in the air, filling the silence. I realise, with dread, that it's *mine.*

His hands drop from my face, sliding down over my sides, around to grip my backside. Two strong hands grip onto my ass, lifting me, pushing me up against his solid chest. He deepens the kiss, and I part my lips hesitantly, allowing his wet tongue to clash against mine, a deep, low growl escaping his throat, causing me to shudder.

He tastes of mint, beer, and pure temptation. My hands slide up his large arms, wide shoulders, hooking them both behind his neck. In doing so, I can't help myself but pull at the curly strands of hair that rest at his nape.

Our bodies still pressed tightly against each other, the world outside this moment fading away. His hard grip on my ass cheeks keeps me in place as he continues to stroke my tongue with his. Savage and unrelenting. That's the only way to describe it.

He bites down on my bottom lip, and I gasp. Swirling his tongue over the now sensitive spot, my tongue curls around his. I am desperately trying to convince myself that this is wrong. But this feels far from being wrong—I've never found myself trapped in such a daze of sudden pleasure. *I don't think I have ever been this aroused. I don't want this to stop.* How far am I willing to let this go?

Xavier lingers for a moment before he slides his tongue out of my mouth, gently biting my bottom lip again, this time with a softer pressure—teasing almost—that sends flutters straight down to my pussy, making me clench.

His hands, strong and demanding, squeeze my ass once more, as he lifts and pushes me up against his bulking frame, his now rock hard and very prominent bulge, rubbing against me. Well fuck.

Hands still gripping me, he breaks the kiss abruptly, and I feel his hot breath on my face. In a deep yet soft tone, he says, "Goodnight, Isla." With that, he turns, sauntering down the stairs toward the entrance door and back out into the night, to his ute.

Dumbfounded, shocked, breathless—*W-what the fuck just happened?*

With shaky hands, I grab onto the door handle and close it as I step back inside my apartment, using the door to support my now-wobbly legs. I lean against it, replaying the kiss in my mind—Xavier's face, the *intensity* in his eyes, the *warmth* of his touch—leaving me with a curious mix of exhilaration and confusion.

I can still taste him on my lips, minty and something else that is just... entirely him.

A sense of disbelief washes over me. I can't believe Xavier Mitchell, the same guy who lingered in my mind all those years ago during high school, the one guy I'd never expected to get to know, just kissed me—swapped *saliva* with me.

Fuck me, the man can kiss.

What does this mean? Did that kiss mean anything to him, or was it just a momentary lapse? My mind races with questions, and as I stand there, still feeling the warmth of his touch, I can't deny the tingling, unsettling excitement that's settled in my stomach.

I am well and truly fucked.

As I walk away to my car, leaving Isla behind, a whirlwind of thoughts consumes me. What the fuck just happened back there? If I hadn't stopped that kiss, I would have fucked her right then and there, on her doorstep. Fuck, I don't even want to consider what could have happened. I just knew I had to stop it before things escalated. Would she have let me? Fuck. I think about Isla, how she had willingly kissed me back, eagerly even, as if she was as desperate for it as I was. How did things take a turn so quickly? Jesus. *Fuck.*

I can't shake the image of her standing there, looking at me with those eyes, those lips. It's like something inside me just snapped, and all I could think about was kissing her. But now, as I walk away, the reality of what almost happened hits me like a ton of bricks.

Isla is the girl from my past, from my high school years. The one I spent countless moments daydreaming about, the one who occupied my thoughts in secret. Memories flood back to me, as if I've been transported back to when I was eighteen years old. I'd told myself all those years ago that she was someone I wanted to know better, but never did I think I'd be able to do that.

Yet, here I am now. The thought is absurd. Now, though, everything feels different. I can still taste her on my lips, feel the warmth of her body pressed against mine. It's intoxicating, and I can't deny that a part of me wants more.

But I can't. I shouldn't. She deserves better than an impulsive kiss on her doorstep. I slide into the driver's seat, the engine purring to life. The temptation to turn around and go back to her is overwhelming, but I know I can't. Not now, not like this. I need to clear my head, to figure out what the hell just happened. Isla was the last person I expected to kiss tonight, the last person I expected to stir up these feelings in me.

But she did, and now I'm left grappling with what to do next.

14

Isla

The morning light creeps through my blinds, and I wake up with a headache pounding like a construction site. It's a familiar feeling, a sense of déjà vu, that has me questioning the choices I made last night. Groaning, I reach for my phone, squinting at the screen—8:44 am. I've got a barrage of missed calls and texts from Imogen, and a more recent text from Claire.

Claire: We need to talk. Can I come by today, please?

"Ughhh." I groan out loud, not ready to face the day or reality.

As I contemplate the impending doom of those conversations, my doorbell rings. At this ungodly hour? And I haven't even had my morning coffee yet. "Seriously," I curse under my breath.

My first paranoid thought is, what if it's him? *No, no way. Surely not.* He wouldn't show up at my doorstep after... that. But the universe likes to play cruel jokes on me, so who fucking knows?

Dragging my feet across the floorboards, I lumber inside to the front door, mentally rehearsing my annoyed face. I swing it open, ready to unleash my morning wrath, and... well, it's not him. To my surprise, I find Claire standing outside my door, holding two takeaway coffee cups and looking like a ray of sunshine.

Her soft smile fades a bit as our gazes lock, and I feel an unexpected tension in the air. Before I can say anything, Claire barges in, wrapping her free arm around me, squeezing tight. I stand there frozen, not expecting such affection so suddenly.

"I am so sorry for last night, Isla. I honestly had absolutely no idea. Things got so out of hand, fucking hell," she says, genuine concern on her face.

Ugh, I was such a bitch last night. I think in my mind, feeling a mix of guilt and relief at Claire's sincerity. "No, I'm the one who should be apologising, honestly. We had a plan, and I messed it all up. Oh my god! You were supposed to stay here. Fuck, Claire. Where did you end up staying?" I say quickly, rattling off. *I am such an idiot.*

"It's okay, honestly. I stayed over at Imogen's babe... You had every right to get angry over what happened. Imogen is so cut up about everything; she really, really wants to talk to you. I think you should–you know, maybe let her explain herself," Claire replies back, her eyes filled with genuine concern.

Ugh, I was such a bitch last night. I can't believe I lost it like that. I am so *embarrassed*. Claire's right, though. Imogen does deserve a chance to explain herself. But what could she possibly say that would make everything okay? I run my fingers through my hair, feeling a knot of frustration building in my chest.

"Fine," I finally concede, rubbing my temples.

"Tell her we can meet up, but I need some time to gather my

thoughts." Claire nods in agreement, and I can see the gratitude in her eyes.

The headache from last night's alcohol isn't helping, and the last thing I need is more stress.

As I retreat to the kitchen, I can't shake the feeling that my life has become an unexpected rollercoaster, and the twists and turns are far from over.

I cringe at Claire's barrage of questions. "Where did you disappear off to last night, *and* with Xavier Mitchell?? You had us both so worried! We called you so many times," she scolds, her tone filled with both relief and reproach. Her words make me wince as I recall the missed calls on my phone this morning.

"Oh my god," Claire continues, her eyes widening with mischief, "the way he defended you last night, fuuuck me." She fans herself with a sly grin, and my confusion deepens.

I frown—so confused at what she's saying. "What do you mean 'defended' me? He basically dismissed me in front of everyone," I reply, recounting last night's awkward encounter at the booth.

"Babe, after you left, he literally threatened those men for disrespecting you," she retorts, and I'm genuinely surprised by the revelation.

"No way!" I exclaim.

"You should have seen the dirty look he gave Imogen and me. My my, if looks could kill. I'd say there's something brewing under the surface there. He was all worked up," Claire continues, placing a hand on her hip as if waiting for me to sparc any information.

My mind drifts back to last night, our moments alone, and that kiss. *Jesus Christ.* It's too early for such thoughts—I don't need to be horny this early. Now well and truly flustered, I look back up at Claire. *Big mistake.*

"Isla, I know you're not blushing right now," she teases, pointing a finger at me. "Oh my GOD! You are, bitch. What are you not telling me? You still haven't answered my question about Xavier," she presses.

Heat rises in my cheeks, a vivid blush betraying the emotions swirling within. Ignoring the question, I busily occupy myself in the kitchen, opening the fridge to grab a cold bottle of water, taking one out for Claire as well.

She must've caught my blush and persists, "Uh, hellooo, I'm waiting... And don't tell me you walked home because that's horseshit."

"How do you know I didn't Uber it?" I retort back, trying to divert the conversation. *Not helping, Isla. You're just digging yourself a bigger hole.* Might as well just tell her. *Fuck it.*

Claire raises an eyebrow, hands crossed over her middle, leaning against the kitchen counter. Damn, this woman is persistent. Fuck, I feel sorry for whoever decides to date her. God love her, though. Taking a big gulp of water, swallowing both the water and my nerves down.

"Fine, Xavier brought me home! There, happy?"

Claire squints her eyes. "No, something else happened. You know my intuition is fucking phenomenal. You can't lie to me, Isla Thompson." I take a deep inhale, mentally contemplating how to go about this.

"Well for starters, he literally chucked me into his ute because he wouldn't take no for an answer and then drove us to the... um, 'Royal Cove Lookout,' I think that's what it's called," I say, trying to recall the name.

Claire interrupts, her eyes going wide, raising a hand to stop me. "He chucked—Wait, hold up, did you guys hookup?" I roll my eyes and tsk.

"Do you want me to tell you what happened or not?"

"Yes, yes, sorry. Hurry up," Claire replies eagerly.

"We just sat in silence for a bit and spoke. It was actually nice; he just took my mind off everything. Distracted me for a bit," I recount, downplaying the intensity of the moment.

Claire pushes for more details, "And then? Is that it?" I refrain from telling her that I had actually tried to initiate the first kiss because that's just mortifying.

"We just talked, Claire. Nothing crazy happened." But the way she's staring at me suggests she's not entirely convinced. The air hangs with unspoken questions, and I can't escape the fact that last night was indeed a turning point, and the mere thought of him sends a flutter of butterflies dancing in my stomach.

"Oh, come on! Quit being a prude for once and live a little. Spill," she teases, taking a sip of her water and leaning in expectantly.

I take another deep breath and huff out, "Fine, he dropped me off home *and* walked me up to my door... and then he fucking kissed the life right out of me."

Claire chokes on her water, coughing and sputtering. "No, he didn't! I fucking knew it! No way. What was it like? *Xavier Mitchell,* who would have bloody thought?" she huffs out a laugh in disbelief.

What was it like?

You know that feeling when someone's lips touch yours, and it becomes intense, electrifying? It's like an explosion of warmth spreading from your lips to every inch of your body. There's this incredible surge of butterflies straight to your stomach, like a fluttering dance of anticipation. It's as if the world fades away, and all that's left is this magnetic connection, leaving you completely breathless and caught up in the sheer intensity of the moment. *Yeah, like that.*

"It was... nice." Downplaying everything currently running in my mind.

"NICE! Just nice? You said he kissed the life out of you, and it was just... nice?!"

"It was like, when his lips touched mine, this crazy warm and tingly feeling took over. Like everything else just vanished, and I couldn't breathe for a second—It was fucking intense, Claire." I pause, attempting to put into words the sensation that still lingers on my lips. I shiver at the thought of it. It'd been a while since I had been kissed like that, or kissed in general, for that matter. I run my fingers through my hair, exhaling slowly as I ponder on these thoughts.

"The way Justin used to kiss me was just normal, mediocre at best, maybe. He'd say things, making me believe I wasn't good enough, or not skinny enough, but then he'd sweeten it up with his excuse of, '*caring too much for me, and just wanting what was best for* '*us*','and I totally fell for it. I was so innocent and naïve back then, unbeknownst to me at the time." His kisses never used to give me *butterflies*. Maybe once or twice at the beginning, but after that, everything intimate just became a chore.

"Honestly, it's... it was fucked, Claire. You have no idea. It's like you no longer feel like the person you used to be. You often wonder if you're being too sensitive. You feel like everything you do is wrong. I just didn't feel like me anymore, you know?"

"Wait. *That's* why you broke up?! You said it was a mutual agreement... *babe?*" she says softly, tears welling in her eyes.

The absence of commitment after Justin never bothered me before, but now it's different. Now, I find myself yearning for something more, someone perhaps? Who will appreciate me without demanding change? *It scares me, you know?* The idea of opening up again after everything that went down with Justin. I don't even know Xavier that well for him to be spurring on these infuriating thoughts after one kiss. Just *one*!

Who is he really? What is he truly like now after all these years post high school? I haven't spent much time with him now to know the true answers to these questions. *Do I even want the answers?* I can't stop myself from wondering this and it both bothers me yet intrigues me. *Why, though? Arghh.*

"Yeah, and no, definitely not *mutual*," I say softly. "Fuck, I've never really said those words out loud," I admit, my voice cracking. Tears start slipping from my eyes, and I blink them away. Claire looks at me, her own tears falling.

"Oh my god, babe!" she exclaims, rushing over to give me a hug. "Why didn't you ever tell me? I knew he could be a bit of a wanker at times, but I didn't realise how bad it'd gotten," she says, sniffling into my shoulder, spurring on my sobs. *No one did. Not even his own family.*

As Claire and I stand there, embraced in a hug that feels like an eternity, she finally breaks the connection, and her words slice through the heavy silence, "You're so much better than him. Fuck that piece of shit. You deserve better, and you must know that now; otherwise, you wouldn't have broken it off with him." I nod, feeling the truth of her words settling into the wounds that Justin left behind.

"You're beautiful, both inside and out. Women would kill to have these curves. I would kill to have them, honest to god." Claire's compliment only intensifies the emotions swelling within me.

She presses on, "It takes a real man to appreciate these things as well as a woman's personality, and the day you find one who does, you better not let him go, because trust me, they're fucking impossible to find in this sea of men. Believe me, I am surrounded by men all day, 24/7, and it's fucking hard. I am convinced all men are useless."

I huff out a laugh, and as I look at Claire's determined expression, a genuine smile forms on my face. "You know," I say, feeling a sense of gratitude, "you always know how to make me laugh, even in the midst of a breakdown. I love you."

Claire grins, gently wiping away the last of my tears. "Damn right, babe. Love you, too! Now, let's forget about that asshole ex of yours and focus on finding you a real man who appreciates you for all that you are. Trust me, he's out there, swimming against the tide of uselessness." Our shared laughter becomes a comforting melody. "I say, get to know Xavier more. You just never know."

"I don't know, Claire," I respond hesitantly. "Maybe it was all just a spur of the moment. Maybe he kissed me because he felt bad…" I trail off. "I don't know." I try to reassure myself as much as I reassure Claire.

She doesn't seem convinced, however, and retorts, "Not with the way he acted last night. He wouldn't have kissed you for no bloody reason. Just… never say never, okay?" Her words linger in the air, planting a seed of doubt in my mind as I ponder the possibilities of what could be brewing with Xavier. Echoing previous thoughts from earlier and last night.

In the quiet moments that follow, Claire's expression takes on a thoughtful cast. "You know, Isla," she continues, "being back home in Wattle Creek suits you. There's something about this place that brings out the best in you. I feel like big things are coming your way." She laughs. "Look at me being all spiritual and shit." I join in on her laughter.

"I guess so," I admit. "I'm just so worried about Dad. I think he needs to see someone, maybe a doctor." *I don't know.* "I've just—I've been gone for so long Claire, I am so afraid I've missed out on so many things—important things."

Claire's eyes soften with understanding, and she places a reassuring hand on my shoulder. "Isla, you've always been there for your family, despite everything that's happened with your mum *and* your dad. No matter what happens, at the end of the day, he's your dad. You'll always need each other. If something's not right with him, we'll figure it out together. You don't have to face it alone."

I nod, appreciating the support and comfort in her words. "Thanks, Claire bear. It means a lot." *I really need to talk to Imogen.*

"Always, babe," she affirms, "that's what best friends are for. We'll navigate these waters together, just like finding you a real man. And remember, your purpose is now here, in Wattle Creek, surrounded by people who care about you."

After Claire left, my place felt like a battleground of emotions, and naturally, my anxiety kicked in. Cleaning, the universal remedy for my chaos, became my go-to. I mean, who doesn't organise when life gets messy, right? I'm that girl who tidies up when the world feels like it's playing Twister with my sanity.

Our laughs hung in the air, bumping into the heavy stuff—Claire's wisdom bombs about Justin, the whole self-worth revelation, and this whole shemozzle with dad. My apartment had soaked it all in, a witness to the aftermath of girl talk therapy.

But Claire's chat got me thinking, especially about Dad, and once again, the home phone kept ghosting my calls. *Hmm.* I made a mental note to dig into that when I got there.

So here I am now, sitting in my car, out the front of the house. His car, a 1990 Toyota Hilux, is parked out front, so I know he must be home. *Home.* A mix of known and unknown.

As I hop out of the car, déjà vu hits me hard. It's like a weird sense of familiarity and uncertainty all rolled into one. The echoes of our last encounter, which hadn't gone well, whisper in the air as I approach the front porch. I shake off the uneasy feeling and walk up to the weathered screen door, giving it a knock.

"Hello? Dad?" The words hang in the air, but the only response is silence, except for the faint sound of the telly playing from inside.

It's weird, you know? Like, I half expect Dad to stroll in from the living room, grumbling about the volume being too low or too high—*like he'd always used to do.* Instead, the quiet just lingers. The screen door creaks as I push it open, and the living room unfolds before me. The glow of the television casts a muted light on the worn furniture—a game of test cricket playing.

Something feels off, like the air itself is holding its breath. "Dad?" I call out again, louder this time, my voice carrying a mix of concern.

I take a step further into the house, the floor creaking beneath me. It's *strange*—the echoes of my footsteps, the hushed television, and the uneasy stillness. My eyes scan the room, searching for any sign of him. *Where the fuck is he?*

"Out here," his deep voice calls from the back. A sense of relief washes over me. I walk towards the back door—the back screen door is directly adjacent to the front door, a long hallway connecting the two together. If you were standing from the front door, you'd be able to see straight out to the back. A memory flashes in my mind of a time when I used to run up and down this hallway, coming to and from the back of the house to the front. My dad was usually on my heels, chasing me with either a playful grin or a stern one. The recollection warms my heart, a moment of innocence amid the complexities of the present. I make my way down the familiar hallway. I open the back door, and there he is, just out in the yard, working on the Strukta Fencing that surrounds the house. Some pieces of timber planks look to have been disjointed, broken off—some fallen to the ground, some hanging downwards.

"What're ya doing here?" he grumbles, but loud enough for me to hear him. Back to his usual self, I see—I think.

I walk out towards him, mentally patting myself on the back for putting on my favourite pair of Ariat Krista western boots, because the grass is quite long, probably in need of a mow right about now, and you just never know what's hiding out in the grass. If I'm not in my steel cap working boots, I'm in these. They just go with soo many outfits, they're cute and practical—*plus they weren't fucking cheap, so I have to get my money's worth, right?*—and the girls always compliment them, so...

It's a bloody scorcher out again—the downside to living out here in the bush, apart from literally every deadly, poisonous animal or creature that can be found here, is the heat. It's about 2:30ish pm in the afternoon, and I'm pretty sure the temp is way past the thirties.

I walk towards him, feeling the heat intensify with each step. He's sweating, a testament to how long he's been working out here in the scorching sun. As I get closer, I can see the familiar lines etched on his face, the wear and tear of a life lived in the unforgiving elements.

"You got any water?" I ask, trying to keep my voice light despite the concern. Dad replies in his usual gruff tone, "Back fridge," nodding up behind me. I turn around, spotting the old fridge tucked away near the back door. Walking back up, I open it, grateful for the cool rush of air that escapes. Grabbing cold water bottles for Dad and me, I close the fridge and make my way back to Dad.

The plastic crinkles as I twist open the cap, taking a refreshing sip. The sun beats down, casting long shadows across the yard. I glance at Dad, his focus on fixing the fencing, hands weathered and skilled from years of manual labour.

"Need a hand with that?" I offer, taking another sip of water. Dad grunts, a sign that he appreciates the offer but isn't about to admit it. I take that as a cue to grab a spare pair of work gloves from the shed.

As I return, I join him in working on the fence. The rhythmic sound of hammering and the occasional creak of the wood become a backdrop to the shared silence between us. The heat lingers, but there's a sense of familiarity in the routine, a connection mended by actions rather than words.

I decide to break the silence, my words clipped and hesitant. "Home phone not working or something? I've tried calling a few times... You never answer."

He doesn't look up from his work, but his expression tightens. "Don't need it ringin' all the time," he mutters.

"But what if it's important? What if I need to reach you?" I press, frustration creeping into my voice.

He finally looks at me, a mixture of irritation and something else in his gaze. "I'm here, ain't I? If there's somethin' important, you come here."

I bite my lip, realising the futility of arguing. Dad mumbles something about people calling all the time, wasting his time.

Confused, I press for more, "What do you mean, calling all the time? Who is it? Like telemarketing or randoms?"

"Randoms, I s'pose. Tryna stir shit," he mutters, a hint of frustration in his voice. I pause in hammering a nail, trying to comprehend his words. "Stir shit?"

He shoots me a stern look, his eyes locking onto mine. "Ain't nothin' important comin' from a damn phone. People talk, spread rumours. I ain't got time for that nonsense."

Recognition forms in my mind about what happened at the bar, the vile words those pieces of shit men had been talking. Fear and unhappiness wrack my body as I recall the demeaning comments that had cut through me like knives.

"Why do you let these people talk like that?" I ask, frustration bubbling within me.

"What'ya been hearing?" he asks, his voice deep, concern flickering in his gaze.

"Nothing, I'm just saying, from what you said..." I reply, my voice trailing off. I want to ask more, to understand why he would let such words slide, but he cuts me off with a stern look.

"Nevermind what I said," he says, his tone final. The unspoken understanding lingers between us. I can't help but wonder if he *knows*. Does he really know what those townies have been saying?

I think back to when I was a kid, hearing Mum and Dad discussing Nan and Pop's battle with dementia. Nan got hit with it early on. I can still hear Mum's words echoing, *"People in the early stages of dementia may understand their diagnosis and its implications. But everyone is different. Some don't."* Nan, she always knew what was going on, but Pop, he might've been in denial. In the end, he was lost to the world, not really knowing what was happening. My heart breaks for my poor dad. *What if he turns out the same?*

I shake off these thoughts. A heavy silence now punctuated only by the sound of nails being driven into the fence. I need to find a way to bring it up without angering him. I know for a fact he'll never just willingly go to the doctor for a visit. He'd always hated them. *How the fuck am I going to do this?* I don't know what the fuck I'm doing.

"Dad," I begin tentatively. "Do you, uh, still keep in contact with Mr. Mitchell?" I ask casually, my curiosity piqued.

It's a question that's been lingering in the back of my mind lately, ever since seeing Xavier. I vaguely remember Dad working with Mr. Mitchell when I was younger, but my memories from that time are fuzzy at best.

At the mention of his name, Dad looks up abruptly, his weathered face scrunching up in disgust. "Why are you asking about him?" he demands, his tone sharp and clipped.

I hesitate, unsure of how to answer. "Oh, well, I just happened to run into Xavier in town, and it got me thinking," I reply cautiously. The truth is, there's more to it than that, but I'm not about to dive into the deets with my father.

Dad's expression darkens. "Stay away from 'em Mitchell boys, Isla," he warns sternly. "If they're anythin' like their father, I suggest you stay away. They're nothing but trouble." *Trouble?* His words catch me off guard, and I can't help but feel a knot of unease forming in my stomach. *What does he mean?* I need to know more.

"But, why? Did something happen?" I press, hoping for a clearer answer. He brushes me off, his expression growing more stern, and I know it's best not to push him further. As he turns away to tend to his work, I can't shake the feeling that there's more to this story.

Clearing my throat, I watch as he resumes working on the fence. My phone then buzzes, distracting me from my thoughts, and I fish it out of the front pocket of my denim shorts. A text message from an unknown number lights up the screen.

"Hey, Isla. It's David, you know, from high school and from the other night at the Loose Lasso? Uh, I was just wondering if you wanted to hang out tonight?

There's a rodeo show happening out in Hilltop Creek next weekend, at the showgrounds. I could pick you up on Sat at, say, 6:30?"

As I glance at David's unexpected message, a small wave of anxiety kicks in. I take a few deep breaths.

Totally didn't see this coming. I hadn't expected him to message me so soon, secretly hoping that Claire's attempt at setting us up had flown off the radar. *Apparently not.*

I mull over my response. Despite the absence of any immediate sparks, there's a lingering curiosity and a touch of intrigue. Plus, I've never been to a rodeo before, so that adds an interesting twist.

Sure. Sounds good.

I shoot back, keeping it cool and casual.

15

Xavier

"**O**i, fucker, it's official. We're in line for the comp. Fuck yeah!" Harrison whoops, Michael joining in. I shoot them an unimpressed look. "What did you two idiots enrol me for?"

Harrison grins, waving a form in my face. "Bronc Riding. You'll kill it, Xav!"

"Of course," I mutter under my breath, shaking my head.

Dragged into this damn rodeo competition by my own will has me in just the most chipper mood. I roll my eyes inwardly. These two nutcases had been on my case for months about signing up. Annoying as it was, their relentless nagging finally broke me, and I caved just to shut them up.

Michael chuckles. "We've also got our names down for Breakaway Roping and Team Roping. It's gonna be a blast, mate."

I resist the urge to roll my eyes. "Just make sure I don't end up on a damn bull or something."

The boys exchange a knowing look, and I can already tell they're up to something. As they continue with their excitement, I can't help but think about the days with Bradley, practising these skills.

The muscle memory's still there, etched into my bones like an old tattoo. Team roping, though? Nah, I draw the line there. The farm's got enough of that action. I'll let the boys handle it. I'm just here to prove a point, maybe relive the thrill of the ride, and endure this rodeo nonsense.

Hilltop Creek Rodeo—a spectacle townies take way too seriously. This place is buzzing with energy, packed to the brim with people and rows of cars stretching for miles. These folks treat it like a national holiday, and I've got to admit, the contagious enthusiasm might just make this chaotic celebration somewhat enjoyable.

The blare of the commentator's voice reverberates through the air, drowning out the chit-chat of the rowdy patrons. The boys, lured by the prospect of the competition, shuffle inside towards a series of small demountables where competitors wait and wind down before the show.

As we walk, Michael keeps turning back, his eyes searching for something—or maybe someone. He suddenly shouts, "You guys go ahead, I'll meet you there." Harrison, catching on to the unspoken signals, nods. "Yeah, mate, sure."

As Michael darts off, Harrison can't resist adding, "Don't be long, we'll be in the demountables!" Michael, always the one to disappear when things get lively, the quieter of the two brothers, always seems to have a hidden agenda. His retreat is predictable, leaving Harrison and me to head towards the demountables, ready for the rodeo chaos that awaits. The energy is palpable, a mix of excitement and anticipation.

"Man, Xav, this is gonna be a bewdy bonza!!" Harrison, bouncing on his heels, exclaims, as we wait in the demountable for our rounds to be called over the PA system.

"Can you believe we're doing this after all these years? Remember when we were little kids?"

I nod. "Yeah, those were the days. Running around the farm, pretending we were in our own little rodeo... Your brother tagging along like a stray pup." Memories come flooding back.

Harrison laughs, "Yeah, good times. And now, here we are, about to ride for real. Life's a funny thing, ain't it?"

There's a sense of nostalgia in the air, and for a moment, I allow myself to be transported back to those carefree days. It's a stark contrast to the present, standing on the brink of adulthood, about to engage in a rodeo that once existed only in our childhood imaginations.

Harrison continues, "The place is chokers, fuck me," sounding a little nervous now.

I glance out the small window, observing the bustling activity and the huge crowds of people surrounding the showground and seated in the grandstands.

I smirk. "Oh, what's wrong, big boy, having second thoughts, are you now? You don't think before you use that thick skull of yours, do you?" I tease, poking his temple, pushing him slightly from the force.

"Fuck off!" he retorts. "I'm not? Are you?"

"Too fucking late to have any now, don't you think?" I quip. As nervous as I am, I can't help but get off on the adrenaline.

Michael returns after his brief absence. Harrison gives him a playful slap on the back. Harrison's energetic spirit persists. "Where'd you run off to, mate?"

Michael, now noticeably more reserved, dismisses it casually. "Nothing, just saw an old mate."

"Yeah, right," Harrisons says just as I snort out loud.

"Oh, fuck off, both of you. Just some chick I know, wanted to have a chat before we go on, that's all!"

"More like a quick blowie before the show? Some pre-show spirit, aye?!" Harrison says as he throws his arm over his brother's shoulders.

Michael, a hint of mischief in his eyes, shoves off his arm. "No. Shut the fuck up," he says, hushing Harrison to avoid unnecessary attention. "Aw, looks who's all shy now."

Michael just rolls his eyes, scrolling through his phone. I watch their exchange, shaking my head, amused by these two idiots.

It's a distraction, a welcomed diversion from the building tension of waiting for my turn in the arena. The smell of hay and dust fills the air, and I can't help but feel a strange mix of nostalgia and determination as I prepare for the upcoming challenge.

Harrison breaks my daze, leaning in. "So, what ended up happening with you and Cal Thompson's daughter?" My eyes cut to him, glaring.

"Yeah, what the fuck! I forgot all about that," Michael exclaims, moving closer to sit next to me.

I shrug off the insistent questioning. "Nothing. Just dropped her off, and I went home. Felt bad for what those fuckers were saying about her dad."

Michael cuts in, his eyes narrowing. "Seemed like it was something, brother. You looked like you were gonna kill those guys." Still sitting too close for my liking.

I shoot Michael a glare. "You boys really don't know the meaning of personal space, do you?"

Harrison chimes in, "C'mon, Xav. What is it with you two? You've always had some vendetta against her." *More like she's had one against me.*

I brush it off with a wave of my hand. "Nothing, leave it." I'm not about to delve into the complexities of my feelings, especially with these two. *Feelings?* I'd trust these blokes with my life, but they both just have too big of a mouth to share shit like this with them... for now, I guess.

Of course Harrison doesn't understand the idea of 'Leave it.' He grins mischievously and nudges me. "Maybe you'll be the cowboy to sweep her off her feet!" He laughs at his own joke, and Michael and I just sit there.

I roll my eyes. "You don't shut up, do you?"

This earns a chuckle out of Michael and he chimes in without looking up from his phone, "Tell me about it," he deadpans.

Harrison sticks the finger up at both of us, and I can't help but chuckle at that.

The dusty air hangs thick around the rodeo arena as the contenders are called one by one. I make my way towards the iron pen fences, the horses lined up behind the bucking chutes, each contender ascending the platform stairs to saddle themselves onto their assigned bronc. I've been around these rodeos enough to understand the drill. Growing up on a farm, I've attended my fair share, even practised at home, though never driven enough to participate.

Three riders have already taken their chances, leaving me as the third in line. Four more are waiting behind me. The goal is simple: ride for eight seconds with one hand on the reins, avoiding any contact with the horse or oneself using the free hand. Both feet must stay in the stirrups, and the spurs must touch the point of the shoulder when the horse's feet touch the ground on the first jump. So far, three riders have gone, the last one falling just shy of the 8 seconds at 7.3 seconds. Tough break.

Harrison and Michael stand beside me on the platform, exchanging banter to ease the tension. "You got this, Xav!" Harrison shouts, a grin on his face. Michael just gives a supportive nod. The challenge awaits, and as I prepare for my turn, my focus sharpens on the task at hand.

The commentator's voice echoes over the speaker, the upbeat music blaring in the background, "And our next contender, ladies and gents, is our very own local farmer, Xavier Mitchell!" The crowd erupts in cheers, the sound reverberating through the arena, people chanting my name. It's a symphony of excitement, a cacophony of voices blending into a unified roar of support.

Harrison and Michael are shouting and hollering from the fence, their words getting lost in the sea of noise. "Go get 'em, Xav!" Harrison yells, and Michael adds a boisterous, "Make it look easy, mate!"

I look down at the black-coloured bronc beneath me, taking a deep breath and exhaling through my mouth. The men surrounding me engage in conversation, making sure everyone is ready to go. I carefully seat myself on the bronc, noticing this one is a bit more agitated than the ones I'd seen earlier. *Fan-fucking-tastic.*

The process of roughstock events is a meticulous dance, a series of steps choreographed to ensure both rider and bronc are ready for the electrifying eight seconds that follow. I feel the familiar sensation of being seated onto the horse, the firm grip on the rein, and the tension in the air as the rodeo men meticulously check all the ropes and flank straps, securing everything in place.

I exchange nods with the rodeo men, their experienced eyes assessing the readiness of the horse and rider. I give the cowboy nod for the man at the gate to see, signalling that I'm prepared for the ride. The hum of the loud buzzer looms into the atmosphere, a moment charged with anticipation. Time seems to stretch as the seconds tick by, the crowd's roar and the thumping of my own heart merging into a rhythmic soundtrack.

Then, in an instant, the gate swings open, and the action unfolds in slow motion. The bronc explodes out of the chute, a flurry of hooves and flying dirt. I grip the rein with determination, my body moving in harmony with the powerful movements of the horse beneath me. The world blurs, and for those eight seconds, nothing else matters.

It's just me and the relentless dance between man and beast.

16

Isla

Hilltop Creek Rodeo is buzzing with energy, a sea of people converging for a night of thrilling events. I take a deep breath, my heart fluttering with a mix of excitement and nervousness. David had been prompt, arriving at my place exactly at 6:30 pm.

The sight of him waiting at my door sent goosebumps down my arms, and for a moment, I was glad I spent a good twenty minutes or so deciding what to wear—which consisted of seeking Claire's guidance via FaceTime—*who did not shut up the whole time about me finally going on a date*—and so I eventually settled on a white ruffle dress with short puffed sleeves. The dress paired perfectly with a blue denim jacket and my trusty brown western boots. *This is not a date!*

My hair, left in loose curls down my back, felt effortless, and I had clipped it up, half up and half down, with loose tendrils framing my face. Makeup was kept light and minimal—Claire's mantra of "enhance, don't cover up." I wasn't one to spend hours in front of the mirror, and tonight was no exception. I'm glad I gathered the courage to pull this look off. *This is new for me.* I am not even entirely sure where this newfound confidence has come from?

I glance over at David, who now has my hand in his as we enter the showground—a smile playing on his lips. He seems awfully cheerful, this one. The men I've encountered recently are usually not so chipper—well... more like *only one*.

The showgrounds are alive with activity, the crowd bustling with excitement. I take a moment to appreciate the lively atmosphere, a far cry from the quiet moments spent at home or in contemplation. Tonight feels different, a step outside my comfort zone, and I'm ready to embrace the experience, even if my heart is doing a little two-step of its own. David still has his hand in mine as he guides me over to the small makeshift wooden bar surrounded by eskies, filled with assorted drinks.

He looks at me with a smile and asks, "What can I grab ya?" But before I can answer, he seems to answer his own question, deciding for me, "Something girly, aye? Fruity?"

Seriously? An involuntary irritation prickles within me. I've never been a fan of people making decisions for me, especially when it comes to drinks—or anything, for that matter. I'm not one for girly concoctions—give me something robust, like a bourbon and coke or a smooth whiskey.

A hint of irritation creeps into my voice as I respond, "Actually, I was thinking maybe a whiskey and coke." I throw in a small smile, silently urging him to catch on.

"Oh, really? Maybe we'll save the hard liquor for later on," he says, winking. *Uh, okay.* The irritation lingers, but I shake it off, opting to keep things polite. David scurries off to the bar to fetch our drinks.

His response raises a silent alarm in my mind. I can't help but wonder what he might be insinuating. Is he suggesting something more than just drinks and conversation? Because that's all this little meetup is—drinks, conversations, and some rodeo fun, *right?* The uncertainty nags at me, and my mind starts spiralling into overthinking mode—why does my mind suddenly drift to Xavier? *Huh.*

Maybe it's the mention of whiskey, reminding me of that unexpected kiss we shared during a spur of the moment. *He wouldn't be here, would he?* The idea sends tingles down my spine. *Why do I care anyway?* There's literally nothing going on—I don't want there to be. Do I?

He kissed me out of nowhere, and that's it? I don't even have his number, nor does he have mine—no other effort has been made on his part or mine. And why would he—or better yet, why would I? I push those thoughts aside, reminding myself to stay in the moment. I'm here with David; I shouldn't be thinking of Xavier Mitchell. Argh. It annoys me now, thinking about how he just left. Why it annoys me, I don't know. But damn him for kissing me like that and just leaving.

David returns, holding two clear plastic cups filled with an orange and red concoction. "Vodka Sunrises," he announces as he hands me one. I take a sip, and the potency of it catches me off guard, the orange juice leaving a bitter taste in my mouth. My eyes widen, and my lip curls in distaste. How people enjoy the taste of vodka is just beyond me. It's just not for me.

David, seemingly oblivious to my reaction, starts up our conversation again, asking about my thoughts on the rodeo. "I can't believe you've never been to a rodeo before," he says, sounding genuinely surprised.

I respond with a subtle reminder, "Well, I haven't been back here in years, remember? The city doesn't have stuff like this, so I'd never been given the opportunity."

"Oh yeah, yeah, that's right. Oh, well, we have these here all the time. They go off."

I apprehensively take another sip of my drink, bracing myself for the bitter taste. David offers a warm smile as he delves into the details of my city life, making small talk to ease any tension.

"So.. where abouts did you live in the city? And work-wise, still rocking the vet life, I see."

I play with a strand of my hair. "Oh, I lived in a place called The Rocks. The apartment I shared with some mates had such incredible views of the harbour. I was actually sad to leave it." I let out a nervous laugh. "As for work, yup, still doing the vet thing. Couldn't leave the animal life behind."

He nods, recalling what he already knows. "Ah, right. City life can be quite something. Sounds like it must've been expensive. No wonder you had to live with roommates." He laughs. "Back to the calm of the countryside, huh?" He nudges my shoulder.

I feel a twinge of annoyance. Is he implying I can't afford to live on my own? I shoot him a sidelong glance. "Well, you know, city living and all. Roommates make it more fun, right? Plus, who needs to live alone when you can split the rent and share the drama?" I force a grin, hoping he catches the sarcasm. "But yeah, back to the roots," I say as I take another big sip of my drink. Maybe some liquid courage might make this a little less awkward. This is going... great. *Give him a chance, Isla.*

We continue to stroll around the lively venue, drinks in hand, soaking up the excitement of the rodeo grounds. The grandstands offer a fantastic view of the large arena, and the air is filled with the scent of hay and the distant allure of food trucks.

David gestures to the right, pointing out the seating area in the grandstands. "Let's find a spot—the next round is about to kick off." The grandstands stretch before us, alive with people chatting, laughing, and cheering. We snag two empty seats in the first row—they're a bit worn, but it adds to the rustic charm.

As we settle into our seats, the buzz of the crowd envelops us. David leans in, his voice barely audible over the chatter and the commentator's announcements. "So, Bronc riding is pretty wild," he explains, a hint of enthusiasm in his eyes. "The rider has to stay on the horse for eight seconds, and they're judged on their style and control."

I nod, taking it all in. The loudspeaker crackles to life as the next round of Bronc Riding is about to begin. The commentators' voices pierce through the noise, and David continues with his rundown. However, my attention drifts as I find myself more focused on his words than the commentator's explanations.

"Watch their form when they're thrown into the air," he says, pointing toward the arena. "The skill is in how they recover and maintain control."

David's explanation sinks in, and I gather that unlike bull riding, where the animal tends to turn in a circular motion, Bronc riding involves a more tumultuous up-and-down movement. Riders are tossed back and forth, their only anchor being the reins held with a single hand. The intricacies of this dance between rider and horse become clearer, emphasising the skill and control required to navigate the perilous ride.

I glance into the distance at the line of men patiently awaiting their turn. Even from this distance, I can't make out their faces, but the array of colours in their shirts and the bold logos on their black vests catch my eye. Their jeans, accompanied by stylish chaps, give off a rugged yet fashionable vibe. And, of course, the cowboy hats add that touch of country charm.

The commentator announces the next rider, named Jackson Hill, who hops onto the horse in the chute, and a loud buzzer goes off. As the first bronc bursts out of the gate, my gaze intensifies, fixated on the rider and horse. The horse's powerful movements ripple through its body, creating a mesmerising spectacle.

The rider skillfully manages to stay atop the bronc despite its relentless bucking. There's a moment where it seems like he might lose his grip, and my breath catches. But in a feat of remarkable balance, he regains control. The air becomes thick with tension, each second ticking away on the larger-than-life timer attached to the commentator's booth.

As the timer rapidly approaches the coveted 8-second mark, the bronc launches one final, forceful move. In an instant, the guy is flung off, rolling to the ground. The crowd erupts with a mix of disappointed sighs and impressed cheers. The commentator's excited voices compete with the background hum, announcing his score of 85.3. *Oof, so close.* With a quick recovery, the rider stands up, brushing off the dust, and hurries off towards the gates. The rodeo atmosphere pulsates with energy, and I find myself eagerly awaiting the next round of daring performances.

David leans in to shout into my ear, attempting to be heard over the uproarious crowd. "Shit, I thought he was gonna make that one. Pretty cool, huh..." His words, however, are swallowed by the raucous cheers and the commentator's voice booming over the loudspeakers, announcing the next rider.

"And our next contender, ladies and gents, is our very own local farmer, Xavier Mitchell!" The crowd erupts in cheers, creating a deafening symphony that reverberates through the arena. My eyes widen, and I freeze on the spot. The realisation hits, and my heart skips an entire beat.

What the fuck? My mind races as I watch the grandstands come alive with enthusiasm. I find myself unconsciously searching for him among the people, trying to catch a glimpse of that familiar figure.

Bloody hell, it was literally not long ago that I had thoughts of him lingering in my mind, and now, it's as if the universe has answered my unspoken questions. What is he doing here? David's exclamation snaps me out of my trance. "Oh, wow! I had no idea he'd be competing. What the heck?" What the heck, indeed.

My eyes find Xavier standing in the same spot as the guy before, flanked by two guys—no doubt offering words of encouragement. They pat him on the back, whispering something in his ears. Just as the previous contender did, Xavier hops over the gate and into the chute, settling onto the horse. This one, however, seems a bit more agitated than the previous horse. My heart skips a beat, and I unconsciously hold my breath. *What on earth is Xavier doing in a bronc riding competition?* I can't help but wonder, feeling a strange mix of surprise and intrigue.

With a nod of his head, signalling that he must be ready, the buzzer goes off again and I'm nearly out of my seat, watching everything unfold in slow motion. My eyes are glued to the intense dance between the horse and Xavier. He does it with seamless effort, like he's been doing this all his life. The air is filled with tension as the timer moves rapidly.

My eyes dance back and forth between the timer and Xavier, captivated by the vigour of his riding—my breath caught in my throat as he's bucked up and down vigorously. I find myself silently chanting, '*Stay on, stay on... Don't you dare fall off.*' I shake my head, ridding myself of the thoughts—my brain just momentarily short circuiting. *Surely.*

There is just something captivating about seeing Xavier in this raw, unfiltered moment. The unexpected rush of emotions catches me off guard, and I find myself invested in whether he can make the eight seconds.

In a split second, Xavier's hand almost loses its grip, and my heart lurches forward. I find myself standing, hand covering my mouth in shock, unable to tear my eyes away. The timer is rapidly closing in on the 8 seconds, and to my complete surprise, Xavier manages to stay on the bucking bronc for the full duration. I release the breath I had been involuntarily holding, exhaling with a big whoosh. "Fucking hell," I mutter under my breath, my eyes still glued to Xavier.

The horse continues to buck, and I wonder how on earth he's going to get off. Just as this thought crosses my mind, two pickup riders fly into the arena, moving up close to Xavier on the still-bucking horse. With seamless precision, one of them manages to wrangle him off, with an arm around his waist and onto his horse, moving him safely away from the untamed bronc. The other guy signals the horse with a whistle, guiding it back to the chutes. Still processing the adrenaline-pumping spectacle that just unfolded before my eyes. I'm left in awe.

As Xavier is safely wrangled back behind the fence, the commentator loudly announces his score—an impressive 93.8. "Wow, now that's a record to beat, gents. Give him another round of applause!" The crowd erupts into cheers. *Shit!* That's the highest score so far, and I can't help but join in with the excitement. I watch as Xavier turns around to the crowd, taking his hat off and throwing his arm in the air, exclaiming his excitement and disbelief. Those two guys from earlier run up and jump him.

In this suspended moment, the crowd's chaotic buzz fades into a distant hum, and all that exists is the spotlight on Xavier. My eyes unintentionally seek refuge in his, and a shiver of trepidation crawls down my spine. I'm caught off guard, my heart skipping a beat as I realise that Xavier has inexplicably locked eyes with *me* in this huge sea of faces.

His gaze is piercing and intense, like a magnetic force pulling me closer against my will. In this vulnerable exchange, his raised eyebrow and the playful smirk dancing on his lips hint at a silent acknowledgment of our shared encounters. It's as if he revels in the clandestine dance of this weird fucking connection we're somehow entangled in. The air thickens with an electric current, charged with a fusion of tension and curiosity binding us together in this peculiar moment.

Despite the horrified realisation that I've been spotted, I just can't look away from his eyes. It's like I'm stuck, completely hooked on his gaze that feels like it's going beyond normal time and space. His eyes catch movement from beside me—*David...Fuck!*—I'd forgotten he was still next to me. I watch as that annoying smirk of Xavier's disappears off his lips, his eyes now shooting daggers at David, who's sitting next to me—completely oblivious to Xavier's silent threat.

Suddenly, it feels like all the air has ditched my lungs. I struggle to catch my breath, my heart now doing some Olympic-level sprints. I grab my drink and skull the rest of the contents down quickly. Wrong decision. It burns its way down my throat, and the potency goes straight to my head.

I need air. No.

I need to get the fuck out of here and away from *him*.

Xavier

Standing on the platform, with Harrison and Michael cheering like maniacs, the chaotic buzz of the crowd around me seems to fade, drowned out by the warm sensation and shivers running down my back. My eyes unintentionally scanned the crowd, and there she was—Isla fucking Thompson. Caught off guard, I locked my gaze on her, wondering what the hell she was doing here, and... with that piece of shit, of all people? *Seriously, what the fuck?*

My gaze narrows as I watch Isla say something to the idiot, who's completely oblivious to my death stares. Then she bolts, slipping through the crowd. Where the hell is she going? She better not be bailing on this, on whatever the fuck this is.

Nah, fuck that.

I quickly rattle off to the boys that I need to "take a piss" and run off in the direction Isla fled.

17

Isla

I'm hauling ass, trying to catch my breath as I search for the damn bathrooms. Not sure how much of that intense stare-down David caught on to, I gave him a quick "I need to hit the bathroom" and dashed off. He looked a bit curious, maybe apprehensive. Who knows? I jog up to the nearest stall and ask the lady at the counter, "Excuse me, where are the bathrooms?"

She grins and says, "Dunnys are just down that way, love, round the corner behind that bar over there." Her hand points in the direction, about 200 metres away.

I sprint in that direction and slip inside one of the empty cubicles, even though I don't really need to... *bloody hell.*

I wait a moment, for good measure, before flushing the empty toilet and head back out to one of the nearest sinks. I rinse my hands and pat some water behind my neck, a futile attempt to calm the heat radiating off of me.

Grabbing a paper towel from the dispenser, I wipe my forehead, eliminating the beads of sweat forming along my hairline. As I stare at my reflection in the mirror, I can't help but notice the disarray my appearance is in—hair slightly dishevelled, eyes wide and still brimming with the excitement from before. It's like the mirror is reflecting the chaos inside me.

Taking a deep breath, I fluff up my hair, fixing a few stray strands that have fallen out of my clip, needing to pull myself together before heading back out and face god knows what... or *who*.

Drying my hands, I toss the paper towel into the bin. With that, I head outside, shuffling past a few girls now waiting in line outside the bathroom. I turn to walk out, but notice an exit to my left. Figuring I need some fresh air, I glance back at the arena, looking for... well, *I'm not even sure.* A feeling of unease stirs within me, and just as I turn to continue walking outside, I collide into something hard and bulky, a soft "Oof" escaping my lips.

The abrupt collision throws me off balance, sending me backward. Before I can land on my ass, two strong arms grab my waist, keeping me upright.

"Going somewhere, love?" A deep voice drawls. I freeze—recognizing that *voice*—even in my slightly dishevelled state. I try to pull away, but it's like trying to escape the gravitational pull of a black hole.

I glance up, meeting his intense gaze. The arena lights cast shadows on his rugged features, emphasising the scruff on his jaw. It's the kind of face that would make most girls swoon, but all I feel is a surge of irritation and a hint of something else that I refuse to acknowledge.

"Xavier," I mutter, my voice low and strained.

He smirks, his eyes dancing with amusement. "Didn't mean to

interrupt your escape, princess. Leaving so soon?"

I scowl at the nickname. "I'm not your princess. Let. Go."

His hands linger for a moment longer before releasing me softly. I take a step back, regaining my composure. "What are you doing here?" I ask, more sharply than intended.

"Just enjoying the rodeo, same as you, I see," he replies. His gaze flickers over me, and I suddenly feel self-conscious in this silly dress.

I narrow my eyes on him. "I highly doubt we enjoy it the same way, and unlike some people, I don't have a death wish."

He chuckles, the sound sending a chill coursing through my body. "Fair enough. But you were looking for something out here, weren't you? Or some*one*?" He adds with a raised eyebrow, "Where's your little date?"

I avoid his probing gaze. "None of your business. And it's not a date," I scoff.

He takes a step closer, his gaze intense. "You seem to have a knack for finding yourself around me, don't you?"

I laugh, a bitter sound escaping my lips. "Oh, please, Xavier. My world doesn't revolve around you." *Ironic*, because lately, it has.

"Hmm, that's three times in a row now. You know what they say, *third* time's a charm, Isla," he says, a smug grin playing on his lips. "It must be fate that we bumped into each other again."

I deadpan, meeting his gaze with a sarcastic smile. "Don't flatter yourself. It's a small town, Xavier. It's bound to happen."

He leans in, his breath warm against my ear. "I dunno, maybe fate is trying to tell us something." I push him away, rolling my eyes.

Being around his presence is so spellbinding, like I forget everything about me and everything that's around me. My head is buzzing, no doubt those sips of alcohol now rushing to my head from this whirlwind of a conversation. I sway on my feet a little, trying my best to avoid looking at him. *I should head back to David.*

But damn it, I'm desperate to fight this attraction I have toward him. I'll be damned if I let that one kiss cloud my judgement. Yes, it was fucking unreal, but that's all it'll ever be. I'm smarter than this.

His expression darkens, and I can practically feel the anger radiating off him. "Are you drunk?" he asks abruptly, his eyes narrowing as he notices my slight sway.

I roll my eyes. "No, Xavier. I'm not drunk. Just needed some air."

He doesn't seem convinced, and his next words are laced with suspicion. "How many drinks have you had?" he demands, his voice low and dangerous.

I bristle at his accusation. "What?—One? Why do you care?"

His jaw tightens. "Because you're swaying on your feet like you're tipsy. This ain't the time and place to get drunk."

"And what? You think I actually came here to get drunk? What do I look like to you? I had *one* drink, Xavier." *Why am I even explaining myself right now?*

"All it takes is one drink and—"

"And what?"

"Nothing." He shakes his head. "Just don't want anyone taking advantage of—" his voice trails off, brows furrowing.

"Of me? I can take care of myself. I don't need you playing hero."

He grits his jaw. "I'm not playing anything, Isla. You haven't been here before to know what goes on around these events. I've seen enough girls been taken advantage—"

I scoff, crossing my arms defensively and cutting him off. "Again... Why do you even care? It's not like we're actually friends. I don't need your chivalry or whatever this is. I can handle my own shit." I know better than to let that happen.

I shift on the spot under his intense gaze. Xavier presses, his expression now edged with anger. "That's what they all say," he retorts, his tone carrying a sharp edge. "Why are you here with him, anyway? On a date, of all things."

I raise an eyebrow, irritation bubbling to the surface. "I don't need to explain myself to you."

He smirks, a spark of mischief in his eyes. "Just making sure you're not settling for less, that's all."

I can't help but laugh, a sarcastic edge to my voice. "And what, like you're any better?"

His smirk widens, and he leans in closer, his breath teasing my cheek. "I bet he can't make you melt into a whimpering mess with just one kiss, can he?"

As he speaks, I can't help but seethe with frustration. How can he go from actually being nice the other day, to kissing the hell out of me the other night, to now, this? There was a reason I disliked him in high school. Who does he think he is? Ugh.

Despite these thoughts, my body betrays me. His words send a shiver down my spine, and I instinctively step back, creating some distance between us. "You wish," I retort, my tone challenging. "But even if he could, it wouldn't be any of your business."

His question needles at me, and the anger that's been simmering beneath the surface boils over. "You know what, at least he takes me on a date, wants to get to know me, not just kiss the fuck out of me and then leave me like nothing happened. What the fuck was that, Xavier?" I blurt out, shoving him with my hands.

Xavier's eyes widen in surprise, his usual composed demeanour shaken for a moment.

"Isla, what the hell are you talking about?" he responds, his voice a mix of confusion and defensiveness. "It was just a kiss. It just happened—in the moment. You're the one who's always kept me at arm's length, acting like you can't stand the sight of me."

I scoff, a bitter laugh escaping my lips. "That's because I can't!" I huff out a breath. *Wait.* "*Just* a kiss? You can't just sweep a *kiss* like that under the rug like it meant nothing. Are you living under some rock, Xavier? People kiss because they care, not just for the thrill of it." *Well, maybe sometimes...* but that's beside my point.

He leans in, his face inches from mine, the tension palpable. "I never said it didn't mean nothing to me, princess."

My gaze narrows. "You have a real funny way of showing. You just left me there, all ....confused. You didn't even have the decency to ask for my number or—or... just anything," I say, throwing my hands in the air, my frustration clearly evident.

He smirks, a challenging glint in his eyes. "Fine, Isla, can I please have your number?" he jokes.

Oh, this wanker. Infuriated, I go to shove him again, but this time he catches my wrists and pulls me towards his chest. In an instant, my heart clenches, and a subtle warmth begins to stir within me.

"You're a violent one, aren't you?" His voice low.

I retort, ignoring his remark. "No, you cannot have my number. That ship has sailed, bud. Nice try."

This spurs Xavier on even more—he just laughs as he presses in closer for more. "Come on, Isla. You can't deny there's something between us. Admit it." His face is now so close to mine, I can smell mint on his warm breath.

Just as this exchange starts to take a bewildering turn—something I can't quite grasp—the tension is shattered when a voice slices through the air, demanding, "Isla, what's going on here?"

David. Shit. Blood drains from my face. I forcefully shove Xavier away, putting some much-needed space between us, and awkwardly address him, "David, I'm so sorry. I needed a quick bathroom break and got caught up."

Now visibly unimpressed, he retorts, "Clearly. Is he bothering you?" He gestures towards Xavier.

"Please, she needed air to get away from you."

I bristle at his comment. "Shut up, Xavier." He's dead wrong, I muse, I needed air from *him*, truth be told.

"Well, the bronc riding round has wrapped up. They announced the winner." David turns to Xavier. "Congrats, mate, looks like you're needed up there." David's attempt to oust Xavier is palpable. He then turns to me, a certain glint in his eyes. "I was thinking of heading out... we could, uh, go back to my place. You know, to hang?"

This irritates Xavier, who now wears a frown, glaring at David. I notice this as I glance up at him, gauging his reaction. *But why?* I shift on the spot. I hadn't planned on heading back home with David. The air thickens with a testosterone-filled standoff between the two guys.

Xavier smirks at David, his tone dripping with sarcasm. "Mate, looks like Isla here is not too keen on your offer. We were in the middle of something before you decided to play the hero and interrupt."

David raises an eyebrow and steps forward. "What was that?"

With a sly grin, Xavier retorts, "Oh, Isla, here, was just about to admit how she's secretly been dreaming about me. Sorry, bud." He looks to David apologetically, but there is not an ounce of genuine apology there.

I shoot Xavier an incredulous look, shaking my head. "I think you're the one who's dreaming, Xavier. Could you be any more delusional?"

David cuts in, clearly unamused, "Alright, enough of this crap. Isla, let's go."

Xavier leans in, his voice a low whisper. "Make sure he knows what he's missing, Isla. A night with me is unforgettable. Just saying." His hands now raised in surrender.

I scoff, rolling my eyes. "You're unbelievable, Xavier."

David scoffs, "If that were true, she'd be the one saying it, not you. Anyway, Isla, let's go. We'll head back to mine." He says it loud enough for Xavier to overhear, nudging my shoulder, smirking, and adding a wink.

I can't help but feel a little uneasy. Going back to David's place is the last thing I want to do right now. I'm not sure if it's because of David standing in front of me or Xavier, who's still standing behind me. David said that loud enough for Xavier to hear, and part of me feels uneasy at the thought that he might be thinking about me going back with David. No, that's not what I want. *What do I want?* I don't know, but definitely not this. I need to leave. This is now all becoming too much for me. I just want to go home, snuggle on my couch while I watch another episode of 'New Girl'.

"Actually, no, I'm not feeling too well. I just need to get home," I declare as I turn to walk off towards the exit, but David's grip on my arm pulls me back.

"Hey, wait! What do you mean? I thought we were having fun."

We were, until *he* came along—I muse in my mind about Xavier. David's grip on my wrist tightens, and my attempts to break free are futile. As I struggle, I catch sight of Xavier stepping forward, clearly noticing David's grip on me.

"Let. Her. Fucking. Go," he seethes.

"Clearly, she doesn't want to 'hang'," he says, raising his fingers to do an air quote sign.

"Back off, Xavier," David says, his voice carrying a firm warning. The air crackles as Xavier takes a step toward David, a threatening glint in his eyes hinting at an impending clash.

I take a deep breath, breaking off this brutish standoff by placing a hand on Xavier's chest. "Stop!" *Fuck this.* "I'm getting an Uber home."

The alcohol's earlier buzz now gives way to frustration and distress. *Do not get emotional. Do not cry.*

As I make my way toward the exit, the familiar sounds of the showground fading behind me, I catch David muttering, "Fuck this." A sentiment I wholeheartedly share at this point. I can sense Xavier trailing behind me—persistent as ever.

"Isla, you're not getting an Uber. I'll drive you home," he insists.

A sense of déjà vu wracks my brain. Not this all over again, I think, the memories of past entanglements replaying in my mind.

As Xavier continues to follow, undeterred, and David disappears from the scene, my patience wanes. I'm insistent on catching an Uber, not entertaining the idea of being driven home by Xavier. I glance at my phone—my Uber app isn't showing any available drivers. I curse inwardly and quickly refresh the app, desperately hoping for a change.

"Isla, don't make me throw you over my shoulder again. Or are you into that, because I'm down if you are?" he quips, his voice low, a hint of playfulness apparent. A wave of flashbacks hits me—memories of that night at the Loose Lasso. I hate to admit it, but there's a part of me that liked being manhandled, and the recollection makes my cheeks burn with embarrassment.

"Seriously, not this again. Don't you have a trophy to collect in there?" I throw back, looking down at my phone, waiting for a driver to accept my request. Ugh.

"Couldn't give two fucks about the trophy, to be honest," he retorts, taking his phone out of his denim pocket to text... someone? *Who cares?*

"Go back to your mates, Xavier, pl—"

I'm cut off as he moves in closer. "Just let me take you home, Isla. Don't make me say it again," he reluctantly admits. "Please."

I exhale a huge breath, relenting. "Fine... but only because there are no drivers." The situation forces my hand, but my reluctance is evident.

I begrudgingly slide into the passenger seat of Xavier's ute—the scent of fresh leather wafts through the air, a stark contrast to the familiar traces of hay and dust I expected. I glance out the window, avoiding eye contact with Xavier as I fidget with the hem of my dress.

I can't believe I'm here again. The rhythmic hum of the engine and the gentle sway of the car trigger memories that I would *rather* keep locked away. *That damn kiss.* The night when everything changed, my world tossed upside down by a single, unexpected moment.

As he navigates the roads leading to my house with an effortless familiarity, my mind drifts back to the high school days. Days filled with torment, where Xavier and his friends found creative ways to get under my skin. He wasn't always the instigator, but he never really stopped it either. *Did he enjoy hanging out with them, or was it all just for popularity? To be cool?*

I'd spent years hating those school days, a time when the boys made my life unbearable. And now, with just a few encounters and that one fucking *kiss*, it all seems swept away. *Ugh*. The complexity of it all leaves me grappling with emotions I'd rather not confront.

Turning my attention to the car's interior to distract my rambling thoughts, I notice the pristine cleanliness of the car–which is surprising considering he works with farm animals all day.

The air inside feels unexpectedly comfortable, and I can't pinpoint why. But one thing is certain—being in this car with Xavier feels safer than it did with David, and that speaks volumes.

Isla, you're overthinking it, I scold myself, trying to push aside the tangled web of emotions. Despite my inner resistance, I can't help but steal a sidelong glance at Xavier. His hands grip the steering wheel with a comfortable familiarity.

As Xavier manoeuvres the steering wheel with practised ease, I catch glimpses of him, his features highlighted by the soft glow of the dashboard. The radio hums faintly in the background, and I can't help but admit he really is attractive. You'd be stupid to deny it.

The mere sight of him instantly arouses me, sending tingles down to my core. It's become a regular occurrence, an undeniable magnetic pull that has me clenching my thighs together, desperately hoping he doesn't notice the profound effect he has on me.

Gaining some form of confidence, I reach for the console, intending to change the radio station. But in my clumsy attempt, I accidentally connect to his phone, and 'Like a Stone' by Audioslave blares through the speakers, disrupting the comfortable silence.

"Shit, sorry," I apologise, feeling a blush creep up my cheeks.

"Nah, you're right," he says, a hint of a smile playing on his lips. "You can leave it... or change it, if you want."

I press the arrow button, changing the song now to 'Happy Song' by Bring Me The Horizon. *What?* My accidental intrusion into his music taste revealing a surprising choice. "You... listen to rock?" I ask.

"Yeah? Why does that surprise you?"

Why does that surprise me? I ponder. "I don't know, I pegged you for more the country genre type or... I don't know, RnB?" I say with a huff of laughter.

"Eh, don't get me wrong. I listen to them occasionally, but it's mostly rock. It's the only thing that gets me going when I'm wor king... or training," he says comfortably.

I sit back in my seat, letting the chords of the guitar and the vocals of the lead singer, Oli Sykes, fill the car. I hum along to the song, surprising Xavier, who turns to look at me with a curious expression. "Wait, you listen to rock, too?" he teases.

"Yeah? Why? Does that surprise you?" I reply, echoing his earlier sentiment.

"Yeah, it does actually. I'd pegged you as more of a pop kinda gal, or what do they call it nowadays, Swifter?" He smirks.

"Swiftie? You mean?" I huff a laugh.

He just looks at me with a smile. "Yeah, that. You're not a Swiftie?"

"Um, I mean, I like her songs. I'm just not a diehard fan. I like rock."

"Interesting," he says, and I can't help but feel a sense of pride in defying his expectations.

What is it about me that surprises him? He turns the corner, pulling into the long driveway near my apartment block. He puts the car into park, sitting back in his seat like he's not ready to get out just yet. "Okay, well, thank you again." The atmosphere turns awkward, and I go to open the door, but find that when I pull the latch forward, the door doesn't budge. *What the fuck?*

"Uh, the door won't open?" I say, puzzled.

"I know," he says matter-of-factly, leaving me frowning. "Not until you say yes to going out with me."

"What?! "A-are you being serious right now?" I exclaim, my mind reeling.

"Dead serious," he replies with a smirk. *Well, fuck.*

18

Xavier

As I sit there, gazing at Isla's puzzled face framed by her long brown hair, I can't help but notice how it sweeps over her shoulder, falling gracefully over her breasts. She'd chosen to wear that little dress and those *fucking cowboy boots* I love on her—all for that *wanker*. I fume—now angry at the fact that she dressed up for someone else.

She looks beautiful, that naturally beautiful type—not caked in layers of makeup like other girls I've seen around town. Her full lips, painted with a faint gloss, beckon me to kiss her or imagine them wrapped around... something else.

Cut it out, you idiot. I silently scold myself, shaking my head subtly to dispel these intrusive thoughts. Ignoring the fact that I've had a semi the whole damn drive by just being in her presence.

"Uh, the door won't open?" she says, puzzled.

"I know," I respond matter-of-factly, leaving her frowning. "Not until you say yes to going out with me."

"What?! "A-are you being serious right now?" Her exclamation suggests her mind is probably reeling.

"Dead serious," I reply with a smirk, locking eyes with her, waiting for her response. "One date. Just one, Isla. So I can prove I'm not just some asshole to you."

She licks her lips, stunned, drawing my attention back to those enticing lips. *Stop it.* My arousal is threatening to become obvious.

"W-what? Why? No, let me out of the car. Now, Xavier," she demands, raising her voice slightly, a tone I find strangely arousing.

She possesses such a melodic voice, and I can't help but wonder what it would sound like as she screams my name in ecstasy. *Yep, there goes the semi*—now morphing into a full-fledged hard-on. I shift in my seat, attempting to discreetly conceal it.

"I think we are getting along just fine right now. C'mon," I press. "Just *ONE* date. That's all I'm asking; it's not a fucking marriage proposal."

"*We* don't even know anything about each other. It would never work. Thanks for the offer, but I'm going to kindly decline. Now open the door," she insists. Oh, *game on.*

"Well, for starters, you're a Veterinarian," I counter. "You work at the animal hospital down at Springbrook Reserve. You're 26... no, wait, 27 years old, and you used to live in the city."

"Everyone knows these things? Nice try. It is a small town, after all," she scoffs.

"Thirteen," I blurt out.

"What?" she asks, confusion written all over her face.

"You have thirteen freckles on your face," I declare, and she just frowns, still confused. *I know this because I've counted every single fucking one on her face.*

"Your favourite subjects are English and art. You used to play the piano and the flute—don't know about now. You're shy, tend to keep to yourself, but around people you're comfortable with, you're extremely bubbly and have the worst foul mouth," I say with a smirk, winking at Isla.

She sits there, stunned, mouth slightly agape. "Does that cover it? I think it's you who doesn't really know me," I assert.

She'd spent most of her schooling years probably hating me and my idiot friends because of the childish things we'd do or get up to, and being a part of their friendship group forced me to become involved in their antics. I'm not who I used to be; I desperately want to prove that to her, and *that* speaks volumes.

"So, what's it gonna be? One date? I promise I'll leave you alone after," I say, throwing both my hands up in surrender. Please say yes. Yes, I have resorted to *begging*. I, Xavier Mitchell, do NOT *beg* for anyone. But she's not just *anyone*. How do I convey that without sounding like a wimp? Suddenly, all my smooth talk goes out the window. I can feel the weight of her gaze on me, analysing, considering. God, I wish I could read minds right now. *Is she intrigued? Annoyed? Amused?* It's like trying to decode a cryptic message written in invisible ink. Come on, Isla, give me something here. Anything. My palms are starting to sweat, and I'm pretty sure I'm about to break into a nervous flop sweat any second now. But I have to play it cool. Can't let her see me sweat.

"Look, Isla, about the other night," I start, my voice softer now, more earnest. Inside, I'm urging her to see what I see, to feel what I feel. There's a spark between us, a connection that's hard to ignore.

"It wasn't just a kiss for me. There's something here, something *mutual*. You can't deny that you've thought about it too."

I can see the conflict in her eyes, the war between curiosity and caution. She's contemplating it, I can tell. She shifts on her feet, and for a moment, I think she might actually agree. I raise my brow, waiting patiently for her response. I could sit here all fucking night, waiting if I have to. I'm known to be quite persistent.

Isla releases a long breath, as if she'd been holding it in all this time. "One date? And you'll promise to leave me alone?"

"Promise, I swear," I say, nodding. *Lies.* But she doesn't need to know that.

She raises an eyebrow, clearly sceptical. "Fine. *One* date... and that's it."

I clap my hands together in eager anticipation. "Thank fuck!"

She rolls her eyes. "Can I go now?" she says, waiting for me to unlock the car.

"Nuh-uh. I need your number, don't I?" I question. She huffs out a breath and rolls her eyes, pulling her phone out of her small bag, which I hadn't even noticed she'd been carrying. She hands me her phone, and I grab it, punching in my number and saving it under my name in her contacts. "Done."

I press a button on my side of the door, and the faint clicking sound of locks opening breaks the silence. "Uh, don't you need mine?" she says softly.

"Nah, you message me. Pick a time and day, and we'll go from there. The ball's in your court, love," I assert.

She just looks at me, and I stare back, wanting to know what she's thinking at this exact moment. "O-okay. Well, thanks for the ride," she says.

"My pleasure," I respond.

She finally manages to open the door, but before she goes to hop out, I say, "You should laugh more often, you know...? It's... nice." *Nice? Good one.*

She offers a subtle smile, barely visible in the moonlit night. With that, she closes the door and walks around the car and into her building. I wait for her to get inside safely before driving off.

Pulling into my driveway, the headlights cut through the inky darkness, guiding me home. The familiar silhouette of the farmhouse comes into view as I park the car. The quiet hum of the engine fades into the night, leaving only the rustle of the wind in the surrounding fields.

I reach for my phone, a soft glow emanating from the screen as it lights up the dark confines of the car.

Harrison: Mate, you missed the team roping event! We killed it!! Where the fuck did you run off to?

Michael: Taking a leak, my fucking ass.

I smirk at their immediate curiosity, typing a response.

Me: Needed to take care of something. Didn't miss much, I'm sure.

Harrison's quick to respond.

Harrison: Yeah, right... You won the bronc riding contest, you flop. Congrats, bro! We have your trophy. Can bring it by tomorrow.

Me: Sure, bring it by.

Michael: Taking care of something, huh? Not a surprise visit from a certain someone, was it?

My lips curl into a smirk as I read his message. The guy knows me too well. I respond with a chuckle.

Me: You've got quite the imagination, bud. But, no, just sorting something out.

I can almost hear Michael's sceptical scoff through the text. With a smile, I lock my phone, grab my keys, and get out of the car.

Walking into the house, the quiet envelops me, interrupted only by the faint murmur of the telly playing reruns of The Great British Bake Off. Mum is perched on the couch, her eyes glued to the screen.

"Xav, that you?" she asks softly.

"Yeah, Ma, it's me."

"You're home late. What'd you get up to?" she inquires.

"Not much. Went up to Hilltop Creek. They were hosting another rodeo in the showground."

"Oh, lovely. You went with the boys?"

"Yeah, Harrison and Michael came along. It's late, Ma. Why don't you go to bed?"

"I'll be up for a few more hours, darl. Need to catch up on these reruns," she replies, her excitement evident as she shifts in her seat.

"Right, well, 'night," I say, making my way toward the wooden staircase. As I ascend, my mind inevitably drifts back to Isla, and then a thought stops me dead in my tracks. Now that Dad is asleep, it's the perfect time to ask Mum what she knows about Isla and her father. Rumours about Isla and her family have circulated through the town, and Mum is usually up to date on all the local gossip. While I remember that her mum lost her battle to cancer years ago, curiosity gets the better of me. I stride back over to her, my eyes questioning her.

"What's up, dear?" she asks.

"Uh..." I run my hand down the back of my hair. "What do you know about Dad and Callum Thompson?" I inquire, attempting to sound nonchalant. Her eyes widen with curiosity, and there's something else I can't quite pinpoint. She pats the spot beside her, gesturing for me to sit.

"What do you want to know? Why the sudden interest?" she asks, her tone genuinely curious.

I sit beside her, pondering her question. The truth is, ever since I ran into Isla, something about her has piqued my curiosity. I want to understand her better, to unravel the mysteries that surround her and her family. But I keep this to myself, merely saying, "Just curious,

I guess. It sounds like there's a long-standing issue there."

"Ah, your father and his damn stubbornness," she sighs, shaking her head. "It stems from a job Callum was supposed to complete years ago. Your father had hired him for some farm work, but Isla's father didn't finish the job."

"There was some issue with the materials. Your father had to cover the cost of materials, and he's..." she sighs, "he's just never forgiven Callum for it, I guess."

I frown. "But why?"

"It's just how he is, dear," she says, placing a hand on my shoulder. "Your father can be... difficult when things don't go his way, you know this." I snort at this. He's the most stubborn bloke I know, apart from Bradley.

"Most of the time, his actions come with reason. I may not always agree with 'em, but he's your father, and my *husband*. He loves you, Brad, and Liv more than anything."

I just nod. She then looks at me with a mischievous glint in her eyes, and I raise an eyebrow, silently questioning her unspoken thoughts. With a smirk, she shakes her head, indicating it's nothing.

I roll my eyes at her playful demeanour and lean in to give her a quick kiss on the cheek.

"Thanks, Mum," I mutter before heading upstairs to my room, my mind still buzzing with thoughts about Isla and her father.

19

Isla

Lounging on my couch, I cradle a glass of Coke Zero with more ice than soda—my preferred ratio. A packet of Smith's chips sits nonchalantly on the coffee table. In my favourite PJs, bra finally off, my girls are free, and the relief is downright glorious. Whoever wished for big tits must be pulling my leg. It's a real mission carting these girls around every day, not to mention the endless back pains. The joys of being a woman.

In the background, the TV plays an episode of 'New Girl', but my mind refuses to tune in. The events of last night, especially the encounter with David, are on constant replay, an unwelcome loop. The urge to message David gnaws at me, a sense of guilt for the abrupt exit lingering. Despite the lack of a spark, he deserves a smoother ending. I type out,

> **Me:** Hey, David, it's Isla. Apologies for the way things went down last night. It's a bit weird right now, but I did have fun. Maybe we can give it another shot sometime?

Taking a deep breath, I decide to call Imogen. It's been too long since our last conversation, and there's a pressing need to sort things out. As the phone rings, I watch the screen intently until she finally answers.

"Bout time you rang," she says, injecting a teasing tone. A ragged breath escapes me.

"Ugh, Midge, I'm so sorry. I should've called sooner. I just didn't know when the right time would be."

"It's okay. I'm glad you called. What are you up to right now?"

A chuckle escapes me. "Nothing much. Just on the couch watching 'New Girl'."

Imogen laughs softly. "Got any wine?"

"Uh, yeah, I do. Bought a bottle recently."

"Beauty! I can be there in ten."

I release a sigh of relief. "That sounds perfect. I'll have two glasses ready." The phone call ends, and I eagerly prepare for Imogen's arrival.

Imogen and I are settled on the couch, each cradling a wine glass, the TV's muted chatter in the background. We navigate the initial small talk dance, dipping into the ebb and flow of recent events.

"So, how's the salon treating you?" I inquire, genuinely interested in Imogen's life as a hairdresser at one of our local salons.

She smirks, setting her glass down. "Oh, you won't believe the drama this week. Pam tried to colour her hair at home, but ended up with neon pink instead of blonde. I had to fix that disaster."

I burst into laughter, picturing Pam with her accidental punk rock look. "Poor Pam. How's Claire adjusting to her new role?"

Imogen leans back, sipping her wine. "Loving it, apparently. She gets to boss all the men around now—she'd be having a field day." Imogen laughs. "Always knew she'd make it big."

"I second that! That's great for her," I say, intentionally leaving out the details of my last night. There'll be time for that later.

As if sensing the weight of the conversation, Imogen takes a deep breath, exhaling it raggedly before speaking. "Look, Isla, I need to apologise. I've heard some stuff in town, and Dad mentioned a few things, but I didn't want to get involved. It's complicated, you know? And now that you're back, I thought it'd be best for you to see how things go with him. I'm sorry if it seemed like I was avoiding it."

I meet her gaze, surprised by the sincerity in her voice. "Midge, y-you don't need to apologise. It's a messy situation, and everyone in town seems to have their version of the story. I appreciate you not wanting to add to the gossip." I smile softly, adding, "If anyone should apologise, it should be me for how I acted."

Imogen's eyes widen in shock, and she quickly responds, "No, no way. You had every right to act that way. I would have done the same if it were me. I'm just sorry I didn't mention anything sooner, and now everything's a big mess."

Her gaze shifts downward, avoiding mine, and a heavy silence settles between us. The weight of unspoken words hangs in the air, reminding me of the complexities surrounding my return to this small town.

I manage a small smile, grateful for her understanding. "Thanks, Midge. It means a lot. Let's just try to navigate this one step at a time."

Feeling somewhat relaxed, a heavy revelation spills out of me. "I've been spending time with him lately, and I've noticed some weird things. He forgets his memories, misplaces things, and one day, he had brought up Mum in conversation.

"He acted like *she* was still around, off at the grocery store. It's like he's stuck in this time bubble of when she was still here. I freaked out, didn't know what to do, so I left. I fucking *left* him there, Midge." Sobs now wracking my body.

"I'm a bloody coward—not willing to accept that he's gone off the rails. You should have seen his face, Midge. Oh my god, he was so happy when he spoke of her." Tears stream down my cheeks, and I let out a frustrated sigh. "*Ugghh*, things would be so much easier if Mum were here. She'd know what to do in these situations." *I miss her so much.*

"Oh, babe," Imogen says, scooting closer, placing her glass on the coffee table to give me a comforting hug. "Your Mumma is looking down on you—she's always with you. She'd be so proud of every-thing you've accomplished—moving to the city, getting the job you always wanted, owning your clinic now. It's what she always wanted for you." Imogen looks me in the eye, tears forming in hers, as I continue to sob.

"It's a tough situation—I can understand that. Don't feel guilty about your actions at all." I nod and Imogen hands me a tissue.

"Maybe it would be best to see a doctor, you know? To get a firm diagnosis or just to see what's going on."

I let out a laugh. "Have you met my father? He hates doctors. There's no way he'd go willingly." Another frustrated sigh escapes me.

Imogen continues, "I know babe, but it's the best chance of understanding what's happening and getting help. Maybe approach it as a routine check-up, you know, just to make sure everything's okay. Frame it as a proactive step for his health, not as a reaction to a problem."

I wipe away the remaining tears and nod, considering her words. "I guess you're right. I'll find a way to talk to him about it. I just hope he doesn't shut me out." *Like he always does—always has.*

Imogen reassures me, "He's your father, Isla. He might resist at first, but deep down, he'll appreciate your concern. And if needed, I can talk to him, too, maybe offer some haircuts at the clinic as a reason to drop by."

I chuckle through my lingering sadness. "Haircuts? Really?"

Imogen grins. "Hey, desperate times call for desperate measures. And who knows, it might just work."

Feeling a bit lighter, I thank her for being there and helping me see things more clearly. The weight of the situation hasn't lifted entirely, but at least now I have a plan, and with Imogen's support, it doesn't seem as daunting. It's reassuring to have a friend who genuinely cares, even in the midst of small-town drama.

I take another deep breath, holding back my laughter. "I-I have some more news..."

Imogen, her eyes wide and curiosity lighting up her expression, exclaims, "What? What?"

A mischievous grin spreads across my face as I spill the details about that unexpected kiss when Xavier dropped me off.

"Soo, Xavier drove me home that night, and we ended up sitting in his car for a bit. He walked me inside, and then out of nowhere, he kissed me. It was so fucking unexpected, and I've been left all flustered and confused ever since."

Imogen reacts with a playful smack on my arm, her eyes widening. "No freaking way! What was it like? OMG, I need all the juicy details. What's happened since then?"

I laugh, shaking my head. "Well, here's the kicker. I went on a date last night with David to the local rodeo at Hilltop Creek. Xavier was there, too. Long story short, he *'somehow'* convinced me to agree to go on a date with him. Now, I'm stuck with these conflicting thoughts and the responsibility to initiate this so-called bloody 'date'."

Imogen, still processing the whirlwind of my story, remarks, "Isla! This is fucking wild!"

I nod, feeling a mix of excitement and confusion. "Tell me about it. I have no idea what's going on."

Imogen, sensing my inner turmoil, asks, "Well, what are you going to do? The decision is now up to you. He's waiting for *you* to message him, right?"

I'm conflicted. When should I message him, or do I even want to? Imogen senses my hesitation and encourages, "He went to all that effort to convince you. What's one little date? If it doesn't end well, then you don't have to see him again. Simple." But it's not that simple though, *is it?*

Ugh. I guess she's right. One little date. I repeat the words in my mind, the weight of the decision feeling heavier than it should. A whirlwind of thoughts spirals through my head like a tornado of uncertainty. *Should I? Shouldn't I? What if it's a mistake? But what if it's not?*

Imogen, watching the turmoil unfold on my face, senses my inner chaos. She leans in, her voice comforting. "Isla, don't overthink it. If you're not feeling it, then it's okay. But what if it turns out to be something amazing? Life is full of surprises, and this might be one of them."

Surprises, huh? I contemplate the idea, my mind echoing with uncertainties. What if it's just a distraction? What if I'm not ready for something new? The prospect of the unknown both excites and terrifies me.

Imogen, her gaze steady, says, "You're not signing a contract, Isla. It's just one date. You'll figure things out along the way. Don't let hatred or fear hold you back from potential happiness." *She's starting to sound like him.*

"I know, I know." I sigh.

Potential *happiness*. The words linger in my mind, and I wonder if I'm brave enough to take that step. Closing my eyes, I take a deep breath, exhaling the lingering doubts. Maybe it's time to embrace the unexpected, to step into the unknown.

"Look," Imogen's voice breaks through my thoughts, "whatever you decide, I'm here for you. Whether it's a wild adventure or a quiet night in, I've got your back."

Her words resonate with comfort, and a small smile plays on my lips. Maybe it's time to see where this crazy ride takes me.

Imogen left not long after that, two glasses down and feeling a slight buzz—leaving me with a sense of contentment and introspection. The weight of the night's revelations lingers in the air, a mix of excitement and uncertainty dancing in the room.

As I lay in bed, my phone dings from beside me, casting a soft glow in the dimly lit room. Seeing David's name light up the screen sends a shiver of anxiety through my body. The anticipation of his response to my earlier message tightens my chest.

David: Hey, no prob, I guess. It looks like you two have some unfinished business to deal with, and maybe until that is all sorted, it's probably best we don't see each other for the time being.

Unfinished business? I scoff inwardly. My fingers tap out a response.

Me: There is no unfinished business. Like I said, it's weird, as we share some history having gone to high school together, but that's it, honestly.

Yeah right, who am I trying to convince, him or me?

David: Yeah, does he know that? I saw the way he was looking at you... you don't have to explain anything to me, seriously. Goodnight.

His instant reply throws me off. *The way he was looking at me?* What does he mean? Confusion swirls within me, adding another layer of complexity to an already tangled situation. I recall Xavier's words, how he had counted every single freckle on my face, how he knew my favourite subjects and pastimes. *Was he always that perceptive?* I gently touch my cheeks, grazing over where my freckles would be. Thirteen? *Do I have thirteen?*

I'm stunned by the fact that he noticed such a detail. When would he have taken the time to notice? It's a strange mix of flattery and discomfort, knowing that someone has paid such close attention to me. The drama I hoped to leave behind in the city seems to have followed me back, weaving itself into the fabric of my small-town life.

This was not part of the plan.

20

Isla

The sun beats down relentlessly, and the air outside today feels akin to the blast when you open the door of a preheated oven. Welcome to Spring in Australia, where a mere two metres of walking is enough to trigger a cascade of sweat. And don't even get me started on the flies—persistent little buggers that seem to have a personal vendetta.

It's just been Katy and me holding down the fort today; Molly's been neck-deep in her exam prep for her upcoming prelims. The day has been slow, typical for a small-town clinic, especially on a Monday. However, amidst the routine, we've become an unintentional halfway house for furry friends.

The hospital wasn't designed for animal sheltering, yet over the past few months now, we've gathered a few stray animals. Katy has been fostering Henry, our charming Italian Greyhound, and just recently, we welcomed a new addition—a timid Australian Kelpie, around five years old, with a brown and tan coloured coat.

I spotted her on my way to work one day, lingering near the hospital. Malnourished and scared, her frail frame revealed a harsh history of neglect. Slowly, I earned her trust, bringing her into the clinic one afternoon. She's now our new resident fur baby, seeking shelter here, who Katy and I affectionately named Luna. She's been responding well to the care, her once fearful eyes now brightening with trust.

It breaks my heart seeing these dogs without permanent homes. We've put up signs and ads, hoping for foster parents or, better yet, adoptive families. Katy helps occasionally, but my apartment can't handle one small dog, let alone two—my landlord might revolt.

So, we patiently wait for someone to step forward, offering a forever home for these beautiful dogs.

For now, they're our little companions at Wattle Creek Veterinary Hospital, with makeshift pens for cosy nights. We're here to keep them company and provide daily care, hopeful for the day they find their permanent homes.

The morning started with a bit of a rush—handling the aftermath of a daring cat's encounter with a prickly cactus. I couldn't help but chuckle at the sight of the disgruntled feline, a reminder that even our four-legged friends can't resist the allure of a plant adventure.

Guess it's not just dogs who find creative ways to keep us on our toes. After that, it's been a steady stream of routine check-ups and minor procedures and just about an hour ago—an elderly Golden Retriever named Max who desperately needed dental cleaning. It's a procedure I'm well-versed in, having tackled it many times before.

We've also recently had a trio of mischievous kittens who've become the clinic's temporary mascots, testing the limits of our patience with their playful antics. Fast forward to the present, just after lunch, and the clinic has settled into a calm rhythm. The events of the morning linger like echoes in the background as hunger begins to nudge its way into my consciousness. I glance over at Katy, who sits at the reception desk, glasses on, staring intently at the computer screen.

"Hey, Katy, feeling a bit peckish. How about I grab us some lunch from the chicken shop down the road? Craving anything specific?" I suggest, the thought of crispy fried goodness already makes my mouth water.

Katy glances at me, an unreadable expression in her eyes, as if she's harbouring some secret amusement. "What?" I prod, my curiosity instantly ignited.

"Maybe hold off on grabbing food. I have a feeling we might have another patient coming in soon," Katy replies cryptically, her tone almost overly cheerful.

"Another patient?" I question, perplexed. "There's nothing scheduled on my planner for the rest of the afternoon. Did someone just call in?" I press for more information, sensing Katy's unusual chipper demeanour.

"Not just now, but earlier, something about a chicken or hen... or whatever. Couldn't quite decipher them over the phone, but they said they'd be waltzing in around..." Katy glances at the clock, squinting at the time, "now, actually."

"You do realise a chicken and a hen are the same thing?" I give her a side-eye, sensing a mysterious vibe in the air. "You're acting strange today. What's the deal?" I probe, my suspicion growing.

"Strange? Me?" Katy feigns innocence with an exaggerated gasp. "Nonsense, just relaying the *riveting* chicken drama I heard over the phone."

"What's the owner's name? Any details, so I'm not caught off guard by a surprise chicken visit?" I ask, detecting a whiff of mischief.

"Nothing, no name, just somethin' 'bout a chicken is all I picked up," Katy quips, her cryptic demeanour adding to the peculiar charm of the day.

Before I can delve further into questioning her, the familiar chime above the door jingles, and I swivel around to find Xavier Mitchell—*in all his glory*—standing there, that damn cowboy hat perched atop his head, and two plastic bags in hand.

"Afternoon, ladies! I picked up some lunch and thought I'd bring some past. Anyone hungry?" he declares, his easy going demeanour filling the room. My eyes narrow at Katy, who feigns innocence with a smile.

"What? Don't look at me, darling. I had no idea..." she says with a sly grin. I shoot her a deadpan expression, leaving me to wonder just how much she's orchestrated this unexpected lunch visit. *Sure you didn't, you sly, sly woman.* But why? And how? My mind races with questions as the pieces of the puzzle slowly fall into place.

The pieces don't quite fit together in my mind. Why would Katy conspire with Xavier to surprise me with lunch? And more importantly, how did she manage it without me catching on?

As if to add to the surreal moment, Xavier presents two bags filled with the tempting aroma of chicken and chips from the local shop. *What? How did he*—This is one big coincidence, surely? I'm taken aback, and Katy, here, seems to be thoroughly enjoying the spectacle.

"Wow, Xavier, you really went all out," Katy remarks, a twinkle in her eye. "Isla here was just about to grab lunch for us, too. What a surprise!"

Xavier grins, and as I stare at his smile, a smile that could melt panties—I stand there stunned. He looks at me intently, seemingly oblivious to any potential conspiracy theories brewing in my mind. "Great minds think alike, I guess. Didn't know what you ladies like, so I got all the favourites—extra crispy chicken, seasoned chips, and some dipping sauces to top it off," he says with a casual air. *Righto.*

Katy then asks if Xavier will be joining us, but he politely declines, saying, "I've got to get back to work—the farm ain't gonna run itself. Besides, I need to finish everything in time before my date tonight." Damn him and his stupid mouth, I think as a warm flutter pools in my belly. He smirks ever so slightly, adding to the turmoil of conflicting emotions.

Xavier continues, "Been waiting for this girl I know to get back to me for a date. But... she's leaving me hanging," he teases, shaking his head. The nerve of this guy. I shoot him a playful glare as he turns to look at me, winking. *So much for the ball being in my court.*

Katy replies, "Oh gosh, how exciting. Well, hopefully, she doesn't keep you waitin' too long." A glint of mischief in her eyes. *Ugh, great.*

Xavier dismisses the two of us politely with a head nod. "I hope so too, Katy," he replies, then turns to me.

"Laters, Doc," his gaze lingering on mine for a moment too long. Why does his stare have to be so intense? My body shudders involuntarily as he leaves the clinic.

Katy then bursts out abruptly, "Well... are you gonna message him or not?" I stand there, completely dumbfounded.

I frown, "How did you—"

She interrupts, "Darling, I may be old, and partially blind, but I ain't *that* blind."

I release a frustrated sigh, muttering, "I just can't catch a break, can I?" Maybe asking the universe... or no one in particular.

Seated in my chair, office lights casting a warm glow, I let out a satisfied sigh as my stomach revels in the aftermath of lunch. The air conditioning works its magic, creating a comfortable coolness that envelops the room.

Sleep Token's 'Take Me Back To Eden' fills the clinic with its soft, soothing chords. Katy indulges my music choice occasionally, as long as I promise to keep it tame. She deems my preferred rock music as the 'Devil's tunes', and I scoff silently.

My mind is a chaotic whirlwind, racing through a million thoughts, buzzing with anticipation and a futile attempt at irritation directed at Xavier. I find myself grappling with these conflicting emotions. But let's face it, resisting that pull is a lost cause.

The idea of messaging Xavier lingers in my thoughts. The pressure is on now; he left the initiation of this date up to me, yet he couldn't resist pulling that bloody stunt today.

A part of me considers going, while another part insists I shouldn't entertain the idea. The internal struggle continues as the gentle melody weaves through the air—but let's face it, resisting that pull is a lost cause.

Imogen's advice reverberates in my mind, 'Don't let hatred or fear mess up a shot at potential happiness'. The mental wrestling match intensifies, and I find myself teetering on the edge, contemplating whether I should take the plunge.

"Ugh. Fine," I mutter, tossing caution aside as I hunt for Xavier's name in my phone. My fingers glide across the screen, crafting a message. I stare at it for a moment, doubts creeping in. I groan, caught in the conflict of uncertainty about how to navigate this.

Backspacing, I start afresh with another message. As I read it in my head, I assess the words. Screw it. Without second-guessing, I hit send.

> **Me:** Alright, Cowboy. You win...

> **Me:** ONE date! Tonight, 6 pm. Don't make it weird.

The message sails into the digital abyss, leaving me to wonder what the hell I just got myself into. As the agonising moments pass, anxiety seeps in, and just when I convince myself he won't respond, those three little bubbles dance on my screen, and his reply pops into view. His response teasing as ever.

I scoff at his audacity. *Typical.* Just as I'm about to put my phone down, it pings again with another message—his playful tone taunting me through the screen.

This bloke's got some real gall. What did I just sign up for?
I will most certainly NOT be wearing a dress.

21

Isla

I caved. I'm wearing a dress. *Pathetic, I know.*

All day today, I've been a complete mess. *Why?* It's not like I haven't been on dates before. Sure, plenty with Justin, but that doesn't count, right? He was my 'boyfriend,' and those dates were never about what I liked or enjoyed. And don't even get me started on the date with David recently—I'm not even going to count that one.

Big public displays of affection—kissing, hand-holding, all that jazz—have always given me the ick. But now, thinking about it, maybe it was just because of my ex. I won't ever know for sure. It's not like I'm planning to settle down any time soon. I'm content with working my dream job full time. No time for distractions, especially with everything going on now with Dad.

I wonder what he's doing right now, and my heart sinks at the thought of him alone on the couch, most likely nursing a stubby, just like he used to do, early in the evenings. *What if he's having another episode?* No one is there with him. *Argh.*

I push aside these thoughts for now, making a mental note to call and check up on him tomorrow morning.

Mentally preparing for what I'm about to walk into, Imogen came over after I'd finished work. My desperate pleas for help resulted in her carrying two dresses on hangers—which I scoffed at, as there's no way her dresses would fit my body. She also brought cases of hair styling irons and makeup.

She is NEVER one to turn down a little glam styling sesh. Midge insisted that these dresses were all elastic and extremely comfy. She had made me try on both, and one of them actually ended up looking nice—surprisingly. It's moments like this that make me grateful for my smaller waist, even though my thighs and hips have always been on the larger side. I'm still no size ten. Don't get ahead of yourself, Isla. It's a stretchy dress; it would fit anyone, really.

"Don't doubt me, bitch—you're not fat. You have the most amazing curves. Show them off," she'd threatened, to which I just rolled my eyes and laughed.

So here I am, wrapped in a short black dress—a tad shorter than my usual preference or the one I wore the other night. Imogen practically strong-armed me into this, claiming it makes my legs look 'hot'. *"Girl, look at those muscly thighs and those calves,"* she'd exclaimed. I wasn't quite convinced, but Imogen is always brutally honest, so I guess that's something. My confidence has gone up lately, and I can't pinpoint why or how?

It has a stretchy shirred bodice and a square neckline that Imogen insists accentuates my silhouette, or, as she likes to put it, my "big tits and small waist"—she can be so crude sometimes. But hey, she's got a point, I guess.

The puff sleeves and flared mini skirt with a ruffle hem add a little playfulness, and I can't help but marvel at how Imogen's dress actually fits me. She's worked wonders with my curls, and the light makeup she's applied enhances my features just enough. But despite her skilled hands, Xavier's mention of my freckles invades my thoughts yet again. Since when has he been so observant? And why does it unsettle me so much?

As Imogen finishes up, packing her things with practised efficiency, she kisses me on the cheek and demands, "All updates, Isla! Don't keep me waiting!"

At precisely 6 o'clock, Xavier pulls up outside my apartment complex. Nerves kick in, somersaulting in my stomach. I take a few deep breaths, attempting to settle them, but they persist. *Get a grip, Isla. You'll be fine.*

As I reach for my small bag on the kitchen counter, the doorbell rings, shattering the silent ambience of my apartment. *Here we go.* I open the door to find Xavier leaning against the frame, his towering height emphasising my smaller stature. He's like a giant, easily over six feet. His intense gaze sweeps over me, slowly, before freezing momentarily, moving off the door frame.

"Nah, I changed my mind," he blurts out.

"What?" *What?*

"You're not wearing a dress," he states matter-of-factly.

"W-what? Why? You're the one who told me to wear one!" I exclaim.

"Yeah, that was before I'd seen—" he nods toward my body, "you... dressed in that!"

"W-what is wrong with what I'm wearing?" *I knew I shouldn't have worn this dress. I should have just worn*—My thoughts are cut off by Xavier's words.

"Absolutely nothing. It's... perfect. That's the problem." He says it so low, it's almost a growl. Oh. *Oh.*

"Unless you want me walking around with a fucking hard on, I suggest you go and change, right now," he growls. *No fucking way.*

"What! What is wrong with you? Must you be s-so vulgar?" I stutter, avoiding his gaze. Do not blush.

"Just speaking facts, princess." He gestures with a nod down to his now clearly evident bulge in his khaki denim shorts. *Fuuuck me.* Just from that bulge, I can tell the man is packing. Surely that's not normal. *Abort mission.*

"This is ridiculous. I am not changing. I did not spend hours getting ready just to change because you can't control your... y-your—" I gesture toward his crotch, "that." I feel warmth spreading across my cheeks and wipe my forehead, now feeling all flushed and flustered around this huge brute. The heat is not doing anything to help me at the moment.

"You spent hours getting ready for me, princess? I'm honoured," he teases, a smirk playing on his lips. I scoff, pushing past him, slamming my door in the process. Why must he rile me up? So much for him not making it weird. I am convinced this idiot does NOT know how to *listen*. Or is he doing it on purpose?

I can hear him laughing as I walk down the stairs to his car, waiting at the passenger side door.

As we drive for about twenty minutes—the scenery changing from rural suburbia to just plains and bush—I can't help but wonder where the hell he's taking me and what kind of date he has planned for us tonight. Xavier eventually turns down a long, narrow road, leading to a large lookout overlooking a vast expanse of our Australian bush—a view that would undoubtedly be breathtaking in the daylight. Throughout the drive, I'd been seated awkwardly in my seat, both hands on my lap, a futile attempt to cover up my exposed thighs. My mind involuntarily drifting back to his confusing reaction to me wearing the dress. *He is such a perplexing man.*

The expanse of the outback unfolds before us, vast and limitless, with a large lake twinkling in the distance under the moonlight. The night sky stretches above us, a canvas of stars scattered like diamonds, and a slight coolness in the breeze now makes me regret not bringing a jacket.

The anticipation builds as he parks the ute, the rear end facing the breathtaking view. We hop out, and he leads me around the back of his ute, where I finally notice a blanket laid out on the tray with a few pillows.

"You just gonna stand there all night?" Xavier teases, a smirk playing on his lips. I respond with a frown, my uncertainty about what to do evident.

"And here I thought you'd planned a dinner or something..." I retort, crossing my arms defensively. The movement catches Xavier's eye; his gaze lingers on my arms crossed over my bust before moving back up to my face. He clears his throat.

"This *is* dinner. I have everything covered," Xavier reassures me as he goes back into the back seat, effortlessly pulling out an esky and placing it on the tray beside the blanket and pillows.

"D-dinner, out here?" I stammer, my words betraying a mix of curiosity and a hint of irony. As I turn around to take in the vast scenery, my mind can't help but conjure images of murderers luring their victims into the woods. *Well, this is not ominous at all,* I sarcastically think to myself. But then again, I trust Xavier, for some odd reason. The man may be confusing, but surely he's not planning a horror movie dinner date, right?

"Relax. It's not like I'm going to drag you into the bush and murder you. Come sit," he says, hopping onto the tray and patting the space next to him. I chuckle, a nervous yet amused sound. Almost as if he knew exactly what I'd been thinking.

"Said every murderer out there. This oddly feels like a scene straight out of Wolf Creek," I say with a raised brow.

Xavier chuckles and puts on his best Mick Taylor voice, saying, *"What the bloody hell are you lot doing out here?"* I laugh but stay rooted in place.

"Just get up here, would you, woman? I don't bite—unless you want me to, then I'd be happy to oblige," he teases, winking, and instantly making my panties damp. A silent shudder wracks through my body—it's become a common occurrence every time he winks at me. Something so simple, yet it has such a dramatic impact. I playfully roll my eyes, deciding to join him on the tray, keeping a respectable distance.

As we both settle on the tray, I stretch out my legs before me, crossing one over the other. Xavier opens up the esky and lays out the food before us. Assorted sandwiches, cut-up fruit, beers, a bottle of wine, and freshly baked muffins create a tempting spread. My curiosity piques, and I can't help but glance back and forth between Xavier and the delicious offering.

His black t-shirt leaves nothing to the imagination, accentuating his muscled arms that ripple and clench with every movement. My eyes are drawn to his left arm, adorned with an intricate array of tattoos. I had glimpsed it briefly that night at The Loose Lasso, but its full expanse is a revelation.

Tattoos have never seemed more appealing.

As Xavier and I dig into the spread, each savouring a sandwich and me enjoying a glass of wine, I'm pleasantly surprised by how delicious everything is. I shoot Xavier a quizzical look while taking a bite of my sandwich, the flavours dancing on my taste buds.

"So, did you put all of this together?" I gesture to the enticing spread, my eyes lingering on the muffins that still emit small swirls of steam, a clear sign of freshness. Did he... bake those.

Xavier, swallowing a bite and taking a sip of his beer, grins. "As a matter of fact, I did."

I raise an eyebrow, teasingly asking, "You baked the muffins?"

He playfully places a hand over his heart, feigning hurt. "Isla Thompson, are you implying I can't cook?"

With a smirk, I reply, "Well, no, but—"

He cuts me off, admitting, "Alright, fine. Mum baked the muffins, but the sandwiches and fruit are all me."

I chuckle, impressed. "Not bad, cowboy. Trying to impress me with your sandwich-making skills?"

He winks, making me flush. "Is it working?"

I playfully roll my eyes, hoping the night sky hides my blush. "Mm, that's what I thought."

We continue to enjoy our sandwiches. After a short moment of silence, Xavier breaks it with a question, "So, Mrs. 'You know nothing about me,' tell me, what was life like in the city?"

I grab a napkin from beside the esky that Xavier has laid out, wiping my hands and mouth before answering, "Busy. Very busy. It took me a while to get used to, I'll admit, but eventually, I settled into a routine not long before finding my first job working at a practice not far from where I was living."

God, the city was a whirlwind—reminiscing about the constant hustle and bustle that marked those days.

He prods further, asking why I decided to come back.

"It had started off great, don't get me wrong," I begin, contemplating how much to share. "But things took a turn. I had recently gotten out of a long-term relationship that didn't exactly end on the best terms. I needed a change, a fresh start. And then the clinic shutting down, looking for new management, was the sign I was unknowingly waiting for."

Funny how life works, I reflect, realising that if it weren't for those unexpected twists, I might not have found my way back home.

Xavier brings up my dad, and his question about the current situation lingers in the air. I hesitate—my father's struggles are personal, and the town has already become a breeding ground for rumours.

Sensing my reluctance, he reassures me, "Look... I'm not one to gossip, but you don't have to talk about it if you're not comfortable."

Part of me doesn't want to delve into the details, but another part, perhaps the one drawn to Xavier's comforting presence, contemplates opening up. For some reason, I find myself considering sharing the burden with him.

"Honestly," I start, "my dad has been going through a tough time. Now that I'm back, I want to be there for him, especially since Mum isn't around anymore, you know?" How could he possibly *know*, though?

"I've missed out on a lot of things, so I guess I'm just making up for lost time—trying to rekindle that connection we once had. It's been gone for so long, I just hope I'm not too late and can fix it now."

Xavier listens quietly, respecting my decision to open up. After a moment of thoughtful silence, he responds, "Sounds like a tough situation. Losing someone and then navigating the complexities of a strained relationship. It takes strength to come back and face it all. I admire that."

His words bring a sense of comfort, a rare understanding that makes me appreciate the genuine connection forming between us. The night sky above, with its countless stars, seems to be silently witnessing the unspoken bond developing during this unconventional little 'date'.

I blush a little at Xavier's response, appreciating the genuine understanding in his words. "Thanks," I reply, a small smile tugging at the corners of my lips.

As the conversation takes an unexpected turn towards my ex, Xavier asks, "So, what happened with your ex? You mentioned things didn't end on the best terms. What did you mean by that?"

As Xavier's question pierces through the air, I feel a familiar discomfort settling in. Taking a deep breath before offering a concise version of the truth.

"Um, well, in the end, he became too demanding, turned out to be a narcissistic asshole," I confess, my gaze momentarily shifting to the vast expanse around us. The memories resurface, the weight of a toxic relationship, the slow erosion of self-worth. "*Always complaining about my looks and weight,*" I mumble softly, quickly brushing it off to say, "Anyway... It's funny how someone you thought you knew could turn out to be a stranger," silently hoping Xavier hadn't caught on to that subtle admission.

But he did. Xavier's eyes darken, a frown marking his face. "Looks? He complained about your... looks?" he questions, his tone edged with a mix of disbelief and anger.

As things start to get tense, I shift in my spot, uncrossing, then crossing my legs again, a feeling of anxiety creeping up my throat, making it hard for me to swallow. I haven't always been an anxious person. Being with and breaking up with Justin had done that—memories now surfacing on the emotional toll it took on me.

"Uh, it's just—J-Justin would complain about my weight," I say, my voice slightly strained, "saying that I needed to be thinner 'for my health', especially if we were going to be 'married' in front of his family." I pause, the bitter taste of those words lingering. "But it was always in ways that sounded 'okay,' I guess?"

Again, *a narcissistic asshole*. I shake my head, attempting to dispel the unpleasant memories.

Xavier sits up abruptly, growling so low, "Nothing about *that* is 'okay', Isla."

I laugh anxiously. "Yeah, I know that now," my voice soft, fingers fidgeting with the hem of my dress. I do everything to avoid his darkening gaze, but that magnetic pull just makes it so incredibly hard.

I glance at him, watching as he stares, his gaze moving from my eyes down to my mouth, then over to my body. A slight tremor runs through me, inviting goosebumps to prickle my skin. I wrap my arms around myself—a futile attempt to shield against the cool breeze or the intensity of his gaze?

"You, cold?" He frowns, but before I can respond, he's up, moving around the back seat, pulling out a thick flannel shirt.

"Here, take this," he says, handing it over. *Uh, okay.* I wrap the flannel over and around my shoulders, his scent immediately enveloping my senses, the aroma washing over me in the cool breeze. Breathing in the heady scent of his cologne and just him sends me into some weird state of euphoria—it's so intense. Intoxicating.

Xavier watches me intently, and I look out into the horizon, a moment of silence passing before he breaks it. "You're nothing like that wanker said you are. You're perfect." I inhale, freezing. Perfect? Me?

"Don't be silly," I reply softly with a scoff, releasing the breath I'd been holding, but he's not laughing.

His gaze darkens further. "Don't start that bullshit with me. I'm not *him*, Isla. I can appreciate beauty when I see it. That fucker must've been blind as a bat not to know what he had in front of him." He says this while somehow moving closer to me. "I'm telling you, you're perfect the way you are," he adds, adjusting my hair tucked underneath the flannel, pulling a strand behind my ear so softly. My breath hitches. Can he really see me that way? After all I've been through—do I believe him? Some part of me *actually* does.

I'm frozen in place as Xavier inches closer, his intense gaze locking onto mine. Uncertainty grips me, and I fidget, not sure where to place my hands in this charged atmosphere. My eyes wander down to his full lips, and an unexpected urge surges within me. *Why do I want to kiss him so desperately right now?* I should resist.

I remind myself that I'm not seeking a relationship, uncertain if I'm even ready. *But who says it has to be anything more than a casual fling?* I'm not getting any younger. Shaking off these conflicting thoughts, I become acutely aware that I'm now moving closer to him, drawn in by an invisible force.

"Stop looking at me like that, Isla," he interrupts my thoughts, his commanding presence towering over me.

"L-like what?" I play coy, trying to deflect.

"Like you want me to kiss you. Be careful, princess. I'm afraid I won't be able to stop once I start this time." Oh, *shit*. Despite the warning, a newfound courage takes hold.

"What if I want you to?" I whisper, testing the waters.

"Want me to what? Use your words, Isla," he growls, intensifying the friction. *Fuck me.*

"To k-kiss me? Not like you haven't done it before," I stammer, feeling the effect he has on me.

"That was different, Isla. I wasn't thinking much then," he confesses.

"And what are you thinking now?"

"That I want to fucking devour you." Seconds pass. "All I need is a yes," he says, closing the gap, his breath brushing over my face.

"Is that what you want?" I place my hand on his thigh, which now touches mine. *Fuck it.*

"Ye—" I'm cut off as he swiftly pulls me closer, one hand behind my neck, slamming his mouth against mine. My body melts against his, sparks flying, butterflies erupting inside my stomach like fireworks.

The tip of his tongue traces the seam of my lips, seeking entrance, and I willingly allow it. A soft whimper escapes me, its volume echoing in the silent night, almost deafening. This only fuels his desire, and he kisses me hard. Aggressively—the kind that leaves no room for restraint.

Xavier wraps both arms around my waist with a possessive grip. With a sudden, commanding movement, he pulls me from beside him, effortlessly lifting me onto his lap. Now, I find myself straddling his hips, the closeness and the heightened connection intensifying our shared desire.

As our kiss deepens, desire surges between us, and Xavier's grip tightens on my waist. His tongue intertwines with mine in a fervent dance. Moving with purpose, his hands trail down my waist, boldly cupping my ass through the dress, which has now ridden up to my thighs. The cool breeze underneath adds a contrasting sensation to the warmth spreading at my core.

Suppressing his groan in our entwined mouths, I quicken my breath as he kneads my ass, urging me to grind against him in his lap. Xavier takes my bottom lip into his mouth, biting down with a primal intensity, a low and deep growl escaping him. I moan in satisfaction, my hands leaving his shoulders to lock behind his head, surrendering to the intoxicating connection we share.

His breath catches, a low "Fuck" escaping him as I continue to grind down onto him, feeling the impressive bulge in his pants. I've never been kissed like this in my life, I think to myself, swept away by the intensity of the moment.

Xavier's left hand traces an electrifying path up the front of my body, curving over my waist before confidently seizing my breast with a firm grip, eliciting a soft whimper from me. He plants a series of kisses along my jaw, then firmly grips my jaw, tilting it to the side for better access to my neck. He kisses and sucks on the sensitive skin, all the while continuing to sensually massage my breast.

Locking his gaze with mine, Xavier silently poses a question, seeking permission to go further. Understanding the unspoken request, I nod. He grabs the front of my dress, the shirred fabric scrunching underneath his grasp before he pulls it down, freeing my breast from the confines of my bra. Xavier cups my breast, his touch gentle yet possessive, his thumb tracing teasing circles around my nipple. Leaning down, he takes the puckered bud between his lips, the warmth of his mouth nearly melting me. He twirls and flicks my nipple with the tip of his tongue, emitting a loud groan against my skin. His gaze, now fixed on my exposed bust, is filled with awe as he mutters, "Fuuck me, Isla. These tits are perfect." I whimper, running my hands through the long locks of hair at his nape.

Just as Xavier snakes his hand back up behind me, grasping my hair and pulling my head back, moving over to the other side to return the favour, my phone rings in my bag, abruptly disrupting the heated moment. I can't help but wonder who might be calling. The ringing stops, leaving a brief uncertainty—perhaps it wasn't important, or just a random butt dial?

I begin grinding over his rock-hard bulge, the pressure building down at my core. I can feel the wet spot forming on his pants, evidence of my arousal, but in this state, I'm too consumed to care. Just as we get back into the rhythm, my phone rings again.

What the fuck, I think, frustration creeping in.

22

Xavier

"**Y**ou gonna get that, Doc?" Her phone has rung now for the second time, interrupting this heated moment.

The night has been a rollercoaster of desire and anticipation between Isla and me. The cool breeze, now picking up, feels amazing against my skin, which is practically burning up from the intense arousal. My dick has been painfully hard in my pants ever since we left her place. If this keeps up, I'll probably need to take care of that soon, avoiding a dreaded case of blue balls. That shit's fucked up.

Isla's on top of me, grinding so intensely that it feels like I could combust any second. *Not helping the matter.*

To distract myself, I pull on her hair, tilting her backward as I continue to twirl my tongue around her other nipple, pulling at it between my teeth before sucking on it.

"That's the second time it's rung now." My mouth releases her nipple with a 'pop' as I move back to her neck, biting down gently.

Isla releases a frustrated sigh and reluctantly moves off of me to grab her phone from her bag. The moment she pulls it out, her face falls entirely, and I'm instantly alert. "What's wrong?" I question, my concern evident.

She sits back on her calves and stares at her phone screen before putting it to her ear. Is she calling someone? When the person she's trying to reach doesn't answer, she exclaims, "Shit. Shit."

Concern now etches my face as I ask the question again, a bit more forceful than before, "Isla! What the fuck is wrong?"

She looks up at me, and my heart lurches on the spot. Confusion, pain, and sadness mar her beautiful features. "My dad, he rang me twice..." she says, frantically trying to call him back. "H-he's, he's not answering, Xavier. What if something happened?"

Tears now glisten in her eyes, reflecting off the night sky. Don't cry, *please*, I silently beg. I'm not sure what I'll do if she does. The thought of her being upset infuriates me. *Fuck, what is wrong with me?*

She abruptly continues, "I need to see him. I need to go over there, Xav. I'm so sorry. This has all been so lovely. I'm sorry to cut thi—"

I cut her off before she can continue, "Isla, please. You don't have to apologise. I'll drive you," I say, moving to start packing everything up—now a mess from us fooling around. Isla starts to help, but I place a hand on hers and add, "Go wait in the car. I got this, love."

After securing everything in the car, I close up the tray, circle around, and slide into the driver's seat.

"Xavier, you can't just show up at my place. I don't know how my dad will react. I need my car."

No chance in hell. "There's no way I'm letting you drive in this state, Isla. I'll park further down so he doesn't spot the car—I promise."

She looks at me with apprehension in her eyes, and I start the car, leaving behind the serenity of the night, our desire still softly lingering in the air, not forgotten.

Seated in the car, Isla guides me with directions. Glancing at her beside me, her worried expression alarms me. She bounces her knee anxiously, fidgeting with her dress—a telltale sign of her nervousness or anxiety that I've come to recognise.

I place my left hand on her thigh, gently gripping it to offer comfort. With my right hand manoeuvring the car, I slowly move my hand up and down her thigh, savouring the smoothness of her skin—almost like silk.

As we pull into the long driveway leading to her family home, the large white house with a huge wrap-around porch comes into view. Lights are on inside, indicating her father must be home. She's probably wondering why he didn't answer the phone. I park, as promised, a bit further down from the house, behind a massive pine tree. Leaving the ignition running, I turn off my lights, not wanting to draw too much attention.

Isla unclasps her seatbelt, but before she can leave, I place a hand on her stomach to hold her back. "Woah, woah. I don't want you going in alone. I'm coming." Isla whips her head back to me, shock in her eyes. "What? No, Xav, no way. You don't understand, my father isn't himself. If he sees you, he'll lose his shit."

Hold up. "Listen, what your father has going on with mine has nothing to do with us. It's all bullshit, old news."

Isla freezes. "W-wait. What? How do you know about that? What do you know?" she asks. She knows? How does she know? *That's a silly question, Xav.*

"Just something about a job, money being owed. It's no big deal, Isla—we'll sort it out. I'm coming."

"Money being owed? What?!" Isla pauses for a moment, as if thinking about something, before quickly saying, "No, Xavier, no! Please. I'll be fine—he's my father. I'll text you if anything." She stares at me intently, her eyes pleading, "Please... just stay here." *So, she doesn't know about the ridiculous feud between her father and mine?*

I sigh in frustration. "If I hear anything, I'm coming in."

Isla nods, "Okay," before heading out and closing the door. I watch with apprehension as she walks up the driveway, up the stairs to the porch, and into the house.

I don't like this. I don't like it at all.

Minutes and seconds drag on, and I find myself restlessly toying with anything within reach to soothe the unease clawing at my throat.

What's taking so fucking long? Snatching my phone from the centre console, I hastily type out a message to Isla.

> **Me:** Everything okay? What happened?

The message delivers, but there's no reply. I wait, fixated on the screen as more agonising minutes and seconds slip away.

A distant noise jolts me out of my stupor. *Huh?* Glancing toward the house, I discern figures moving in the dim glow seeping through the windows. There's a commotion inside—something clattering, voices in a frenzied exchange. I'm too far to catch the words. *Fuck this.*

I kill the engine, snatch my keys and phone, and step out. With a click, I lock the car behind me, trudging up the driveway. Thunder rumbles overhead, and dark clouds gather—a storm on the horizon, the inevitable result of the scorching heat we've endured. Just great.

My thoughts flit to the farm, the animals grazing in the pastures. I hope Dad senses the impending storm and guides them to the shelter of our barn.

Drawing closer to the house, the clamour intensifies. Isla's father shouts urgently, his movements frantic. Isla's gentle voice intertwines with his, a stark contrast to his deep, gruff tone.

As I reach the front porch, the escalating voices become clearer, and I can distinctly hear Isla and her father engaged in a heated argument. Tension hangs in the air, and I strain to catch the words.

Isla's voice maintains a steady calm, a stark contrast to the turmoil unfolding within the house. My gut tightens. Something's seriously wrong.

I hear her father's distressed words, a worried inquiry about his misplaced belongings. He's desperately trying to contact his wife, and panic drips from his every word. "Where is her damn phone?" he bellows.

Isla's reply, though composed, holds a depth of understanding. "Dad, please. Just calm down. Mum's not here. Remember?"

His confusion and desperation strike a chord in me. Is this what Mum warned me about? Poor Cal Thompson, grappling with dementia. The realisation stings, and I feel a pang of sympathy for him.

Then, the sound of something shattering pierces the air. My protective instincts kick in instantly. I dash up the porch steps and pound on the locked screen door. Damn it, Isla.

My knocks echo through the turmoil inside. I don't care about the consequences; I need to ensure Isla's safety. Her father seems to be teetering on the edge, his agitation escalating into something more aggressive.

"Isla! Open the damn door!" I yell, the urgency seeping into my voice. I can't stand idly by, oblivious to whatever chaos is unfolding inside. My heart races, matching the tempo of the storm brewing both outside and within the walls of this troubled house.

23

Isla

I step into the chaos of our home, a place that's supposed to be a haven—now transformed into a battleground of emotions.

The air reeks of alcohol, assaulting my senses as I find Dad in the kitchen, a hurricane of frustration tearing through him. Drawers and cupboards open and close with a violent urgency.

"Dad, what's wrong? Why did you call?" I ask cautiously, my tone tinged with apprehension. Slowly, I move towards him, trying to gauge the storm brewing within him.

"Please, calm down," I plead, my eyes searching for a connection with the man who once held my world together. I raise my hands in a placating gesture, my voice soft yet laden with understanding.

"Don't tell me to fucking calm down. Where is her damn phone?" he bellows, his anger a tempest that threatens to consume everything. I keep a safe distance, unsure of how he'll react, not wanting to push him further into the abyss of his own anger. The memories of my mother being the soothing balm in these situations play in my mind, but now, I am alone in navigating this turbulent sea of emotions with him.

"How much have you had to drink, Dad?" I ask, my voice edged with concern. He just grunts, his frustration continuing to spiral as he searches relentlessly for the phone. The crash of a phone book hitting the floor reverberates through the room, a harsh punctuation to his anger. I recall the words I'd read about handling dementia-induced aggression—stay calm, reassure, address the underlying feelings, distract.

"Where do you think you saw it last, Dad?" I ask gently, my voice a calming melody amid the chaos. He's agitated, his eyes darting around the room as if the phone might materialise before him.

"It was on our bedside table," he replies with clear frustration. "Now it's not there, and I tried callin' it, but the damn fucker goes straight to voicemail." His words carry the weight of confusion and anger.

I take a deep breath, remembering the importance of maintaining composure. "Okay, Dad. Let's look together. Maybe it got moved somewhere else," I suggest, hoping to redirect his focus.

He slams a drawer shut before moving into the lounge room, a tempest leaving chaos in his wake. I follow, my heart aching for the man he once was, grappling with the storm within his mind.

"NO! It couldn't have moved; I never touched it. Where is she?"

Dad's anger echoes through the walls, and I find myself grappling with the knowledge I've gathered about dementia. The guide in my mind speaks again, suggesting a gentle reminder for those lost in a confusing reality. My heart is heavy, so I decide to navigate this delicate terrain.

"Hey, Dad," I say, keeping my tone soft. "Let's sit for a moment. I want to talk to you."

He eyes me suspiciously, still seething from the frustration of the missing phone. "Talk 'bout what? No time to fuckin' sit." His words slur, no doubt from the amount of alcohol he's consumed.

I guide him toward the couch, a small oasis of calm in the storm. "Just... about Mum," I say cautiously, choosing my words with care.

"Remember the funeral? We went through the order of service together. Maybe looking at it again will help." The mention of her brings a flicker of recognition to his eyes, a momentary pause in the tempest.

Hesitantly, he follows me to the couch. As I retrieve the funeral program from a nearby shelf, I hope that, somehow, these tangible connections to the past can anchor him in the present.

The mention of Mum's passing only fuels Dad's confusion, and a volatile anger sparks in his eyes. "She ain't dead. What the bloody hell are'ya talkin' bout?" he retorts, the words a harsh rejection of the reality I'm desperately trying to navigate.

In his frustration, he seizes a small vase from the coffee table, filled with delicate daisies, and hurls it to the floor. Glass shatters, scattering across the room. As the storm within the house intensifies, a distant echo reaches us. The sound of persistent knocks on the door.

As Dad's rage shatters the fragile calm, a distant voice echoes through the turmoil. "Isla! Open the damn door!"

The urgency in the voice seeps into my veins, and I recognize it as

Xavier's. His pounding echoes through the chaos, a resounding plea that refuses to be ignored.

My father, now even more agitated by the unfamiliar voice, demands, "Who the fuck is that?" The question hangs in the air, unanswered, as the storm within the house matches the tempest outside. Xavier's fervent knocks persist.

Fucking hell, Xavier. Why can't he ever listen? The glass crunches beneath Dad's boots as he trudges over it, heading toward the door. He swings it open to reveal Xavier, his expression a blend of concern and anger. "What the fuck are ya doin' on my porch, boy?"

Dad's voice bellows, the anger palpable. Recognition flickers in his eyes, and he turns back to me, suspicion etched across his face, probably connecting the dots about my dress. "You with... *him?*" Dad seethes, the disgust evident in his tone.

Panic seizes me, and I instinctively step forward, forgetting about the glass scattered on the floor. Xavier notices my movement and reacts swiftly. "Isla, don't fucking move. There's glass everywhere. Are you okay?" he says, his eyes searching mine.

"What the fuck did I say about those Mitchell boys, huh?" Dad's anger escalates, and I feel the weight of his disappointment. *Shit, this is just getting worse and worse*—caught in the crossfire of Xavier's concern and my father's rage.

I walk up to the door, the glass crunching beneath my feet, and face my father as he steps forward towards Xavier. "Dad, please." I place a hand on his shoulder. "You need to calm down. He was just leaving," I implore, my voice a desperate plea.

Xavier, his eyes never leaving Dad, steps closer, a protective force that sends ripples through the tension-filled air. "Isla, he's been drinking. He's too disoriented right now. I'm not going anywhere," he asserts, his tone resolute.

My face flushes with heat, embarrassed that Xavier has to witness this. He's my father, I shouldn't feel this way because of him, but damn it.

Dad seethes, his voice a thunderous demand, "I ain't gonna ask you again. Get lost, boy. This doesn't concern you."

"Absolutely fucking not," Xavier counters, refusing to back down. "Anything to do with Isla does, sir. You should listen to her. You need to calm down."

I can feel the weight of their confrontation, a precarious balance between a protective instinct and a father's fury. The familiar warmth of Xavier's presence grounds me, but the chaos in the room threatens to pull me under. Dad's anger, fueled by confusion and frustration, is a tempest I can't control. *Why does everything have to be so complicated?*

Dad's anger intensifies, the threats escalating. Storming off, he leaves us on the porch, the remnants of his fury lingering in the air.

Xavier instinctively wraps a protective arm around me. "Are you okay? I'm sorry, I had to come in," he says, concern etched in his features. Tears well up in my eyes, embarrassment flushing my cheeks more.

"Please, Xav, just go. I'll be fine. I can control it. Just leave—you'll only make things worse," I plead, my voice shaky. But Xavier remains resolute, tightening his grip around me.

"I'm. Not. Fucking. Leaving. You here with *him*," he seethes, each word a declaration of unwavering determination. "He can threaten me all he wants."

Just as Xavier asserts himself, Dad returns, now brandishing a shotgun. Panic grips me, fear taking root in my chest.

"Dad! What the fuck? Put the gun down," I plead, my voice desperate. Never before have I witnessed my father resort to such extreme measures. The gravity of the situation dawns on me, and I find myself teetering on the edge of a precipice, unsure of what comes next.

Dad's words slur with a mix of anger and alcohol. "You're not welcome 'ere, mate. Get the bloody hell out before I make ya." His threat is thick—the shotgun, a menacing punctuation to his words as he points it towards Xavier.

Xavier stands his ground, his protective stance unwavering. "You're outta line, mate. Put the damn gun down," he demands, his voice steady despite the tension crackling in the air. Unfazed, raises his hands in a gesture of surrender, his eyes locked onto Dad's. There's not a trace of fear in those intense blue eyes. *How can he remain so composed in the face of this chaos?*

"Ya think you can waltz in 'ere and take my girl? Not on my bloody watch!"

I tremble as the standoff unfolds before me, caught between the man I've known my entire life and the one who's become only recently my *anchor*.

"Dad, please, this is insane. Just put the gun down," I implore, the desperation in my voice echoing the chaos in my mind.

Dad's eyes, bloodshot and cloudy, flicker between Xavier and me. "I warned ya, Isla. Get rid of him or both of ya will be sorry," he slurs, the shotgun wavering in his grip.

Xavier's jaw clenches, his protective instincts colliding with a fierce determination. "Isla, go inside. I'll handle this."

"No, Xav, please," I whisper, tears streaming down my face.

My heart pounds in my chest, fear and determination waging a battle within me. "Dad, please, put the gun down. We can't go on like this. You're scaring me, and I can't bear to see you like this," I plead, desperation and fear lacing my words.

Dad's eyes, bloodshot and wild, flicker with a mix of anger and confusion. "You stay outta this, Isla. This ain't your concern."

"But it is, Dad. It is my concern," I assert, my voice firm. "I won't let you hurt him or yourself."

I step in front of the barrel, gripping the gun with both hands. Xavier, still with his hands raised, interjects, "ISLA! What the fuck are you doing?" His words bellow loudly.

"No! Dad, please, put the gun down. We need to talk, not fight," I implore, my grip on the gun tightening. The once-familiar porch now feels like a battlefield, and I'm caught in the crossfire, torn between protecting the man I—*what do I feel?* My thoughts are conflicted—The man I *care* about and my father, who's spiralling out of control.

"Isla, ya foolish girl! Get the fuck out o' the way," he threatens, his voice laden with frustration.

I stand there, determined but scared shitless, praying that my actions can somehow defuse the chaos.

I know the gun isn't loaded. Years of growing up with my father, out hunting and learning about guns, taught me that. As Dad goes to pump the shotgun, the chamber where shells are normally held is empty—a glaring sign that he hadn't loaded any shells into the shotty. It's something he'd taught me to notice really well—now a detail he must've overlooked in his dishevelled state.

The sky has now darkened completely, thunder rumbling in the sky, rain starting to patter on the roof and behind us. The tension is palpable, a storm both outside and within.

Xavier roars, "Put the fucking gun down, Callum," as he moves closer to me, gripping the barrel of the shotgun, pointing it upwards to the roof.

"Isla, MOVE!" In the chaos, my father is knocked off balance and Xavier yanks the gun from his grip.

"Don't you ever fucking do that again, Isla, do you hear me?" he roars, his proximity unsettling.

"I had to fucking stop him—he wasn't budging."

Xavier pumps the shotgun's barrel back in an attempt to empty the shells, but realisation dawns—it's already empty. His piercing and intense gaze locks onto mine, a silent exchange of tumultuous emotions. "Please, just go!" I urge, frustration now building, pushing him.

"Isla, I'm not fucking leaving you here with him." My desperation echoes in the air.

"Just go back to your car!" I plead.

He resists, so I press harder. "Please!"

My voice, usually gentle, now feels alien as it cuts through the chaos. Xavier mutters something—I don't quite catch it but hear 'unbelievable' under his breath as he storms off to his car. Why do I have shit luck with dates? I turn to my father, who is now resting on the edge of the lounge chair.

I rush over to him. "I-Isla," he repeats, my heart doing somersaults.

"I'm here, Dad, I'm here," I say, my voice wavering as I redirect him inside onto the couch.

"What time is it? What happened?" His confusion is disorienting—does he have no recollection of what just happened?

"Just rest, Dad, stay here. I'll get you some water," I say, frantically rushing to the kitchen to grab a glass, returning to place it in front of my father—who has now passed out on the couch. I nudge him softly as panic courses through me. His chest moves with soft movements and I exhale a breath in relief. I grab a blanket folded on the chair beside the couch and throw it over him. Then I sweep up the broken glass carefully and toss the shards in the bin inside the kitchen.

Lights in my peripheral vision catch my attention. Xavier's car is still down the dirt path, lights on. *He's still here.* Closing the front and screen door, I rush off down the stairs towards him. He needs to *leave*—what doesn't he understand?

The rain pelts down, unrelenting, soaking through my clothes as I rush towards Xavier's car, lights piercing through the darkness. Thunder still rumbles overhead.

Xavier sees me approaching, frustration etched on his face as he steps out into the downpour.

"How could you fucking do that, Isla? Are you fucking stupid?" he seethes, standing defiantly in front of me. "You never put yourself in front of a barrel like that. Ever. AGAIN—Didn't your father ever teach you anything?"

Infuriated, I defend myself against his anger. "He would have shot you if I didn't intervene." I place my hands on my hips. "The gun wasn't even loaded! So, *YES*, Xavier, my dad did teach me something," I retort, my voice cutting through the drumming rain. My heart pounds, a mix of frustration, fear, and lingering adrenaline.

Xavier's frustration boils over, and he practically snarls, "That's not the fucking point, Isla."

The rain lashes down on us as we stand in the storm, a physical manifestation of the tempest between us. "You can't just throw yourself into harm's way like that, especially not for me," he continues, his voice a low growl. My own frustration flares.

"What about you, Xavier? What were you thinking, storming in like that? You could have gotten yourself killed! You have to trust me to handle things."

His jaw tightens, the tension between us thickening as he roars, "Trust? Isla, you can't just expect me to stand by when you're clearly in danger. I didn't want anything to happen to you."

I clench my fists, the rain mingling with tears on my cheeks. "Danger?" I scoff. "I don't need you to be my knight in shining armour, Xavier. I need you to *understand* that I can take care of myself. You don't get to barge in and dictate everything," I say as I shove him. "Why do you care so much? You should have just left—-anyone else would have."

"I'm not anyone else. I've told you before, I care about you," he insists, frustration etched across his features. He cares for me, *but why?* My mind still can't comprehend why.

"This... whatever the fuck this is... isn't going to work," I exclaim loudly, gesturing between us. The relentless rain paints a blurry backdrop to our heated exchange. "You said *one* date, and that's all it'll be, Xavier. Just leave, please, for the hundredth time—" I say as I turn to walk back into the house. Yet, I'm abruptly halted as Xavier seizes my wrist, forcefully pulling me back to him. In an unexpected move, he slams his lips to mine.

The world around us dissolves into the storm, the taste of rain and desperation lingering on our lips. I try to pull away, my palms pressing against his chest, attempting to create distance, but the intensity of the kiss keeps me anchored.

The rain cascades around us, an unyielding force echoing the tumultuous emotions that entwine us in this moment. My head wages war with my entire body, fighting the addicting attraction I have for him. Kissing Xavier is like tasting the sweetest poison.

The friction of his body against my flimsy dress has me panting into his mouth. The entire world fades away as we tease, nip, kiss.

Our tongues duelling against one another for dominance. He pulls away with a ragged breath. "I told *you*, for the *hundredth* time, I am not leaving." He stares down at me, his blue eyes piercing mine with an intensity that kindles a warm and fuzzy sensation within.

"Deny it all you want, princess—trust *me*, I've tried—but there *is* something here." There's that word again—trust.

"If you want me to stop, then tell me. I need your words," he murmurs, his breath warm against my ear.

"What?" I whisper, but I heard him loud and clear. Fuck, I shouldn't want this. *Especially not now.*

"Yes, or no, Isl—" he doesn't have time to respond. I slam my lips back to his, eliminating any lingering doubts. A low growl rumbles from deep within him, the vibrations resonating through both of us. With effortless strength, he lifts me, carrying me to his car. Fumbling with the door handle, he yanks it open and gently tosses me into the back seat, following closely behind.

As I settle into the backseat with him, he guides me to straddle his thighs. I instinctively clench my thighs together. The air in the car crackles with a newfound tension as Xavier's lips find their way back to mine. My breath hitches, caught in the dance of desire and restraint.

His hands, rough yet gentle, trail along the small of my back, the warmth of his touch sending shivers down my spine. As our lips meld, he pulls me even closer, and his voice, gruff and low, breaks the silence.

"Stepping in front of that gun... it means something, Isla," he murmurs against my lips, his breath a warm whisper. "Means you care, too."

His words hang in the air, adding a layer of complexity to the charged atmosphere. He persists, his lips leaving mine to trail kisses down my neck. "Admit it. Admit you care about me too, princess."

I manage to find my voice. "I can't explain why," I breathe, the admission escaping in a whisper that gets lost in the heat of the moment.

He prods, "I didn't ask you to explain it to me—I asked you to admit it."

"Fine, Xavier. I care about you, too."

He returns his mouth back to mine with a growl, and as our lips connect once more, the electricity between us intensifies.

When he breaks the kiss, his husky voice pleads, "Don't ever do that again, Isla. Please."

I take a moment to catch my breath, our eyes locked. "I won't," I admit, my voice carrying a hint of sincerity and a dash of playfulness.

He runs his hands up and down my body, the warmth of them burning against my cold skin from the downpour of the rain. His clothes are soaked, and so are mine. My hair is probably a ratted mess.

In the silence of the car, he murmurs, "Fuck, I shouldn't want this as much as I do. But I can't fucking help it. You have me hooked, Isla."

I can't help but whimper at his words. In that moment, his confession mirrors the sentiments echoing in my head. My own thoughts align with his, and I find myself entangled in the magnetic pull between us, unable to resist the undeniable connection that has taken root.

"Are you wet for me, Isla? If I run my fingers over your pussy, will you be drenched for me?" His words draw a soft whimper from me.

Xavier's words, filthy and laced with desire, echo in my ears, sending tingles down my back. The raw intensity of his question hangs in the air, leaving me breathless.

Am I wet for him? The answer is undeniable—I can feel it, a physical manifestation of the desire he's ignited within me. It's a sensation I can't quite explain, unlike anything I'd ever felt with Justin.

Xavier has an inexplicable effect on me, an allure that elicits an arousal I've never felt before—the sensation almost bordering on pain. Frustration builds deep in my core. Desperately needing some form of relief, I continue to gyrate my hips over his—his now incredibly hard bulge rubbing my sensitive spot.

"Why don't you see for yourself," I whisper.

24

Xavier

Isla's perfume wraps around me like an aphrodisiac—an intoxicating blend of floral notes that ignites my senses. The delicate fragrance clings to the air, creating an invisible thread that pulls me closer to her. It's more than a scent—it's a sensation that infiltrates my very being.

"There's no going back after this," I declare, my tone promising.

"Fine by me. *Please*, Xavier," she pleads, whimpering whilst grinding herself harder against my stiff cock. Isla tugs at my hair at the nape of my neck, adding a touch of pain.

"Please what, baby?" She forces my neck to the side, granting her access to kiss the column of my neck. I groan, continuing, "Use your words."

"Touch me," she pleads. The warmth of her neck inviting beneath my lips.

I respond with a growl that makes her tremble. "Touch you where?" I purr, my voice low and gravelly, sending shivers down her spine.

"My... my pussy," she declares, and that's all the permission I need.

I rake my hand down her back, over the large round globes of her ass, drifting lower underneath. My fingers tease the outside lining of her underwear, and just as I'd suspected—she's fucking drenched. *Fuck me.*

"Has a man ever made you come by fingering you?"

She shakes her head, so slowly, I almost miss it.

"Did *he* ever try?"

She nods.

"Why didn't you come?" My voice sounds like gravel.

She shrugs. "I-I... just couldn't. It wasn't enough."

Moving her slightly to the side, I continue to glide my fingers over her pussy, through the drenched cotton, before moving it over to the side to run my fingers up and down her wet folds.

Her breath hitches, and she moans in my ear. I thought Isla's giggles were compelling, but the breathless moans she releases are fucking intoxicating. I never want to stop hearing them.

"Mm." I hum. "You are drenched." I dip a finger inside her, moving slowly, in and out. Her pussy is so tight, clenching around my finger, and she sucks in a breath, hissing when I add in a second, feeling her stretch around them.

"Fuck, Isla, your pussy is so tight."

I bite down on the sensitive area between her neck and collarbone and she moans loudly as I continue to finger fuck her. My hand slides up to her throat, my fingers brushing over her pulse point.

She gives my hand a little squeeze with hers, giving me her silent approval. Fuck, does my girl liked to be choked. *My girl?* Is that what she is? Fuck, I'm a goner for this girl. There is no way I'm stopping now.

With a groan, I move my mouth to her ear, biting her lobe. "You like that, baby? My hand on your throat, my fingers in your cunt."

She whimpers in response, her body melting into me.

"That's it, ride my hand. Show me how you're going to ride my cock." Isla moves her hips with my hand, riding me as she releases a breathless moan. I let that hand at her throat squeeze, and she catches her breath, sharp and sweet.

I give her clit a little friction with my thumb, moving it from side to side and her tight pussy clenches around my fingers. I kiss her neck, nipping at her ear again.

"Oh god," she pleads, squirming on my hand. She's right fucking there, I can feel it. In every moan, every breath.

The way her tight walls suffocate my fingers, pulsating inside with every movement that I make. I curve both fingers upward in a 'come here' motion, massaging her G-spot. I'm not taking her pussy until I feel her shatter on me.

"Fuck, Xav," she whimpers. "*Please*, don't stop."

Stop? As if I'd fucking stop now. Fuck, I'm already right there—my dick strains against my shorts, painfully, no doubt leaking pre cum.

"*Yes*," she moans, her hand trailing from mine around her neck down to her perfect, large breast, tugging at her nipple through the fabric of her dress.

I continue to curl my fingers inside her along her G-spot and whisper in her ear, "*Come* for *me*, come all over *my* fingers." I growl. "That's it."

And fuck me, she does. She comes all over my fingers, her body shaking in my arms as she quivers and moans, riding out her orgasm, her pussy pulsing around my fingers. Releasing a breathless moan, her body goes slack against my chest as she continues to tremble through her release.

I release my hold from her throat, moving to grab her waist, grounding her against me. I slip my fingers out of her soaking wet pussy, lifting them to my face—her arousal dripping down them.

I don't even attempt to stifle my moan as I place my fingers into my mouth, sucking them clean—she tastes like pure sin. Warm and incredibly sweet. Isla watches with pure satisfaction.

I move in closer, brushing my lips softly over hers. "Taste yourself. See how perfect you fucking taste." I dip my tongue into her mouth, hers moving obediently with mine. She moans as I deepen the kiss, spreading her arousal from my tongue to hers.

I hum a low growl. "Fuck, baby. If you don't let me have you right now, I'm going to fucking explode." My cock is throbbing in my pants, aching to be released. She didn't know what she was starting. She didn't know what the fuck she was doing to me. The fire that was roaring within me. The restraint I was using to not rip this dress off her.

"Then take me," she whispers, her face flushing with heat. I love the effect that I have on her.

In the confined space of the backseat, beads of sweat form on my brow—a testament to the heat radiating off our entwined bodies. The windows fog up as rain continues to tap out a soothing rhythm outside, accompanied by distant thunder. The car's tight space wraps us in silence, interrupted only by her soft moans blending seamlessly with mine.

"Take my cock out, Isla," I say, shifting her off my lap to allow her room to move before me.

Sitting in front of me, her breath hitches as she shifts, her eyes meeting mine, now squinted and hooded from her recent waves of arousal.

This girl has every potential to ruin me. She just doesn't know it yet.

25

Isla

I feel bold. *Reckless.*

Xavier fucking Mitchell just made me come with his *fingers.* Something I hadn't thought to be possible for me. It's something I had always struggled with, something I had always *wished* to experience. Until now. Sex has always been pleasurable for me, but over the years, Justin had made it feel like just another ordinary chore—never really paying attention to my likes. Sometimes I wouldn't even finish. This is all so incredibly new for me.

I sit in front of Xavier, his eyes hooded, looking down at me—hunger dancing in them. *Fuck me.*

"Take my cock out, Isla." He voices. *Fuckity fuck fuck.* This is happening. I am really going to do this. I move my hands to his belt, unbuckling it with a clack as I move it out of the way. My hands are shaking; I can't fucking stop it.

"Hey," he says softly. "We don't have to do this. I don't want to force you to do anything you don't want to." *My heart.* It aches. Where did this guy come from? Why does he have to be so perfect?

Ugh.

"N-no. I want to," I say, swallowing the lump in my throat. "I want this."

He hums so low, the sound resonating audibly despite the pouring rain hitting his car. Then, with a sudden move, he takes off his hat and throws it to the side. He shakes his head, water droplets falling onto his chest, before raking his hands down his long mane. His hair—his damn hair—it's become an obsession of mine.

"I'll help you. Unzip my shorts." I do exactly that, wasting no time. My shaky hands latch on to his zipper, pulling it down. He lifts his hips up slightly to make moving his shorts and briefs down much easier. His cock springs free and I freeze. *What the fuck... do I do with that?!*

Had you asked me a few weeks ago—or better yet, *years* ago—if I'd be sitting in front of Xavier Mitchell, with his cock out in front of me, I would have just laughed at the absurd thought.

Look at me now.

His cock is fucking huge. Like *huge,* huge. I have never seen a more good looking penis in my life. He is *much* bigger than Justin, I'll tell you that. He is also uncut... something I have not experienced before. There is no way he's going to fit. RIP to my pussy.

"Jesus fucking Christ. How do you keep all of... *That...* tucked away in there?" I say, exhaling a breath in disbelief.

He laughs, tilting his head back against the seat—it's so deep, so masculine—smooth like a fine whiskey. "You're cute, princess." That *nickname...* he's mentioned it a few times tonight, and it makes me flutter—Every. Single. Damn. Time.

His thick thighs are nothing but muscle, dusted with dark hair. Fuck, I'd known Xavier was attractive, fuck, but him sitting in front of me with his shorts halfway down his huge thighs, rigid cock on display in the back seat of his car, is absolutely devastating. Is this even real? Or am I dreaming?

"Touch me, baby. Wrap your hand around me," he goads. Nope... *Definitely not dreaming.*

This position is so fucking awkward, I'm seated in front of him, resting my ass half on the centre console, and my knees now on the floor—I'm not exactly the smallest of girls. Thankfully, his backseat actually has quite a bit of room for the both of us—yet, I'm just too fucking horny to care.

Xavier's gaze follows me as I trace the thick vein down his shaft.

His breathing grows heavier as I wrap my hand around him gently, impressed by the girth. My fingers don't even touch. *How?*

Surely this is going to do some damage... and I start to rethink all of my decisions as nerves start to kick in. He places his large hand over mine, urging me to move up and down, giving mine a squeeze.

"You don't need to be gentle. You can use more pressure."

I sigh, stroking him from root to tip with an eager hand, applying pressure—his bulbous head now leaking precum at the top. His skin is so velvety smooth. I could touch him all day.

"That's it, good girl. Keep doing that," he groans, as he watches me intently. Fuck, I want to taste him—I need to. I want to learn everything he likes. I want to be good at this for *him.*

His groans spur me on, and I build up the courage to replace my hand with my tongue. I start tentatively at first, licking the tip, tasting his arousal—warm and salty. I hum in the moment and he growls. "Fuck, *yess*. Do that again," he hisses. *Oh my.*

I continue to hum on his cock as I wrap my lips over his head, my mouth stretching wide open to accommodate his girth. Feeling brave, I cup his balls with my other hand, massaging them softly, and his hips surge forward as he hisses through his teeth, groaning loudly. His arousal continues to coat my tongue as I switch between deep sucks and long strokes of my tongue. Xavier's hands find my hair, grabbing two fistfuls, gently guiding my head up and down as I move.

"If you keep going with that, Isla, I'm not going to last. The thought of coming in your hot mouth sounds like fucking heaven... but I need to fuck you." *Well fuck.*

"Come here," he growls, beckoning me to sit up.

His entire body shudders as I give him one last suck. He lets out a hiss of air when I release him before sitting back up. He grabs me by the waist, settling me over him and when his cock nudges my pussy through my undies, I just about melt—right then and there. I whimper.

"You ready?" he quips, smirking at me.

"*Yess,*" I moan.

"Take off your undies. Show me that beautiful pussy. Show me what I'm about to fuck." I'm pretty sure I am *that* wet, that it is now dripping down my inner thighs.

I lift and hook my underwear with two fingers and pull them down, carefully manoeuvring over him to take them off. I throw them to the side of the seat. I sit back on the console, spreading my legs—my dress still resting in front of my thighs. *C'mon, you literally just sucked the man's dick—there is no time to be shy now, girl.*

"Lift your dress a little for me."

I hesitate, feeling helpless as my insecurities start to surface. But after a moment, I do as he says, moving it up hesitantly and I swear his eyes darken—his eyes molten, the blue all but swallowed by the black of his pupils.

"*Fuccck,* you have the most perfect pussy. All wet for me. I can't fucking wait to devour you. Feast on your perfect cunt," he growls. Fuck me, *his mouth.* I never pictured these words coming out of his mouth. It's doing things to me that I just can't explain. I shift awkwardly in my spot, now avoiding his gaze.

"Hey," he murmurs as he sits up. "Look at me." I don't know what he sees when I lock my eyes with his, but they *soften.*

"You're beautiful, so fucking perfect. Don't hide from me, ever," he warns, his voice so low it sends a shiver through my body.

"I'm going to make you feel so good, Isla," he says, grabbing me and hauling me back over onto his lap, his cock resting against his t-shirt that has now ridden up slightly—catching a glimpse of the dark hair dusting his abdomen and that incredibly sexy 'v', leading straight towards his cock. I'm dying to see the rest of his body.

"I have a condom. Grab it from the centre console," he says, and I lean backwards, lifting the small compartment to find two condoms inside, grabbing one.

"You keep condoms in your car?" I ask, raising an eyebrow, questioning him with a glare.

He laughs again, and I want to listen to it forever, on repeat. *How can a man's laugh be so fucking sexy?*

"A guy can never be too sure." He winks. *Smug prick.*

My mind can't help but wonder how many girls he has fucked in this car. Feelings of insecurity creep up my throat, and I question whether I'm making the right decision. He must sense my thoughts as he says, "I haven't fucked anyone in months, Isla. I didn't put those there with the intention that I'd be fucking you tonight. I had forgotten they were there until now," he reassures me, and I believe him. *Damn him and his ability to read my mind.*

"Me too." I sigh. "It's been... a while for me, too. My *ex* was my last," I admit.

At that he nods, as he takes the condom, tearing at the foil with his teeth, nodding his head to me. "Put the condom on me, Isla."

I aim the tip of his crown and carefully roll the condom down. Once it's secure, I lift my gaze to his.

"I-I... don't think you're going to fit," I say and unease flickers deep in my gut. He laughs, a deep baritone erupting from him.

"Please don't break me," I plead, and this earns me another deep chuckle.

"I'll be gentle, princess. I promise." Another *promise*. He slides his hand down to his shaft, gliding his tip up and down my folds gently. He notches his dick at my entrance, easing in slowly. I tense, bracing myself.

"That's it. Such a good fucking girl," he praises. My pussy clenches with eagerness as he pushes up inside further as I press down on him slowly, using his shoulders as leverage. I gasp at the fullness, shutting my eyes, succumbing to the burn as he stretches me.

"Almost there," he goads. Fuck, fuck, fuck. This shit is *painful*.

I push against him, my body shuddering as I clamp around his cock. I swivel my hips, which makes his eyes roll back into his head. He looks back down at where our bodies are joined, his dick still halfway inside of me. *Fuck, how much more?*

I adjust over him, tilting my head, revelling in the sensation that has now turned into a sweet mix of pleasure and pain. I lean forward, my lips finding his neck, and I nip at the skin.

Xavier's fingers quiver against my hips as he releases another groan.

"You feel so good. So *big*," I hum against his neck.

He thrusts in a final time as I push down, burying himself to the hilt. I moan with pleasure, gripping his shoulders harder as I start to ride him, my body trembling as I move.

"You are—" a groan takes over his words "—breathtaking."

He captures my mouth with his again, biting on my lower lip before dipping his tongue inside my mouth. Each time I rise, I withdraw right to his tip, making him suck in a breath before I slam back down. Xavier's eyes lock on to mine and something snaps inside of him. He takes full control, his biceps straining against his t-shirt as he lifts me before pulling my hips back down.

"Fuck, baby. Hold on to me tight," he croons, and his thrusts become relentless. With each punishing stroke, my breath gets knocked out of me. The only sound filling the car now—as the rain outside subsides—is our breathy moans and skin slapping on skin.

"You're gonna come for me again, Doc," he says, his voice strained from his vigorous movements—it's not a question, it's a *demand*.

Pleasure starts to build up my spine again. I close my eyes as black spots fill my vision and when Xavier lifts his hand over to my clit, rubbing circles over my sensitive bud, I explode. Stars burst, sparkling to life behind my shut eyes.

"Ohmygod—f-fuck..." My body shakes as pleasure rushes through me.

Xavier's entire body trembles as he comes with a strangled groan, muttering under his breath, "*Fuck–fuck–fuck.*" I feel his dick pulsating inside of me, and I don't know how, but I swear his girth thickens inside me as he comes. My pussy is stretched wide, that pain I'd once felt, now dissipating into the most addictive sensation of pleasure.

I don't stop moving my hips until we're both breathless and limp as we come down from our highs together. Xavier is still seated deep inside of me. After a moment, he pulls out of me and we both groan. My body feels airless, so incredibly light, like I'm high—a pleasant euphoria and sense of relaxation.

Xavier leans over and presses the automated button, rolling down the window slightly, a cool breeze instantly whooshing inside the car, sending chills down our bodies. I feel Xavier's body tremble underneath mine.

The rain has now completely settled, and the thunder has ceased. Xavier and I remain close, our bodies still emanating heat around us.

"Well, that didn't go the way I planned," I huff out with a nervous laugh, feeling the weight of our actions sinking in. I hide my face, trying to mask my embarrassment.

Xavier notices and gently turns my face to look at him. "No, it definitely did not," he drawls. "Still gonna deny that there's something here?" His deep voice sends tingles throughout my body. I can't bring myself to answer. Xavier squints, shaking his head slightly. He's definitely not amused at me dodging his question, but I just need a moment to process everything that just happened. Our date, that kiss, my father, and Jesus Christ, just *him*.

As I watch his expression, I notice his eyes are so dark, hooded from his arousal. Intense. I look away for a moment, trying to distract myself from the intensity by picking up his black cowboy hat—well technically it's an Akubra hat—resting on the seat to my left with a playful smirk, and placing it on my head.

We just fucked... I just had *sex* with Xavier Mitchell—*car sex*, if we're being technical. I've never had sex in a car before. I softly breathe a laugh through my nose, the sound barely audible but full of amusement, at the thoughts running through my mind.

"Something funny, Doc?" Great.

"No, not at all. I just—" I shudder. "I can't believe we just did that."

"I can," he says matter-of-factly, "and it was fucking incredible. You're incredible." I take a deep breath in, taking in his words.

He tucks a rogue strand of my hair—now a complete mess—behind my ear. He then adjusts the hat on my head.

"Perfect," he murmurs, and I feel my cheeks burn with a deep blush. He then gently pulls me closer, my body naturally leaning into his. Our breaths synchronise, creating a perfect moment of intimacy. Butterflies flutter in my stomach, and my mind is consumed by the warmth of his body and the unexpected connection we've just shared.

What happens now? Where do we go from here? The thought stirs a feeling of unease within me, at the uncertainty of what lies ahead. All I am certain of, is that this is what it feels like to be alive—to be consumed by desire and tangled in the aftermath of a storm.

And that both terrifies and excites me.

26

Xavier

It's been four days since the tumultuous encounter with Isla's father—the man is genuinely troubled. The memory of that night stirs unease within me. His drunken state, wielding the shotgun, was a stark reminder of the fragility of life and the unpredictable nature of human behaviour.

At home, things have settled into its usual routine. Bradley, my younger brother, is enjoying a day off today, having officially become a police officer after completing his training in Goulburn. Liv, on the other hand, has been nothing but an annoying ball of energy since finishing up her course at uni. She's already planning stuff for Christmas—*it's bloody three months away*. Her over-enthusiasm just really irks me. The September spring has brought scorching temperatures, making me dread the impending heat of summer that I know we'll face during the upcoming holiday season.

I'm sprawled on the couch, grateful for the cool respite from the scorching heat outside. Dad's been up since the crack of dawn, off handling business down in Sydney, leaving the house to us for the day. With Mum, Bradley, and Liv scattered about, I'm left alone with my thoughts.

My mind drifts to Isla. The memory of our intimate moment in the car lingers, altering the atmosphere between us. There's a potent mix of desire, arousal, and something more elusive that I can't quite grasp. Thoughts of her dance through my mind, her presence lingering in the air like a sweet, intoxicating fragrance.

Isla has lodged herself in my thoughts in a way no other woman ever has. The intensity of our encounter in the car has left an indelible mark, unlike any experience I've had before.

I woke up thinking about *her*. I went to bed with *her* face behind my eyelids. I pumped my cock in the shower this morning, visualising *her* body, *her* moans, and the way she tastes.

I couldn't understand why I was feeling this way. Where had this sudden shift come from? After years of being contentedly single, of never sticking with a woman for more than a night—whenever that happened—this woman who had vanished from my life for so long, not even crossing my mind, until *now*, was stirring something deep within me.

I tried to resist it, to push it down. But it was futile. She had crept back into my thoughts, weaving herself into my consciousness in a way I couldn't shake.

I couldn't fight it. Even if I tried.

A soccer match blares on the screen, and Bradley is beside himself, shouting at the TV screen, hurling colourful phrases at the referee. It's so unlike him, but with soccer, he's a different person. I join in, unable to resist the adrenaline of the game. Olivia, on the other hand, looks utterly uninterested, scrolling through her phone and releasing an annoyed huff.

"Ugh, you both are so boring. I need another female in this household. Too much testosterone in the fucking air," she complains, her face twisted in disgust. My mind immediately jumps to Isla, imagining what it would be like if she were here, blending into my family chaos. The thought brings a smile to my face, a *rare* occurrence, unless I'm around Isla.

My mother's voice cuts through the banter from the kitchen, admonishing Liv, "Olivia! Language."

Olivia throws her hands in the air, pointing between me and Bradley. "What? Seriously, so these brutes can swear, but I can't," she protests, her frustration evident.

Her words trigger thoughts of Isla again, and my smile lingers. Olivia directs a question my way, breaking me out of my stupor. "Remind me, why did I come back home again?" I just smirk.

"To be honest, I don't know why you did. You were probably better off there," I reply, teasing her. Olivia looks at me funny, and her lingering gaze unnerves me.

"What, mate?" I quip, trying to brush off her scrutiny.

"You're... smiling? Hold on, let me rub my eyes real quick to make sure I'm not delirious," she says, frantically rubbing her eyes and scrutinising me. I roll my eyes at her dramatics.

"Something is different, Xav. You *never* smile," she remarks, narrowing her eyes.

Bradley catches on, turning his head to look at me, too. "You're never here, Liv. How would you know? I smile all the time," I dead-pan. Bradley snorts and returns his attention to the TV.

Mum, chiming in from the kitchen, says, "I noticed, too, Liv. He had a spring in his step this morning."

Olivia stares at me like I've grown two heads.

"If you ask me, I believe it has to do with a certain someone... a *she*, perhaps?" Mum suggests with a mischievous grin. I shoot her a glare. My mother is way too perceptive for my liking.

"Get the fuck out! Xav has found himself a girl? Brad, did you know?" Bradley, engrossed in the game, shushes her with his hand.

"You're both delusional," I retort, rolling my eyes. Olivia, unde-terred, invades my personal space.

"Who is she? Do I know her? What's her name?" She bombards me with questions. I push her away.

"Back off, would you? It was quiet around here before you came back."

Olivia's disbelief hangs in the air, and she tries to pry more infor-mation out of me, but I keep my lips sealed. She stands up, defeated, and concedes, "Fine, be mysterious, you grump. But I'll find out eventually. No secrets in this family!" she declares before giving up. I stifle a laugh at her theatrics.

"It's hot as fuc—" she pauses mid-word, correcting herself, as Mum pins her with a glare, "Fudge. I'm going for a swim. You two knuckleheads are welcome to join. A game of volleyball sounds like a fabulous idea." I contemplate her words—she's not entirely wrong.

After she leaves, Bradley and I share a mischievous glance. The match has finished anyway, so Bradley decides to join me. He turns off the TV, and I stand up, heading outside with Bradley trailing behind me. The prospect of a swim seems like a good idea to shake off the tension that's been lingering since the other night with Isla.

The chaos of water and laughter surrounds us in the pool, Olivia and Bradley bickering about fairness in our comically disastrous attempt at volleyball. Olivia, a force of nature, exclaims, "Oi! You two are not fair. Stop hogging the bloody ball, you damn buffoons!" splashing me and Brad in the face.

I chuckle, shaking off the water from my face, the droplets lingering on my skin. With a glance around the pool, I realise we're short on players. The game needs at least three or four more to turn it into something resembling an actual game. A mischievous idea forms in my mind—it could either be genius or spectacularly dumb.

Swimming over to the poolside ledge, I reach for my towel and phone, the vibrant energy of the game echoing around me. Checking my phone, it reads 3:52pm. Harrison and Michael would be finishing up from the shop anytime soon, perfect timing. As my fingers dance across the screen, I pull up the group chat with Harrison and Michael, ready to introduce a new level of chaos into the mix.

Me: Volleyball at the house. Get your asses over here ASAP.

Harrison's swift response is filled with excitement.

Harrison: Volleyball?

Harrison: Fuck yes!

Michael: This idiot is jumping up and down. On our way.

Contemplation brews within me as I consider messaging Isla. The idea sparks a silent battle in my mind—if she joins us, will it set off alarms to the others? We're friends though, right? Well, friends who've now had mind-blowing sex, among other things. But then again, what exactly are we? The uncertainty lingers, leaving me in a moment of internal conflict.

Me: You putting that cowboy hat to good use yet? 😅

That night, Isla had insisted my hat looked better on her—and damn, she was right. I pushed her to keep it, telling her seeing her in something of mine drove me wild. She resisted, but I eventually persuaded her. After a few moments, she responds.

Isla: Indeed I am.

Isla: It's doing a real good job keeping the sun out of my eyes as I wash my car.

Fuck—my mind wanders to Isla, covered in soap, bending over, washing the car while sporting my hat and those damn cowboy boots—painting a vivid image in my mind. *Fuck me.* Now I'm hard.

Me: Washing your car... In this heat?

Isla: Hey, it was in desperate need of a clean. I've neglected my poor girl.

Me: How long will you be, you reckon?

Me: My brother, sister and I are currently swimming in the pool. Come join me?

Another moment passes...

Isla: Oh, I don't know. I don't know your siblings. Won't it be awkward?

Me: Why would it be? They're harmless though. Liv can be slightly dramatic sometimes, but that's about it. I'll introduce you to them.

Me: Brad doesn't even speak much.

Isla: I don't know...

I can sense her apprehension through the phone. She doesn't reply straight away, so I keep the convo going to avoid her getting stuck in her thoughts.

Me: I won't force you. I just... want to see you. And these nutjobs are doing my absolute head in. Come save me, please? *Prayer hands emoji*

Fuck, I sound *desperate*. But *I am...* and I don't even give a fuck at this point. I can't help this urge that I have. I want her here. *Need* her here. I can't explain this shit.

Isla: Lol. Fine. I can be there in 15?

Thank fuck.

I waste no time in replying, my fingers flying over the keyboard.

Harrison and Michael are now here, adding more chaos to the mix. Between Liv, Bradley and those fuckers, it's like a damn circus out here. Not even farm animals cause this much shit—well, except Franklin, our cream-coated five-year-old alpaca. He's a menace, that one. Only seems to be friendly around Mum and that's it.

Twenty or so minutes pass before I hear Buddy start barking, running around to the front, signalling that someone is here. *Isla.* I swim over to the shallow end, drying off my hair before announcing that *I'll be back* to the group. As I make my way back up to the house, I faintly hear Harrison ask, "Who's here?" and Olivia responds with a casual "Noo idea."

Jogging up through the house, to the front, I spot Isla and Imogen getting out of her car.

"Ladies," I drawl, nodding to them both.

Isla turns around, freezing when her eyes lock onto me and then my naked chest. I smirk, curious about the dirty thoughts swirling in her mind.

I nod towards her car, sparkling in the sunlight. "Not bad, Doc. You should take up car washing as a side gig. I'd pay you." I wink, maybe a bit too suggestively—hoping her friend didn't catch on to that. Isla rolls her eyes, stifling a laugh.

As the girls approach, Imogen leisurely lowers her sunglasses for a more discerning gaze. I can sense her eyes tracing the contours of my naked chest. I've invested sweat and discipline into maintaining my frame, a testament to the demanding labour endured day in and day out.

The satisfaction of knowing my body is a reflection of this dedication tempers my awareness of the attention, yet a subtle discomfort lingers—something about another woman ogling me makes me feel... uneasy. While she is attractive in that girl next door vibe, with blonde hair and a small frame... I only have eyes for one woman at the moment—she's all woman—curves for days and that perfect foul mouth that I love about her when she's all riled up.

As we enter my house, I see no sign of Mum—she's probably out running errands. Guiding Isla with a hand on the small of her back, we walk down the pathway that leads to the large expanse of our backyard—our pool, just hidden down a hill by a row of trees.

The backyard is still a mess of chaos, with the idiots in the pool splashing around. I grab their attention, placing two fingers in my mouth and whistling loudly. The splashing stops as they turn to face us. Isla tenses beside me, and I quietly reassure her, sensing her apprehensiveness. "Don't be shy, princess. I'll introduce you."

I take a step forward, guiding Isla with me, and address the group. "Guys, this is Isla, and her friend, Imogen." Imogen and Isla both wave at them.

"The quiet one with the shaved head is Michael," I say, pointing to where he sits on the step of the pool. Harrison whistles loudly, a smug recognition forming on his face when he looks at Isla. He winks at me, and I roll my eyes.

"The loud fucker next to him, covered in tats, is Harrison, his brother. You'll get used to him, eventually," I add with a laugh, and Isla just smiles.

I then point to Brad, who's sitting on the edge of the pool, nodding back to the girls. "That's my brother, Bradley." Finally, I introduce Liv, who swims to the shallow end to exit the pool, now overly excited about more girls joining the scene.

She squeals, "Oh my! Xavier has lady friends? Pigs must be flying." She laughs, and I can't help but roll my eyes again. Isla giggles beside me, and I turn to look down at her. Olivia watches our interaction with a curious glance.

"Omg, hi, I'm Olivia. The better Mitchell sibling." She laughs, and I shake my head.

Isla chuckles softly and introduces herself, "Hey, I'm Isla," she says with a blush.

Olivia can't resist expressing herself. "You're so gorgeous... wow!" Her exclamation catches Isla off guard, and to be honest, me too. I can't help but notice the way Isla's cheeks flush slightly, her eyes sparkling with surprise. For once, I find myself internally agreeing with my sister, silently acknowledging Isla's beauty and the charm that seems to radiate from her. Olivia continues, "I feel like I know you both from somewhere..."

Imogen steps in. "We both went to Springbrook High School. You might recognise us from there."

Olivia, now connecting the dots, exclaims, "Oh shit! Yes, that makes sense." She turns her attention to Imogen. "I love your hair, who colours it?"

Imogen chuckles. "This is all natural, babe. But I am a hairdresser if you're ever looking for one."

Olivia beams. "Oh, I love you even more now. Come, come. We were just about to play a game of volleyball," she says, playfully dragging Imogen toward the pool, leaving Isla and me alone.

As Isla stands by my side, I catch a glimpse of her apprehension, her shyness lingering in her gaze. "Hey, you all good?" I inquire, my voice a gentle reassurance. She looks up at me, her arms wrapped around her mid-waist, a subtle defence.

"Yeah," she responds, a hint of uncertainty in her tone. Her attire complements the sunny day—a black sundress and thongs, a beach bag casually strapped to her arm.

As I place my hand on Isla's back, the subtle warmth resonates between us. "Ready to play some volleyball?" I inquire, and she responds with a shy nod, a delightful blush colouring her cheeks. Guiding her down to the pool, I relish in the warmth building inside me. Reaching the group, Imogen is now in the pool, engaging with

Olivia. I urge Isla to put her stuff on one of the lounge chairs and join the others.

"Just drop your things on one of those chairs," I say, attempting to make her feel at ease. Olivia, always the instigator, beckons for everyone to start the game.

Isla reluctantly drops her belongings, throwing her sunglasses on top of her towel. I notice her searching for reassurance, her eyes seeking mine for guidance. The way she looks at me does things to me, awakening a protective instinct. *My shy girl*. But why, all of a sudden, am I thinking of her like that? It's not a way I've ever thought about someone before. The thoughts sound so foreign to me, yet they persist, swirling in my mind as I try to make sense of them.

As Isla begins to undress, the air is momentarily knocked out of my lungs as I admire the graceful curves of her body. She's in a black one-piece that clings to every curve and dip, and I find myself at a loss for words, my eyes tracing the contours of her figure. The sight of her in that cozzie leaves me momentarily speechless, and I can't help but feel a surge of desire just staring at her.

"Did you wanna borrow my shirt?" I offer, hoping to ease any nerves she might have, although it's clear she doesn't need it.

"I think I'll be okay," she says with a smile, catching my eyes as they linger over her body. To distract myself from the intensity of the moment, I urge Isla to join the others in the pool with a nod, and I follow suit, submerging myself in the water.

She eases herself into the water, entering a realm of laughter and splashing. The vibrant energy of the group envelops her, and I can't help but feel a sense of pride as I watch her gradually blend into the lively scene. Olivia watches my movements, her gaze flicking between Isla and me. She's way too observant, and I'm not subtle enough.

Harrison, the noisy fucker, whoops out loudly, "Alright fuckers, let's do this."

Bradley seizes the opportunity to chime in, "But we have odd numbers. How's it gonna work?"

Michael quickly responds, "I'll ref, leaving you with six—3 on 3."

Olivia eagerly suggests, "Alright, but it's girls vs. boys."

Imogen adds, "Oh, that's not fair—the boys are going to beat us."

She laughs, and Isla surprises me by chiming in, "That's if we let them." I catch her eyes, and we share a look that says 'game on'.

Olivia beams. "Alright, ladies, let's do this."

And with that, the games begin.

27

Isla

In the centre of the long pool, a makeshift net is set up for our 'volleyball' match.

The boys, including Xavier, are on one side, and us girls are on the other. Laughter echoes around as the game unfolds, with heated arguments breaking out between Imogen and Harrison, who seem to be getting along *real well*. Olivia, who I've realised is very competitive, seems to be in her element—which is to be expected being surrounded by older brothers all her life.

Bradley, Xavier's brother, remains mostly silent, watching everyone intently, chiming in occasionally—he's a real quiet one. Very reserved. I wonder what he does for work? As my eyes drift toward him, I note the contrast between the two brothers. While Xavier is tall, like really tall and lean, Bradley looks to be more muscular. They both share the same attractive, tanned, rugged features. His hair is lighter compared to Xav, cut shorter on the top. It's a subtle difference that gives him a distinct allure.

Much like Bradley, Michael is also quiet, yet a bit more outspoken than Xavier's brother, but he seems like a real chill guy. Unlike these two, however, Harrison never shuts up. I like him; he's so outspoken and loud. He gives off those real golden retriever vibes—goofy and incredibly friendly. His appearance, however, is contradictory to his personality. He's got a scruffy beard, dark hair shaved on the sides and longer on the top, tattoos covering both of his arms—undoubtedly attractive, I must admit. His brother, Michael, and he couldn't be any more opposite.

Xavier just laughs at the chaos, and Michael rolls his eyes at the ongoing banter. The dynamic is like a sitcom, and I can't help but be entertained by the contrasting personalities.

Despite the initial nerves, I find myself thoroughly enjoying the game. These people, once strangers, are turning out to be a really fun bunch. Xavier, while not saying much, engages in friendly arguments about the rules, often involving Michael, who proves him either right or wrong.

Every now and then, Xavier glances over at me, and my pulse quickens. Warm tingles spread over my body each time his gaze meets mine, and his winks make my craving for him inevitable.

He's like a forbidden drug that I can't help but want more of—a single taste, and I'm hooked. Conflicted thoughts swirl in my mind.

With a tumultuous relationship with my father and the scars of my past relationship still fresh, my guard is high. Uncertain about what to expect from others, the familiar feelings of pain and doubt linger. Yet, as Xavier's eyes lock onto mine, I feel that guard dropping, if only for a moment. Now up close near the net, Xavier moves over to me, from the other side of the net.

"You're pretty good at this, Doc," he remarks, flashing a mischievous grin.

"I could say the same about you, Cowboy. Seems like you've got a few tricks up your sleeve," I reply, a playful glint in my eyes.

His laughter ripples through the water. "You have no idea," he says, low enough for just me to hear, and I blush, my face now probably fifty shades of red.

Harrison repeats my words, "Oooo cowboy, huh? That's a new one." He teases Xavier, who responds by splashing him in the face. Harrison shakes off the water with a deep laugh.

I catch Olivia's eyes lingering on us. She smirks knowingly, and I clear my throat, shaking off the subtle survey. Returning my focus to the game, I dive back into the water, leaving the unspoken connection with Xavier lingering beneath the surface.

As the game progresses, Michael announces that the score is now 2-1 in favour of the girls.

"We're smashing it," I exclaim to Imogen, who gives me a high-five in celebration, our teamwork shining through in the poolside match.

When it's my turn to serve, I muster all my strength, ready to make a splash—quite literally. However, my aim goes awry, and I accidentally smack the ball too hard, sending it careening into Xavier's unsuspecting face. The pool erupts into laughter as he turns, a mischievous glint in his eyes.

"Oh, that's how it's gonna be?" he teases, water dripping down his face.

Innocently, I retort, "It was an accident. Maybe you should pay more attention." He shoots me a playful glare.

"It was a friendly fire." I add, with a mischievous grin.

Our banter continues, the back-and-forth exchanges making the game even more enjoyable. Before it escalates, Harrison interjects with a snarky comment. "Now, now, love birds, settle down."

I feel a flush of embarrassment rising, but Xavier, sensing my discomfort, retaliates by splashing Harrison and playfully dunking him underwater. Imogen laughs heartily, and Olivia, ever the observer, comments with an amused smile, "Boys." I share a laugh, shrugging off the playful chaos in the pool.

Xavier, ever the provocateur, mouths words that tease curiosity and heat into my cheeks. 'Game on,' he mouths slowly, his eyes locking onto mine.

A shiver runs down my spine as I decipher his message, leaving me both intrigued and flushed. The question lingers: what does he have in mind, and what does 'game on' entail? A spark of anticipation dances in my eyes.

The passing hours slip away unnoticed, lost in the laughter and playful banter. Bradley's keen eyes notice the shifting sky. He redirects our attention to the impending grey clouds. Harrison dismisses the potential rain confidently, claiming, "Nah, it's probably just a passing cloud. I doubt it'll actually rain."

However, the rapid formation of angry clouds defies his assurance, and just as he utters his scepticism, thunder crackles, accompanied by a light drizzle.

"Thanks, dickwad. You jinxed us," Michael snorts, delivering a playful smack to his brother's head.

Xavier, slipping into protective mode, declares, "Alright, guys, fun's over. Let's go inside."

Olivia protests with a grumble, "You're such a party pooper."

Xavier retorts sternly, "Hey, you know better than to swim during a thunderstorm. Out. Now!" he commands. Always so gruff.

Olivia playfully salutes. "Yes, Dad!" She rolls her eyes as she exits the pool, and I follow suit. Amidst this exchange, thoughts bloom in my mind about Xavier as a father. The notion elicits a wave of warmth coursing through my core. He would make a sexy daddy—my thoughts flirting with a provocative idea.

Chastising myself to hush the wandering thoughts—my body and mind seem to operate on different wavelengths, *clearly*.

We retreat inside, the laughter and merriment echoing in the air now confined by walls. The distant rumble of thunder crescendos, and the rain intensifies, a staccato rhythm against the windows.

Just as the tempest outside gains strength, Xavier's mother bursts through the front door, her arms laden with bags of groceries. Without missing a beat, Xavier steps up to liberate her from the grocery load.

"Thanks, love," she breathes, glancing around the room. Her eyes widen with surprise as she spots our gathered group on the lounge.

"Oh my, hello, everyone." We say hi back in unison. "This bloody damn rain. What a shit-show. Some ol' townies reckon it'll be our worst one yet."

My heart drops at the realisation. How will we get home? Imogen, sensing my unspoken concerns, addresses me directly. "We should get going then, Isla."

Before we can make a move, Xavier's mother dismisses the idea with a firm declaration.

"Oh, nonsense. No way! There is no way you girls are going to drive out in that storm. They've closed off most roads. Started floodin' already." The situation is clear—we're stuck here.

An undercurrent of panic begins to seep in as the realisation hits—we can't stay here, imposing on Xavier's family. Questions about where everyone will sleep echo in my mind.

Xavier echoes his mother's declaration. "She's right, no one is driving anywhere."

Michael groans and Harrison nudges him. "Ouch, you fuck," he exclaims.

"Manners, idiot. Don't act like you don't want to cuddle me tonight." He wiggles his eyebrows and Imogen, Olivia, and I just chuckle.

"Piss off, wanker," Michael retorts.

"Don't be so worried, dears. You can all crash here."

Bradley reassures, but scepticism lingers as he questions the available space. "Here? Do we even have the room?"

"Yes, Bradley, in fact, we do. We have the pullout lounge here and downstairs," Xavier's Mum responds, shooting him a look.

"Sure thing, Ma," he says, busying himself with his phone.

Imogen turns to me then, concern etched on her face. "We can't stay here, Isla. I feel bad."

I whisper back, "I know, so do I," shooting her a sympathetic look. At that moment, I raise my eyes to Xavier, who's undoubtedly watching me. He nods slowly, silently acknowledging my inner turmoil and questioning.

Trying to soothe Imogen's nerves, I whisper, "It's okay. It's just one night. We'll leave in the morning." I'm trying to calm her, but in truth, I'm also trying to reassure myself. The thought of spending the night at Xavier's is both exhilarating and nerve-wracking. It's a step into the unknown, and while a part of me is excited about the possibility, another part is anxious about what it might mean for us.

She nods, and adds a playful remark, "You know, this is perfect timing for you. What are the bloody chances." She nudges me with her shoulder. "Maybe you'll finally get to shack up and ride the cowboy?" Oh, if only she knew.

I plan to tell her—I just... want to savour this fleeting moment I've found with Xavier a little longer. I'm not sure what it means yet. "Shhhh," I admonish, and she giggles.

Xavier observes our exchange from the kitchen, raising an eyebrow in silent inquiry. I respond with a subtle shake of my head, feeling my cheeks warm with a blush.

His mother invites everyone to get comfortable as she heads off to prepare dinner. I take a moment to retrieve my phone from my bag, only to discover it's on its last 10% of battery life. Shit, I'll need to charge it.

I rise from my spot on the couch and approach Xavier. "Hey, is there anywhere I can charge my phone?"

Recognition flits in his eyes. "Yeah, come, I've got one in my room," he says, leading me toward the wooden curved staircase that ascends upstairs. The layout of their home is stunning—wood and thick stone, with large beams adorning the ceilings. The open staircase leads us to a loft, maintaining visibility of everyone downstairs in the living room.

Xavier guides me to the last room down the hallway. As he opens the door, I am immediately enveloped in his scent—masculine and distinctly him. A mixture of pine, cologne, and his soap—it's so addictive.

Xavier takes my phone and places it on charge near his bed, nestled on the bedside table. Surprisingly spacious, his room boasts tiled flooring and wooden beams that grace the ceilings.

His bed—massive and likely super king-sized—suits the stature of this large man. A bay window adjacent to the bed offers a breathtaking view of their backyard and its vast expanse. As I approach the window, the stunning scenery captures my attention. "I could wake up to a view like this every morning," I sigh, soaking in the beauty.

Xavier creeps up behind me, gently sweeping my damp hair to the side as he leans down to place a tender kiss on my exposed shoulder. Goosebumps ripple across my body, and I shudder as he continues trailing kisses up the column of my neck, his touch tenderly stroking my arm up and down. "I haven't been able to stop thinking about you," he confesses. My breath hitches, and I shudder anew as his lips explore my neck.

"About your moans and whimpers. That incredible pussy of yours," he murmurs, inhaling deeply to savour my scent. "Your scent is so addictive," he adds. *I could say the same.* "What are you doing to me, Isla?" he asks, gently turning me to face him, his eyes locked onto mine.

"I don't know." I whisper, meeting his gaze.

A low hum, almost a growl, escapes him. "I need to kiss you. I've been thinking about these lips every single fucking minute," he confesses, leaning in with a hungry anticipation.

Noticing he is still shirtless, I seize the opportunity to run my hands up the expanse of his chest, exploring every ridge and divot. His chest, chiselled and imposing—almost as solid as the stone that surrounds this home. My hands shake as I move them up over his large pecs, over the dusting of hair covering his chest.

"What are you waiting for, then?" I goad, and he slams his mouth to mine with a growl. I whimper as his tongue seeks entrance into my mouth, moving seamlessly with mine.

As we kiss, Xavier's hands trail down to my ass, cupping each cheek firmly in his hands, gripping them tightly before giving them a shake.

"This ass," he murmurs. "I can't wait to fucking spank the shit out of it," he declares. Oh, this man and his mouth. So, so *dirty* and *unexpected.*

He takes my lips again, swallowing every whimper and moan that surfaces, our groans echoing the same rhythm. Just before the kiss becomes too heated, I gently push against his shoulders, breaking our connection.

"Xav, your family is downstairs. We can't. We should head back down before they wonder where we've gone," I say, attempting to regain some semblance of control.

A growl rumbles in his chest. "We're not finished here, Isla."

It's a promise I know he will somehow fulfil, and the thought sends a shiver wracking through my body.

Seated at the massive wooden dining table, an extravagant spread of food unfolds before us, courtesy of Mrs. Mitchell. The rain continues its relentless pour outside, now bordering on torrential, accompanied by the occasional crack of thunder. Damn, this weather can't catch a break.

Laughter and banter fill the room as we indulge in the feast. My eyes flick to Xavier every now and then, and it's as if he senses me because he does the same. The table becomes a symphony of voices, clinking cutlery, and the delicious aroma of food.

I place my napkin on the table, and as I look up, I catch Olivia watching me with a smug grin. This isn't the first time she's caught on to me staring. Uncertain of what she's thinking, I shift my gaze to anywhere else but at Olivia or Xavier.

Imogen and Harrison are going at it, locked in a heated conversation while the rest of us enjoy our dinner. Their lively exchange draws the attention of Xavier and Olivia, who eagerly join in with their own remarks. Bradley and Michael, on the other hand, remain quiet, their occasional eye rolls or shakes of the head indicating their amusement or exasperation.

They've been at it since our volleyball game earlier today. I can't tell if they really just don't get along or if they just need to work out the tension that surrounds them like an aura. Knowing Imogen, it's probably the former. I can sense the way she feels about him from a few seats down. She's a force to be reckoned with, that one.

As I listen to their back-and-forth, I can't help but admire Imogen's quick wit and Harrison's playful charm. Their dynamic is entertaining, to say the least, and adds a lively spark to the evening.

"Harrison, do you ever stop talking? It's like living with a permanent human radio," Imogen retorts.

"Hey, I'm just keeping the atmosphere lively. Can't let it get too dull."

Imogen rolls her eyes. "Your idea of lively is borderline exhausting. I'm surprised even the crickets outside can't get a word in."

"Hey, I provide free entertainment," Harrison retorts. "You should be thanking me."

"Sure, Harrison, keep telling yourself that," Imogen quips. "Maybe you should take up stand-up comedy. Oh, wait, your jokes might put people to sleep faster than counting sheep."

He chuckles. "Touche, Immy. But at least I'd have a captive audience."

"Captive being the operative word," she teases. "—and my name is Imogen," she spits.

Olivia, unable to resist, chimes in with a playful tone. "This is the best fucking thing ever. I think this is better than watching Xav and Bradley bicker. Come on, you two!"

"Olivia! Language," Xavier's mum retorts, and we all chuckle.

"Sorry, this is just too funny. This is why we need more females around the house," Olivia says, shooting a playful glance at the boys.

"Too many males, *ugh*. No offence."

Imogen snickers. "He's the one that started it. He's like a mosquito buzzing in your ear—annoying and impossible to get rid of."

Harrison smirks. "Sure thing, sweetheart. Deep down, I know you secretly enjoy talking to me. Admit it."

"Hard pass. I'd rather spend my time watching paint dry," Imogen scoffs. "You must be so used to women falling at your feet, huh?"

Michael, who sits beside Harrison, just smirks as he watches the two of them bicker. Xavier chuckles, joining in the banter.

"You don't even know me, sugar," Harrison replies.

Imogen scoffs, "And that's perfectly fine with me. I don't need to know you well to know what you're like."

"You know, I have been told I'm unforgettable."

"Doubt it."

"We'll see," he says sarcastically, sending her a wink. She just rolls her eyes.

Xavier's mother, who has watched this whole exchange, just chuckles before saying, "Now, now, you two. Let's not get too carried away."

My eyes flit back and forth between them. Imogen and Harrison—now that's a combination that would be the funniest match, chaotic and potentially explosive. They only just met and act like they've known each other for years. I suppress a laugh at the thought, imagining the sheer unpredictability they could unleash on each other. Caught in my silent musings, I feel Imogen's eyes on me, and I offer her a small smile, silently acknowledging the entertainment her banter with Harrison provides. She raises an eyebrow in response, her expression a mix of amusement and challenge, as if daring me to join in their verbal sparring.

I shake my head slightly, deciding to remain an observer for now. I glance at Xavier, who catches my eye and gives me a knowing smile. Mrs. Mitchell rises from her seat to collect everyone's plates, and I instinctively stand up to help. Xavier watches my movements, and his mother reprimands me with a warm smile.

"Oh, honey, sit. I've got this."

I know better than to let someone else do all the work, especially when they've been gracious enough to host us.

"No, please, I insist. It's the least I can do to thank you for cooking for us and allowing us to stay."

She appreciates the gesture. "Oh, dear, you're too sweet. Thank you." As we walk up to the kitchen to start washing and loading the dishwasher, I take a moment to express my gratitude.

"Dinner was lovely, Mrs. Mitchell."

She responds with warmth. "Please. Call me Grace. Mrs. Mitchell makes me feel like a granny." I blush, letting out a chuckle at her lighthearted comment.

While rinsing the dishes, I can hear the laughter and banter still echoing from the dining table. Imogen is likely bickering with Harrison, and Olivia is probably not doing anything to help the situation. Michael and Bradley remain quiet, and Xavier... well—*need I say more?*

As my mind gets lost in these observations, Grace's voice breaks through my thoughts. "You're good for him, you know." I freeze, not entirely sure if I heard her correctly.

"I'm so sorry. What was that?" She chuckles.

"My boy, he's smitten. I haven't seen him like this before. You make him smile... laugh." I smile shyly, avoiding her gaze. Her intensity is almost as palpable as Xavier's. *I do?*

Grace remains confident. "Oh, indeed, dear." *Oh shit.* Did I say that out loud? I hadn't realised. "He hasn't been able to take his eyes off you, and you with him."

I feign a blush, unsure how to respond. "I don't even realise..."

Grace interrupts with a knowing smile. "Darling, I see the way you look at him." I'm left at a loss for words, feigning embarrassment at having been caught out.

"We're... we're just friends," I think.

"Mhm, we'll see about that." She remains unconvinced.

After finishing up in the kitchen, we return to the lounge. It's dark outside now, and everyone looks to be exhausted. With pull out beds fixed for us, Harrison, Michael, and Bradley having excused himself to his room, it's just the girls and Xavier left in the room. Mrs. Mitchell had also thoughtfully left out towels for us to use if we needed to shower. After the boys had descended downstairs and Olivia had signed off for the night, Xavier bid us a 'goodnight,' his lingering gaze on me eliciting goosebumps across my skin. Imogen caught on to the unspoken tension and whistled softly as Xavier ascended the stairs. I just rolled my eyes, dismissing her teasing.

As Imogen and I had only come here for a swim, we had brought just a clean change of underwear and bra. Olivia had graciously offered spare clothes, which we accepted with thanks, but there was no way Olivia's clothes were going to fit me. She's like, tiny, easily a size ten, yet, I accepted them, anyway, out of gratitude. Imogen took her clothes and hopped into the shower on the first floor, with the boys downstairs likely occupying the laundry, as Xavier's mum had described. That meant I'd have to wait for my turn. Unease stirs within me as I lift up Olivia's clothes to check if they'll fit, a sense of insecurity settling in.

I sigh, realising I'll have to make do with what I have. Deciding to check on my phone, hoping it had charged fully by now, I cautiously make my way upstairs. Approaching Xavier's room, I hear the faint sound of a shower running.

I knock, but there is no response. Assuming the room is empty, I open the door to find his room deserted, but the light in the en-suite is on. He's in there. Showering. *No shit sherlock.* Heat rushes to my face at the thought of him naked, water and soap cascading over his sculpted body.

My eyes fall on a framed photo on his bedside table. It's a picture of him with his family, smiling and happy. I can't help but smile at the sight, imagining what it must be like to grow up in such a close-knit family. As I head to retrieve my phone, lost in my thoughts, the sound of Xavier clearing his throat startles me. I whip around to see him, leaning against the bathroom door, dressed in nothing but a towel wrapped around his waist.

"Oh my god. S-sorry," I stutter.

As I regain my composure, my gaze involuntarily drifts over his sculpted chest, and my mind froths over the sight. Despite the numerous times I've seen him shirtless, especially earlier in the pool, witnessing him now, almost naked, wrapped in just a towel, remains an image I can't seem to get over. The allure of his physique strikes me once again, and my thoughts begin to dance on the edge of something I can't quite put into words.

"I, uh, I just came to grab my phone," I stammer, turning my head, embarrassment flooding my cheeks.

Xavier releases a breathy laugh, and I turn back to look at him—mischief lighting up his eyes. "Isla, I've literally made you come—twice... and you're embarrassed about me being in a towel?" he says in disbelief. I smile shyly and look away.

"Have you showered yet?" he asks.

"Uh, no. I'll wait until Imogen is done," I reply.

"Shower here. I have clean towels in the cupboard, shampoo, and all that… stuff. Just none of that girly scented stuff you use…" he says with a smirk, waving his hand casually as he pads over to his wardrobe.

"No, no, it's okay. I don't want to impose," I insist.

"Isla, just use my shower," he murmurs.

"Okay—my clothes are downstairs," I begin, but before I can move, he tosses an oversized t-shirt at me, and I catch it just in time.

Righto, then. Well, *this has a better chance at fitting me than Olivia's tiny clothes.*

I make my way into his en-suite, and his lingering scent fills the air, instantly arousing me. His bathroom is surprisingly luxurious, adorned with all-white tiling, a bathtub strategically placed in front of a large window offering a view of the vast plains of his farm, and a fancy-looking shower that seems larger than my entire bathroom back at my apartment. *Jesus.*

I strip down, placing my clothes over the drying rack, and step underneath the shower-head mounted at the top of the ceiling. The warm water instantly envelops me, and I sigh in relief. Wasting no time, I begin to wash my body and scrub my hair until it's squeaky clean, revelling in the idea that I'll now smell like him.

The sound of the rain outside amplifies the cosy ambiance of the bathroom, and I take my time, letting the water soothe away any lingering anxieties. The bathroom is filled with a cloud of steam as I eventually turn off the shower. Wrapping myself in one of Xavier's oversized towels, I feel a strange mix of vulnerability and exhilaration. The thought of Xavier just a few feet away, separated by a door, adds an unexpected thrill.

I step out of the en-suite, the damp air from the shower still clinging to me. Xavier sits on the edge of his bed, engrossed in his phone, thumbs tapping away at the screen. The glow from the device illuminates his striking features. His brows are furrowed as he works on his phone, the long strands of his dark hair—still damp from his recent shower—hang down over his brow, and the hair at his nape starts to curl. How can a fucking *haircut* be so attractive? He really takes a mullet cut to the next level.

"Hey," I say, my voice betraying a mix of nerves and curiosity.

Xavier looks up, a smirk instantly playing on his lips. "Hey. You good?"

"Yeah," I feign a smile. "Your shower is amazing, by the way," I say with a smile.

He chuckles. "Glad you liked it. Help yourself anytime."

I nod, unsure of what to respond to that. His t-shirt provides both comfort and a strange sense of intimacy. Arousal flushes through my core as the realisation hits me—I'm wearing his t-shirt without underwear. I can't help but feel a little naughty and so, *so exposed.* Xavier pats the space beside him on the bed, inviting me to join him. I hesitate for a moment before making my way over.

"What were you working on?" I ask, attempting to shift the focus away from my impending self-consciousness.

"Just some work emails. Can't seem to escape them even on the farm," he replies with a sardonic expression.

We sit in companionable silence for a moment, the hum of the rain outside faintly reaching our ears. I steal a glance at Xavier, and his gaze meets mine, the coolness in his blue eyes sparking a sense of comfort.

"Thanks for letting me use your shower," I finally say, breaking the silence.

"Anytime," he replies, his smirk making me melt. "You look good in my shirt," he says, his tone gravelly.

A subtle warmth spreads through me at his words. *Does he really think I look good in his shirt?* The thought plays in my mind, and I can't help but let a small smile grace my lips. It's a simple compliment, but it feels nice, adding a touch of sweetness to the moment.

"You should smile more," I suggest, the words slipping out without much thought.

He chuckles, and a playful glint lights up his eyes. "Then you need to be around me more," he replies, his tone holding a teasing edge.

His response catches me off guard, and a blush creeps onto my cheeks. He wants me around more? The idea lingers in my mind as I ponder his words. Things have taken an unexpected turn, and part of me wonders how different it all would be if we hadn't crossed that line in his car that night.

The connection between us feels palpable, and for a brief moment, I consider staying longer. However, the rational part of my brain kicks in, reminding me that boundaries are crucial, especially in this situation.

"Well, I should probably head downstairs," I say with a small smile, attempting to mask the inner conflict.

His eyes squint, sussing me out. "You sure?" he asks, a hint of disappointment underlying his words. He studies me for a moment, his gaze lingering as if trying to decipher my unspoken thoughts. There's a magnetic pull between us, a gravitational force that's hard to ignore.

"Yeah... it's been a long day," I reply, avoiding the intensity in his gaze.

He nods, but the atmosphere in the room shifts ever so slightly. It's like leaving a movie halfway through, wondering about the ending you're missing out on. Despite my resolve to maintain distance, a part of me wishes I could *linger* a bit longer.

As I turn to leave, Xavier stands up, closing the distance between us. There's a fleeting moment where it seems like he might say something more, but instead, he offers a genuine smile.

"Alright. Goodnight, Isla," he murmurs, and the way he says my name sends a shiver down my spine, stirring something deep in my core. The warmth in his voice lingers in my ears, and as he gazes at me with those intense blue eyes.

I return the sentiment, "You, too, Xavier." And with that, I head back downstairs, leaving the enigmatic allure of his room behind.

Xavier

Glancing at the screen on my phone, it reads 12:44 am. The day's events replay in my mind—the pool, dinner, and now. Isla's presence has completely enveloped my thoughts, and I'm at a loss for how to handle it. Part of me revels in her captivating allure, while another part is unsure of what this all means. *Do I even want these thoughts to stop?* Her effect on me is undeniable. She stirs up a whirlwind of emotions that I struggle to grasp. Her scent lingers in the room, a constant reminder of her presence.

I close my eyes, attempting to clear my mind, but she's all I can think about. I find myself wondering if she feels the same pull, if she's wrestling with her thoughts about me. The way she avoided my gaze as she left, it felt like there was something unsaid between us. I want to understand her, to know what she's thinking.

With a heavy sigh, I acknowledge that I can no longer ignore this attraction. Surely she must feel the same. I realise that I can't keep denying this attraction. Isla has stirred something in me, something I haven't felt in a long time. I can't shake the feeling that she's changing everything, and deep down, I'm not sure if I'm ready for the changes she might bring.

Is she awake, thinking about me as I am about her? She should have fucking stayed. *God, I wish she stayed.* Fuck, the thought of her here, in my bed, makes me instantly hard. I re-adjust myself in my briefs, cursing at the fact that my mind can't just shut the fuck up.

This insomnia can suck it.

As the urge to reach out to Isla grows stronger, I resist the impulse to grab my phone and text her. Should I text her, or should I just leave it and go the fuck to bed? I don't think I'd be sleeping anytime soon, with this hard on. I shift uncomfortably under my sheets.

What if she's awake too? Maybe a quick conversation would help me settle down, push away this restlessness. Maybe I can distract myself for a bit and then try to sleep again. *But it's late, and I don't want to disturb her if she's already asleep. Plus, what would I even say?*

I grab my phone, my thumb hovering over the screen, debating whether to message her. After a moment of hesitation, I decide to text her. *You awake?*

Fuck it, no going back now. Nerves kick in. What the fuck? Why am I nervous? Thirty years old and I'm starting to sweat like a prepubescent boy, as if I'm talking to a girl for the first time. My stomach actually flutters. Oh, fuck me.

Please be asleep, I chant in my head. I can only hope that she's asleep and doesn't see my message, because if she does, I don't know if I'll be able to control myself.

28

Isla

The rain has finally settled, and the house is wrapped in a tranquil quiet, with only the distant sounds of crickets serenading the night. Since leaving Xavier's room, I've been unable to find peace, tossing and turning in the dimly lit space. Beside me, Imogen sleeps soundly, seemingly undisturbed by the world. That girl could sleep through anything—possibly the world's heaviest sleeper. A small smile tugs at my lips at the thought.

My mind is a tempest—a torrent of thoughts racing through a thousand scenarios. Every interaction with Xavier from today plays out in my mind, the reel looping back to that night in his car. The moments, the words exchanged—they form vivid scenes, each more intense than the last. The more I try to quiet my mind, the louder the thoughts become, wrestling with the reality of what has transpired between us.

His touch, his kisses, the warmth of his embrace—they linger like a whisper in the shadows. I can't escape the magnetic pull drawing me toward him. My eyes wander to the window, wondering about Xavier. Is he asleep or awake? What is he doing right now?

Thirsty and restless, I decide to break free from the conundrum of my thoughts. With quiet determination, I slide out of bed and grab my phone, careful not to disturb anyone. I reach the kitchen, the cool tiles underfoot making my body shudder. I open a cupboard, grab a glass, and pad over to the humming fridge, a soft lullaby for the night. As I stand in the kitchen, the cool glass pressed against my lips, my phone vibrates in my hand, startling me in the silence of the night.

Glancing at the screen, I notice the time—12:44 am. The soft glow reveals a text message from Xavier, a simple yet charged question.

Xavier: You awake?

My heart lurches forward at the sight of those words. He's reaching out to me, and the late-night air suddenly feels charged with a different kind of energy. Anticipation and nerves intertwine as I quickly type out a reply.

Me: Yes. Couldn't sleep.

Seconds later, my phone buzzes again.

Xavier: What's keeping you up?

Me: Just thinking. You?

Xavier: Same. Just... thinking about a certain someone.

My heart does somersaults. He continues.

Xavier: Her smile, her breathtaking body, those sounds she makes when she comes.

Well, *fuck me*—my mind goes into overdrive. A blush creeps up my skin as I muster the courage to keep whatever this is going.

> **Me:** She sounds... alright.

I type out, downplaying his thoughts.

> **Xavier:** Just alright? She's bloody perfect. I'm so hard thinking about her.

I love the way he refers to me in the third person. My phone dings again, this time with an image attachment. *Oh my god*—my heart skyrockets. I open the image, and my screen is immediately filled with Xavier's grey briefs concealing his massive hard on, his cock straining against the fabric. Shit, *I do that to him?* Not so much a question, but a reassurance for my own mind.

My eyes widen at the image on my screen. Heat rushes through me, settling low in my belly. Xavier's arousal is on full display, and the realisation that I'm the cause sends a thrilling jolt through me.

"Fuck," I mutter under my breath, unable to tear my eyes away. His next message arrives quickly.

> **Xavier:** What about you? Thoughts?

I bite my lip, debating how to respond.

> **Me:** Maybe.

I type, teasingly cryptic. His reply is swift.

> **Xavier:** Come on, Isla. I've been hard for you since the moment you left my room.

My pulse quickens, and I can almost feel the intensity of his gaze through the words.

Xavier: I can't get you out of my head.

I hesitate for a moment, my fingers dancing over the keys before I confess.

Me: I can't get you out of my head either.

A flutter of nerves mixes with the arousal that already courses through me.

Xavier: Prove it.

My heart pounds, and my breathing quickens. The desire to see him, to feel the connection that has ignited between us, overwhelms any reservations. I type a tentative response.

Me: How?

Xavier: Come to my room.

Fuck, fuck, fuck.

Standing outside Xavier's door, nerves clashing with desire—I hesitate to step inside. When I push the door open, Xavier is there, sitting at the edge of his bed. His eyes, molten and dark, lock onto mine, and I'm captivated by the intensity within them. Nerves kick in, and

I berate myself for the hesitation—it's not like I haven't already been intimate with him.

He senses my internal struggle, and his command, uttered in a low, husky tone, cuts through the air. "Come here."

The invitation hangs in the space between us, and I approach slowly, the magnetic pull too strong to resist. The subtle scent of his cologne envelops me, heightening the intoxicating allure of the moment. Xavier's hand reaches out, a silent directive, and I find myself drawn into his embrace. His grip tightens around my waist, fingers curling around the fabric of my t-shirt—*his t-shirt*—that I'm still wearing, as well as a clean pair of underwear. Standing between his legs, I look down and notice that his hard-on is still present, possibly now even larger than his picture. His cock—now straining against the waist-band, peeking out from the top against his abs.

"Xav," I breathe, but he doesn't respond—he just lowers his hands to my ass, gripping tightly as he urges me to move forward and sit on top of his lap. His hands squeeze my ass underneath the shirt—leaving a burning trail across my skin.

Then, in an instant, he grabs my waist with one strong arm before flipping me around onto the bed. He hovers above me, his presence commanding the room. My breath hitches as he lowers his face to mine.

"Do you want me to stop?" he asks, his voice a low murmur that reverberates through the charged air.

"No," I breathe, anticipation coursing through me.

"Thank *fuck*," he replies, his words laced with primal desire. Without hesitation, he crushes his lips against mine with a low, guttural sound—swallowing my breath and any insecurity bubbling to the surface.

His lips meld with mine, our tongues dancing with each other in a battle of one of the most panty-melting kisses I have ever experienced. With a protective grip around my throat, his mouth devours mine—swallowing every whimper and groan—as I try to remain as quiet as I can.

His forearm is braced beside my face, while the other trails down my body, igniting a trail of heat in its wake. As his hand reaches the hem of my shirt and begins to tug it upwards, I freeze. It's been months since I've been entirely naked in front of anyone, and a surge of vulnerability washes over me. Yet, Xavier's touch is both commanding and reassuring, his fingers tracing patterns on my skin, so I let him. I let him raise the shirt up and I lift forward, allowing him to tug it up and off me, throwing it across the bed. I lay there naked and incredibly exposed in front of him. My hands instinctively move to cover my breasts. Xavier growls low, the sound sending shivers down my spine.

"What did I say about hiding from me?" His words hold a possessive edge, and I'm left breathless. "Fuck everyone else. This body is fucking phenomenal." I tremble.

Xavier takes his free hand and gently grabs my hands, moving them out of the way.

"This body is *mine*," he growls, and I just about melt, then and there.

He descends on my breasts, taking his time to leisurely lick, suck, and nip at both swollen buds. Soft whimpers escape my lips as pleasure courses through my body, each touch sending a tantalising wave of sensation.

He releases a nipple with a soft pop. "Fuck, these tits. You're killing me, Isla," he murmurs, grabbing a handful of one, giving it a soft squeeze before giving it a jiggle.

Xavier's lips continue their journey, moving lower, and my breath catches in anticipation. As he reaches the sensitive skin just above the waistband of my g-string, he pauses, his gaze meeting mine. The intensity in his eyes is palpable, a silent question that lingers in the air. I nod, giving him the unspoken permission to continue. He hooks his fingers into the waistband, slowly pulling the fabric down my thighs and off completely—revealing more of me to his hungry gaze. I shudder, now *entirely* exposed and naked in front of him. My pussy no doubt glistening with my arousal.

His lips leave a trail of heated kisses along my thighs. I let out a soft moan, unable to contain the pleasure that courses through my body. He moves lower off the bed, dropping to his knees, and grabs hold of my ankles. I gasp as he jerks me forward, dragging me to the edge.

Xavier on his *knees* before *me*—it's a sight that will be forever ingrained in my memory.

His thumb brushes over my clit, and I jerk. He moves his thumb lower, softly massaging my lips, feeling him slide up and down so quickly.

"Fuck, you're so wet," he says, before sliding a finger inside me, pumping it in and out slowly.

He looks up at me, his blue eyes hooded with lust. "You ever come from being eaten out, baby?"

"N-no... I've never... done that before," I stammer.

"No one has ever eaten you out? Not even your ex?" he says in disbelief, his voice husky.

"No... he never wanted to?"

"What a fucking *wanker*. His loss," he growls. "I've said this before, princess, but I'll say it again. I am going to fucking devour this cunt." I shiver at his words.

His warm breath fans over my clit as he says, "Don't be shy for me, okay? You tell me what you like, yeah?" I sit up, propping up my body on my forearms to watch.

Keeping his eyes on me, and before I can reply, he lowers his mouth to my pussy, circling his tongue around my clit—his finger still pumping slowly. I groan out in pure fucking bliss.

He removes his finger and does exactly what he promised not once, but *twice* now—he fucking *devours* me.

"That feels good," I tell him. "Xav, don't stop—"

This man holds nothing back. He ravages me with his tongue, flicking, sucking—learning what makes me whimper and completely desperate for more.

Xavier

Fuck, I am so painfully hard—I'm trying my absolute hardest not to fucking explode in my briefs right now. Isla's pussy is so fucking addictive. To think that pathetic flop of an ex of hers never went down on her completely baffles me. I bet he's that type of wanker that doesn't kiss a girl after she's sucked his dick. *Fool.*

As I continue to devour Isla's pussy like a man starved, her arousal coats my tongue and my eyes roll into the back of my head. Her groans match mine. I lift her legs and place them over my shoulders, sliding my hands underneath her ass to lift her up to me as I feast, delving my tongue deep inside her. She tastes perfect, so fucking sweet—like honey—and I just can't get enough.

Her words filter in the air, and I continue my assault on her clit with my tongue. I suck her clit into my mouth, and Isla releases a breathy moan and I just about come in my briefs from the sound. I lift my arm and glide it over her stomach to grab a handful of her luscious breasts, squeezing and kneading it as I move my tongue.

"Fuck, Xav, I think I'm gonna com—"

"Come for me, baby," I croon, cutting her words off. Her breathing quickens and her back arches off the bed, now laying down flat. She's so close, I can tell from how her arousal coats my tongue in waves. I fucking love the way her soft shaven skin feels against my mouth, no doubt my stubble adding in a little friction for her.

"Come all over my tongue—let me taste how fucking sweet you

are." I slide my finger into her, adding in a second, curling them upward towards the soft tissue, applying pressure while alternating between sucking on and licking her clit.

"*Oh-oh, my god,*" she moans, fisting the sheets beside her. She moves a hand to grip my hair, and I don't dare stop now. Her pussy clenches tightly around my fingers as she tips over the edge, and I groan as her body trembles from her climax, her walls pulsating around my fingers.

I slide both of them out slowly, leaning up and over her, my face still buried between her legs.

"Suck," I growl, my wet fingers tracing her lips. Her breath hitches, and she sucks on them, licking them clean.

"What a good fucking girl," I murmur. *My dirty fucking girl.*

She whimpers at my words and then suddenly, she sits up, pulling me towards her chest with a playful grin. "Your turn," she declares, mischief gleaming in her eyes. Before I can react, she seizes my arms and deftly turns my body. Now, I'm perched at the edge of the bed, and Isla is on her knees before me.

"You don't need to repay the favour. Making you come is more than enough for me," I murmur, my eyes locking on to hers, as I tuck a loose strand of hair from her face behind her ear.

"No. Trust me, I want to. *Please,*" she croons. Fuck me, this girl. She can have me anytime, at any moment, and I'd willingly say yes, *every time.*

My cock, straining against my briefs, begs for attention, peeking out from the top. As Isla kneels in front of me, her hands glide up my thighs, using her nails to scrape against my skin, causing a shudder to run through my body. She's in charge now, she's running the show.

She hooks her fingers in my briefs, pulling them down, all the while never breaking eye contact. My heart races as desire courses through me, and I can't help but marvel at the intensity in her gaze. It's as if every move she makes is a deliberate invitation, and the anticipation makes my skin crawl. My cock springs free, resting against my abdomen, and her eyes widen at the sight. She grabs hold of it with one hand, while the other rests on my thigh. Isla tentatively strokes my cock once and I groan at the contact. Her thumb rubs over my tip, at the precum pooling at the top. Isla then leans forward to lick it before swallowing me down into her mouth completely.

"Fuck," I groan, grabbing a fistful of her long hair. I hold it at the crown of her head—keeping it out of her face as she bobs up and down on my cock. She takes my length as far back as she can, expecting her to gag with her mouth full of my cock, but to my surprise, she doesn't. *Fuck me, no gag reflex?*

I'd come then and there if I didn't have such good restraint. *Well, sometimes.* She keeps her pace slow and steady, licking my tip each time she pulls back before taking me all the way to the back of the throat, her cheeks hollowing out with each pull, and my head falls back with a groan.

She hums on my cock as she continues to suck me off, applying a harder suction now, as she relentlessly swallows me down. "*Fuck,* you look so fucking sexy with your mouth full of my cock." She whimpers, her hooded gaze locking onto mine. "You like it when I talk dirty to you, don't you?" I croon, and she nods with my cock still in her mouth. She lifts her mouth before releasing me.

"Spit on it," I prod.

She looks up at me, her eyes wide. Without any delay, she complies. Isla spits on me before running her hand up and down in a circular motion, coating me with her saliva. She takes me back into her mouth and I groan aloud. Isla doesn't slow down, keeping the same pace now, adding in her hand every now and then to stroke my cock while she sucks on my tip.

"Good girl. Fucck, keep going," I groan, as I watch her with fascination, and she literally sucks the life out of me.

"Fuck, *yes*, fuck, Isla," I groan. She works her hand tightly over my length, sucking hard on my crown as I tip my head back, groaning out in pure ecstasy. I feel her hand trail down, *lower*, beneath my shaft, and all it takes is for her to grab hold of my balls and tug before I'm muttering complete nonsense as I tip over the edge.

"*Coming*-I'm coming," I growl. With her mouth full, she moans—creating that vibration I fucking love—and I shoot my load into her mouth, my body wracking with intense waves of pleasure. She swallows it all down, like a fucking pro. Sucking me dry and clean until my body feels limp and spent. Popping her mouth off me, she wipes her lips with her fingers, cleaning any spillover.

In a rush, I'm hauling her up off her feet, pulling her into my lap so she's straddling me, and I slam my mouth to her—my tongue stroking hers, hands in her hair.

"Fuck, Isla. I think that was the hardest I've ever come." My legs are fucking shaking, and she giggles. She rakes her fingers through my hair as she tugs on the hair at my nape. In this moment, we're the only people in this universe. Nothing else matters. It's just us. Yet, in the quiet space, with nothing but our heavy breathing, a quiet storm rolls in my mind.

I've never encountered this kind of connection before—it's throwing me for a loop. I'm not one to get all sentimental and shit, but there's something about Isla that's got me questioning the usually *laid-back* me, and I'm also not about to spill my guts and risk freaking her out.

As our eyes lock and the world outside fades away, I wonder if she feels the same magnetic pull. The chemistry is there, no doubt, but decoding her thoughts is like solving a puzzle blindfolded. Is it as real for her as it is for me? It's like walking on eggshells, trying not to mess up the good thing we've got going. I'm no relationship guru, but this?

This is uncharted territory.

29

Isla

My car engine hums softly as I navigate through the quiet streets, since leaving Xavier's—the gentle purr providing a backdrop to Imogen's lively chatter. She sits beside me, a whirlwind of energy and enthusiasm, filling the confined space with her animated tales.

Imogen, with her boisterous spirit, spends the last leg of our journey unravelling her thoughts.

"Olivia is just the best, you know? I mean, who wouldn't love her? And don't even get me started on Harrison. Ugh, that fucker just infuriates me!"

I offer a soft chuckle, letting her vibrant expressions wash over me. Imogen's vivacity is a stark contrast to my own quieter demeanour. The contrast is somehow comforting, like the ebb and flow of a familiar rhythm.

"I swear, Isla, if you don't tell me something is going on with you and Xavier, I'm going to combust!!

"He couldn't take his eyes off you the entire time we were there. It was like you had this magnetic pull on him."

Despite my efforts to downplay my reaction, I can't help but remember the intimate moments we shared, the midnight mischief that led to us falling asleep together. I had quietly slipped away early in the morning, retreating back to the sofa bed, leaving him undisturbed.

As I drive, the events of last night replay in my mind. Xavier had pulled me onto his bed to lie down, despite my refusal. I remember feeling both nervous and excited, my heart racing at the thought of being so close to him. And then he had wrapped his arms around me, pulling me into a warm, comforting embrace.

I, Isla Thompson, cuddling with Xavier Mitchell. The thought still feels surreal, like something out of a dream. I feel the warmth spreading across my cheeks, betraying the thoughts swirling in my mind. Imogen, ever perceptive, notices my blush and turns to me, her gaze intensifying with curiosity. She narrows her eyes, leaning in for a closer look, and I can almost hear the wheels turning in her head.

"Hold the fuck up," she exclaims loudly, her voice tinged with excitement. "There is, isn't there!!! Oh my god, you little cow, why didn't you tell me? ME, your best friend of ALL time!"

She pouts and places her hand on her heart dramatically. I can't help but chuckle at her theatrics. Such a drama queen.

"You better tell me everything. Don't spare any detail, or I'll riot!" Her eyes widen with anticipation, waiting for every juicy detail. I take a deep breath, feeling a mix of nerves and excitement as I begin recounting the night at my father's place, the incident that Imogen is already familiar with. However, as I delve into the aftermath, the moments shared in Xavier's car after leaving my father's, Imogen's eyes widen even further.

"Wait, you never told me about that part!" she exclaims.

I continue, sharing the details of last night. Imogen, usually full of words, sits there stunned, processing the revelations. The air hangs heavy with the weight of my untold stories, and as I finish, a profound silence envelops us, punctuated only by the soft hum of the car engine.

Imogen's stunned silence triggers a pang of worry within me. Imogen is *never* silent.

"Uh, you good?" I cautiously inquire.

Imogen raises her hand in the air. "I need a minute to process the thought of my best friend fucking Xavier in his car AND sucking him off—right under my nose, I must add!"

I try to lighten the atmosphere with a playful giggle, feigning a blush. Imogen breaks her silence with a dramatic gasp.

"So, how do you feel about everything now? Have you both spoken about your feelings? Do you have feelings for him?" Imogen bombards me with questions, her curiosity relentless.

Externally, I offer a tentative response, "W-we're just friends... I guess. We haven't really spoken about anything. It's more like a mutual attraction, you know? I don't *really* know how he feels."

Internally, my thoughts are a messy whirlwind. Xavier's charm, the unspoken moments, and now Imogen's genuine concern all weigh heavily on my mind. A conflict brews within me, a flurry of emotions that I find myself navigating without a clear path.

Imogen shoots me a worried glance as I respond to her barrage of questions. "Isla, I don't want you to get hurt," she says softly, concern etched in her eyes.

"After everything with that pathetic excuse of a man, I don't want you rushing into something only to get hurt again, you know?"

I'm caught off guard by the sincerity in her words, and a warmness spreads through me. Imogen's concern resonates in my mind, and for a second, I feel an overwhelming wave of love for her. I couldn't have asked for a better friend. Claire included. Damn, I miss her.

"I know, Imogen. Trust me, I don't want that either. It's just weird. I've never felt so drawn to someone, and the fact that it's him of all people really rattles my brain, you know?" I confess, my voice carrying a mix of bewilderment and vulnerability. After a beat, Imogen breaks the silence, her voice filled with compassion.

"Isla, you deserve happiness. Just take things one step at a time. If there's anyone who can navigate this, it's you."

I guess she's right. Keeping things casual for now sounds like the only foolproof plan as I run it through my head—the perfect way to protect my heart while having some fun. With everything happening now with dad, major distractions are the last thing I need.

Maybe keeping Xavier at arm's length while exploring these desires might just work. Can casual be enough without complicating things, though?

I hope so.

The afternoon sun casts a warm glow over the backyard as Dad and I sit on the porch, nursing cold VB stubbies. The air is thick with the hum of cicadas and the distant melody of birds chirping—the soundtrack to a scorcher of a day. Despite the heat, Dad seems to be in a better mood today, a subtle shift from the cloud that usually hangs over our visits.

We just finished cleaning out the shed at the back of the house, a task that involved more grunts than words from Dad, but he managed a smile or two. I consider it a win. The memories of that night, when Xavier faced the business end of Dad's shotgun, lurk in the corners of my mind, but we've danced around the topic, and it hasn't surfaced in our conversation yet. My body shudders at the mere thought. As we sip our beers in the silent ambience, I let my guard down a bit, indulging in the cold beverage. Beer isn't my favourite, but here, in my father's company, it feels right. The metal cap clinks as I take a sip, and the familiar bitterness lingers on my palate.

Dad breaks the comfortable silence, catching me off guard with his question. "So, life in the city, uh? What's that like?" His words carry a genuine curiosity beneath the gruff exterior. I hesitate for a moment, my mind flickering through the images of bustling city streets and crowded cafes.

"It's different, Dad. Busy, you know? Always something happening. Work was demanding, but I enjoyed it," I respond cautiously, trying to gauge his reaction.

He nods, taking a swig of his beer. "Oh, ye? Sounds like'a different world. What 'bout the people? They treat ya right?" His eyes, weathered by time, meet mine, searching for a glimpse into the life I've led beyond these familiar walls.

I offer a small smile, appreciating the effort in his question. "Yeah, Dad, they treated me well. It's just... different. More opportunities over there, but I found myself missing the quiet of home sometimes. I guess that's what brought me back." The unspoken truth lingers in the air—the pull between the life I had built in the city and the roots that ground me here.

Dad grunts, a simple "Righto," and I sense the weight of his unspoken thoughts. After all these years, I've come back for a work opportunity, not specifically for him. What he may not understand is that I always yearned to come back home, to see him. It's something I've failed to let him know, unable to build up the courage to express this deep desire. How do I tell him that home isn't just the place—it's him, too?

In that moment, my phone chimes, and I see Xavier's name lighting up the screen. My heart quickens as I open our text message thread.

Xavier: You get home alright today? I meant to text you earlier but got caught up. Sorry.

His message warms my heart, and a slight smile creeps onto my face. I quickly respond,

> **Me:** Yep. All good. No need to apologise.

His reply is instant.

> **Xavier:** Ok, good.

> **Xavier:** What are ya doing?

My heart rate picks up. Texting Xavier Mitchell was not something I ever imagined, but here I am. I smile as I type,

> **Me:** Nm, just with dad. Helped him out a little today.

> **Xavier:** What is 'Nm'?

I can't help but internally laugh at his question. He's joking right? The amusement adds a lightness to the moment, and I read on as he continues.

> **Xavier:** That's good, princess. How is he today?

> **Me:** LOL! You really don't know what Nm means?

> **Xavier:** Wouldn't be asking if I did, would I?

> **Me:** Right, I forgot you're old. It means 'Nothing much'.

> **Xavier:** Old, huh? I'm three years older than you bud

> **Me:**

I stifle a laugh, and in that moment, I glance up at my father. He watches me with a stern look, a curious glint in his eyes, as if trying to decipher the source of my amusement.

> **Xavier:** You weren't calling me old last night when I had my face buried in your pussy were you?

> **Xavier:** Looks like I seem to be doing pretty well for someone that is, 'old'.

A flush of warmth creeps up my cheeks, and I hastily rattle off a response.

> **Me:** Xav, my dad is right next to me, you perv.

> **Xavier:** Will you spank me for being naughty? We can take turns 😏

> **Xavier:** Because I'm into that if you are 😈

Oh boy. This man.

> **Me:** Shush. Gtg!

> **Me:** That means 'Got to go' by the way.

> **Xavier:** 😂😂

> **Xavier:** You watch and see what happens when I see you next.

> **Xavier:** I'll find a way to occupy that smart mouth of yours.

Not if, but *when.* The thought sends a shiver down my spine. As I anticipate seeing him again, excitement flares up inside me. As we sit in the serenity of the outback that surrounds us, the sun casting a warm glow over the familiar landscape, Dad breaks the quiet with another question. "That the Mitchell boy you messagin?"

My pulse stutters. His warning about steering clear of the Mitchell boys echoes in my mind, creating a tension in the air. I'm uncertain about how he'll react if I confess. However, the thought of lying to him doesn't sit well either. A touch apprehensive, I reply to my father, "Yes. H-how did you know?"

"Just a guess. I told you, stay away from 'em boys. They're nothing but trouble."

I can understand why he must be thinking that. Xavier and his brother did have a bit of a reputation growing up, causing a ruckus everywhere they went, stirring up problems both at home and out.

"If he ain't treat you right, I won't hesitate to bring my shotty out... again." I freeze, realising he does remember. The memory of that night when my dad wielded his shotgun.

"You remember?" I ask, my eyes widen momentarily in shock.

"Course I remember, I may not be all there, but I remember that now," my dad responds.

My heart drops, and my expression saddens. So, he is aware he hasn't been doing too well. Gathering courage, I bring up that night. "Dad, about that night with Xavier—" There's a moment of heavy silence before he nods, inviting me to continue. The weight of the unspoken hangs in the air, a shared acknowledgment of the challenges we've faced. I take a deep breath, my words carefully chosen.

"I know you were just trying to protect me, but Xavier—he's proven to not be like who he used to be. He's... different—older, more mature. I've gotten to know him a bit now, and there's more to him than what people say."

My dad listens, his expression a mix of sternness and curiosity. "I ain't sayin' he's a bad kid, just that them Mitchells come with their own kind of trouble. You be careful, Isla," he warns, his concern evident in his eyes.

"What trouble, Dad? You keep saying to stay away," I ask with a raised brow.

He clears his throat, running a hand through his grey mane. "Them boys used to run riot when they were youngins. Had their fair share of stoushes..." His voice trails off, and then he mumbles something under his breath about their old man being a stubborn prick. He quickly dismisses it, not keen on laying out the dirty laundry.

I frown as I ask, "Dad, Xavier mentioned something about you and his father? What happened?"

He pauses, running a hand through his hair, before finally sighing. "We were doin' a job together. Things got messy. Had a fallin' out with his old man.

"But that's ol' news. No need for you to get bogged down'n the details. Just keep ya wits about ya, yeah?" Dad drawls.

His nonchalant response leaves me with more uncertainties and questions. That wasn't helpful. There are pieces missing, gaps in the story that I'll need answers to, eventually. I can feel it lingering, a mystery begging to be unravelled.

"I will, Dad. But things have changed, and I think Xavier might be someone worth giving a chance," I explain, hoping he understands.

He grunts in response, a reluctant acceptance of my words.

"He's got you smilin', though. I like seein' you smile," he says out of nowhere.

Caught off guard, I murmur back, "He's a friend. A-a good friend... I guess."

My dad probes further with a furrowed brow, "Just friends?" Uncertain of what to say, I merely shrug, my cheeks tinted with a blush.

"I'm proud of you, Isla. For going out and doing all that..." he waves his hand in the air, "you know, vet stuff," he says, changing the subject suddenly.

I freeze. I can't remember the last time my father said those words to me. I can't even recall the last time he told me he loved me. I remain quiet as he continues.

"I may not always say it. I may not be like I used to, but I still see things, know things." He taps the side of his temple with his index finger.

"Your mumma would be proud. It's what she wanted for you, you know." He nods to himself, as if reminiscing about something. Tears well up in my eyes.

"Yeah, I know, Dad," my voice clipped from the emotions surfacing. "Thank you." We linger in a heavy silence, a shared understanding hangs in the air.

In this unspoken moment, the gaps between us seem to narrow, and the weight of our history feels a tab bit *lighter*.

30

Xavier

As a new week begins, I immerse myself back into the grind of work. The late afternoon sun beats down on our farm, a relentless force casting long shadows across the rugged landscape. With Brad back, he's been a welcome presence, lending a hand whenever the opportunity arises. I find myself knee-deep in farm work, the tasks multiplying with each passing day. Having an extra pair of hands, especially Brad's, proves to be an invaluable asset. Occasionally, Harrison and Michael join in, offering their assistance when they can. Liv's been an expert at avoiding it, as always. Country girl through and through, but the farm life never quite grew on her.

We're in the barn now, the air thick with the scent of aged wood and hay. Bradley and I are knee-deep in the grind, shuffling out old hay into wheelbarrows, creating space for the fresh bales—sweat dripping down our foreheads. Dad's back from his Sydney trip, leaning against the barn wall with a cigarette dangling from his fingers. Buddy, loyal as ever, rests beside him. The old dog's getting on in years, slowing down. It's a sight that tugs at my heart.

Dad's presence brings a mix of emotions. On one hand, there's a sense of pride working alongside him, picking up the slack he can no longer manage. On the other, I wonder when I'll get a moment to catch my breath. The farm demands constant attention, and as much as I love it, sometimes it feels like a never-ending cycle.

As we work, I steal a glance at Dad. His eyes, weathered by years of hard work and hardship, watch us. There's a sense of approval in his gaze, a silent acknowledgment of the responsibilities I've shouldered. As Bradley and I rhythmically shuffle out the old hay with well-worn rakes, the coarse fibres catch on the times before tumbling into the nearby wheelbarrows. The dust hangs in the air, caught in the rays of sunlight that filter through the openings in the barn walls.

I turn to Bradley, beads of sweat clinging to my forehead.

"I got this, can you start bringing in some of those new stacks outside?" Bradley, as stoic as ever, just nods. Words aren't his forte much—never have been.

People might think I'm bad at communicating, but they haven't had the pleasure of getting to know Bradley. He makes me look like a chipper fuck on a good day. His silence is a language of its own, a quiet strength that I've come to appreciate more with each passing day. With a nod between us, Bradley heads toward the fresh bales stacked neatly outside the barn, and I get back to the task at hand, the steady rhythm of our work filling the air.

As Bradley moves with the precision of a man who measures every step, I can't help but think he's found his calling. God knows this shitty town needs better law enforcement. His calculated and observant nature, the quiet way he takes in his surroundings, it's a skill set that serves him well in his line of work. I can't imagine him doing anything else. *I'm proud of that fucker.*

I don't tell him often, but maybe I should. There's a strength in him, a quiet resolve, and it deserves acknowledgment. As Bradley and I work, the stack of hay growing steadily, he breaks the silence with a casual, "So, what's going on with Isla?"

I pause, the rake stilled in my hands. Bradley's gaze is fixed on me, a silent demand for answers. I shrug, attempting nonchalance. "Just friends, mate."

He narrows his eyes, a sceptical look that cuts through the casual facade. It's a look I know too well—Bradley isn't convinced, and deep down, I understand why. I haven't exactly been subtle about my—-my what? Attraction? Feelings? I'm not even sure. Is it like this? Or something more? The uncertainty twists in my gut, and I find myself unable to look Bradley in the eye.

My mind drifts to Isla, thoughts of her mingling with the rhythmic sounds of the barn work. Images from Saturday night play like a vivid film in my mind. The touch of her hands, the warmth of her skin, her moans, her beautiful face when she came all over my face—they create a lingering sensation.

"Come on, Xav," Bradley prods, his voice low but insistent. 'I've seen the way you look at her. Don't bullshit me."

I run a hand through my hair, a nervous habit. "I don't know, Brad. It's complicated. We're just figuring things out."

Bradley's gaze shifts towards the front of the barn where our dad is stationed, and he asks, "Does he know? You know how he feels about her father... although I don't know why he hasn't gotten over it." I shake my head, still wrestling with the uncertainty swirling within me.

"No. I'll tell him when I'm sure of what this is between us, and you know what he's like. Old man has been holding grudges since he came out of the womb."

Bradley laughs, a sound that breaks the seriousness of our conversation. "Just... hope you know what you're doing. I like seeing you happy. I don't wanna see you fuck up something potentially good, you know?"

His genuine concern warms my heart, and I tease, placing a hand over my chest dramatically, "Shit, my heart, it hurts. Bradley just told me he loves me."

He retaliates by picking up a hay bale and launching it at me, hitting my shoulder and knocking me off balance.

"Such a dick," he says, a smile playing on his face. Despite his gruff exterior, Bradley's protective side always manages to shine through.

After wrapping up our work in the barn, Dad retreated inside, and Mum's call informed us that lunch was ready. Though the prospect of a meal awaited, my appetite seemed to have abandoned me. Lost in my thoughts, I couldn't shake the wondering of what Isla might be doing right now.

Fuck, I'm pathetic. My once quiet mind, a sanctuary from the chaos around me, is now filled with thoughts and images of her. *I'm fucked.*

Unable to resist the pull, I cave and pull out my phone. I decide to text her, my mind momentarily drifting back to the other day when she teased me with acronyms, having the audacity to call me 'old.' As if I don't know what 'Nm' means—I wasn't born yesterday. I just enjoyed riling her up. I could imagine her face and reactions vividly when I had said that.

> **Me:** Wyd?

She responds after a few moments.

> **Isla:** Just finished playing detective with a bunch of sneaky cats and sassy dogs.

> **Isla:** The real question is, wyd?

> **Isla:** Probably bossing everyone around and intimidating innocent farm animals?

A chuckle escapes me at her witty response.

> **Me:** People? Always. Animals? Never 😔

> **Me:** What are you doing later tonight?

> **Isla:** I'm about to head into town to get some groceries for dinner. You?

An idea springs into my mind, and without overthinking, I type.

> **Me:** How bout I get some groceries, bring them over, and cook for us?

It's not a typical move for me; I don't cook often, not because I can't, but because it's just not my thing. I fucking love to cook—when I get the chance to, of course. Yet, now, some part of me wants to do it for her—wine and dine her, do all that sappy shit. She *deserves* it.

I sense her hesitation. The three little dots dance on the screen and disappear twice, before a message finally pops up.

Isla: Uh, you sure? You don't have to..

Me: I'm sure. I'll be at yours around 6?

Isla: Okay xx

I stand outside Isla's apartment door, plastic bags filled with groceries in hand. Giving a gentle knock, I wait patiently. As she opens the door, the scent of her apartment engulfs me instantly—a comforting mix of vanilla and a hint of lavender. She stands there, clad in simple yoga pants, a loose t-shirt, her hair pulled back into a messy bun. Even in this casual state, she takes my breath away. Isla's natural beauty shines through effortlessly, and she doesn't need makeup to enhance it.

As I enter her small apartment, my eyes wander, taking in the cosy space. The soft glow of warm-toned lights casts a comforting ambiance. A few framed pictures on the wall capture moments of her life, and a bookshelf filled with novels reflects her love for reading. The simplicity of her space resonates with me, offering a glimpse into her world.

Isla watches me intently as I take in the details of her apartment. After a moment, she blurts out, "Sorry, it's not that crash hot here. It's a little small, but it'll do for now."

I turn to her with a reassuring smile, "Hey, it's perfect. Size doesn't matter when it feels like home." I hope my words convey the sincerity behind them, letting her know that I appreciate the space she's opened up to me.

Isla guides me around the kitchen, her gestures pointing out ingredients and utensils as I prepare us dinner—my favourite dish, chicken pasta bake. While I'm immersed in the cooking process, she sits at the kitchen island, gracefully sipping on a glass of wine. Then, without missing a beat, Isla rises from her seat and casually asks, "Mind if I prepare a salad?" I meet her gaze and give a nonchalant nod.

Despite the familiarity we've built, a nervous energy creeps in. I can't quite place why—it's not as if we haven't been on a date or shared intimate moments. This feels different—domestic, normal, like we've been doing this for ages. I revel in the comfort of being around her, finding solace in the simple act of preparing dinner together.

Now seated at her small round dining table, steam wafting from the pasta bake, I notice Isla's hesitation as she portions her plate—a slight nervousness evident. That won't cut it. I can't have her going hungry on my watch. Snatching her plate from her hands, I add a more substantial serving of both salad and pasta bake, setting it back down with a gruff, "Eat. Don't be shy around me, Isla."

Her face flushes, caught off guard, but I can sense the internal debate. She replies back with a nod of reassurance and I then proceed to pile a mountain of food onto my own plate. She watches with wide eyes and a smile. "Fuck, I'm starving," I mutter and wink at Isla—and with that, we both dig in. My mouth waters at the taste. *Not bad*, Xavier.

As we sit on her couch, a comfortable silence lingers after the satisfying meal. Isla, however, breaks it with a warm, "Thanks for dinner, Xav. It was really nice."

I respond with a smirk, "No prob, it was nothing."

Curiosity sparks as she asks, "Do you cook often?" Swirling the beer in my hand, arm casually resting on the back of the lounge.

"Sometimes. Learnt from young, though. Mum taught us all the basics, and I love to experiment with food here and there. What about you? Can you cook?"

I raise an eyebrow, teasing a bit. She smiles softly, but her expression shifts as her gaze drops to her hand, fiddling with her nails. "Um, yeah here and there. My Mum also taught me a thing or two. We used to cook together all the time, but now... I don't do it as often."

The change in her tone doesn't go unnoticed, and she seems almost sad. "I'm sorry, I didn't mean to bring up anything," I quickly apologise.

Shaking her head, she reassures me, "No, that's okay. I should talk about her more, you know. I have nothing but fond memories of her."

I can understand this, having lost my grandparents, although I can't even begin to imagine what it would be like to lose a parent—I do know, however, that sometimes embracing happy memories can be a healthy coping tool and a source of comfort.

I bite the bullet and ask, "What was she like? Your mum, if you don't mind me asking." Isla looks at me intently, still twiddling her pointer finger and thumb.

She takes a moment, then softly begins, "Mum was... she was incredible." She sighs.

"Warm, you know? Always had this way of making you feel safe and loved. She loved animals, just like me. I remember the days when she'd teach me about different species, their behaviours, and how to care for them. She had this endless patience."

A hint of a smile plays on Isla's lips as she continues, "She used to say that animals could sense the good in people. That's why I chose to be a vet. I'd developed a strong love for the idea and she always pushed me to pursue it. She had this gentle strength about her. Always there to listen and provide comfort."

I listen attentively, appreciating the glimpse into Isla's past. It's a delicate topic, but one that carries a certain warmth, a celebration of a life well-lived. I find myself captivated by Isla's words, her fond memories casting a glow over the room.

"She sounds amazing," I say sincerely. "You must've learned a lot from her. I think you're doing a great job carrying that legacy forward."

Her gaze softens, and she gives a small nod. "Thank you, Xav. It's not always easy, but I feel connected to her when I'm helping animals. It's like she's with me in those moments."

I sense a profound connection between Isla and her mother, one that goes beyond words. "I'm sure she'd be proud of the person you've become," I say, meaning every word.

Isla's eyes turn glassy, and she shakes and clears her throat. "I hope so. Anyway, enough about me. Tell me more about your family, about Brad and Liv.

"Bradley has always been the quiet one—a man of few words," I chuckle, recalling memories of our mischievous exploits. "But don't let that fool you. When it came to pranks when we were younger, that guy was a mastermind. Olivia, on the other hand, had a knack for getting us out of trouble with her charm. She'd flash that smile, and suddenly, we were off the hook."

Isla joins in with a laugh, her eyes sparkling with amusement. "Sounds like you had quite the dynamic trio."

"Oh, you have no idea," I grin as I resume, "Now that we're older, Bradley and Liv have conquered the art of getting under my skin. Bradley's the agitator, always finding new ways to rile me up. Liv, she's the mastermind of making things worse. She's twenty-one, but I swear she acts like a child. They tag-team like pros." I roll my eyes. Isla giggles.

As we navigate through the stories of my family, high school somehow slips into the conversation without a conscious thought. I notice a subtle shift in Isla's demeanour. Her eyes widen, and she seems to squirm uncomfortably in her seat. A twinge of regret hits me, realising that high school wouldn't have been the easiest time for her. I decide to tread carefully, choosing my words more considerately.

"Fuck, high school wasn't my finest hour," I confess. "I've had my fair share of regrets, especially with how I treated everyone, and *you*. Fuck, honestly, if I could go back and change things, I would."

As those words leave my lips, memories of the immature antics of my high school friends flood my mind. I wince at the thought of what Isla had endured from that group. Anger builds up within me, knowing I was part of that toxicity.

"Isla," I begin, my voice firm with remorse, "I was a dick back then. Not just to everyone, but to *you* especially. I should've put a stop to those juvenile stunts, but I didn't. I regret every moment of it. I'm not that boy anymore, and I'm sorry if my past actions hurt you or made those years harder."

There's a brief silence, and Isla appears apprehensive. I await her response, my gaze focused on her, hoping she understands the sincerity in my apology. A heavy sigh escapes her lips. The weight of the past seems to linger in the air, and she finally speaks, her voice a touch hesitant.

"I appreciate you saying that, Xavier. High school was... not the best time for me. But, like you said, it's in the past. People do change—" her voice trails off.

In a moment of vulnerability, I add, "Isla, I need you to know something. You've always intrigued me. From the moment I saw you, I wanted to know more about you. You were always so quiet, had this allure to you," I admit, the truth hanging in the air. "Because of that fascination, I acted out. Hated the fact that you infiltrated my thoughts, so I just went along with my mates' dumb antics to hide it. I was an idiot—fuck, you don't know how sorry I am."

As the weight of my words settles, Isla stammers, clearly shocked and not sure what to say. I reassure her, "I don't expect you to say anything. I just wanted you to hear me out."

"People do change—-" her voice trails off.

I nod, sincerity lacing my words, "And I'll show you every day from here onwards that I have. I owe that to you, at least."

A playful smirk plays on my lips, an attempt to lighten the mood. "So, what do you say? Second chance?"

Isla, considering my words, teases back with a playful smirk, "I'll think about it." A genuine laugh escapes me as I take the last swig of my beer.

As we banter back and forth, the air between us seems to lighten. Isla's balcony doors are open, allowing a cool draft to sweep inside. I notice her body shiver, and my gaze intensifies, drifting to her lips. An irresistible urge to kiss her washes over me, a desire to erase any lingering negative thoughts from her mind. She catches my gaze, her blush deepening as she turns her head down shyly.

In a low, deep murmur, I find myself saying, "Come here."

The distance between us suddenly feels too far, and I need to be closer. Isla inhales through her nose, releasing a deep breath, and as she inches closer, a sudden impulse seizes me. Without overthinking, I gently grab her waist and lift her, guiding her to straddle my lap. Loving feeling the weight of her on top of me and her ass in my hands. I give each round globe of ass a hard squeeze—each with more than a handful, and she whimpers softly.

The shift in our positions creates an intimate closeness, her warmth now fully melding with mine as she arches into my touch. She looks at me with a mixture of desire and affection.

"Glad you came back into my life." I admit, and I sense her body shudder in response—without hesitation, I lean in, capturing her lips with mine. Her groan vibrates in my mouth, and when she sucks on my tongue—*fucking hell.*

She's everything, and *I don't plan on letting her go now.*

31

Isla

Tuesday rolls over and today at the clinic, a couple came in asking about sweet Luna, our Australian Kelpie with a heart as big as the Outback. I spent a good half hour this morning trying to charm them into seeing that Luna is the paw-fect fit for them. But, alas, my powers of persuasion were not enough.

After a lengthy discussion, they narrowed it down to their 'back-yard' being too small for Luna's zest for life. Ugh, really? Luna's a furball of energy—she'd be content with a patch of grass and some sunshine! It's moments like these that tug at my heartstrings. I just want these adorable fur babies to find their forever homes, filled with love and belly rubs. Why can't everyone see how amazing Luna is? Sigh, the struggles of a veterinarian who's a little too emotionally invested in her patients.

Despite the heartbreak with Luna, the clinic has been a whirlwind of activity today. We had a parade of new furry friends and a few familiar faces—there was Max, the mischievous tabby cat who thinks he's the king of the world, and Nala, our spoiled rottweiler with a penchant for slobbery kisses.

While I do my veterinarian thing, Katy, provides some comic relief. She has this way of turning even the most mundane tasks into a stand-up routine. As I jot down notes on Nala's health check, Katy leans over the counter, a smirk on her face.

"You wouldn't believe what Max did today. He tried to stage a coup against the goldfish in the waiting area aquarium. I had to break up a full-blown underwater rebellion!" *Ah, so that's what that ruckus was earlier, I ponder.* I can't help but laugh. "Max is quite the troublemaker. Maybe he's just trying to add 'aquatic conqueror' to his resume."

Katy grins, "Well, at least he's ambitious. But seriously, Isla, you're a superhero for dealing with all this chaos. How do you do it?"

I shrug, "It's all in a day's work. Plus, the wagging tails and purring cats make it worthwhile. Plus, I'm used to chaos," I say with a lopsided smile, and she returns a soft smile back, a look of understanding in her eyes.

While I scribble down a few more notes, Katy exclaims and bursts into a grin that's practically ear-to-ear. I glance up, and she can barely contain her excitement.

"Oh, guess what, Isla? Our saviour is returning! Molly's done with the worst of her exams, and she'll be back tomorrow." Relief floods through me.

"Oh wow! That's so soon. That's great," I exclaim. I could really use the extra pair of hands around here again. And let's be honest, the clinic just isn't the same without Molly's chaotic charm.

Katy nods in agreement, "Absolutely! I've missed her constant stream of coffee-induced energy. It's been way too quiet without her." I can't help but laugh at that.

As Katy leaves the reception area, I feel a sense of anticipation for Molly's return. The clinic is like a family, and having our energetic and vivacious vet nurse back will undoubtedly inject a burst of life into our little animal sanctuary.

My phone buzzes with an unknown number flashing on the screen. I hesitate for a moment, contemplating whether to pick up or let it go to voicemail. Eventually, my curiosity gets the best of me, and I answer. "Hello?"

A familiar, lively voice bursts through the speaker, "Isla! It's Olivia. I hope you don't mind—I totally pestered Imogen for your number." Olivia's laughter dances through the phone, and I can't help but smile, shaking my head. Of course, Liv would pull a stunt like that.

"Hey, Liv! What's up?" I ask.

"Hiii! Um, what are you up to?" Liv's voice buzzes through the phone, as she exclaims further, "Isla, I am so fucking bored out of my brains at home, and my brothers are doing in my head."

In the background, Xavier's voice booms loudly, demanding, *"Liv, get your ass over here. These cows aren't going to milk themselves."* My pulse flutters at the sound of his voice.

"Just at work, you know, the usual stuff." I reply, glancing around the clinic, and I continue.

"Seems like you have your hands full with that one."

Olivia whines over the phone, "Please save me, Xav is making me milk a fucking cow—a COW, Isla." I laugh out loud. I can hear a commotion happening in the background, cow's mooing and people talking. Then, Olivia goes silent for a second before blurting out, her excitement overflowing,

"Omg, you should come and help me milk the cows—we have five of them here, *FIVE*, and Xavier is making *me* do it all. Come and save me?" I can't help but laugh at Liv's enthusiasm, her voice breathless from her rambling. Just as I'm about to respond, Xavier's unmistakable voice booms in the background, demanding to know, "Who are you on the fucking phone to?"

Over the phone, Olivia answers Xavier's questioning voice, "Isla! You know your *girrrlfriend*," she says with a teasing tone. I freeze at this, I'm not his... *girlfriend*, but before I get to correct her, Xavier's voice cuts through the phone.

"Doc, do I even want to know how my sister got your number?" I let out a soft laugh, "Hey, it wasn't me. Apparently Imogen gave it to her."

"Good luck, she'll never leave you alone now." I snort at this, and in the background, I hear Olivia exclaim, *"Hey, don't be rude, you big asshole."*

Ignoring her, he says, "So how's your day so far, Doc? You missing me yet?"

I snort at his question, a smirk forming on my lips. "Oh, terribly," I retort, feigning sarcasm. "My day is just so dull without you, Xavier. How will I ever survive?" I smile at my own words.

He chuckles on the other end, and without missing a beat, Xavier fires back, "Now, now. Don't be getting all sassy with me, woman. You'll hurt my feelings. Don't lie, I know you miss me."

"In your dreams, Cowboy." But the truth is, I do miss him. Tragic.

Olivia chimes in, *"What feelings? You don't have any. Stop flirting and give my phone back."* I blush at this. Flirting? Is that what we're doing?

Xavier's voice joins the banter, and as he shifts his tone sternly to Olivia.

"Don't you have cows to milk? Move along," attempting to shoo her away, and I can't help but roll my eyes at his futile effort. As if Liv would listen to him. It's both amusing and incredibly arousing to witness his commanding side. My mind drifts for a moment, wondering what it would be like to have him boss me around in bed. The thought sends a tingling warmth through my body, and I quickly push it aside, focusing on the present banter. Yet, a nagging question lingers—*what am I into?* I've seen Xavier's dirty side, but I haven't explored my own desires. Justin was so... vanilla, and vanilla is just not my cup of tea, *evidently.*

"You didn't answer my question," Xavier remarks, his tone teasing. *Question?*

"What question?" I ask, momentarily confused. He chuckles softly, the sound rich and deep.

"I asked, how's your day so far, Doc?" he repeats, his voice laced with amusement.

"Oh, that question," I reply, feeling a flush creeping up my cheeks. "Uh, pretty quiet now. The morning was busy. That's how most days are. That's why we shut the clinic early most of the time."

"If you're up for it, and have nothing else to do, you should come past. Liv here is hopeless and could really use your skill set or two in milking these cows," Xavier suggests.

I let out a huff of laughter, "And you think I'll be any better? I have never milked a cow before."

"Well, it's never too late to learn, right?" he replies, the mischievousness evident in his voice. As I ponder his invitation, Katy walks back into the room, a mischievous look in her eyes.

"Hm, true," I respond, trying to sound nonchalant. Xavier repeats his previous question, "Anyway, no pressure, the invitation is there. Liv is going to bust my balls until you say yes, just saying," he says casually.

Liv chimes in, "Isla, you're a lifesaver. Please say yes."

I consider it for a moment. "I'll see how I go here at the clinic. But no promises," I add with a chuckle.

"Oh, I'm sure we'll be seeing you soon, byeee!" Liv cheers, her voice filtering clearer onto the phone now, and then she hangs up. Katy watches me with a raised brow, a knowing smirk playing on her lips.

She keeps staring at me, her eyes filled with mischief. I finally break the silence, "What?"

Katy smirks knowingly. "Oh, nothing. Just wondering if you're really going to *help* Liv, or if it's just an excuse to spend time with a certain cowboy."

"How much of that conversation did you hear, huh? Do you have supersonic hearing or something?" I ask in disbelief.

She chuckles, "Well, let's just say I have a sixth sense when it comes to juicy gossip."

I roll my eyes. "It's just helping out with the cows. Nothing more."

She chuckles, "Sure, *'Doc'*. Just don't forget your veterinary expertise while you're at it, and make sure you give those *cows* a thorough check-up," she says while wiggling her eyebrows.

I shake my head, laughing. "Hm, why do I get the feeling that when you say *'cows'*, you mean nothing of the sort, huh?" Katy smirks, hinting at something dirtier.

"Hey now, you said it, not me," she raises her hands. I feel the heat rising in my cheeks, and I playfully shove her shoulder. "Katy, you're such a dirty woman."

"Now, now, dear, I think you're the dirty woman here, Miss Isla, with her head in the gutter." I roll my eyes. Katy laughs, and I can't help but join in. The banter between us is always entertaining.

After a moment she informs me that there are no other scheduled appointments, so I can actually take off. Is heading to Xavier's farm really a good idea? I contemplate this, my mind caught between practicality and the allure of curiosity. I mean, it's just cows, right? Yet, there's a little voice inside me whispering about more than just bovine check-ups.

I let out a sigh, my curiosity winning over caution, and I grab my keys from the front desk, calling out to Katy that I'm leaving and to call if she needs anything—ready for whatever awaits beyond the clinic doors.

As I prepare to leave, a twinge of anxiety creeps in. The thought of encountering Xavier's father, the source of past disputes, tightens my chest. A bubble forms in my throat, and I run through my breathing routine to calm my nerves—*In, out, in, out.*

But then I think, screw it. My father is not an indicator of who I am as a person. I refuse to let past ruffles tarnish my reputation. They need to understand that my father hasn't been himself for a while, and if anyone questions it, I'll set the record straight.

With a determined exhale, I stride outside to my car.

Pulling up to Xavier's place, the familiar nerves dance in my stomach as I find myself around him again. A text message from Xavier lets me know they're just around the back, near the barn. Rounding the side of the house, I come across a chaotic scene—Olivia is wailing about having milk all over her, exclaiming how sticky it is, while Xavier seems to be losing his patience, visibly irritated. Bradley stands to the side, leaning against a wooden beam, wearing a smirk.

Approaching cautiously, I walk up to Bradley, and he surprises me by muttering, "They've been at this for the past half an hour. I think they need your help." His words catch me off guard—I think it's the most he's uttered to me so far. I can't help but smile and nod, before trudging over to Liv and Xavier.

As I walk towards them, their conversation becomes clearer amidst

Olivia's wails and Xavier's grumpy and frustrated demeanour.

"Can you fucking relax, Liv? It's just fucking milk. I showed you how to do it. It's not rocket science," Xavier grumbles, lifting his hat off his head—running a hand through his hair in apparent irritation. Olivia shoots back with a playful pout.

"I did it, like you showed me!" She exclaims. "I was trying to help, and this stupid cow decided to shake its tail right when I was standing there." I notice a small bucket of milk tipped over, and Xavier leans forward off the small stool to pick it up, saving the last remaining bits of milk. He places it back underneath the cow's udders, his movements showing a combination of frustration and expertise.

I notice his frustration etched on his face, his hair sticking to him with sweat underneath his cowboy hat. The rugged charm intensifies as I take in his attire—a white t-shirt that clings to him with sweat and those blue washed jeans that I've seen him wear before.

His outfit is completed by a pair of brown steel-cap Booma boots. There's something about this rugged look that I love—a magnetic pull that makes him even more irresistible.

I can't help but appreciate the way he wears the farm life—casual yet effortlessly appealing. It's as if he belongs to this landscape, the sweat and dust adding a layer of authenticity to his allure.

Shaking off the distraction, I clear my throat and flash a playful smile.

"My, my. What do we have here?" At the sound of my voice, Xavier turns in my direction, and his frustration-marred face instantly dissipates. In its place, a look of relief appears, followed by a smirk that doesn't go unnoticed.

Xavier grins, "Well, look who decided to grace us with her presence. Liv, your saviour has arrived."

Olivia cheers, "Isla, you have no idea how badly I needed your help. Xavier was about to murder me." She frowns at him, poking her tongue out. I stifle a laugh.

Xavier lets out an annoyed sigh. "Well, it's about time. Liv here was making a mess," he grumbles, his irritation still evident.

Olivia sticks her tongue out at him, again, and I can't help but chuckle at their playful banter. "I tried my best," she defends herself, a mischievous glint in her eyes.

Xavier rolls his eyes and shoots me a grateful glance. "Thanks for coming, Doc. Liv's enthusiasm for farm chores tends to backfire more often than not."

I walk over closer to where Xavier is sitting on the stool, the playful banter between Olivia and him still echoing. Olivia crosses her arms in a huff.

"Why do I have to do this anyway? That bastard over there is doing nothing." She nods to where Bradley is, I'm assuming, still standing. "Why me?" she whines, giving Xavier a pointed look.

Xavier smirks, unfazed by her complaints. "Because you're good at doing *nothing*, Liv. It's about time you did something useful," he retorts, a teasing glint in his eyes. I suppress a laugh at their dynamic.

Xavier successfully shows me how to milk the cow, Olivia standing nearby. His closeness makes my body shudder. I'm sitting on the stool, and Xavier's towering frame bends over me, his muscular arms next to mine as he guides my hands on how to grip and pull the udders to get a stream of milk flowing. My face flushes with heat, but I remind myself that I'm in the presence of his sister, so I need to calm down.

Olivia, from beside us, whines, "That's not fair, she makes it look easy."

Xavier retorts, his face close to mine, "That's because it is."

Olivia huffs, "Whatever."

Xavier is so close, I can feel his breath on my face as we continue to milk the cow together. He whispers in my ear so only I can hear, "Hm, you've got a good grip there, princess."

"I'm getting hard imagining you gripping my cock, like that." He murmurs, his voice low. I shiver as his breath tickles the side of my face.

My mind races at his words, and I can't help but feel a flutter run straight to my core. Heat flushes to my face, and I nudge him, "Your sister is right there, shush," I whisper.

Olivia mutters, "Ugh, gross. Can you two not?"

Xavier feigns innocence as he stands up behind me, "What? I didn't do anything."

Olivia says, "Oh yeah, sure.. That's why she's blushing, aye?"

Xavier just glares at her, and I look away to hide my uncontrollable blush.

"You know, you two are really cute together. I definitely ship this!" Embarrassment courses through me, and I clear my throat.

Xavier says, "Right, I think that's enough for today. Liv, you're done."

Liv releases a sigh, "Oh thank fuck! I'm out, see you later, love-birds."

As Xavier wraps up the equipment, I follow him into the barn with the cow. Sweat glistens on his skin under the hot sun, and as he locks up the gate, his arm accidentally brushes against mine, leaving a sheen of sweat on me. I playfully wrinkle my nose. "Ew, you're all sweaty," I tease, wiping at my arm with a smirk.

Xavier turns to me, his grin mischievous. "No shit, Doc. It's scorching out here."

He pauses, then mockingly growls, "Is my sweat 'ew,' huh?" With a playful twinkle in his eyes, he wipes his hands across my face and arms, leaving me covered in his perspiration. I burst out laughing, feeling a bit icky but strangely exhilarated at the same time.

"You won't be complaining when my sweat is all over you the next time I fuck you," he says with a suggestive tone. My cheeks heat up, and I can't help but think that maybe a little sweat isn't so bad after all.

He moves closer to me, closing the gap between us, his chest brushing against mine as he looks down at me. Just then, Olivia comes rushing into the barn, breaking up the moment, saying, "Oi guys, we're going to the Loose Lasso tonight, you know, to celebrate your birthday, Xav. You old fart."

I break apart from Xavier, stopping in my tracks. *His birthday?* It's his birthday? Why didn't he say anything? I look at him, shooting him a confused look. "Your birthday?"

Olivia chimes in, "Well, technically it's tomorrow, but I thought it would be nice to go out tonight." She falters, "Wait... didn't you tell her, Xavier Mitchell?" He rolls his eyes at her use of his full name. The moment becomes awkward, and I shuffle my feet, feeling a bit embarrassed. Twentieth of September. I make a mental note to remember for next time.

Xavier shrugs, running his hand behind the hair at his nape, "It's nothing important, really. It just never came up in conversation, and honestly, I'd forgotten until now."

"Why am I not surprised that you'd forget," she deadpans and then turns to me, "Well, this old codger's birthday is tomorrow, he's turning, hmmm, fifty?" She teases with a finger to her lip.

"Ha, ha. You're hilarious. and you're what, twelve?" Xavier teases back.

"Twenty-three, asshole," she says with a smirk, her hands on her hips—sometimes I forget how much younger she is. She's the baby of the family, no wonder Xav is so protective.

I feel a little out of place, not having known it was his birthday. Olivia chirps in, "So, we're all going, yes? Isla, you're invited."

"Oh no, it's okay. I don't want to impose," I reply.

Olivia scoffs, "What! You're not," at the same time Xavier interjects, "Don't be silly, Isla. It's not an imposition."

Xavier adds, "I'll only go if Isla says yes to coming." They both look at me, awaiting my response.

I sigh in frustration, feeling a bit cornered.

"Okay—I'll come," I concede with a playful roll of my eyes.

Xavier winks at me, and Olivia whoops loudly in response. I can't help but blush.

32

Xavier

L oud music, pulsating lights, and the scent of alcohol linger in the air.

This type of shit is not exactly my scene, but with Isla by my side, it somehow feels more tolerable. Imogen, Bradley, Harrison, Michael, and Olivia are all here tonight. Bradley, the stubborn one, had to be convinced to join, much like myself.

Big night outs and drinking have never been my thing. I did it for a while when I was young, but that's about it. Now with age, I find myself preferring the quiet of the farm over the chaos of a crowded bar.

Olivia just let us know that she'd invited Amelia, an old childhood friend we hadn't seen in ages. I remember her from our farm days, always following us around, with my sister—and by 'us', I mean Bradley. Back then, I had a hunch she'd had a little crush on my brother, though the oblivious fool never noticed. *I could be wrong.* I wonder how she's changed after all these years. She hasn't arrived yet, leaving an air of anticipation tinged with nostalgia. The bar is a sea of people, and it's no surprise given the night is young and the allure of The Loose Lasso is hard to resist.

Isla seems a bit uneasy, and I can't blame her. The last time she was here, it didn't end well. She leans into me subtly, silently pressing for reassurance. I look down at her and offer a reassuring smile. "Hey, it'll be fun."

She looks up at me with appreciation, and my chest warms at the sight. It's moments like these that make the chaos of the night seem a little more manageable, a shared understanding that we're in this together. That I've got her, for as long as she wants me.

We're all crammed around the bar, waiting for an available table or booth like a pack of wolves sizing up potential prey. The air is charged with the promise of a good night out, and each of us holds a drink in our hands. Olivia, with her vivacious spirit, had taken charge of the first round, shouting for drinks. The guys and I had opted for cold beers, while the ladies indulged in those overly sweet, fruity concoctions. Not my Isla, though. She's a woman of taste, ordering a scotch and coke. I love that about her—she's got a distinct flair that sets her apart. We all clink our drinks together.

Liv's eyes light up as she spots an empty booth in the corner. "Found a spot, guys!" she announces, and we collectively decide to make our move.

My gaze lingers on Isla, her presence grounding me. We might be at a funny place, dancing on the fine line between friendship and something more, but I can't help the surge of protectiveness I feel around us. She's mine, whether she acknowledges it or not. The realisation settles in, and I can no longer deny the depth of my feelings for her.

Tonight, amidst the pulsating music and the laughter of friends, I can't escape the truth—*I'm falling for Isla, and there's no turning back.*

As we settle into the booth, the energy of the place envelops us. The low hum of conversation, the rhythmic thumping of the music surrounds us. I pull Isla into the booth to sit next to me. Imogen takes a seat beside Isla, and the rest of the crew cram into the booth, determined to make it work. The leather upholstery creaks underneath our weight.

As the group settles into the booth, the lively energy of the place surrounding us, Imogen and Harrison, true to form, break out into a comfortable bickering session.

"Imogen, you can't seriously think pineapple belongs on pizza!" Harrison exclaims, a mockingly incredulous expression on his face.

Imogen scoffs, rolling her eyes dramatically. "Harrison, if you had any taste buds left, you'd know the sweet and savoury combo is divine. You're just a culinary caveman!" Harrison puts a thumbs down in the air. Michael and I collectively groan out loud.

Imogen leans forward, her eyes narrowing in on Harrison. "I appreciate the finer things in life, unlike you, Neanderthal."

Harrison smirks, undeterred. "Call it what you want, sugar, but I'll take a classic Margherita over a fruit salad pizza any day."

Olivia jumps into the fray. "Well, I also love pineapple on my pizza," she declares with a mischievous grin, fully aware of the chaos she's about to incite. Imogen high fives her, smacking their hands together and Harrison just glares at both of them.

Michael, clearly exasperated, interjects, "Who even brought up this stupid conversation?"

Imogen and Olivia, in perfect unison, point accusingly at Harrison. "He did!" they exclaim simultaneously.

The banter between Imogen and Harrison continues, their voices blending into the lively soundtrack of the night. Isla leans into my side, her presence a comforting weight against me. And in the midst of this lighthearted chaos, I can't help but appreciate the simple joy of being surrounded by friends who have become a second family, Isla now included.

As we settle into the booth, Olivia's infectious excitement bursts forth, announcing Amelia's arrival. She declares her intention to fetch Amelia from the entrance, leaving the booth.

Bradley, seated across from me, seems to subtly adjust in his seat. His expression remains unreadable, hidden beneath layers of familiarity and, perhaps, a hint of discomfort. I'm no mind reader, but something's definitely on his mind.

Moments later, Olivia returns with Amelia in tow, their camaraderie evident from the way they navigate through the crowd. Amelia greets the group with a friendly wave, and Olivia proceeds with introductions.

"Everyone, this is Amelia! Amelia, meet the crew," Olivia says, gesturing to our eclectic bunch.

Amelia's gaze lands on Isla, and Olivia continues the introductions. "And this is Isla, our new resident vet."

Isla waves from her seat, smiling shyly. "Hi!"

"Pleasure to meet you, Isla," Amelia says with a warm smile, waving back.

Olivia, ever enthusiastic, redirects Amelia's attention to Bradley and me. "And, of course, you remember Xavier and Bradley, *right*?" she asks, playfully. Amelia's eyes flicker with recognition as she greets us. "Xavier, Bradley, it's been way too long. How've you both been?"

I exchange pleasantries with a polite nod and a smile. Bradley offers a reserved response, his gaze lingering for a moment before he shifts his attention elsewhere.

With everyone now gathered, Olivia takes charge and announces another round of drinks. This time, Bradley surprises us by standing up abruptly, offering to shout for the round. He saunters off to the bar, leaving the rest of us to speculate about his sudden enthusiasm for generosity.

Amelia watches his departure, her gaze lingering for a moment before returning her attention to the group. There's a quickness to Bradley's steps that catches my eye, sparking a mischievous thought. Isla, sensing something, turns to me with a quizzical look in her eyes. "Is there something going on there?" she asks, her curiosity piqued.

Leaning down into her ear with a sly grin, I decide to have a bit of fun. "Secret lovers," I tease, winking at her. Isla's eyes widen in mock shock.

"No, really?" she questions, genuinely surprised. I chuckle softly in her ear. "Nah, I'm kidding. I know just as much as you do." She just nods.

As the lively chatter continues, Amelia turns her attention to me, breaking the flow of the conversation. "So, Xavier... how's that farm of yours going? Still running?" she inquires with a warm smile.

I smirk in response, a familiar pride in my voice, "Yep, 'til the day I die probably. What about you? Still interested in educating young little minds?" I ask, genuinely curious—remembering her saying, a few years back her, she'd wanted to become a teacher.

Amelia's face lights up with enthusiasm. "Yes! I work at the local primary school, down at Koala Creek, teaching kindergarten. It's so fun!"

This revelation piques Isla's interest, and she jumps into the conversation, "No way, that's awesome. I love little kids." The warmth in her voice mirrors the image of her being surrounded by playful children, and I can't help but feel a surge of affection. She'd make a good mum someday—warm and nurturing.

Amelia, turning her attention to Isla, continues the conversation. "Yeah, they sure keep you on your toes! What about you? I hear you're a vet. That must be fascinating work!" she remarks, genuinely interested.

Isla, with a warm smile, responds, "Oh, it's definitely challenging, but it's an incredibly rewarding job. I get to help animals every day, and there's always something new to learn."

Unable to resist chiming in, I add with a proud grin, "Yeah, Isla's the best in the business. There's no one else I'd trust more with our animals."

Amelia nods in agreement, "That's amazing! It takes a special kind of person to do what you do, Isla." She blushes at the compliments, and looks up at me, appreciation in her eyes.

"Thank you, Amelia. It's my passion, and I love every moment of it."

As Isla and Amelia delve into their shared love for animals, their conversation takes an unexpected turn towards their common interests. They discover a mutual fondness for the TV show 'New Girl—absolutely no clue what they're on about—as well as a shared passion for coffee.

Amelia excitedly remarks, "You *love* 'New Girl' too? That show is *hilarious*! Schmidt is my favourite character."

Isla grins in agreement. "Oh, absolutely! His quirky personality is just too good. And don't get me started on Nick and Jess."

Amelia laughs, "Right? Their dynamic is everything."

Isla nods, "Oh, I agree!"

Observing the animated exchange, I mutter, "New what now?" Clearly lost in their discussion about a show I'm unfamiliar with, I watch with a bemused expression.

Isla, appalled that I have no idea about the show, exclaims, "You've never watched New Girl? Oh, we'll have to fix that. It's hilarious! Full of quirky characters and ridiculous situations. You'd love it." She shoots a playful grin in my direction.

I shoot a smirk her way and respond, "Mhm."

Amelia watches the two of us with a curious glint in her eyes before blurting out, "You two are really cute. How long have you been dating?"

Isla freezes beside me, clearly caught off guard by Amelia's assumption. Stammering, she begins, "O-Oh, we're just... we're not—"

I cut her off, answering for both of us, "We're friends," I say.

Isla blushes beside me, and I can't help but notice the way her cheeks turn a rosy hue. In the back of my mind, a voice whispers, friends who secretly fuck and fool around. The words taste bitter in my mouth. *I don't want to be just friends with Isla.*

Amelia's assumption falls flat, and she awkwardly apologises, "Oh, I'm sorry. I didn't mean to assume."

Isla, still a bit flustered, manages to say, "All good."

Imogen then jumps in, "So, have you tried the nachos here? They're amazing!" she exclaims, steering the conversation away from the momentarily awkward topic. The group joins in on the discussion about the menu, successfully shifting the mood to a lighter, more comfortable one.

Bradley had returned shortly after with the drinks, and I handed them out to the group. Isla wasted no time grabbing hers and taking a few big sips.

Olivia whooped loudly, "Oh righto, let's get this party started," as she grabbed hold of Amelia by the hand, coercing Imogen and Isla to join in the dance. The girls hit the dance floor, moving to the rhythm, while the guys and I remained seated at the bar.

I'm now watching Isla's every move, sipping on my second beer for the night. The atmosphere in the bar is lively, the music pulsating through the air—Luke Combs' voice echoes in the distance, his music blaring through the speakers as the girls lose themselves in the dance. I can't help but be drawn to Isla's energy as she loses herself in the music.

As I watch them dance, my eyes scan the crowd surrounding us. A couple of old couples sway nearby, another group of young girls and random men scattered around. Unease settles within me. I can't shake the feeling that she's out there, surrounded by other men. *I don't like it.*

Harrison starts, "So, Xavier, how about we have a barbecue tomorrow at the farm for your birthday? Maybe even set up a bonfire. What do you think?"

Michael adds, "Yeah, that sounds like a great idea. Count me in."

But my attention is elsewhere, focused on Isla as she dances. Harrison clicks his fingers in front of my face, saying, "Earth to Xavier..."

I reply nonchalantly, "Yeah, yeah, BBQ sounds good."

Harrison raises an eyebrow. "You sure about that? You seem a bit distracted." I tear my eyes away from Isla to focus on the conversation.

Michael speaks up, "Xav, you've been staring at Isla like a lovesick puppy. What's going on?"

I feel a blush creeping up my neck, but I clear my throat and try to play it off. "Nothing. Just watching."

Michael smirks, "Watching, huh? Fuck, someone's got it bad."

I glare at him. "Shut up, Michael."

The boys chuckle, and Harrison chimes in, "So, have you made a move on her yet?"

Ignoring him, I feel the flush creeping up even more. Michael notices and says casually, "Oh, he has, alright. It's obvious how much he's obsessed."

Harrison exclaims, "Seriously? Xavier, you old dog! You better tell us!"

I shoot a teasing look at Bradley, who's wearing a smug grin, as if he is amused at this. Deciding to turn the tables, I remark in a snarky tone, "What about you, Bradley, huh? You seemed to rush off real quick earlier, when Amelia got here."

The boys echo my teasing, and Bradley raises an eyebrow, caught off guard. "What? What are you on about?" he says casually. Harrison looks back and forth, confused, before turning to Michael, who adds, "No clue."

Returning the smug look back at Bradley, I respond with a knowing, "Mhm, sure," while Bradley shakes his head, pulling out his phone.

Harrison, with a laugh, says, "Is there something in the air turning you fools into lovesick idiots? Let me know because I want in."

Michael deadpans, "Yeah, good luck with that one, brother."

I play it off, downplaying the situation, and say, "I don't know what you're talking about," smirking as I take a swig of my beer.

Returning my gaze back to the girls, I'm struck with a pang of anxiety when I notice they're no longer on the dance floor. My heart drops, and I sit forward in my seat, scanning the crowd until I spot them at the bar, downing shots together. I exhale in relief, but narrow my eyes as I watch them.

As I observe, I notice some bloke, clearly full of himself, and his mates, making their way toward the girls. They engage Imogen and Amelia, and Imogen seems to be having a good time with their banter. Isla and Olivia, on the other hand, remain aloof, observing from a distance. But then, the mate of the wanker starts heading in Isla and Olivia's direction.

Not a chance in hell, bud.

I find myself on the edge of my seat, leaning forward with my elbows on the table, my gaze fixed on the unfolding drama. Thoughts race through my mind as I glare at the scene, ready to step in if things get out of hand. The audacity of these pricks to encroach on Isla's space pisses me off to no end. She's not just some girl. She's *mine*.

Well, not really, but she *should* be. The idea of some random bloke thinking he can just waltz up to her makes my blood boil. The fact that Liv is there makes it even worse.

My fists clench involuntarily as I witness the situation escalating. The guy at the bar leans in closer to Isla and Olivia, invading their personal space. Anger simmers beneath the surface as I see the discomfort on their faces. I glance at the guys beside me, and Harrison, meeting my eyes, just nods, acknowledging the need for intervention.

I look at Brad, who has his eyes narrowed on the escalating situation. "Yeah, fuck that," I mutter, frustration boiling over, as I stand and saunter over to the girls.

As I approach, I notice one of the men, and recognition flashes through me. Billy Sawkins. *What a wanker,* I think, recalling our high school days, where he was a year above me.

The men persist, and Billy has the audacity to place his hand on Isla's arm. My jaw clenches, and a surge of rage courses through me. No one lays a hand on her without permission, and these idiots are pushing all the wrong buttons. I step forward in front of Isla—my presence looming over them like a storm cloud.

"You need to back off," I growl, my voice low and menacing. Isla and Olivia seize the opportunity to distance themselves from the unwanted attention. Billy, still thinking he's smooth, smirks. "Well, well, well, if it isn't Xavier Mitchell," Billy sneers, his tone dripping with sarcasm. I fix him with a glare, not in the mood for his antics. I never really did like this cunt.

"Woah, big tough guy now, huh?" Billy turns to look back at Isla. "She your girl or some shit?"

The comment only adds fuel to the fire, intensifying the tension in the air. My temper flares, jaw clenching at Billy.

"Yes, she is. Now back the fuck off," I retort with a low, threatening growl. I hear a gasp, but I'm too fucking angry to notice who it came from.

"Easy, easy," he jeers. "We were just having some lighthearted conversation, mate. Ain't that right, girls?" The girls don't respond.

He just can't take the hint. "So, Xavier Mitchell, crushing on the daughter of the town's loony? That must be a tough gig, bro."

"Back off, Billy," I warn. In my peripheral vision, I notice Bradley, Harrison, and Michael are now standing beside me.

Billy scoffs, muttering, "Bitch seems too frigid, anyway," before pointing to Olivia. "She looks more fun," his words slurred as he winks at my sister. That's it. I snap. Rage blinds me, everything turning red. The bar explodes into chaos as I seize him by the collar and slam my fist into his smug face. He staggers backward, crashing into the bar stools.

Shouts and gasps fill the air. "Oh shit, it's going down!" someone yells.

"Xavier!" Bradley's voice cuts through the commotion. But I'm beyond reason, fueled by rage. I ignore the pleas and continue my assault. Billy tries to fight back, but I'm relentless, fueled by a protective instinct for both Liv and Isla and boiling anger at the disrespect thrown their way.

Amidst the chaos, Olivia's voice pierces through the air like a beacon, screaming my name.

"Someone call security!" an older woman's voice cries out.

"He's going to kill him!" This comes from Amelia as she gasps.

My adrenaline surges, drowning out the chaotic noise around me. I'm focused on one thing—making sure Billy regrets running his mouth.

Isla's voice cuts through the chaotic scene, a sharp command to stop. For a split second, my movements falter at the sound of her voice. In that brief pause, Harrison and Michael seize the opportunity to step in, their strong grips pulling me away from Billy.

I'm seething, ready to continue, but their combined strength prevents me from retaliating. The other guy, however, seizes the opportunity and throws a punch at my face, and the impact jars me momentarily. Bradley then intervenes, yelling at me, "What the fuck, Xavier! Calm the fuck down!"

A pair of security guards arrive, each grabbing one of us by the shirts. I look up and find Olivia and Isla, wide-eyed, as they watch the scene unfold. Amelia looks shocked, while Imogen covers her mouth in disbelief.

I'm still growling in anger as I watch Billy stumble backwards, but manages to shout something incoherent. In the midst of the struggle, I mutter to the security guards, "That cunt started it."

"You're out of your mind. I didn't do a damn thing!" he yells, attempting to regain his balance, and I lurch forward.

"Stop!" I hear Isla scream, her voice cutting through the chaos. For a brief moment, my movements falter at the sound of her voice, but then Harrison and Michael step in, restraining me backward.

Unimpressed by his protests, the security guards now at our sides, guide us all toward the exit.

So much for a fun filled night.

33

Xavier

The night air is thick with tension as we step outside, the chaotic energy from the bar brawl still pulsating through me. The cheers and jeers of the townies create a cacophony around us, but in my mind, there's nothing but the echo of my own thoughts.

What the fuck just happened? How did things spiral so out of control? I've never lost my cool like that before, not in front of everyone, not like that. It's like I was someone else entirely in that moment, someone fueled purely by rage and protective instinct.

I rub a hand over my face, trying to shake off the remnants of adrenaline coursing through my veins. My knuckles ache from the impact of my fists against Billy's face, and I can still taste the metallic tang of blood in my mouth.

As the group grills me, questioning my actions, I take a deep breath to calm the wave of anger that just subsided. "What the hell, Xavier?" Olivia demands, her arms crossed. "I've never seen you lose your shit like that."

"What the fuck even happened?" Imogen adds, her eyes wide with concern, as she comes up beside me.

Harrison chimes in, "Mate, you really need to learn to control your anger."

My jaw tightens, my temper still smouldering. "Let it go," I growl. But for some fucking reason, they just can't let it go. Isla marches up to me, her face a mixture of anger and concern.

"Why would you do that? You could have been arrested, you—"

Bradley steps forward. "She's right." *Fuck, I'm really not in the mood to hear all this now.*

"What the fuck did you want me to do? Just let that cunt run his mouth about Isla, about Olivia—our own fucking sister, Brad!" I'm seething, anger radiating off me in waves.

"Hey, I don't blame you for retaliating, but you need to be smart. Shit like this can get you locked up, bud. What if he presses charges, huh? What are you gonna do then?" I don't answer him, my gaze fixed on Isla, my chest heaving with heavy breaths.

Bradley continues, "I get that the guy was a complete asshole, but you could have handled it differently. Now you're risking getting yourself in trouble."

"You didn't have to punch him," Isla asserts.

My eyes narrow, and fuck, I can feel my anger bubbling to the surface again. "Isla, you don't understand. He crossed a line, insulted you and Olivia, and I couldn't just stand there."

"But you have to think about the consequences," she argues, but her eyes show a different kind of emotion, like she's battling thoughts in her head. "Bradley is right."

I run a hand through my hair, frustration most likely evident in my features. "I don't give a fuck about the consequences." I notice Isla shudder, no doubt from the glare I'm currently sporting. Fuck, I really need to calm down.

"If you girls hadn't gone to the bar, none of this would have happened," I bark, frustration boiling over as Olivia and Imogen quickly defend their actions.

"Hey! We were just getting another drink and some shots. There's nothing wrong with that," Olivia retorts, and Imogen cautiously adds, "Yeah, it was my idea."

I remain relentless, my concern for their safety driving my words. "What if those fuckers had spiked your drinks? And you just let them get close to you. You need to be smart, Liv. I thought I taught you better."

Olivia tries to argue back, but Bradley intervenes, commanding her to let it go. She huffs in frustration and storms off, walking down the street, Amelia trailing behind her.

"But there's nothing wrong with us talking to a bunch of guys. It was harmless," Isla retorts.

"They had no business talking to you, Isla."

"Why? I mean, we're just—" I cut her off before she can finish that sentence. I'm done with hearing excuses. There's no chance we're just 'friends', and she can't be that blind to know or see how I feel.

"Don't," I growl, my voice sharp and commanding, "you dare finish that sentence."

As her words hang in the air, I'm hit with a wave of realisation. Earlier, I might have said we were 'friends' to ease any tension, to make things less awkward. But now, standing here, looking into her eyes, I know. I know I can't deny it anymore.

I've made a decision, one I've never made before. This woman in front of me, Isla—she's mine. Whether she likes it or not. And it's time I make that clear.

Harrison mutters a low, "Oh, shit."

"When you damn well know we are not *just* friends, Isla," I declare, my voice carrying a weight of intensity. She must understand. "I defended you because I care about you, Isla. Whether you'd like to admit it or not."

"No one touches what's mine," I grumble, my voice low, anger simmering beneath the surface. The thought of another guy putting his hands on Isla ignites a fierce protectiveness within me, a primal instinct to defend what's mine.

An audible gasp escapes her lips, her chest rising and falling rapidly. I can almost see the thoughts swirling in her head, the confusion, the realisation. It's a tumultuous storm, and I've just thrown a stone into the heart of it. As our voices escalate in the heated argument, the two security guards from the bar reappear, yelling out, "Oi, you lot need to get the fuck outta here!" The urgency in their tone is clear, and another one of them adds, "Now!"

Harrison and Michael, sensing the need to diffuse the situation, chime in, "Xav, let's go!"

I'm hearing their voices, but I can't tear my eyes away from Isla, waiting for something. Anything. At that moment, caught up in the tension, she looks at me for a second before blurting out, "I-I need to get home." She turns to Imogen, searching for support. "Imogen, you coming?"

It all happens so quickly, the guards pushing us further onto the street, Billy and his lowlife mates long gone. This isn't over. She can't just fucking leave now. I watch as the girls flag down a passing taxi and open the doors. Imogen says something to her quickly, placing a comforting hand on her arm. Isla glances back at me before disappearing into the taxi and vanishing down the street.

Fury boils inside me. There is no way I make a declaration like that for her to run away. She needs to stop running away. I'll be damned if I let her get away from me again. My emotions are a chaotic whirlwind—anger, frustration, and a deep, undeniable yearning. She needs to understand, needs to see that I'm not going to let her go that easily.

I stride forward, my steps purposeful, my mind set. Isla may have run this time, but she won't get far.

I won't let her.

34

Isla

The taxi drops Imogen off first, and even though she offers to stay, I assure her I'll be fine. As I step into my apartment, frustration still lingers from the night's events. I kick off my boots, dropping them by the door with a heavy thud, the echo of my annoyance.

Heading further into the apartment, I undress, shedding the layers that carry the remnants of a night gone awry. Wearing jeans and a frill off-the-shoulder top, the fabric falls away, leaving me with a sense of vulnerability, raw emotions simmering beneath the surface.

Xavier's confession tonight has sent shivers down my spine. In that moment, the unspoken tension between us surfaced, laying bare the hidden emotions that we had both tried to ignore. We've danced around the truth, claiming 'just friends'. Yet, hearing his raw admission then, I couldn't deny the undeniable connection that lingered between us. Fuck, fuck, fuck.

As the taxi sped away from the scene, I found myself doing what I'd become adept at—running away from my problems. It was a familiar pattern, one I'd repeated in the past, yet it seemed nothing had changed. Imogen sensed my unease, warning me before we got into the taxi, well more like questioning me if I really wanted to leave. I was too conflicted, scared of the emotions that suddenly overwhelmed me, so I left.

The mess I'm in now only tightens the knot of anxiety in my chest. I swallow repeatedly, trying to push down the bubble creeping up my throat. Here in my apartment, these feelings are still raw and swirling inside me, refusing to be ignored.

Grow up, Isla.

Breathe. Stop acting this way.

You'll be fine.

I'll be fine—but will I?

The overwhelming nausea, a physical manifestation of my anxiety, claws its way up my throat, threatening to suffocate me. I stumble to the bathroom, desperate to rid myself of the churning turmoil within. With a gut-wrenching heave, I empty the contents of tonight's doings into the toilet, gasping for air between retches. The acidic taste of bile lingers in my mouth, a bitter reminder of the chaos that has consumed me.

With a few deep breaths, I do my best to compose myself—wiping at my face with a wipe to rid it of all makeup, and brushing my teeth. Deciding a hot shower would feel amazing right now, I move toward it, turning on the hot water.

As I step in, the water cascading over me is a soothing balm to my frazzled nerves. The steam fills the air, cocooning me in a warm embrace, and I let out a long, slow breath, feeling the tension begin to melt away.

I towel off, the fabric rough yet reassuring against my skin, and prepare for bed, hoping that the familiar routine will bring some semblance of peace to my restless mind. Maybe some 'New Girl' or the latest episode of 'Bridgerton' will provide a temporary escape from the whirlwind of feelings I have for Xavier.

But deep down, I know I can't ignore these emotions any longer. I need to confront them head-on, like a woman. Like a *strong* woman. The thought both empowers and terrifies me. I'm done fighting against what I feel, but fuck am I scared of what this all might mean. I slip into my pyjamas and head inside to grab a bottle of water. As I'm about to grab it from the kitchen, the sudden sound of a car pulling up and a door slamming outside catches my attention. My curiosity piqued, I move towards the window overlooking the front courtyard.

A jolt of surprise courses through me as I spot Xavier's ute parked outside. Frozen in place, I watch as he makes his way toward the entrance. *What will I say to him, and what does he have to say?*

With a furrowed brow, I wait, the unexpected visit sparking a mix of apprehension and anticipation. Nervously, I fidget while standing in the middle of my living room, my eyes flicking between the door and the window overlooking the courtyard. Just as the thought of an impending knock crosses my mind, a heavy rapping echoes through the silence.

I take a deep breath, steeling myself, and approach the door. Hesitating for a second, I find myself staring at it, uncertainty gripping me.

"Open the door, Isla. I'm not leaving until you do," Xavier's voice murmurs from outside, breaking through the quiet tension. I exhale a shaky breath, my nerves always seeming to get the best of me around him. It's a feeling I still have grasped yet. With a determined exhale, I reach for the doorknob and slowly open the door, meeting his gaze.

"Thought you could just run away from me, huh?" Xavier growls, his tone rough as he steps into my apartment, swiftly closing the distance between us. Instinctively, I take a few steps back, but he continues forward, matching my movements until I'm backed up against the kitchen island.

"Xavier, you drank tonight. You shouldn't have driven," I express my worry, the concern evident in my tone. However, he only glares down at me, his imposing presence sending goosebumps across my skin.

"I got here in one piece, didn't I?" he retorts, his words laced with defiance. The tension between us thickens.

"I wasn't done talking to you," Xavier growls, his words carrying a weight that leaves me frozen, too stunned to speak.

"I-I—," I stammer, attempting to form a coherent sentence, but Xavier presses further, his tone intimidating.

"I'm not going to apologise for my actions tonight—that dick deserved it," he declares, his gaze unwavering. I glance up at his face, noticing a slit in his eyebrow with dried blood around the wound from the punch. I raise my hand slowly, softly running my fingers over his injured brow. His eyes remain locked on mine, intense.

"I should ap-apologise for mine," I say softly, my words stuttering with nervousness. I struggle to find the right words.

"It's just... I didn't want you doing anything stupid, f-for nothing," I admit, the concern evident in my voice.

He responds firmly, "It wasn't for nothing. No one touches what's mine." His intense gaze holds mine, and I read between the lines. *'Mine'*—the word echoes in my mind again, and I'm unsure how to process it. This intense attraction is new, and it makes me nervous. I don't respond, and Xavier presses further.

"You have five seconds to tell me to leave—*five* seconds, Isla. Before I take you into your room and fuck you until you're screaming out my name." His countdown begins, and my breath hitches.

"Five," he starts, his eyes flicking between mine.

"Four," his gaze drops to my mouth.

"Three," his hands grip my waist, pulling me towards him.

"Two," anticipation builds, and a shiver runs down my body.

"Last chance, Isla," he growls.

"One," and before I can respond, he slams his lips to mine.

In an instant, he lifts me effortlessly and carries me to my bedroom, kicking the door open, and throws me onto the bed. The room feels cramped with our bodies, his towering frame heightening the intensity. I sit up on the bed as Xavier stands at the edge, his eyes unwavering.

"Take your clothes off, Isla," he commands, his voice low and demanding. Under his intense, watchful gaze, I comply. I lift my shirt up and over my head, baring myself in front of him. At this point, I don't even care about the vulnerability—it's as if something has shifted within me. I'm left in my G-string, and I wait for him to say something.

"Everything, *off*," he growls, his tone brooking no argument. The air in the room thickens as I remove the rest of my clothes, leaving me entirely naked in front of him.

"Come here," he beckons, and I slide over to him on the bed.

"Take my belt off. Unzip my jeans," he commands. Aroused and intrigued, I comply. His commanding presence, something I've seen with others, takes on a different, more intimate tone in this situation. It's everything I expected and *more*.

As I undo his belt and jeans, I realise the power dynamics at play turn me on. There's a certain thrill in being told what to do, a delicious surrender to the moment that heightens the intensity between us.

He gestures for me to pull his pants down over his ass. As I do this, he grabs the back of his shirt behind his head and pulls it off, revealing his immaculate bare chest and those incredible tattoos on his arm. The play of shadows accentuates the contours of his body, and the sight is mesmerising. As I pull his jeans and briefs down, his cock springs free, bobbing in front of me—incredibly hard and leaking with precum. I pump it a few times softly, and a growl resonates deep within his chest.

"Say it, Isla," he demands.

"W-what? Say what?" I whisper.

"Say you're mine. I want to hear you say it—because this," he gestures to himself, "all of me, is yours." *Fuck me.*

It's been a few weeks of dancing around this so-called 'friendship' of ours, and finally, we have something to move forward with. I'm nervous—the memory of my last relationship still haunts me, but deep down, I know Xavier is nothing like my ex—nothing alike *indeed*. Goosebumps creep all over my skin.

"I want you. I-I'm yours," I whisper, locking eyes with him. He growls and pushes me back onto the bed before stepping out of his pants. He reaches for a condom from his wallet in his back pocket, but unease stirs within me, a desire for more. I don't want him to wear a condom—I want to feel all of him.

"Wait—," I say, placing a hand on his stomach. "I–I, we don't need the condom," I murmur, and he frowns, looking at me confused.

"What?"

"I want to feel *all* of you—*bare*. I'm on the pill," I admit as I wait for his reaction.

Xavier's eyes narrow at my words, a mix of surprise and intensity crossing his face.

"You're on the pill?" he repeats, his voice low and husky.

I nod. "No condom. I want to feel you—I want to feel you, come inside me," a slight blush stains my cheeks. His fingers tighten around the condom in his hand, and with a deliberative move, he tosses it to the ground.

"So fucking dirty," is the last thing he says before, with a smirk, he grabs me by my jaw and captures my mouth, his tongue moving my lips. As I part my lips, his taste immediately infiltrates my senses—that woodsy scent, mixed with mint from his gum. I can't get enough.

Of him.

His hands are everywhere, pushing me back, so I'm now laying on the bed, his hands roam all over my body, caressing with a firm touch. Over my collarbone, my breasts, my stomach and my thighs as he brings one up beside his body.

"Xavier," I moan and my hands slide into his hair tugging on it roughly, eliciting a groan from him as he continues to kiss me.

I grip the hair at his nape and pull to move his tongue off mine. "*Please*, fuck me."

He moves his hand down my body, swiping a finger through my folds. "Fuuck, you're always so ready and wet for me, baby." He groans.

"This pussy is *mine*," he says enunciates the word *mine* with a growl, and I just about explode from that. My body quivering, shaking, yearning for him. I need him inside me, like *now*. He senses my urgency as I hum and moan. Gripping his cock, he runs it up and down my folds a few times.

"Lift your thighs up, baby and spread them," he instructs. I lift my thighs up so they're resting against my stomach, spread open, wide.

He positions himself at my entrance, and I momentarily hold my breath, bracing myself for the burn. "You're going to feel so fucking good," he groans.

I know he isn't all the way in yet, just pushing forward slightly and retreating back out—but he is so big, his crown so wide, it feels like much more.

"I need you," I cry out. My nails find his hands, pressing down on my thighs, and I run them up his arms. "Please, Xav I—" I moan, drawing in a breath, despite everything feeling so tight. I don't even get my words out, because in an instant he slams into me, right to the hilt. I cry out, and groans rumble from deep within his chest.

I've never had sex without a condom, and this is just insane. So fucking incredible. I've never felt anything so smooth, no barrier between us, just the two of us. He moves in and out smoothly, and I whimper at the sensation of being full—so fucking full.

"*Isla*," he stammers, "this... feels... fucking incredible," his voice strained, low and husky.

I know. I feel it, too.

But with the way his hips move in and out of me, the way his hands grip my thighs, pushing me down further into the bed, the way he moves his hand to rub at my clit with his thumb—I'm rendered fucking speechless. I'm at a loss for words. Yeah, we've fucked around before, but this—I am never having sex with a condom. Ever. *Again.*

I can feel my body start to tremble, that familiar sensation building up deep in my core, sending chills throughout my body. But then it fades.

Xavier pulls out of me abruptly. "On all fours, now," he growls, and grabs me by my hips, twisting me so I'm resting on my elbows, my ass up in the air. His hand comes down on my ass, and a loud crack whips through the air, breaking the silence—apart from our heavy breathing.

I moan, loudly. He does it again, smacking the other cheek with the same ferocity. Gripping me by the hips, he positions himself at my entrance. "I'm going to fuck you *hard* now, Isla.

"Tell me you're ready," he says as he leans forward over my back and murmurs in my ear, "Don't hold back for me baby. I wanna hear you loud and clear, okay?"

"Yes, *yes.*" I whimper, and he doesn't hold back. In a second, he's slamming back into me, his thighs slapping against mine, and I drop face down onto my elbows.

"Such a good fucking girl," he groans, and the fullness causes my orgasm to start building again. At this moment, my body doesn't even belong to me—it's all his.

Xavier falls into a more relentless pace, fucking me so hard, my body jolts forward with each movement. His strokes are deep. Relentless. I push back against him with each thrust, and we both groan.

"I'm almost there, Xav," I manage as I arch my back more, my tits grazing the bed from the momentum, adding in extra friction that sends tingles down to my core.

"Yes," he groans. "Come all over my cock, Isla." He grabs hold of my hair, twisting it in his hold, pulling my head back. He leans forward over me, capturing my lips, plunging his tongue into my mouth, and I whimper with need.

I feel it, then. The intense waves radiating from where Xavier is driving into me. I can feel my pussy spasm, gripping him tighter like a vice, and when he slides his hand underneath me, his fingers grazing my clit, I explode. Chanting his name over and over as I come, his ferocious thrusts tearing me apart at the seams.

"Fuuuck," his voice is thick as he moans, and I continue to push against him—riding out the waves of my orgasm. "I'm going to come, *fuck.*"

"Yes, Xav. Come inside me," I moan, and his movements never falter. I don't know how, but his thrusts become harder—his body slapping against mine as he fucks me so hard. Xavier lets out a deep growl as he comes, instantly filling me up inside. I feel a gush of warmth spreading within me, and his warm cum starts to leak down my thighs. Xavier's movements become slower, his breathing turns deeper as he tries to regain his composure.

He leans forward, pressing kisses at the nape of my neck, trailing them down my spine. I feel complete, whole. In this moment, one thing is crystal clear—I don't want whatever this is between us to end.

And later that night, after many rounds of intense orgasms leaving me quivering and limp, there is an undeniable connection that's lit a fire within me.

And I'm not ready to let it burn out.

35

"Alright, folks! Who's ready for a BBQ feast?" Harrison's voice booms with infectious enthusiasm, a twinkle in his eye as he brandishes a pair of tongs. "Let's turn this place into a carnivore's paradise!"

Michael can't help but let out a dramatic groan, and I roll my eyes at Harrison, who's standing on the porch, clapping the tongs together like some barbecue maestro. The man's enthusiasm for grilling is unmatched.

Harrison and Michael, true to their word, have organised a barbecue at my farm. The lingering vibes from last night's chaotic events have given way to a more relaxed setting.

The familiar group from the bar is now gathered around a small bonfire near the back porch of my farmhouse. The time is around 5 pm, and the sun is gracefully making its descent, casting a warm glow on the surroundings. A gentle breeze has picked up, a common occurrence in the bush at this time. Days are scorching, but the evenings bring a welcome coolness.

I find myself at the barbecue with Harrison and Michael, tending to the grill and enjoying the laid-back atmosphere. The rest of the gang—Bradley, Liv, Imogen, and Isla—along with my mum, are settled around the bonfire. Laughter and chatter fill the air as everyone unwinds and enjoys the camaraderie.

About twenty minutes later, the aroma of the freshly grilled and smoked meats wafts through the air, signalling that the feast is ready. Harrison, ever the showman, calls everyone to gather around the outdoor table.

The table is laden with an assortment of meats, from perfectly grilled burgers to succulent smoked ribs. Side dishes and condiments complete the spread. We all take our seats, and a comfortable silence settles over the group as we dig into the delicious offerings.

Isla, in the midst of the festivities, moves to sit beside me. With a wink, I pull out the chair for her, a small gesture that doesn't go unnoticed. My mum catches the exchange and shoots me a warm, knowing smile.

As the night unfolds, Bradley stands up, raising his glass high for a toast.

"Here's to Xavier, the old man of the hour! Happy birthday, mate!" The sentiment is met with a chorus of cheers, glasses clinking together in celebration.

Olivia, always the lively one, chimes in with her trademark enthusiasm. "And here's to the guy who's officially one year closer to needing reading glasses!" Her playful jest earns a round of laughter from the group. I roll my eyes but can't help but laugh.

The atmosphere is charged with camaraderie and warmth. The

bonfire crackles, casting dancing shadows on our faces as we continue to celebrate my birthday in the heart of the bush, surrounded by good friends and great food. Having Isla by my side makes it all the better, and I find myself grateful for her presence.

As the plates are cleared away, the women return, my mother leading the charge with a massive birthday cake in her hands, adorned with scattered lit candles on top. I can't help but roll my eyes at the sight. "Oh, c'mon, I said none of this shit," I groan.

"Now, now, Xavier. Don't be stupid—a birthday cake is a must," my mother retorts, and I can't deny the knowing grin on Isla's face. This is undoubtedly her doing. Her smiling face warms my centre, and I find myself appreciating the effort.

The rendition of 'Happy Birthday' begins, led by Isla, and the group joins in. I run my hands down my face, attempting to hide my embarrassment when Harrison starts the 'Hip hip, hooray' routine. Reluctantly, I blow out the candles upon their relentless prodding.

My mother hands me the cake-cutting knife, and I hesitate. Nevertheless, I take it because, let's be real, I can't say no to my mother. The knife touches the bottom of the cake, and Imogen seizes the opportunity to stir the pot.

"Ohhh, it touched the bottom! Quick, you need the nearest person," she announces, her eyes mischievous as they land on Isla, who's now blushing furiously.

Olivia joins in the teasing. "Awwww, Xav, you need to kiss a *girl*, and it ain't gonna be Mumma this time, so..." This earns a laugh from the group.

Shaking my head, I rise from my chair, facing Isla. The group starts chanting, "Kiss, kiss, kiss," and I can't help but search Isla's eyes for permission. She smiles, biting her lip, blushing, and nods, granting me all the permission I need—so I grab her chin, playfully planting a kiss on her cheek.

"There you go. Happy?"

"OH C'MON!" Imogen prods further.

"You can do better than that, mate," Harrison shouts. I look at Isla, and she smiles, biting her lip as she blushes and nods once again.

This time, I don't hold back—not caring that we have an audience. Fuck it. She's mine and I want everyone to know it. I grab her face with both hands and plant a kiss on her lips. Instinctively, her hands go to grip my arms as I deepen the kiss, arousal flooding straight down to my cock.

An "Awwww" emanates from my mother.

"Alright, that's enough now. We said one kiss, not eat each other's faces," Olivia feigns disgust, and I break the kiss, Isla now giggling, turning her face away.

"Alright, happy now?" I tease, and the group chants a resounding, "Yes."

Later that night, my father comes home. Wearing an easy smile, he strolls over, and his hand lands on my shoulder in a familiar, friendly gesture. "Happy birthday, you old dog," he quips, the teasing twinkle in his eyes mirroring the glow of the bonfire.

"Relax, I'm only thirty-one. You're the old dog," I tease, and he laughs. The rest of the group has shifted back to the bonfire, leaving a bit of distance. An old gazebo adorned with flowers, meticulously kept by my mother over the years—'*It makes the perfect romantic spot*'—she'd always say.

Coincidentally, the girls settle inside the gazebo, surrounded by fairy lights Olivia put up this afternoon. Amelia had arrived just after we cut the cake, apologising for being late due to work drama. As I stand against the railing of our porch, my attention is drawn to Isla as she sits with the girls, and my father breaks the silence.

"So, you and the Thompson girl, uh?" he says with a bit of disdain in his voice, a subtle disapproval lingering.

"Isla, her name is Isla, Dad," I correct him, defending her with a touch of irritation.

He raises an eyebrow, his tone revealing an unspoken history. "Isla. Right. I just hope you know what you're doing, you know, before it becomes serious."

I glance at him. "Well, I think it's a little too late for that."

Dad sighs, the lines on his weathered face deepening. "Xavier, I just don't want you getting involved in something messy. Relationships come with their own baggage, and some are heavier than others."

He huffs, a disapproving tone lingering. The unease settles in my stomach. I want my father to be happy for me, to let go of the old grudges he holds against Isla's father.

"Dad, you know Isla's dad isn't doing well," I say, hoping to evoke some understanding.

My father waves his hand dismissively, "Those people and their problems. You don't need that, Xavier."

I sigh, frustrated with his unyielding stance. "Dad, Isla is nothing like her father. You need to get over it," I say, my tone carrying a mix of irritation and pleas.

"For now, I'll tolerate it because of your mother. She's been ramblin' non-stop about the two of you, and I can't get'er to stop," he admits, his voice trailing off.

With a shake of his head, he saunters off back inside, leaving me to mull over the strained conversation. The knowledge that my mother supports us brings a small sense of relief, but I can't shake the frustration that lingers in the pit of my stomach.

"Good chat," I mutter to myself, a wry smile playing on my lips. Just as I turn to head back towards the lively bonfire, Harrison spots me from where he sits beside the fire with Bradley and Michael. He raises his hand and whistles sharply, beckoning me over with a sly grin.

I lock eyes with Isla and she shoots me a look—her lips curling into a playful smile. I can't help but smirk back. There's a twinge of defiance bubbling up inside me, echoing against the old man's warnings. Sure, relationships have their baggage, but I've never been one to shy away from a challenge. As I walk towards the guys, I feel a newfound determination settling in. Whatever hurdles come our way, I'm all in, and I'll stand by Isla's side, no matter what is thrown at us.

As I settle into a seat beside the crackling fire, the laughter of the girls under the gazebo drifts across the night air. The guys break into a random conversation, topics bouncing from work escapades to the latest sports highlights. Michael leans forward, eyes sparkling with the excitement of a recent sports event.

"Did you guys catch that NRL game the other night? Our team played like they were attempting to set a record for the most fumbles. It was painful to watch."

Harrison lets out an exaggerated groan, his frustration apparent. "Don't remind me. I swear, I almost launched the remote at the TV. How do they manage to mess up such a straightforward play?"

The collective disappointment over the game lingers. Harrison then glances over at Bradley, curiosity evident in his eyes. "Bradley, how's work going?"

Bradley, always stoic, responds with a clipped, "Good. No news here."

Harrison interjects, "You're a braver soul than I am, Bradley. I can't imagine dealing with all that you do. I'd rather stick to fixing cars. At least when something goes wrong, I don't have to read anyone their rights. I just tell them their transmission's fucked, and that's it."

Bradley smirks, leaning back slightly. "We're not in America—we don't read their rights out. You just tell them why they're under arrest."

Michael shakes his head, a playful exasperation in his expression. "You're an idiot, I swear. Sometimes I forget that you're the older one." We burst into laughter, but not Harrison, who in mock offence, just sticks the finger up at his brother.

My gaze lingers back on Isla, and I can't help but admire her from afar. I've got it bad. Bradley nudges me, bringing me back to the present as my eyes keep gravitating toward Isla.

"You, uh, planning on staring a hole through Isla or what?" he teases, a mischievous glint in his eyes that doesn't go unnoticed by the others. I roll my eyes at him.

There's a brief pause, and then, almost nonchalantly, I find myself saying, "I think I'm falling for her." The words hang in the air, blending with the crackling of the fire.

"Seriously?" Bradley asks, raising an eyebrow.

I nod, my tone casual despite the weight of the admission. "Yeah, seriously. It's just—I don't know, man…" my voice trails off.

"About time you admitted it," Michael chimes in.

Harrison, taking a sip of his drink, spits it out dramatically, choking and sputtering. Michael just laughs. I shoot them both a glare, the vulnerability I've just laid bare now floating in the air.

Smirking, Michael adds, "As if we didn't already know that with the way you gawk at her all the time, and that *kiss* before—c'mon man."

"Wait, you're going to have to repeat that—I think my brain just shat itself," Harrison exclaims, with amusement written all over his face.

I roll my eyes again. "Oh, fuck off. You're the two idiots that always say I need to open up more. I'm not repeating myself."

The guys exchange glances, a mix of surprise and amusement on their faces. Bradley wears a smirk, and Michael raises an eyebrow, clearly enjoying the revelation. Harrison, still recovering from his dramatic sip, grins widely.

Before any of them can say more, the laughter of the girls under the gazebo catches our attention. Isla, Olivia, and Amelia start making their way over to us, their curiosity evident. Isla's eyes meet mine, a playful glint in them, as if she senses something has transpired during our absence.

As the girls join us, Isla takes a seat beside me, her presence comforting. On the other side, Amelia and Olivia settle down on either side of Bradley, who looks pleasantly surprised by the turn of events. Imogen, however, seems to be left without a seat.

Harrison, always ready with a quip, takes the opportunity to tease her. "You can sit on my lap, sugar. It's nice and toasty from the fire." We all share a laugh, anticipating Imogen's response.

Imogen glares at Harrison, not amused. Bradley, being the gentleman, stands up, ready to offer his seat. But before he can say anything, I watch as Imogen holds up her hand, "It's okay, thank you," and boldly plonks herself right onto Harrison's lap. I can't help but smirk at her boldness, finding amusement in the situation.

She turns to look behind and issues a playful threat, "If you put your hands on me, I'll elbow you in the face. Got it?"

Harrison smirks before nodding. "Yes, ma'am."

Leaning back in my seat, Buddy contentedly sitting at my feet, I listen silently as the others share about their day.

Harrison, taking a swig of his drink, grins. "Same old, same old at the shop. Just another day of dodging wrenches and pretending to know what I'm doing."

Amelia smiles, her eyes lighting up. "Today with kindy, we had finger painting. Let me tell you, it's both adorable *and* chaotic. I left with a bloody rainbow on my face. I had to go home and scrub my face," she huffs with a smile.

"How's work at the clinic going, Isla?" Amelia asks.

Isla takes a sip of her drink before responding. "Slow, but there's never a dull moment with our two fur babies, Henry and Luna," she says with a smile. I can't help but smile at her.

Olivia then chimes in, "Aww, you *have* to tell us more about them."

Isla smiles, her eyes lighting up. "Henry, our little Italian Greyhound, is a bundle of fun and curiosity." She chuckles, fondness evident in her voice. "Always getting into some mischief, that one. Poor thing can't move as much as he'd probably like, though—he has a bad hip.

"And Luna, she's our most recent addition—an Australian Kelpie—she's a bit more timid, still getting her bearings around other people." Isla pauses, her expression softening at the memory. "I found her stranded on the side of the road."

Olivia's eyes widen. "Stop, omg. What happened?"

"I have no idea. She was just there, looking so helpless and starved. I couldn't leave her there, so I brought her in."

Amelia tilts her head, concerned. "Have you found homes for them yet?"

Isla shakes her head, frustration evident in her expression. "No, and that's the odd part. We've been trying, but it seems like no one wants to adopt them. It breaks my heart."

As Isla shares the story, I can't help but feel a twinge of remorse for the dogs. Animals have always held a special place in my heart, and the thought of them not having a home stirs something inside me, making me feel uneasy.

"Hopefully someone adopts the little babies soon," Amelia says, with hope in her eyes. Isla nods in agreement. The group continues their conversations, laughter blending with the warm night air. My gaze never strays far from Isla, arousal flooding deep down as I take her in. I'll never get tired of the sight of her—she's fucking beautiful, so beautiful. I just want to keep her all to myself—for the rest of my life.

She senses my gaze and subtly nods toward the direction behind us, where the farmhouse stands with the barn just beside it. I get the message; she wants to be alone, and so do I. I have to kiss her. The realisation makes me feel like some pathetic simp—and I've never been one to cling to another, but I can't deny the craving for her touch.

Isla announces the need to head inside to the bathroom. I take the welcomed invitation and declare, "I'll walk you."

To my left, Michael mutters, "Bathroom my ass," and the rest of the group laughs. I shoot him a glare as both Isla and I rise.

I walk her toward the house, stealing a glance back to make sure the group isn't watching. They've resumed their conversations, oblivious to our departure. My hand finds hers, and I pull her toward the barn. Thankfully, the door is already open. The anticipation builds with every step, the desire to be alone with her overpowering any other thought.

As I pull Isla into the barn, the atmosphere thick with anticipation, she doesn't have a chance to say anything. I grab her, pulling her toward me with an urgency that surprises even me. Without hesitation, I crush my lips onto hers. She whimpers at the sudden contact, but it's not a protest. It's a shared desire, an unspoken agreement. The world outside the barn seems to fade away as we lose ourselves in the heat of the moment. Every touch, every kiss, is an affirmation of the craving we've both been feeling.

Her tongue melds with mine as I deepen the kiss. I slide my hands down to her delectable ass, and grip it hard, pulling her up against me so she's standing on her tippy toes. I don't know how long we stand there kissing, but it feels as if time has frozen and it's just her and I. Lost in a battle between tongues, lips and groans. I break the kiss, releasing my firm hold on her as I murmur, "Fuck, I've been dying to kiss you since we cut my cake. I've fucking craved it."

She groans, a blush forming on her face. "Me, too," she murmurs back, looking up at me as she continues, "But I wanted to do this more."

She cups my bulge, now evident through my jeans, and before I can say anything, she's dropping to her knees in front of me, unbuckling my pants. *Fuuuck.*

I'm now on my knees in front of Xavier, a surge of raw hunger in my eyes as I unbuckle his pants. The desire to give him something special for his birthday has been on my mind since I got here. Every touch, every move, is an embodiment of the longing that's been building between us.

Glancing up at him, a deep rumble escapes his chest as he growls. He caresses my cheek, his touch lingering on my jaw before his thumb swipes over my lip.

"Fuck, baby. You, on your knees, for me. It's a sight I'll never fucking get over," he murmurs low, his husky voice sending tingles down to my core. I shudder as I reach inside his briefs and pull his cock out. He's so hard and just so velvety soft at the same time. He's so big that I can't wrap my fingers entirely around his girth. I'll never tire at the sight of him, so big—just all *man*.

I squeeze him in my first, applying the pressure that I know he loves as I move my hand up and down his shaft. I pump him from tip to base before leaning forward to take him into my mouth entirely—there's no hesitation now, no uncertainty or timidity. I suck on his tip, lapping at the precum seeping out of him and he groans—losing his hands in my hair as he grips my scalp.

There is nothing that can compare to how Xavier looks right now. His head is tilted back, the thick column of neck exposed, his Adam's apple bobbing as he swallows.

I take him into the back of my throat and suck hard, creating a suction with my mouth—just how I know he likes it. It's moments like this that I praise myself for not having a gag reflex.

"Fuck yes, princess. Deepthroat my cock, just like that," he growls.

I continue to bob my head, taking him all the way to the back of my throat before moving back to the tip, pulling my mouth free—a string of saliva connecting us. It's so fucking dirty, erotic, and unbelievably sexy.

"Fuuuck... don't think I'm gonna last long," his grip in my hair tightens. "You take my cock so well down that pretty little mouth." I whimper at his dirty words, them only spurring me on.

I hum around his cock, not letting myself up for air as I move quickly, now working him with both my hands pumping him and as I suck. I alternate between twisting my hand around him whilst sucking on his tip before deep throating him. He has both hands in my hair now, his breathing becoming ragged, more shallow.

"Fuuuck, *fuck*," he groans, his voice strained. "I'm coming, Isla, baby," and I whimper, taking him to the back of my throat as he shoots his load down my throat—his salty taste warm in my mouth.

Xavier's movements falter and his grip on my hair loosens, but I continue my relentless suction—wanting to taste every last drop of his come in my mouth.

"Hmmm," he hums, and once I'm sure I've sucked him dry, I slowly release his cock from my mouth, wiping my mouth of any saliva that dribbled down. He grabs me by my shoulder and pulls me up towards him abruptly, burying his hands at my nape, and slams his mouth to mine, tasting the remnants of himself on my tongue. He moans into the kiss, and I melt into his body, holding on.

Xavier breaks the kiss, looking down at me attentively. His eyes are hooded with lust as he rests his forehead on mine, whispering, "That was... fucking amazing. You amaze me every time, Isla."

He raises his head, his hand caressing my cheek before cupping my jaw. "You're something else, Isla Thompson," he murmurs, and I lean into his touch, smiling. In the silence of the barn, animals shuffling quietly in the background, he declares, "Mine," with a growl.

Xavier leans down, kissing me one more time before we head back out into the night to join the others.

36

Isla

As I visit my father early in the morning, Molly has returned to help out at the clinic, giving me a bit of time before I need to be at work. Stepping into the familiar surroundings of my childhood home, a sense of both nostalgia and apprehension washes over me.

Dad is having an off day again, his demeanour mirroring the stormy clouds outside. Despite our recent interactions, which have been somewhat better compared to the past, there's a heaviness in the air as I approach him. The tension is palpable, a reminder of the delicate balance we've been trying to strike in rebuilding our relationship.

This morning is another one of those days where Dad seems to lose his grip on reality. It starts with him misplacing the TV remote, a seemingly trivial incident that spirals into an anger meltdown. I have to remain calm, my patience tested as we search the house for the elusive remote. It turns out to be in one of the kitchen cupboards, and Dad curses loudly, throwing out every expletive under the sun in frustration. Honestly, I have no idea how it ended up there, but I have to keep my composure.

As we sit in the living room, he seems to have calmed down after the remote incident, and we carry on with the morning routine. However, a shift occurs when he slips back into an old memory, speaking of my mother as if she were still alive. In his confused state, he asks about my exams, and I stand there, trying to decipher which exams he means. I play along, saying, "Good, Dad. Stressful, but good."

"Well, gotta study hard if you wanna go to that big school, whaddya call it again?" he mutters, and I softly reply, "Uni." My heart aches at how surreal the conversation sounds.

He then starts talking about my mother, mentioning how she is out again, probably getting groceries. The lines between past and present blur, and I find myself navigating the delicate balance between comforting him in his confusion and grappling with the reality that she is no longer here. The weight of these moments hangs heavy in the air, a reminder of the fragility of Dad's memories and the complexity of our relationship.

As Dad continues to speak, the emptiness in my chest deepens, and I can't help but long for a time when he was the sturdy anchor of our family. The weight of his reality, slipping away like grains of sand, settles heavily on my shoulders. I want him to get better, to break free from the chains of this merciless disease, but deep down, I know there's no going back.

Worry for him is a constant companion, a shadow that looms over my every interaction with him. I hope for good days, always, but I've witnessed the ravages of this disease before, seen how it consumed my nanna and pop. In the end, their bodies couldn't cope, their brains couldn't function, and they left with a sense of peace. They were no longer suffering.

As these thoughts swirl in my mind, tears well up in my eyes. I shake my head, swallowing down the lump in my throat, refusing to let the tears spill over. Standing from the kitchen table, I muster a shaky smile and ask him if I can go out and pick some wildflowers and daisies.

His eyes light up, and he nods enthusiastically. "'Course... yes. Ya know, they're your mumma's favourites."

I nod, the weight of the moment pressing down on me. "Yeah, I'm going to pick a few to take to her in town. I think she'll like the surprise."

Dad's response is a mixture of joy and longing. "Oh, yes, she'd love that. Tell 'er she needs to hurry up and come home. I'm waiting on 'er apple pie."

Tears threaten to spill again as I choke on my words. "I-I'll do my best, Dad," I say, my voice breaking slightly. I head out to pick the flowers, a bittersweet task that brings a mix of comfort and sorrow.

When I drive away, leaving my father standing on the front porch, waving with a smile, the ache in my heart deepens.

I pull up outside Wattle Creek cemetery, a familiar ache burning through my chest. Sitting in the car, I take a few deep breaths. While driving, my phone buzzed a few times, and a quick glance revealed two unopened messages from Xavier. My heart warms at the sight. He's been texting me a lot lately, something I've grown accustomed to but still find surreal. There are moments when I pinch myself, unable to believe that I'm actually here, with Xavier, and as he's declared before, he belongs to me. The fact that we've been intimate still hasn't quite sunk in.

It's been a while since I've come here. After Mum passed away, I used to visit every weekend, never missing a Sunday. Dad would occasionally join me, but that didn't last, especially not with me. He struggled with Mum's death, turning to alcohol and aggression. I couldn't bear to be near that anymore, so I applied to university. After being accepted, I packed up and left small-town life behind. Now that I'm back, it feels like the missing pieces I've lived with my whole life are finally starting to come together, with Xavier at the centre of it all.

I've visited Mum a few times since my return, but I regret to admit that I've neglected to come more often. Guilt eats away at my heart as I turn off the car, taking a few deep breaths before stepping out. Walking up to Mum's plot, a wave of nausea and deep sorrow washes over me. The cemetery feels heavy with memories, each step echoing the ache in my chest.

Approaching Mum's grave, tears well up in my eyes. Surprisingly, my anxiety hasn't been as overwhelming since moving back home, especially compared to the city and the dark days with Justin. Panic attacks were a daily norm then. He scolded me for taking anti-anxiety medication, claiming it would make me worse, insisting I just needed to get over it. I can't help but think, *I fucking hate him.*

Swallowing down the bubble forming in my throat and resisting the nausea threatening to resurface, I take a few deep breaths, blinking away the tears. Focusing on the task at hand, I fit wildflowers and daisies into each vase beside Mum's grave. Kissing the top of the tombstone, I whisper, "Hey, Mumma," before taking a seat in front.

Crossing my legs, I take in the surroundings, surrounded by thousands of graves, each holding the memories of loved ones no longer here. I apologise first, my hand resting on the tombstone, tears welling up again.

"I'm sorry for not coming around more often," I murmur, my voice choked with emotion.

Nervousness creeps up as I speak to Mum, recounting how things are going at the clinic. I share stories about the little furry animals I've looked after, imagining her delight at seeing them. Tears roll down my face as I speak, a mixture of sorrow and longing woven into each word.

"I miss you so much, Mum," I choke. "The clinic is going well, and I wish you could see the animals. You would have loved them," I say, my voice trembling. "I... I still struggle, you know? But being back home has brought some peace."

"And Xavier—he's... he's been a light in this darkness. I can't help but feel like things just might be coming together, but it hurts that you're not here to see it." I sigh. "Oh, Mum, I wish you could meet him now. He's so... just so different. Not what I expected at all," my voice falters, breaking.

"I think Dad is still trying to wrap his head around it, but, Mum, he's just all man—protective and so caring. I feel like you would have liked him."

A heavy silence hangs in the air, the weight of my emotions palpable as I continue our one-sided conversation. Wiping away tears with the back of my hand, I take a shaky breath and lower my gaze to the ground.

"I've missed you so much, especially during those dark days in the city. Life was overwhelming, and I felt so lost. Xavier's been a constant support." Leaning closer to the tombstone, as if sharing a secret, I add, "He makes me feel safe, in a way I never thought possible."

With a sigh, I continue to update Mum on the intricacies of my life, the pain of her absence mingling with the hope that she can somehow hear my words from wherever she is.

As I sit before Mum's tombstone, tears stream down my face, and my voice trembles with emotion. "Dad," I sigh. "*Argh*, he's sick, Mum. Like Nan and Pop. It's all my *fault*—I should never have left."

A sob breaks free, and I continue to cry, allowing the pain I've kept bottled up to spill out. The cemetery echoes with my cries, a silent testament to the weight on my shoulders.

"He's been forgetting, Mum, thinking that you're still alive," I confess, my voice choking with grief.

"He has meltdowns, anger bursts. I can't cope, Mum. I'm trying my best to be there for him, comfort him the moments when he needs it, but I—" I sigh heavily. "What should I do?"

The air remains silent, offering no answers to my desperate questions. I feel a deep sense of helplessness, my heart aching for my father and the struggles he faces.

"I just need help," I cry harder, the weight of my emotions pouring out like a flood.

"I don't know how to handle this. I'm stuck, and it feels like everything is falling apart. I wish you were here, Mum. I need your guidance more than ever."

As I sit in the silent embrace of the graveyard, my tears gradually subside, leaving behind a dull ache in my chest. The wind rustles the leaves on the nearby trees, offering a soft, comforting hum that seems to echo the quiet solace I seek.

After a while, I glance at the time on my phone and realise that I should probably head off. The responsibilities of daily life call, and the clinic awaits. Work is a necessary distraction, a way to temporarily escape the heavy burdens that weigh on my shoulders. I stand up, brushing off the dirt from my jeans, and take one last look at Mum's tombstone.

"I'll be back soon, Mum," I whisper, my voice carrying a mix of determination and sadness. "I promise."

Turning away, I walk back to my car, the memories of our conversation lingering in the air. The drive to the clinic is quiet, the weight of my thoughts accompanied only by the rhythmic hum of my car's engine.

As I pull into the clinic's parking lot, I take a deep breath, preparing to face the challenges that lie ahead. With each step toward the entrance, I carry the memories of Mum and the weight of my father's struggles.

Work becomes a refuge, a place where I can momentarily escape the complexities of life. The routine tasks at the clinic provide a sense of normalcy, a temporary respite from the emotional storm brewing within.

Deep down, I know that I'll be back at the cemetery, seeking solace and sharing my thoughts with Mum. Until then, life must go on, and I embrace the challenges that await me at the clinic.

After a busy day at the animal hospital, where the tasks ranged from treating adorable puppies to comforting distressed pet owners, I found myself mentally drained. The clinic had been bustling with activity, but my mind kept drifting to the lingering worries about Dad and the challenges he faced with his deteriorating health.

During the afternoon, Xavier's calls interrupted the steady rhythm of my day. I answered reluctantly, not in the mood for conversation. Despite his persistence, I couldn't find the energy to engage, offering only short and clipped responses. He sensed my sombre mood but didn't press further, respecting my need for space.

As evening settles in, Xavier has invited himself over, declaring his intention to spend the night at my place. Now, we sit on the couch, wrapped in the comfort of each other's presence. An episode of 'New Girl' plays on the screen, providing a distraction from the weighty thoughts that linger in the corners of my mind.

Xavier, ever curious and eager, begins asking questions about the show. "So... who's your favourite character?" he inquires, attempting to draw me into a more lighthearted conversation. I respond with brief replies, my mind unable to fully engage in the banter.

Sensing my detachment, Xavier turns to look at me, his concern evident in his gaze.

"Hey, what's up with you? What's wrong?" he asks, his brows now furrowed and his voice laced with concern—yet gentle and reassuring. I hesitate, the words caught in my throat. His persistence nudges me to open up.

"It's just... Dad. His health isn't getting any better, and I don't know how to handle it. I feel so helpless," I sigh. "I–he just needs to see a doctor, badly—" I mutter as I shake my head. "That's a battle I just know I won't win."

Xavier listens attentively, his presence a comforting anchor. He reaches over, gently squeezing my hand as a silent gesture of understanding.

"I'm sorry, baby, that you're going through this," he says softly, his rugged features softening in empathy.

"I visited Mum this morning," I continue. "I just needed to talk to her, you know?" I whisper, and he nods, murmuring, "Of course."

"It's been a while since I've been there, and I wanted to share everything that's been happening. But, seeing Dad struggle and then missing Mum—it's a lot to handle."

Xavier continues to nod, his eyes filled with a mixture of compassion and concern.

"I've said this before, but can't even imagine how tough this must be for you. But you're not alone in this, Isla. I'm here for you—whatever you need—I'm not going anywhere," he declares. We just sit here in comfortable silence, 'New Girl' playing in the background. I turn to look at Xavier, my eyes searching his face for answers.

"Xavier?" I ask shyly.

"Yes, love?" He looks down at me with a smirk.

"Can you tell me what exactly happened between my dad and yours? I-I just need to understand what's going on." The concern in my voice is evident as I seek clarity on the complex situation.

There's a brief silence before Xavier takes a deep breath, his eyes meeting mine. "I didn't know about all of this until I asked my mum," he admits, his gaze momentarily shifts away, his expression troubled.

"Apparently, it's about some jobs my dad asked yours to do," he continues, his tone grave.

"But—" he sighs. "Well, they were left unfinished. There's something about your dad owing money, but trust me, my old man will get over it, eventually." I shake my head, determined to make a difference.

"Please, Xavier, just tell me how much he owes. I want to help."

"It doesn't matter, Isla. I'll sort it out, trust me," he insists, avoiding the specifics.

"Xavier, please," I press, my voice tinged with desperation. "I just need to know."

Reluctantly, he reveals the amount. "About two grand." *Shit.* I sigh, shaking my head slowly. *Fucking hell, Dad.*

Without another word, I abruptly stand, telling Xavier I'm grabbing something from my room. I leave him on the couch, heading into my room. I open my wardrobe and retrieve the wad of cash I'd been saving over the years. The bundled notes now carry the weight of my determination to help my father.

With two grand in hand, I return to the living room, where Xavier waits with his arm outstretched. The room feels heavy with unspoken words, and I stand in front of Xavier and he looks up at me curiously. I hand over the money to Xavier.

"Take it. Consider it my way of helping, of making things right."

Xavier's gaze drops to the bundled cash in my hand, and his expression shifts from disbelief to anger. His brows furrow, and a tense silence settles in the room.

"What the hell, Isla?" His voice is sharp, carrying a mix of frustration and concern. "I'm not taking your money. This is between our fathers, not us."

"I know, Xav, I know... but please, just give this to your father. It might help ease the situation a bit," I plead, my eyes reflecting my earnest desire to assist.

Xavier's frustration intensifies, and he becomes visibly upset. "Isla, you shouldn't fucking have to give my dad money. He's an old man. It's been years now—we're not worried about the money, baby. It's my father. The old bastard just can't seem to let grudges go."

"I understand that, but I can't sit idly by, Xav. Let me help in my own way," I persist, my determination unwavering.

Xavier's frustration is palpable, and his voice sharpens further. "Isla, you shouldn't have to be involved in this."

"But you don't understand, I am. It's *my* father, Xavier. I just want his fucking approval. I want him to be okay with everything."

"This is about approval? For what?... Us?" he questions with furrowed brows. "Who gives a fuck what they think? What's between us is exactly that, Isla—between me and you. Nobody fucking else," he grumbles.

I shake my head, releasing a breath. "I want to make things a little easier, not just for my dad, but for us, too, Xav," I reply, my words tense and clipped. "It's not just about the money."

He runs a hand through his hair, visibly agitated. "This isn't the solution, Isla. I need to figure this out without dragging you into it. Just let me deal with my father."

The tension from our argument lingers in the air as we remain locked in a silent standoff. Suddenly, my phone rings on the coffee table, breaking the quiet tension. We both turn to look at my phone—it's a number I don't recognise. Frowning, I pick up my phone.

"Answer it," Xavier says in the silence, despite the phone ringing. I hesitate, but I decide to answer it, *unaware of the impending catastrophes that lie ahead.*

The mood in the room undergoes an abrupt shift, the air thick with tension and angst, as I lift the phone to my ear and cautiously say, "Hello."

The voice on the other end introduces themselves, and a chill runs down my spine. Xavier instantly stands up, his expression etched with concern. He bombards me with questions, but I'm not paying attention—I'm frozen, hanging on every word from the call.

The voice on the other end, a nurse from Wattle Creek Hospital, delivers the devastating news. *My father has been in a car accident and was rushed to the hospital.* The details blur as panic seizes me, my breathing becoming erratic.

"Your father is in critical condition, ma'am. We advise you to come in as soon as possible." The phone slips from my trembling hand, clattering to the floorboards.

"Isla, what the fuck is wrong?" Xavier's urgent question echoes in my ears, but I can't answer. *I can't breathe.* The world around me blurs, and a tight vice grips my chest, squeezing the air from my lungs. My heartbeat reverberates in my ears like a drum, each thud louder than the last. My vision tunnels, focusing on nothing but the fragments of my own ragged breaths. A cold sweat breaks out on my forehead, and my hands tremble uncontrollably. The sensation of drowning overwhelms me, trapped in the constricting embrace of a panic attack that refuses to let go.

Xavier is immediately in my face, urging me to breathe in and out, his hands rubbing my arms, asking questions about what happened and who rang me.

As my body continues to shake with the remnants of the panic attack, Xavier's soothing words and touch gradually bring me back. "It's Dad, my dad, Xav. He's been in a car accident. I-I—" I stutter, attempting to regain control of my breathing as tears well up in my eyes.

When I look at Xavier, he mutters a low, "Fuck," before rushing to grab his keys and my bag from the kitchen table. He ushers me out of the door.

"Come, I'll drive you," Xavier says urgently, the weight of the situation evident in his tone.

The air is charged with urgency and fear as we quickly head towards the car, and I cling to the hope that Dad will be alright. With a trembling breath, I choke out a whisper, "Please, Mum... guide us through this."

The words are a quiet plea, a desperate reach for solace in the face of the unknown.

As I utter my silent prayer, Xavier senses the weight of the moment. His hand finds its way to my thigh, a gentle touch offering reassurance when words seem inadequate.

Xavier murmurs, "We'll get through this, baby. Your dad will be alright."

His voice carries a comforting tone, a lifeline in the tumultuous sea of emotions, and I silently chant in my mind.

He'll—he'll be okay. He'll be okay.

37

Xavier

The hospital looms ahead, its sterile facade a stark contrast to the chaos of emotions swirling inside me. Isla sits beside me, her eyes a reservoir of tears threatening to spill over. Fuck, I can't stand the sight of her crying. It twists something deep within me, an ache that mirrors her pain.

As we pull up to the entrance, I steal a glance at her. Her hands tremble, and her gaze is fixed on the ground. I reach for her, fingers intertwining mine with hers.

"Isla, we're here. We'll figure this out together," I assure her, my voice steady despite the turmoil in my mind, I reassure her, "Deep breaths, remember." She nods, looking up at me, pain etched across her features, tears staining her beautiful face.

Entering the hospital, the antiseptic scent assaults my senses. I guide Isla towards the reception, my grip on her hand offering a reassurance I *hope* she feels. The nurse behind the desk looks up, and Isla manages to croak out her father's name.

The nurse updates us on Mr. Thompson's condition, revealing that he's currently undergoing emergent surgery. She elaborates, providing intricate details about his injuries—multiple broken ribs, a fractured collarbone, and extensive scratches and bruises. Isla winces at her words, trembling as silent tears fall down her cheeks.

"We've been updated, however, that the surgery is going well," the nurse assures, her professional demeanour attempting to instil confidence. With a gentle hand on Isla's back, I guide her towards the waiting room as the nurse instructs. The stark, sterile environment amplifies the tension in the air, and we take our seats, bracing ourselves for the uncertain hours ahead. Time drags on, each passing minute a testament to the vulnerability of life and the fragility of the moments we often take for granted.

Isla is silently fidgeting with her top, her distressed eyes revealing the turmoil within. Unable to bear her quiet suffering, I turn to look down at her, and the sight of tears in her eyes tightens a knot in my chest. Reacting instinctively, I wrap her in my arms, offering what little comfort I can in this moment of uncertainty.

She silently sobs into my chest, and I rub her back in gentle circles, murmuring assurances into her ear. I remind her that her father is a strong man, reiterating the nurse's words about the surgery progressing well. With her face buried in my chest, her breathing gradually slows, and she nods in acknowledgment.

Feeling the weight of the situation, I gently ask, "Do you want to call anyone? Imogen or..." My voice trails off, leaving the question open-ended. She looks up at me, her lips swollen and puffy from crying, her eyes red-rimmed.

"I'll call Midge now," she says, wiping her eyes.

As she dials Imogen's number, I can faintly hear her friend's voice answer the phone. Isla immediately starts crying into the phone, "Midge, oh my god." I just hear Imogen's frantic voice through the phone, questioning what's wrong. "It's Dad, Midge, he was in a car accident—" but her words trail off as she cries. Imogen is talking to her, but Isla isn't paying attention anymore.

I gently grab the phone off her, looking at Isla for permission, and she nods. I place the phone to my ear, hearing Imogen's voice clearly, "Isla, hello? Oh my god, where are you now?" Her frantic questioning fills my ear, and I start speaking into the phone.

"Imogen, it's Xavier," I begin, my voice steady but laced with concern. "There's been an accident. Isla's father is in the hospital, undergoing surgery right now."

Imogen's gasp is audible through the line, and she stammers, "Surgery? What happened? Is he going to be okay?"

I glance at Isla, who is still grappling with her emotions, and continue relaying the information. "He was in a car accident. The situation is critical, but the doctors are doing everything they can. Isla needs you here."

Imogen's panic rises as she processes the severity of the situation. "Oh god, I'm on my way. Is she okay? Is Isla okay?"

I reassure Imogen as best I can, "Physically, she's fine, but emotionally," I sigh, "Just... get here safely. We're in the waiting room."

Imogen assures me that she'll be here soon and hangs up, leaving the tense atmosphere of the waiting room hanging in the air. I return the phone to Isla, offering her a supportive glance.

As Imogen arrives, rushing through the doors of the hospital, her eyes lock onto us immediately, and she runs over. Isla stands up, and Imogen pulls her into a tight hug. Tears are now streaming down Imogen's cheeks as she speaks to Isla in her ear. Their conversation is muffled, but I can see the mix of emotions playing across Isla's face.

Imogen's eyes turn to me, and she steps back, still holding Isla's hands.

"Xavier, what happened? Tell me everything." Her voice is filled with concern and a hint of panic. I take a deep breath and try to relay the details of the accident and Isla's father's critical condition.

The three of us stand there, a knot of worry and grief binding us together in the sterile hospital corridor. The air is heavy with the uncertainty of what lies ahead.

As an hour passes, Isla rests her head on my shoulder, her hand in mine and the other holding Imogen's hand. I had texted my brother, letting him know what happened, and he'd said he'd be here as soon as possible. Our farm was a little further away from here compared to Isla's place, so it'll take him at least twenty-five or thirty minutes before he arrives.

Just then, a nurse enters the waiting room, calling out, "Ms. Isla Thompson," and we all look up and stand simultaneously. She introduces herself as Shelley before informing us that the surgery went well, as expected, and, "He's in the ICU. Follow me."

Every step echoes with uncertainty, and my thoughts race. What the fuck happened to her dad? Will he be okay? My mind is a whirlwind of unanswered questions, but I push them aside, focusing on being there for Isla.

In the quiet hum of the hospital corridors, I squeeze Isla's hand, silently offering my support.

We follow the nurse through a labyrinth of hallways, the stark fluorescence casting an unforgiving glow on our surroundings. Each step feels heavy, laden with the unspoken fear that permeates the air. Isla's grip in my hand tightens, seeking solace in the warmth we share.

The distant hum of medical equipment becomes more pronounced as we approach the Intensive Care Unit. The nurse halts at a set of double doors, her eyes meeting ours with a mix of empathy and professionalism. "He's just in here. You can stay for a while."

Before we go in, however, Shelley warns us with a comforting tone, preparing us not to be disheartened when we see Mr. Thompson's state. Isla, overcome with emotion, lets out a sob, and I instinctively put my arm around her shoulders, offering whatever comfort I can in this distressing moment. Imogen just gasps, putting a hand to her mouth.

"Fucking hell," I murmur under my breath, a surge of helplessness coursing through me. The atmosphere of the ICU does little to quell the chaos within our minds. We exchange a glance that speaks volumes, sharing the weight of uncertainty that hangs over us.

We follow Nurse Shelley into the ICU, and the sight that greets us is gut-wrenching. Isla's father, Mr. Thompson, lies in the hospital bed, surrounded by a web of tubes and monitors. His face is battered, adorned with cuts and bruises. Strapped up to thousands of cords, he appears fragile and helpless. A ventilator mask covers his face, and a long tube is attached to it, providing the artificial breath he needs. The rhythmic beeping of the monitors creates an eerie symphony in the background.

The nurse approaches, her voice gentle, yet probing. "Is Mr. Thompson on any medication? Does he have a history of drug or alcohol abuse?" Her questions hang in the air, and my concern deepens as she mentions the bottle of Jack Daniels found in the car. It's a grim reminder of the circumstances leading to this moment.

A cry breaks free from Isla, escaping her lips as she processes the nurse's words. She nods, her voice trembling as she answers, "Y-yes. He does." She sniffles. "He drinks. I'm not sure about medication though. He... he hasn't been doing too well. His memory is a little foggy." Her words struggle to come out, her voice cracking under the weight of emotion. I place a comforting hand on her back, offering silent support during this difficult moment. Nurse Shelley, with a gentle and composed demeanour, begins to explain the situation.

"I understand, dear. I'll make note of this on his file. Mr. Thompson..." She clears her throat. "Your *father* has sustained multiple injuries, including broken ribs and a collarbone. The ventilator is helping him breathe while his body heals. The next few days will be critical, and we'll monitor his progress closely."

Isla stands frozen, her eyes fixed on her father's battered form. Imogen, her voice shaky, steps forward. "What about his head? Is there any head injury?"

Nurse Shelley nods understandingly. "Yes, he sustained a mild concussion. We're keeping a close eye on that, too. The priority right

now is stabilising him and ensuring his vital functions are supported."

Imogen furrows her brows, worry etched on her face. "And the cuts on his face?"

"They're superficial, mainly lacerations from the accident. We'll clean and dress them regularly to prevent infection." Shelley reassures. Isla, still processing the information, looks at Imogen, appreciating her friend's concern for her father.

As the weight of the situation becomes too much for Isla, tears stream down her face unchecked. Unable to bear seeing her father in such a vulnerable state, strapped to machines and battling for his life, Isla moves to stand beside his bed, grabbing onto his hand as she cries. My heart breaks as I watch her, the depth of her pain cutting through me. Bradley, who had arrived shortly after this, offers a comforting hug, but Isla's sobs persist, refusing to be silenced by even the most sincere gestures of support.

Imogen, grappling with the shock of the situation, has seated herself on the couch beside the bed. The room is filled with the heavy atmosphere of grief, each person grappling with their own emotions in the face of tragedy. In a hushed tone, Bradley lets us know that he'll be waiting just outside, understanding the overwhelming grief filling the room. Isla, however, reaches a breaking point and declares she needs some air.

As Isla makes her way towards the door, Imogen rises from beside the bed, concern etching her features. "Isla, sweetheart, let me come with you. You shouldn't be alone right now."

Isla halts for a moment, glancing back at Imogen with tear-filled eyes. "No, Midge. I just need a moment by myself. I'll be okay, I promise."

The harsh lights cast a glow as Isla steps into the corridor, her steps heavy with grief. I follow closely, sensing her need for support. As we reach the end of the corridor, Isla comes to a halt, her body hunching over as she tries to catch her breath. The air is thick with sorrow, and I approach her, a silent presence offering solace.

"Isla," I say gently, my voice a low murmur as I step close to her, keeping a respectful distance.

She doesn't respond immediately, yet after a few minutes, she finally speaks, her voice raw with emotion. "I just need a moment, Xavier. Please," she says as she releases a deep breath.

I respect her request, rooted to the spot, unsure of how to navigate this storm of emotions. Isla begins to pace back and forth, the weight of the situation causing her to tremble. Tears continue to stream down her face, and I ache, witnessing her struggle.

She huffs, and for a second, it almost sounds like a laugh, a sound that doesn't match the sombre surroundings. Confusion sets in as she repeats it, a nervous laughter escaping her lips. I can't comprehend it, and my concern deepens.

"Are you... are you laughing?" I ask.

She does it again—laughter intermingled with the chaos of emotions. Isla starts to ramble, wiping at her eyes, her words pouring out in an unfiltered torrent of despair.

"I can't believe this. I thought coming here would be a fresh start—a fresh start from living in the city, an escape from that shitty fucking life I was stuck in with Justin. I felt so fucking trapped there, and ironically," she huffs a laugh, "I had thought escaping to the city would have been my freedom—freedom from this shitty fucking town, from my mother's death, from my father's alcoholism, abuse, and here I am, back here, and I haven't fucking escaped anything."

Her voice breaks, and the strength she's been holding onto crumbles. Tears fall freely, and the weight of her words hangs heavily in the air.

"I just can't catch a fucking break. I don't know what to do, Xavier. I'm fucking drowning here, and this..." she gestures around us, to where we are, "this is all my fucking fault." Her voice breaks, cracking, shedding every ounce of her stability, strength, and her tears start to fall.

"This is all my fucking fault." She repeats her words with a strangled sob.

My attempts at reassurance falter as I say, "Baby, it's okay," but she cuts me off, her voice frantic.

"No, nothing about this is fucking okay, Xavier, nothing. MY FUCKING FATHER IS IN THE HOSPITAL, sitting in a fucking bed with tubes down his throat and more strapped to his body, he is in a fucking coma, and it's all my fucking fault," she says, waving her hands around.

She's breaking right in front of my fucking eyes, and I don't know what to do. *Fuck*.

Isla continues, shaking all over, "I should have been there, I should have been with him, I need to be with him 24 fucking 7. He's not in a right state of mind, and I fucking left him, and he drove his fucking car and got into an accident, who knows what happened, he could have..." her voice falters, sucking in a breath, "what if he forgot how to fucking drive? Oh my god, Xavier, he could have fucking died, what if he—" her words trail off.

"Don't finish that sentence. I can't tell you how things are going to be, but I can tell you that your father is fighting for his life in *there*." I raise my arm, pointing back down the hallway.

"He'll need you to be strong, strong for him. None of this is your fault," I emphasise, trying to anchor some sense into the chaos of her emotions.

But Isla, in the throes of her breakdown, insists otherwise. "But it is my fault," she retorts, her voice laden with guilt. "Because instead of trying harder to be there for him, I've been too busy with work, with—" as she tries to articulate the weight on her shoulders, her words trail off. I can sense the unspoken word, the guilt that claws at her.

"Finish the sentence," I dare her, my tone firm. Isla falters, her eyes meeting mine with a mix of regret and sadness.

"Instead of being there for my father, I've been too busy swept up with my emotions, with this newfound, whatever it is, that I haven't made the time for him," she finally confesses, the weight of self-blame hanging heavy in the air. An uneasy feeling settles in the pit of my stomach.

Whatever it is?

"This is," I wave my hands, gesturing between the two of us, "*whatever*, huh?" I shake my head in disbelief. I thought we had established what this was between us. This is bullshit—I'm unable to comprehend the complexity of emotions unravelling before me.

Isla tries to brush me off with an apology, insisting, "I'm sorry, I just—I need to be there for him now, any chance I can get. I don't have time for distractions," Isla says, her voice strained with the weight of her emotions. I can read between the lines.

"Isla," I insist, my voice tight, "what are you not saying?" I ask, wanting her to say the words I know I will fucking hate to hear.

She looks at me with pleading eyes, her voice breaking as she confesses, "I just need space, Xavier. I need to be alone. I need time... to work all of this out."

I pause for a moment, trying to bear my thoughts as I frown.

"You can have that time. I'll be here with you, to support you. I'm not going anywhere. I've told you this. I want nothing more than for you to work this all out, for your father to get through this, baby." She winces at the endearment.

"Please, Xavier, don't call me that. Not right now," she croaks, her voice raw. "I think you should just go. It's late, Imogen is here. I'll be fine. Thank you," she sighs, releasing a shaky breath, "for everything. I..." She cuts off her words, wiping at her tears.

"You want me to... leave?" I say with pure confusion.

At this moment, Imogen—not entirely sure how long she'd been there and how much she had heard, decides to break the silence with a clearing of her throat. "Isla, what's going on here?"

"Nothing, Midge. I think... Xavier was just about to head off." Is she for real? If she thinks I'm going to fucking *leave* her here, she's got fucking Buckley's.

"I never agreed to fucking leave," I growl, frustration and determination lacing my words. "I'm not going anywhere. You can't shut me out, Isla, not after everything we've been through. I'm not one to fucking beg, and it'd be wise not to mistake my kindness for weakness. I'm here because I want to be," I respond sharply. "You're not pushing me away, Isla. Not when you're hurting like this."

She shakes her head, frustration evident in her eyes. "Please, Xavier, I just need you to understand. I need space. I can't deal with everything at once."

I laugh bitterly, the sound echoing in the corridor. "Understand what, Isla? If I leave, then what?" She can't be that blind—she can't be that blind to not understand my feelings for her. Does it have to be spelled out?

"You're shutting me out for what? For what fucking reason?" My voice now a tad bit raised. Imogen, sensing the tension, steps forward cautiously. "Guys, maybe it's best if—"

I cut her off. "You'll get your space, Isla, but I'm staying right outside that door," I declare, crossing my arms defiantly. "I'm not abandoning you."

"Xav, I just think we should take a break," Isla says, her voice trembling.

"A break? From fucking what?" I question, searching her eyes, my jaw clenching.

"Us. This... whatever it is between us," she replies, her gaze avoiding mine.

Anger flares within me. "But why? Why do you keep saying that?"

"It's not about you, Xavier. It's about me and sorting out my priorities right now."

"Bullshit," I retort, frustration evident in my voice. "I've been *here* for *you*, supporting *you*, and now you just want to throw everything away?"

"It's not that simple," she insists, tears welling in her eyes.

"Then, make it simple, Isla," I retort. "Don't shut me out like this. We can get through this together." I'm left standing there in silence—shock and hurt no doubt evident in my expression.

Her lips tremble—her eyes watering, as she stands there with her arms wrapped around her midsection. Unbelievable.

"Okay," I mumble, nodding once. Her silence is the only answer I need to understand what she wants. Complete and utter disbelief surges within me. Why is she doing this?

I raise my hands in surrender. "I'll go. If that's what you really want, Isla, I'll leave. I'm gone." I mutter, my words laced with complete sympathy for her.

With that, I take one last lingering gaze at Isla, and I turn to leave. Her choked sobs echo through the walls, and I briefly hear Imogen's voice soothing her. While walking down the corridor, I spot my brother, Bradley, leaning against the wall.

As I approach, ready to continue my exit, Bradley puts a hand on my shoulder, attempting to form words. "Xav, I—" but I cut him off with a stern "Don't." That's all I offer as I stride towards the lift, desperate to leave this suffocating place behind.

As I enter the lift, it's a painful departure from the only thing in my life that gave me purpose, the light in my shitty, lonely world I'd succumbed to over the years.

The weight of the realisation hits me like a tonne of bricks—Isla is the one person, after all these years, I actually thought I could spend the rest of my life with, like she was *made* for me.

And here I am, leaving behind the one person who felt like home.

With every step as I exit the hospital, I let her slip away, and the echoes of what we could've had linger with each heartbeat.

38

Isla

I wake up to the light seeping through the hospital blinds, the exhaustion of the previous night clinging to me like a heavy fog. The nurses had kindly allowed me to stay the night, and I opted to sleep in the small lounge in the room. The couch, though far from comfortable, served as my makeshift bed.

Sleep eluded me as I tossed and turned on the cramped sofa. Every few minutes, I found myself getting up to check on my father, the rhythmic sounds of the machines providing a haunting backdrop. The weight of the night, the worry for my father, and the unfamiliar surroundings contributed to my restlessness.

Imogen, sensing my fatigue, returned in the morning and insisted that she would keep watch over my father. Reluctantly, I allowed myself a few hours of sleep, knowing that Imogen was there, a reassuring presence in the room. Despite the small reprieve, the exhaustion clung to me like a second skin as I faced another day in these small confines of the hospital room.

As I rouse from my fitful sleep, the hospital room comes into focus. Imogen sits by my father's bedside, her presence a source of comfort. I quietly get up from the small lounge, my body protesting against the awkward sleeping position.

Imogen looks up, concern etched on her face. "Hey," she says with a weak smile. "How are you feeling?"

I manage a small, tired smile. "Not great," I mutter, wiping at my sleepy eyes. "Thanks for taking over."

Imogen nods, her gaze shifting to my father. "The nurses did their rounds a while ago, and everything seems okay for now. One of them said she'd be back to check his fluids."

Imogen glances at her phone and then back at me. "I've reached out to Claire. She's catching the next available flight and will be here as soon as possible."

Relief courses through me at the thought of Claire's presence, but worry lingers. "Thank you. It means a lot that she's coming."

Imogen smiles softly, reaching for my hand. "We'll get through this together."

I join her by the bedside, our attention focused on my father's still form. The machines continue their rhythmic symphony, a constant reminder of the fragility of life.

"He needs to wake up, Imogen," I say, my voice barely above a whisper. "I can't stand seeing him like this."

Imogen places a comforting hand on my shoulder. "He's strong, Isla. It'll take time, but he'll pull through. You'll see."

I nod, trying to absorb the medical information while keeping my emotions in check. Imogen reaches over and gently squeezes my hand, offering silent support.

The door eases open, and a nurse steps into the room, her gentle greeting breaking the silence.

"Good morning, Ms. Thompson. I've just come in to check on your dad's IV drip," she says, her soft smile offering a hint of reassurance.

As she moves around the bed, meticulously examining the IV, tapping the bag, and securing the tubes, I can't help but feel a knot tighten in my stomach. The nurse then turns her attention to the whiteboard, scanning my father's chart.

In a moment of vulnerability, I ask, my voice quivering, "Are things going okay?"

Adjusting her glasses, the nurse begins, "Your father's vital signs are stable—heart rate, blood pressure, and oxygen levels are all within the normal range. The sedative is maintaining him in a controlled state for healing.

"So, in essence, we've placed him in a medically induced coma to shield him from intense pain during recovery and preserve higher brain function after the trauma. Regarding his fractures—two ribs and the collarbone—the surgical team has addressed those issues successfully. The ventilator is aiding his breathing, and we're closely monitoring for any signs of infection or complications."

She then turns serious, mentioning the most critical concern.

"His brain suffered multiple injuries, causing bleeding within. We're doing everything we can, but it's a delicate situation."

My breath catches, and I nod, my eyes searching for any signs of hope or solace in the nurse's face.

Imogen, always one to seek answers, interjects, her concern evident. "Any idea when he might wake up?"

Maintaining her professional composure, the nurse replies, "Predicting is challenging. Each patient responds differently. We'll closely monitor his neurological status, gradually reducing sedation when appropriate. The next twenty-four to forty-eight hours are crucial for assessing his responsiveness."

"The neurology team is on top of it, though—conducting assessments to evaluate his brain function. We'll adjust the treatment plan accordingly. It's a critical aspect of his recovery, and we're dedicated to doing everything we can."

"I must also add, the MRI scans performed last night revealed some concerning findings," the nurse begins, choosing her words with care. "There's unusual brain activity that the medical team has detected. While it's not definitive, it has led them toward a tentative diagnosis of Alzheimer's disease."

My heart tightens at the confirmation, a cold realisation of the suspicions that had lingered in the recesses of my mind. I'd suspected it all this time, certain myself that he'd had it, but hearing it out loud confirms all my worst thoughts.

"Fuck," I mutter under my breath, the weight of the word carrying the gravity of the situation.

The nurse, attuned to the emotional turmoil in the room, places a gentle hand on my shoulder. "I know it's a lot to take in," she says, her voice a soothing cadence. "Your father is in good hands here. We're dedicated to providing the best care possible for him. If you have any questions or concerns, feel free to ask."

I nod, appreciative of her reassurance, but the reality of the situation hangs heavy in the air.

My mind races with worry, and I swallow hard. "Thank you," I manage to whisper.

The nurse offers a compassionate smile before leaving, leaving me alone with the weight of the information pressing on me. Internally, I grapple with the uncertainty, desperately hoping for signs of improvement in the next crucial hours.

Time stretches on, and I steadfastly refuse to leave my father's side. The room becomes a cocoon of beeping monitors and sterile scents, and I feel like the only anchor in my dad's tumultuous sea of unconsciousness. I manage to find a moment to dial Katy's number at the clinic. The phone rings, each tone echoing my own anxiety. Finally, she picks up.

"Katy, it's Isla," I start, my voice holding a tremor.

"What's going on?" Katy's voice crackles through the phone, panic palpable even through the connection.

I take a steadying breath, my words measured. "It's Dad. There was a car accident. I'm at the hospital with him. Things are... not good."

Silence hangs on the line for a moment before Katy responds, her voice now softer, filled with concern. "Oh, goodness gracious me, Isla. I'm so sorry to hear that darl. I'll... I'll manage things here."

"No, no, I can't possibly ask that of you.... I have to come in to help," I insist.

"Don't you dare. Don't be silly," she retorts over the phone and a few moments pass before she speaks again. "You know we could close the clinic—just temporarily, you know—until your father has recovered." Katy's concern pours through the phone, and I can almost picture the chaos at the clinic. "We can't just carry on like nothing happened. I'll manage things here—you focus on your dad," she insists.

I nod, even though she can't see it. "I know, Katy. But shutting down the clinic, even temporarily, that's a big step. What will you do without work?"

"It's the right step. Your family comes first. I'll handle everything. Don't you worry about me. We've got a great clientele, and they'll understand. Besides, I can send out an email to our patients; let 'em know there's a temporary closure due to unforeseen circumstances," Katy reassures, her determination cutting through the panic.

I hesitate, torn between gratitude for Katy's support and worry about the clinic. "Are you sure? What if this affects our business?"

"Business can wait, Isla. This is about you and your dad. We've built something good at the clinic, and our patients will understand, darling. I'll draft an email right away. You don't need'a worry about anything here," she says, her words offering a rare comfort in the midst of chaos.

"Thank you, Katy. I owe you one," I say, feeling a weight lifted off my shoulders.

"No need for that. Just take care of your family. That's what matters," Katy replies, her voice firm.

"I appreciate it. I'll keep you posted," I say with a heavy sigh.

Ending the call, I feel a mix of emotions. Relief that Katy is taking charge, yet a lingering worry about the impact on the clinic. It's a sacrifice, among many, and I wince at the thought—but for now, my focus remains on the hospital room where my father lies, fighting his silent battle.

As midday arrives, my stomach rumbles loudly in the quiet hospital room, a stark reminder of the passing hours. Imogen, a steadfast presence by my side, hasn't left since morning. I glance at her, the worry etched on her face mirroring my own.

"I'm so grateful you're here, Imogen. But you've got work, your own commitments. I can't ask you to stay here all day," I say, my voice laced with concern.

She squeezes my hand gently. "Isla, stop. Your dad needs you. I've taken care of a few things remotely, plus I don't have too many clients at the moment. It's all good."

Torn between gratitude and guilt, I manage a small smile, acknowledging her kindness. "Thank you, Imogen. I just don't want to burden you."

Imogen reaches out, gently squeezing my hand. "Hey, I know you shut Xavier away, Isla, but I won't let you shut me out, too. We're best friends, and friends stick together, always."

Her words strike a chord, and the mention of Xavier brings forth a flood of conflicting emotions.

Thoughts of our encounter last night linger, and pain resurfaces its way back up, settling heavily in my chest. I exhale loudly, unable to shake the haunting question that creeps into my mind. "I fucked up, didn't I, Midge?"

Imogen's expression softens, and she squeezes my hand again and sighs, before answering me.

"You're going through a lot right now, and sometimes things get messy. Just focus on your dad, and we'll figure everything else out together. What happened last night, it's not the end."

Imogen's reassurance provides a fleeting comfort, but as I sit by my father's bedside, my thoughts betray me, replaying the scenes from last night. I asked Xavier to leave, brushed off his feelings as if they were inconsequential. The memory of his face, etched with pain and disappointment, has become a haunting image imprinted in my mind.

How could I be so stupid, so selfish?

The weight of my actions bears down on me, and a surge of guilt tightens my chest. I exhale shakily, feeling the sting of tears threatening to spill once more. Turning to Imogen, who has been a constant support, I find solace in sharing my inner turmoil.

"But I think it is," I cry out. "No, no, no, I really fucked up, Midge," I confess, my voice cracking with emotion.

"I asked him to *leave*, pushed him away when all he was doing was just trying to help. And his face... the pain in his eyes. I can't shake that image." With a choked cry, tears fall down my cheeks, betraying the depth of my regret. Imogen, always intuitive, places a comforting hand on my shoulder, a silent acknowledgment of the pain that words often fail to express.

"Oh, Isla," she murmurs, her voice a soothing balm.

"These are tough times, and emotions are running high. You're dealing with so much right now, and it's okay not to have all the answers and react impulsively. Maybe he'll... understand when things settle down, you know? You can always try to talk to him then. That man is smitten. I see the way he looks at you. He'll come around."

A heavy sigh escapes me as I contemplate Imogen's suggestion.

"Ugggh, I want to, Midge. I really want to fucking talk to him," I huff out, "I just... I'm scared. Scared of what I might hear or, worse, what I might not hear." The tears won't stop, and my nose is all blocked up again.

Imogen squeezes my shoulder gently, offering silent support. "You won't know until you try, Isla."

I wipe away at my tears impatiently. "But what if he doesn't? What if I've ruined everything?"

"If he cares about you, he'll understand. And if not, well, then maybe it wasn't meant to be." She offers a reassuring smile.

"I just wish I could go back and handle things differently," I mumble, almost a whisper.

"I know, babe. I know. It's alright, let's just focus on your dad, the rest will fall into line later," Imogen suggests.

As the afternoon rolls around, a revolving door of unfamiliar and vaguely familiar faces passes through the hospital room. Some are strangers, their concern etched on their faces, while others are old acquaintances from my childhood. The small-town grapevine works fast, I suppose. Word travels swiftly, and eventually, everyone knows everyone's business.

Imogen, after offering unwavering support, had left not long ago to freshen up, promising to return soon. Now, in the quiet of the hospital room, it's just me and dad. I sit beside his bed, my face resting on the edge, seeking solace in the rhythmic sounds of the medical equipment.

Then, the door creaks open again.

I look up slowly, and to my surprise, it's Bradley who walks in. His face carries an empathetic look, a stark contrast to the austere mood that usually lingers around him. Of all the people, I hadn't expected to see him here.

He approaches cautiously, breaking the silence, clearing his throat. "I know I'm the last person you probably wish to see, but I just..." His voice trails off as I sigh, bracing myself for whatever words follow.

"I wanted to check up on you, you know, after last night," Bradley says, his eyes reflecting genuine concern.

Bradley moves to stand beside me, and there's a clipped edge to his response, "I know we don't really know each other that well, but despite everything, with you and my brother, I can't ignore the fact that you're going through a lot." His voice is laced with genuine concern. "I just want you to know that I'm here—for anything."

His words hang in the air, and for a moment, I'm unsure how to respond, but I find myself nodding in acknowledgment. "Thank you, Bradley," I choke on my words. "It's been a rough day."

"How's he doin'?" Bradley asks.

I relay the information from the morning, watching as Bradley sucks in a breath, absorbing the gravity of the situation. The beeping sounds of monitors fill the room as silence settles in. It's a heavy quiet, one that hangs between us.

Breaking the silence, I gather the courage to ask, "Is—" my voice falters, and I sigh. "How is he?" I ask, referring to his brother.

His gaze meets mine, and I see a reflection of the pain that Xavier must be experiencing. "Isla," Bradley's voice is measured, "he's hurting. Last night... fuck, it hit him hard. I've never seen him so riled up." He runs a hand over his short, dark hair. "He cares about you a lot, and seeing you in pain, it's affected him more than he lets on."

A heavy silence settles in the room as Bradley's words linger. I glance down at my hands, fingers intertwined in a nervous dance. Xavier's pain, a consequence of my own selfish request, echoes in my mind.

My breath catches in my throat, a mixture of guilt and longing swirling within me. "Bradley, I just don't know," I confess, my words carrying the weight of indecision. "I have so much on my plate right now, and the thought of getting into a new relationship, especially with everything going on, it just doesn't sit right."

Bradley remains silent, nodding his head slightly as he processes my words.

"I didn't mean for it to be this way, Bradley," I admit. "Last night... I needed space—from everything. It wasn't just directed towards him, and I thought it was the right thing to do. But now, hearing this," I hesitate. "*Fuck*—I just... I never meant to hurt him." How did everything get so tangled up? Is there a way to untangle it, or have I irreversibly messed things up?

Bradley's eyes hold a mix of understanding and concern. "Look," he says gently, "we can't control every outcome, especially in moments of chaos. But what you can control is how you handle it moving forward. If you care about him, if you want to make things right, talk to him. Clear the air. Relationships are resilient, but they need communication to thrive."

His words surprisingly hold a lot of comfort. I'd been an only child all my life, never having experienced the comfort of a sibling, and being here now with Bradley feels just like that—how I'd imagined a brother talk to his sister.

I feel a sense of gratitude for his presence, a brotherly assurance that brings an unexpected warmth to the hospital room. "Thank you, Bradley," I say, sincerity in my voice. "I appreciate your perspective, and... it means a lot, talking to you."

A hint of a smile plays on Bradley's lips, and he attempts to lighten the mood. "You know, my brother can be strong-headed, but when he wants something, he'll work hard for it. He doesn't hold grudges, but he can be a stubborn fuck, much like our father," he says with a shake of his head.

I chuckle, appreciating the effort to bring a moment of levity into the heavy atmosphere.

Bradley smiles. "But seriously, I've said it before—I've never seen my brother like this. He's been alone for so long, and the change is good for him. It might be worthwhile just hearing what he has to say about how he feels about you."

Bradley's words hang in the air, and I'm stuck in the middle of my own mess, unsure whether I have the guts to face Xavier and the storm I stirred up. His advice, with that brotherly touch, makes me think, but it's like untangling earphones—frustrating and complicated.

I sit alone with my thoughts, wondering if maybe, just maybe, listening to Xavier might bring some clarity. He's hinted at his feelings before, but Bradley's words make it sound like there's more beneath the surface.

The road ahead is foggy, uncertain, and probably full of more complications, but Bradley's nod gives me a weird sense of comfort. Maybe, just maybe, there's a chance to sort through the chaos, even if it's just to understand the unspoken words between Xavier and I.

39

Xavier

The weekend sun crawls into the room, illuminating the silence that's been suffocating me for days. Sunday morning, and I haven't heard a damn thing from Isla. Not a text, not a call. Nothing. It's like I've been erased from her world.

Bradley, the bearer of unwelcome news, had ambushed me on Friday. He said he'd had a 'civilised conversation' with her. The words hit me like a sledgehammer. My chest tightens, the air sucked out of my lungs. She's talking about me with Bradley, and I'm left grappling with the aftermath. That's how it's been since Thursday—a vicious cycle. Wake up, immerse myself in the grind, forget to eat, endure my mother's nagging, sleep, and repeat. Anything to avoid dwelling on the fuckery that's become my life.

I'm fucking angry. Fuming. Seething. How the hell could she be so blind? I get the whole 'needing space' thing with her father in a coma, but to dismiss what we have as 'whatever'—that's a kick deep in the gut. The kind that makes you hunch over in pain.

I'm not some soft pushover, but I can't shake these damn feelings. Can't stop thinking about it. I need a distraction before I do something I'll regret. So, I bury myself in work around the farm, ploughing through the fields, letting the physical exertion be a pathetic substitute for the emotional turmoil I'm drowning in.

She's pushed me away, and we never even got the chance to begin. I'm fucking lost, angry, and confused. I need to find a way to dull the sharp edges of this pain, even if it's just for a moment. Anything to silence the thoughts of her that won't stop echoing in my mind.

I need to drown out the noise in my head, and the rhythmic routine of herding the cows might just be the distraction I need. Old Buddy, loyal but showing his age, lumbers beside me as we head to the paddocks. His steps aren't as spry as they used to be, and I've been contemplating getting another dog.

We reach the paddock, and the cows graze lazily, oblivious to the turmoil in my mind. Buddy and I work in tandem, a dance we've perfected over the years. The herding process is a well-choreographed routine—a mix of whistles, commands, and the occasional nudge—to keep the cows in line. The dust swirls around us as we guide them to the fresh pasture.

As we wrap up, Buddy panting by my side, the thought of a new dog lingers. But where the hell do I find one? Then it hits me—Isla mentioned an Australian Kelpie they look after at the clinic. A surge of hope courses through me.

I pull my phone from my pocket, dialling the clinic's number. It rings for an eternity before being unceremoniously dumped into voicemail. I brace for whatever bureaucratic message awaits, and sure enough, Katy's voice spills through the speaker.

"Hello, this is Katy from Wattle Creek Veterinary Clinic. Due to unforeseen circumstances, we regret to inform you that the clinic will be temporarily closed. For any inquiries or urgent matters, please contact me directly at—" and she rattles off a mobile number, "We appreciate your understanding during this challenging time."

I wince at the formality and the inevitable chaos these circumstances have unleashed. Regardless, I mentally jot down the number Katy rattles off and dial it, the tone chiming as I wait for her to pick up.

The phone rings, each tone intensifying my impatience until, finally, Katy answers. Her voice is rushed,

"Hello, this is Katy. Wattle Creek Veterinary Clinic," she answers, the undertone of stress evident in her voice.

I clear my throat, "Uh, hi, it's Xavier... Mitchell," I reply, my tone gruff but laced with a thin veil of politeness.

"Oh, Xavier, dear. I'm so sorry to hear what happened with my dear Isla. How is she going? I tried to call her, but she must be busy with... you know—" Katy interjects.

I sigh, my frustration momentarily giving way to a sense of understanding. "Not sure. I haven't been with her since Thursday—" I trail off, steering the conversation back to the matter at hand. "I was calling about that Kelpie you guys have. Is she still up for adoption?"

There's a pause on the other end before Katy responds, concern evident in her tone. "Thursday? Oh my, why? What's happened?"

"It's a long story," I dismiss, not in the mood for details.

"Oh my, okay, dear. You mentioned Luna?" There's a pause on the other end before Katy responds, "Yes! She still is," she exclaims. "Are you sure about this, Xavier?"

"Yeah, I'm sure. I've been needing another farm dog, and I remembered Isla mentioning her, so I thought—" His words are cut off.

"Oh my goodness, this is amazing news! Why don't you come by the clinic when you're ready, and I'll meet you there with our Luna, so you can meet her," Katy concedes, her tone softening. "We can sort everything out there."

I hang up, pocketing the phone as I whistle for Buddy. He pads over, loyal eyes meeting mine, and we head back to the ute. The engine roars to life as I steer the wheel, the rhythmic hum offering a brief respite from the whirlwind inside my head.

As we drive, the familiar landscape blurs by, each tree and field a backdrop to the internal turbulence. The idea of a new canine companion grounds me, and I can't help but feel a sense of purpose in providing a home for the Kelpie waiting at the clinic.

Buddy settles into the back tray, his long coat catching the wind. I glance at him, contemplating the imminent change in our routine. The road stretches ahead, winding its way to the clinic where a new chapter might begin.

I pull up at the clinic, the engine's growl fading into the quiet hum of idling. As I step out of the car, Katy emerges from the front doors, wearing a soft smile.

She walks up to me, her eyes reflecting both sympathy and genuine concern. Unexpectedly, she pulls me into a hug, a gesture that catches me off guard. My body tenses, not accustomed to this level of physical comfort from anyone other than a specific someone. The mere thought of her sends tingles down my spine, and a shudder ripples through me. Katy releases the embrace, her gaze holding an unspoken understanding.

"Xavier, thanks for coming. I can't even imagine what a rough time it has been for both you and Isla," she mutters softly.

"Yeah," I mutter, my usual gruffness returning as I clear my throat. "So, about that Kelpie."

She nods, guiding me towards the entrance. "Let's head inside, and I'll fill you in on everything."

We step inside the clinic, the air heavy with the scent of antiseptic and the distant murmur of animals in the background. The soft whir of the air conditioning adds a gentle hum to the atmosphere as Katy leads me through the familiar reception area.

"Bud," I call, and the old dog pads in behind me. He sniffs the air, tail wagging as he takes in the unfamiliar scents of the clinic.

Katy leads us to a small, clean room where the Luna awaits. The dog, a sleek and alert Australian Kelpie with a coat that gleams in various shades of brown, looks up as we enter. Her eyes lock onto Buddy, and the two dogs exchange a series of tentative sniffs.

Katy watches the dogs interact, a fond smile on her face. "Luna here is a sweetheart. Isla found her on the side of the road a while ago. She was frail, malnourished, and completely abandoned."

My gaze softens at the thought. "Abandoned? Who the fuck would do that?"

Katy sighs, her eyes reflecting a mix of sympathy and frustration. "Unfortunately, it happens more often than you'd think. People just discard animals like they're disposable. But the good news is, Isla brought her in, and we've been taking care of her since. Luna's got a resilient spirit, though. Despite what she's been through, she's a loving and gentle dog."

I nod, absentmindedly bending down to run my hand over Buddy's back as he stands by my side, his curiosity piqued by Luna.

Katy, observing the interaction, smiles knowingly. "Seems like they're getting along just fine."

The idea of someone abandoning their dog strikes a chord, and a newfound determination settles within me.

Katy watches Luna's energetic display, a chuckle escaping her lips. "Luna can be a bit much for some folks. We've had a few people interested in adopting her, but her boisterous energy scared them off."

As if on cue, Luna starts barking loudly, her excitement contagious. She sniffs Buddy enthusiastically, and the two dogs embark on an impromptu game of chase around the clinic. Katy shakes her head, a smile playing on her lips. "Looks like she's found a playmate in Buddy."

She turns her attention back to me, her eyes assessing. "Xavier, you might be the perfect person for Luna. Running a farm and all, she seems like she could use a setting like that. I think she came from a similar scene. A farm dog—what do you think?"

I watch Luna and Buddy weave through the clinic, their playful antics filling the air. The idea of Luna finding a home on my farm resonates with me. "Yeah, I think she'd fit right in. I've got the space for her to run around and burn off that energy."

Katy nods, a satisfied expression on her face. "Great. Let's get the paperwork sorted, and Luna can join your pack."

With the paperwork sorted, Luna sits proudly next to Katy, her eyes flickering between us as if seeking reassurance. Katy nudges her gently, saying, "It's okay, girl. You've found your new daddy."

The term of endearment catches me off guard, and a warmth seeps through me. "Dad," I chuckle, looking at Katy. "Never thought I'd hear that term associated with me."

Katy grins, understanding the novelty of the situation. "Well, Luna seems to think so. Give her a chance, and you might just grow into the role."

Bending down, I get eye level with Luna. She watches me cautiously, her tail wagging in anticipation. I cautiously raise my hand for her to sniff, a gesture to introduce myself to the newest member of the pack. Luna, ever curious, leans in, taking in my scent before giving my hand a friendly lick.

I straighten up, a newfound sense of responsibility settling in. Luna looks up at me, her eyes filled with trust and a hint of excitement. A farm dog, a companion in the making. The weight of the term 'Dad' lingers in the air, and for a moment, the clinic feels like the starting point of something uncharted and surprisingly comforting.

"Thank you, Katy," I express my gratitude, still processing the sudden shift in my routine.

Katy waves off my thanks, a beaming smile on her face. "No, Xavier, I must thank you. You have no idea how happy you've made me. We've been wanting this for so long. I can't wait to let Isla know."

"If it's okay, could you just hold off on telling Isla for now?" I interject. "I'd like to be the one to share the news with her when she's ready to talk to me."

Curiosity flickers in Katy's eyes as she tilts her head. "Oh, of course, dear," she quips and then interjects, "Did something happen between the two of you? If you don't mind me asking. Something's different." She squints her eyes, trying to suss out my expressions.

With a heavy sigh, I mutter, "It's... complicated."

Katy's eyes soften with understanding as she absorbs the information. "Life has a way of throwing curveballs, doesn't it?"

I nod, a heavy sigh escaping me. "I thought I was helping by giving her space. She asked me to leave, and I didn't want to be another burden on her plate."

Katy pats my shoulder reassuringly. "Xavier, you're not a burden. She's dealing with a lot right now. You know... with Isla," she reassures me, placing a comforting hand on my shoulder.

"She's got a way of pushing people away when things get tough. But she's been working with me long enough for me to know her patterns and her personality. Since she met you, she's changed. Give her a chance, Xavier. Isla is stronger than you think."

I just nod.

She continues, "It's her way of coping. Just give her time, and things will fall into place."

I appreciate Katy's attempt to provide comfort, but the uncertainty lingers in the air. Isla's actions still echo in my mind, and the path forward seems clouded with unresolved questions.

I'd swung by the local pet store to grab a new collar for Luna after I had left the clinic. I had made a mental note that I'd be needing to get a personalised one for her online—matching Buddy's, you know, to make it all official.

Now as the afternoon sun strolls in, casting a warm silhouette along the horizon against the fields before me, I sit in the lounge chair on the back porch—arms resting on my knees, with both Buddy and Luna idly at my side. Luna seems to have taken to farm life well, and I can't help but wonder if Katy was onto something with her farm-friendly background. She's warmed up real fast to the animals and even the horses—it had taken Buddy a while to get used to those big bucks. She's a natural.

I can't shake the desire to reach out to Isla. It gnaws at me, a persistent ache in the quiet moments. The thought of picking up my phone and sending her a text lingers like an unresolved chord. But I resist. Stubbornness takes the reins, fueled by a need to respect the distance she's put between us. I hate it, every damn second of it.

The back screen door creaks open, and my father steps out, standing next to me in silence. Irritated by the lingering presence, I glance at him and mutter, "You just gonna stand there all afternoon doing fuck all or what?"

He retorts with a smirk, "You gonna sit around and mope all day like a fool?"

Touche. I just shrug.

My father, a man of few words, eventually brings up Luna. "New addition to the family, I see."

"Yeah," I reply, my tone shifting into something more contemplative. "Felt like we needed a new addition for a while. Old Bud's getting on, and I figured a companion for him wouldn't hurt." My father nods an acknowledgment.

"Your uh—your Mum told me about Thompson," he says with a sigh. "Damn pity, that is. His alcoholism would've caught up to him soona or later," he adds matter-of-factly.

"That 'Thompson' guy is Isla's father, and he's in a fucking coma, Dad. Show some respect," I retort sharply, frustration bubbling up. "Is this why you came out here, to rub it in my face or something?" I grumble.

"Watch your tone, boy," he warns.

"No, you watch it! I'm not twelve years old anymore, Dad. I'll say it how it is," I snap back, fighting against the tide of emotions.

He responds with a nonchalant "hm"and a knowing look. "You

got a whole lotta pent-up anger. What's really botherin' you, huh?"

"You—this whole damn situation between her father and you. The man is in a coma, and yet you still hold bitter resentment for the bloke. Get the hell over it now," I retort, my frustration pouring out.

"Xavier," his tone a warning. "Just give it a rest."

I stand up, the anger boiling over. "No, I don't give up on things that matter, unlike some people," I shoot back, my voice escalating. "You can't just dismiss everything and everyone like it's nothing, Dad. Isla's going through hell right now, and all you can do is pass judgments. You're fucking heartless!"

"The other night, she fucking offered me *money*, the money her damn father owes *YOU*! Don't you realise how fucked up that is, Dad? This is fucked. Get over your petty vendetta with her father. I won't have it interfering between Isla and me. You need to grow a pair and get the fuck over it!" I shout, causing a scene on the porch, not caring about the attention it draws.

He says nothing, so I press further.

"Who knows how long he has, or if he'll ever fucking wake up. This ends now. You get over the bullshit between you and her father, or that's it," I threaten

He gets in my face, challenging, "Or what, boy? What are you gonna do?"

With a clenched jaw, I fire back, "That's it, I'm done. This farm *runs* because of ME. It makes us *money* because of ME," I assert, my voice carrying the weight of finality. "Figure out your issues or be prepared to lose your son and this damn fucking place."

His eyes widen at the abruptness of my statement.

Before he can respond, Bradley and my mother rush out, their faces etched with concern.

"What the fuck is going on?" Bradley barks, stepping between us, while my mother directs her worried gaze between me and my father.

Bradley steps firmly between my father and me, creating a physical barrier that matches the tension in the air. "Xavier, back off. That's enough," he barks, his voice carrying the weight of authority.

I seethe, my fists clenched at my sides. "If you can't let go of your damn resentment, then I'm gone," I growl at my father, my eyes lock onto his. "I won't let you ruin what I have with her."

His response is dismissive. "Seems like things already are, if you ask me."

That's the breaking point. I lurch forward, ready to unleash my pent-up frustration, but Bradley intercepts me, standing his ground. "Xavier! Enough!" he commands, his voice sharp.

My mother, now visibly distraught, cries out, "Stop it, both of you! Please!"

My father's provocations continue. "What's the fixation on her? You in love, are ya?" he taunts.

"YES, I fucking am," I roar back, the admission ripping from my chest. The air becomes charged with tension, and my mother gasps audibly, the weight of my declaration hanging in the air like a storm about to break.

I can't remember the last time I was this close to losing it. Better yet, I can't even remember the last time I was ever in love with someone—I don't think I ever have been, to be honest. Before things escalate further, I push off Bradley, storming away, my emotions in turmoil. My mother's distressed cries ring in my ears as she calls out, "Xavier!" Her voice becomes a distant echo as I make my way towards the barn, seeking solitude to cool off.

Amidst the escalating tension, my mother's distressed cries cut through the air again, and I can hear her say, "Dom, listen to your bloody son! Stop this! He's hurting!"

Her voice, filled with desperation and concern, echoes in the open space, pleading for understanding. The words hang in the air, a stark reminder of the pain that now reverberates through our strained family dynamic.

Bradley says something in response, but the words become muffled, drowned out by the growing distance between us. The world blurs as I walk away, emotions running wild, and I can't shake the feeling that I've just unleashed a tempest that might change everything.

In the dimming light, I stride into the barn, a mixture of frustration, anger, and hurt boiling within me. Blue, my loyal companion, awaits in his stall, a comforting presence in this storm of emotions. Swiftly, I unhitch the latch, throw on his saddle and bridle, and mount him with practised ease.

With a click of my tongue and a nudge of my boot, Blue responds with eagerness, galloping out into the field. The wind whistles in my ears as I ride, the rhythmic thud of Blue's hooves on the ground echoing the thunderous beat of my own heart. I don't look back—I don't care that the darkness creeps in. All I need is to escape, to outrun the chaos that engulfs me.

As the landscape blurs, my mind races in tandem. The admission of my feelings for Isla hangs heavy in the air, a declaration I hadn't planned to make. Tears, unshed for far too long, prick at the corners of my eyes, but I grit my teeth against them and I furiously wipe at my face.

The open field offers no judgement, only the solace of speed and distance. I ride, seeking refuge in the cold embrace of the night, leaving the agitation behind.

If only for a moment.

40

Isla

The days blur together in a miserable haze since the accident. Xavier, a haunting absence, has not crossed my path since that night. I *yearn* for him, an *ache* that claws at me every damn day. The clinic has begrudgingly resumed operations, with Molly and Katy shouldering the responsibilities. When I tried to throw myself into work, they gently ushered me away, insisting that I need this time to be with my father.

Dad's condition remains the same. The weekend brought no reprieve—stagnation lingered, and blood clots emerged in his legs, demanding immediate attention from the doctors. Claire had arrived Saturday night, and the sight of me and dad had reduced her to tears. We crumpled together on the hospital floor, drowning in shared despair.

In this painful limbo between home and hospital, the latter is fast becoming a second dwelling. There are nights when I linger too long, and the nurses, compassionate souls, let me find solace within their walls.

Today, around 11 am, I drag myself through the revolving hospital doors. The nurse at the front desk greets me with a sympathetic smile. It's a different face today—older, with glasses and a short brown bob—that oddly reminds me of my mother and Katy. There's a warmth to her, though, a familiarity in the midst of the ever-changing hospital staff.

I manage a weak smile. "Hi, my father is in room 213, Callum Thompson. Any changes?"

She looks at me with recognition. "Ah, Isla, is it? I'm so sorry to hear about your father," she murmurs, and I smile politely.

"It's okay, just praying every day, you know?"

"Of course, we all are," she says as she types something into the computer looking for any updates and then shakes her head, her expression empathetic. "I'm afraid no updates, dear. Still holding on."

I exhale a heavy sigh, my shoulders slumping, "Thank you."

As I shuffle to leave, she blurts out that a few people have come and gone this morning to see my father. I nod, but scepticism tugs at me. Town folks don't have many kind words for him, so I find this very odd. They couldn't possibly care about my father.

She then leans in, as if sharing a secret. "Oh, Isla, now that I have you here, I thought I'd mention, now that I remember," I brace myself for her words, not sure what to expect. "There's a man who's been visiting your father when you're not around. Just checking in, asking for updates, and then he leaves."

My brow furrows in confusion. "Who? What does he look like? Is he young or old?"

She hesitates, and then a brief description follows. "He's younger, *very* good-looking, tall—*very* tall."

My mind races through possibilities, and I freeze at the thought—it's not... Xavier, *is it?* I don't think it would be him, not after the way I handled things. Is it Bradley? Maybe Harrison? But then the nurse adds, "He wears a backward cap—"

Xavier rarely wears caps, usually opting for his beloved cowboy hat. My thoughts churn with possibilities. Bradley or Harrison? But the nurse drops a bombshell. "Oh, *tattoos*. Tattoos on one of his arms."

My breath hitches. The realisation hits me like a tidal wave. It's *him*.

My mind grapples with the thought that he's been here, visiting my father. The idea that Xavier has been silently supporting us, even in my absence, cracks my heart just a little more. The nurse must sense my recognition, and she says, "He seems to care a lot about your father. Comes in quietly, spends some time, and then leaves without causin' a fuss. Just thought I'd let ya know."

I nod, a mix of gratitude and confusion swirling within me. "Thank you for letting me know."

"Of course, just thought he might be someone important," she adds, her tone understanding. The weight of his unspoken support adds to the emotional turmoil. I manage a weak smile, appreciating the unexpected comfort in the midst of my father's struggle.

"I guess I should be grateful for that, at least."

The nurse nods sympathetically. "He seems like a good man. Is he a relative, or...?" she trails off, leaving the question open-ended. I shake my head, a bittersweet smile playing on my lips.

"No, he's—" I sigh. "Definitely *not* a relative." I huff a laugh. "It's... complicated."

The nurse smiles warmly, as if putting two and two together. "Ah, 'complicated' often means there's a lot more to the story."

"I guess so," I say with a shrug. And with that, I wave as I turn to leave.

I push open the door to my father's room in the ICU and find Imogen and Claire sitting on the small lounge. My eyes widen in surprise.

"What!? What are you two doing here?" Tears well up in my eyes. "Don't you have work, Midge? And Claire? You're still here? What about your job in the city?"

Imogen offers a soft smile. "To hell with work. We're here for you, Isla."

Claire brushes it off with a dismissive sound. "Pft, please, I took some time off. I practically run that place. They could never fire me." She adds a snarky tone to lighten the mood.

In the small lounge of the ICU, tears welling up in my eyes, I approach them. They both stand up simultaneously, pulling me into a tight hug. Claire breaks the silence. "Baby girl, I've missed you. You have to fill me in on everything." Since Claire arrived, we hadn't gotten much of a chance to catch up, really. She'd been in and out of here, staying with Imogen in the meantime.

As we sit down, Imogen pulls tissues from her bag and hands them to me. She offers a comforting smile. I take a moment to collect myself, wiping away tears, and then I begin to share the chaotic events of the past few days. My voice trembles as I recount the accident, the MRI scans, and the tentative diagnosis of Alzheimer's disease.

Claire listens intently, her hand on my shoulder, while Imogen wipes away my tears, silently offering support.

Claire interrupts gently, "Oh, sweetheart, I'm so sorry. I wish I could have been here for you all this time. You've been through so much," she says, with tears welling up in her eyes.

I manage a small smile, appreciating her sincerity. "It's okay, Claire Bear. I'm just grateful you're here now. Thank you for staying."

She squeezes my shoulder, and her expression turns concerned. "And what about Xavier? How's he holding up?" My gaze shifts to Imogen, and I wince. Imogen sighs, and Claire, noticing the subtle exchange, looks between both of us, her curiosity piqued.

"What? What have I missed? Tell me," she urges, concern etched on her face.

I take a deep breath, feeling the weight of the truth pressing down on me. "We were doing well, Claire, *really* well. But the night of the accident—everything changed." My voice quivers as I relive the events of that painful night.

"He just—he's been so helpful and so caring. I freaked out, like the fucking coward I am," I begin, the words catching in my throat.

"I... I didn't want to burden him. I was scared and just worried. So, I—I pushed him away, and it turned into this... *argument*. He left, and I haven't seen him since."

Imogen squeezes my hand, her eyes reflecting the understanding of shared pain. "Isla, sweetheart," she murmurs gently.

"But I fucked up," I admit, my voice breaking. "I fucked up so bad. I—I fell for him, and then I brushed things off like a selfish idiot."

Both girls gasp at my admission, their expressions a mix of surprise and concern.

"You... you fell for him?" Claire says softly, as her eyes light up. "Are you in love with him?"

Sighing, I nod. "Yeah, I think I am. I can't explain it, but I've never felt these emotions before, and we'd made such strong connections."

"Babe, love can be messy. But messy doesn't mean it's over," Imogen says in a soft voice.

Claire asks gently, "Have you—have you spoken to him? Texts? Anything?"

I respond with a shaky, "No," my lips trembling.

"*I* pushed *him* away. Why would he contact me? And—" my voice breaks, "he—he's been visiting Dad. I just found out, and, *uggghh*—," my voice falters as I turn my head to look up at the ceiling, inhaling a hard breath and exhaling it.

Claire leans in, offering a reassuring hug. "Look, I know nothing about love—" She shudders with disgust and I smile—Claire has never been the one to settle down. She's too work-driven, says she 'doesn't have time for useless men and working with them every day has turned her right off' I recall her past words.

"Sometimes we make mistakes, and it takes time to fix them. Just be patient and give him the chance to come back. Love has a way of finding its path, even in the messiest situations," she reassures me.

Imogen chimes in, "And, plus, if he's been visiting your dad, it shows he still cares. He'll come around."

It's lunchtime, and Imogen kindly offers to run down and grab lunch from the café. Claire decides to stay with me.

I get a text from Olivia, saying she and Harrison want to swing by. They won't stay long, as Harrison needs to get back to work, and he will pick Olivia up on the way. I assure her that it's okay. Meanwhile, Amelia has been texting me incessantly since we exchanged numbers on Xavier's birthday. I genuinely appreciate her friendliness, and honestly, her texts are a welcome distraction.

Shortly after this, while Imogen is still grabbing us lunch, Olivia and Harrison come in, offering their get-well wishes for my dad and hugging me instantly. Harrison turns to Claire with a curious look, and I realise I've neglected to introduce them.

"Oh, sorry! Claire, this is Olivia and Harrison. Guys, this is Claire, my best friend who lives in the city."

I introduce Olivia as Xavier's sister and Harrison as his friend, but Harrison cuts me off, saying, "Hey, I'm *your* friend, too." I give him a playful smile, and we share a laugh. Olivia rushes up to Claire, expressing that it's nice to meet her.

Claire smiles warmly, extending a hand to both of them. "Nice to meet you both. Thank you for coming."

Imogen walks in, her movements faltering as she takes in the presence of Harrison and Olivia. A subtle frown creases her forehead, and I can almost sense the internal agitation behind her eyes.

"Hi, guys," she quips, offering a forced smile to Olivia before shooting a sidelong glance at Harrison.

He responds with a low whistle. "Nice to see you too, sugar."

Imogen releases an audible groan and plonks herself down next to me and Claire. Olivia gracefully takes a seat on the small chair on the other side of the bed, attempting to steer the conversation.

"So, how's everything going with Isla's father?" she inquires.

Imogen doesn't hold back, offering a detailed update on the situation. As they talk, Claire turns to whisper in my ear, "What's up with the two of them?" She gestures discreetly to Imogen and Harrison, her expression curious and slightly amused.

I respond softly, "Beats me. They have this silent hate game going on, and if you ask me, I reckon it's because she finds him attractive and hates herself for it. Always complaining he's too childish. I don't know why, though—he's a catch."

Claire nods enthusiastically. "You're telling me! I mean, hello! Look at him—tattoos, dirty scruff, backwards cap... oof." She fans herself, and I can't help but giggle softly.

As Imogen and Harrison exchange snarky comments, Olivia smoothly changes the topic, asking about my plans and how I'm holding up. I update them on my daily routine, the hospital stays, and the ongoing struggle with my emotions. Olivia and Claire listen intently, offering their support in their unique ways. Claire suggests a change of scenery, a break from the hospital walls. Imogen proposes a weekend getaway once my father stabilises.

"Oh my god! YES! I think that's a perfect idea, once things are better with your father, Isla, of course," Olivia exclaims.

"I think that would be nice. We'll just see how we go with Dad," I say softly. "Plus, your brother and I..." I sigh. "He and I are not really..."

"Oh, screw him!" she says with a huff, and Harrison coughs out a 'she already has' and proceeds to cover it up with more coughs. Imogen smacks him on the arm—hard—muttering, "Idiot," and he winces out loud.

"Ouch, woman! Why are you so violent?" he exclaims, and Imogen just rolls her eyes. We all laugh out loud.

Olivia continues. "Anywhooo, you don't have to explain, Isla," she says with a reassuring smile. "Bradley kinda told me what happened... I hope that's okay?" she says with a worried expression.

I kind of had a feeling he'd mention something to Olivia sooner or later, but that's okay. I give a reassuring smile and shrug.

"He'll come around; he's been moping around every day. Bradley and Mum keep pressing him to do something about it, but alas, he's a stubborn mule—and not even Duchess or Blue are that stubborn." I can't help but chuckle lightly at this.

Imogen and Harrison, though engaged in their own silent war, manage to maintain a façade of civility as the conversation continues. Imogen's disdain is thinly veiled, and Harrison, with his devil-may-care attitude, doesn't seem bothered by it. For a moment, the weight on my shoulders eases. These friends, old *and* new, bring a warmth that contrasts with this gloomy environment.

Eventually, as lunchtime winds down, the group disperses. Imogen makes a swift exit, exchanging curt nods with Harrison. Olivia gives me a reassuring hug before she and Harrison take their leave. Claire promises to visit again soon, squeezing my hand before heading out.

Alone in the hospital room, I let out a sigh. The visit has brought a mix of emotions, leaving me both comforted and conflicted. I find solace in the camaraderie of friends but can't shake the unspoken tension lingering in the air.

I move to sit beside my father, grabbing hold of his hand and squeezing it, feeling the warmth that brings a small comfort. I take a deep breath, absorbing the sight of him. The cuts and bruises are slowly fading, a hopeful sign, yet the uncertainty about his internal condition lingers.

Just then, one of the regular nurses enters the room, accompanied by Dr. Anderson, a male doctor I've briefly met before. He greets me, asking how I am. I'm fed up with people asking this question, each time a reminder of the difficulty I'm facing, yet I respond politely.

Dr. Anderson's voice resonates with a calm assurance. "Isla, it's been a few days, and your father's body is responding quite positively to the treatment. The clotting issues are being managed effectively. In light of his progress, we are considering a significant step forward in his treatment plan. We plan to initiate the process of weaning him off the medically induced coma."

His words hang in the air, a delicate mix of hope and uncertainty. He continues, choosing his words with precision, "This step is taken cautiously, with the intent of allowing him to gradually regain consciousness. We'll be monitoring his responses closely throughout the process to ensure it's as smooth as possible."

My breath catches at this revelation, unsure of what to think or say. His words hang in the air, a delicate mix of hope and uncertainty. I take a deep breath, my weariness evident, "How—how is he going to respond to coming out of the coma? Are there any risks or… complications I should be prepared for?"

Dr. Anderson acknowledges the gravity of the situation, "So, the process is gradual, and we will closely monitor his vital signs, neurological responses, and overall stability. While we aim for a smooth transition, there are inherent uncertainties in such situations. It's a critical phase, and your father will receive the best possible care."

As Dr. Anderson imparts the crucial information, the nurse and he move around my father's bedside with a methodical precision. The soft hum of medical machinery blends with the low murmur of their voices, creating a symphony of hope and tension. The nurse then explains the intricacies of the process. "Isla, we'll begin by gradually reducing the medication that initially induced the coma. This step allows your father to wake up slowly. Our ultimate goal is to withdraw the medication completely. Simultaneously, we'll transition the ventilator to a mode that encourages your father to regain natural breathing functions." Their movements are synchronised, adjusting tubes and interacting with the various medical devices that surround him.

The room becomes a theatre of meticulous care, each gesture a step toward my father's potential recovery.

41

Isla

A few weeks have passed since they weaned my father off anaesthesia, and the weight of his comatose state lingers in the air, a persistent worry gnawing at my insides. Desperation for a distraction led me back to work, Katy and Molly reluctantly allowing it. The routine provides a semblance of normalcy, yet my anxiety has surged since the accident, threatening to spill into panic attacks.

The news of someone adopting Luna briefly lifts my spirits. I'm grateful she found a loving home, even if it's just a momentary reprieve. Katy's suspicious dismissal of my inquiries about the adoptive parents doesn't go unnoticed, but I decide to set it aside, making a mental note to dig for more details later on.

The contemplation of messaging Xavier dances at the edge of my thoughts, a relentless loop of doubt and longing. I was the one who asked for space, but how long is he willing to let this silence persist? The fear that he might have moved on, decided it was for the best, gnaws at me. Each day, the panic seizes me, making it difficult to breathe. I resist the pull of my medication, determined to face the restlessness and nausea head-on.

Today, I decide to visit my childhood home, seeking a distraction, perhaps emptying out the bins. My father's car, now a write-off, fetched a meagre cheque, just shy of $2,000. The irony isn't lost on me—the money a bitter reminder of the night I offered Xavier payment for my father's debt.

A dull ache settles in my chest, and I instinctively place a hand over my heart, as if the touch could ease the pain. It's futile. I just really miss Xavier and the comfort he provided.

I pull up in front of the house, a wave of nausea threatening to overtake me. Stepping inside, the familiar scent of my father surrounds me – a mixture of alcohol and aged wood. I take a deep breath and get to work. The sink full of dishes calls for attention, and I start by cleaning them, then move on to emptying the dishwasher and taking care of the bins out front.

After dealing with the bins, an unexpected urge draws me back inside. For the first time since returning home, I find myself ascending the stairs to the hallway. A peculiar sensation tightens my chest—an unfamiliar pull that guides me upward. Call it intuition or whatever you want, but something compels me to explore. After all, I'd been here countless times before, and not once did I have any inclination to head upstairs—no need for it, until now.

Turning to face the hallway, I'm greeted by rows of pictures adorning the walls, capturing moments from my childhood. The timber trimmings, once pristine, now exude a weathered and rustic charm. The floorboards creak beneath each step. Nausea rises in my throat, and I instinctively place a hand over my mouth, swallowing down the impending bubble of anxiety.

Each picture on the walls holds a profound memory, a visual narrative of my childhood. Some feature both my parents, frozen in moments of shared joy. Others showcase just my mum or dad, and there are even baby pictures—innocence frozen in time. A bitter-sweet smile graces my lips, tears welling up in my eyes.

Continuing down the hallway, I reach what used to be my old room. I take a deep breath, expecting to walk into an empty space—considering I hadn't been here in over 7 years. As I open the door, my breathing falters.

I push open the door, and a wave of nostalgia washes over me. The room, frozen in time, tells the story of a girl who once lived here, dreams and memories etched into every corner. Sunlight streams through the half-closed curtains, casting a warm glow on the familiar surroundings.

Everything is exactly where I left it. The bed, neatly made, appears untouched, as though awaiting my return. The walls, adorned with posters of rock bands and movies from my teenage years, now seem like relics of a bygone era. The desk, cluttered with notebooks and doodles, reflects the chaotic creativity of my adolescence.

On the desk, amid the scattered objects of my past, a picture frame catches my eye. It holds a snapshot frozen in time—a moment that encapsulates the essence of our friendship. Imogen, Claire, and I, in our school uniforms, smiling like we owned the world.

The memories flood back to me vividly. It was an afternoon after school, and we'd decided to head to one of the local parks. There, beneath the shade of a towering tree and perched on a large rock ornament, we spent hours sharing our dreams, aspirations, and the naïve expectations we held for our futures.

I recall the laughter and the comforting aura of that day. Life had been carefree then, surrounded by the once-loving presence of my father and my beautiful mother. She was still alive at that time, though her health was a battle she fought silently—a venomous disease that ultimately took her from me, far too young, far too soon.

As I stand in the room, the image of that photograph resonates with a bittersweet intensity. The innocence captured in that frame contrasts sharply with the complexities of the present. Life has sculpted us in ways we could never have predicted back then, and the passage of time has etched its mark on each of our lives.

Tears blur my vision as I realise how much has changed since those days. The vibrant energy that once permeated these walls and this part of life has given way to the quiet and solitude of an abandoned space.

Moving with purpose, I find myself drawn to my parents' room. The door stands slightly ajar, a silent invitation to revisit another chapter of my history. As I push it open, a rush of familiar scents greets me—hints of ageing wood and the faint remnants of my father's cologne.

The atmosphere in the room is both comforting and haunting. I run my fingers over the surfaces, tracing the outlines of the furniture, absorbing the emotions embedded within them. Closing my eyes, I take a deep breath, savouring the familiar scent that wraps around me like a gentle embrace.

Walking over to my mum's side of the bed, I notice the top drawer slightly ajar. It's kind of odd – maybe Dad left it like that before.... well—before *everything*. I push away those grim thoughts and open the drawer wider, revealing a mishmash of crumpled papers, a couple of trinkets, and a bunch of sealed envelopes.

Old photos are scrambled at the bottom—snapshots of my folks in their younger, happier days. A delicate silver locket with a worn chain catches my eye and my breathing falters—mum's locket chain bracelet. My eyes blur with tears. I pick it up and hold it in my palms, like it's the most delicate thing in the world. She used to wear this all the time and I used to always play with it when I was anxious or whenever I used to hold her hand. *When did my father take this? I thought it had been buried with her?*

Tears spill out the corners of my eyes, and I quickly wipe at them, to avoid blurring my vision further. I clasp it tight into my palm, before putting it into my pocket. My eyes lock back onto a bunch of envelopes. Sealed envelopes that have been neatly stacked like they don't belong here.

I take a seat on the edge of the bed. Picking them up, I see my mum's elegant handwriting on the first one. It's a letter, addressed to me. No, there are multiple letters—all addressed to *me*. My breath catches in my throat and I involuntarily hold them in my hands.

I look at the first one, the simple letters forming my name—*Isla - 21 years old.* A lump forms in my throat, and a profound sadness washes over me. My mind flickers back to the time when Mum passed away, just after I turned 18 and graduated from Year 12 in high school. The memory of her witnessing my high school graduation remains a cherished echo, a moment for which I am immensely grateful.

Tearing it open, my eyes focus on her handwriting, and with a shaky breath I begin to read it.

Dear Isla,

If you are reading this, my love, it means that I am no longer with you. I want you to know that I fought endlessly for you, I fought to live for you. The love we shared, and the beautiful person you are, were my reasons to fight. Life is a fragile, fleeting gift, and in my last moments, all I could think of was you. Hold onto our memories, and let them be the guiding stars in your night sky.

As you stand on the cusp of 21, I want you to embrace the journey ahead with courage and curiosity. Life is an ever-changing tapestry, and with each passing year, you weave your own unique story. Remember, amidst the highs and lows, you possess a strength that can weather any storm.

May your days be filled with joy, laughter, and the pursuit of your passions. Never forget that setbacks are not failures but opportunities for growth. Embrace the unknown, for it holds the potential for beautiful surprises.

Cherish the bonds you forge and hold on to the love that surrounds you. Life may take unexpected turns, but the connections you nurture will be your constant anchor. You are capable of incredible things, my dear Isla, and I believe in the boundless potential within you.

With all my love,

Mum

As the last words of the letter settle in my heart, tears flow freely and a choked sob escapes me. I instinctively cover my mouth.

Tears stain the paper as I continue reading my mother's words again for a second time. With tear-filled eyes, I move on to the next envelope, labelled—*Isla - 25 years old.* As I tear it open, my mother's handwriting, once again, unfolds another chapter of love and wisdom.

Well, look at you, my beautiful girl, officially a quarter of a century! I hope this finds you surrounded by the things that make your heart sing. By now, I imagine you've achieved that dream of becoming a veterinarian, just like we'd spoken about—a force to be reckoned with in the world of healing our four-legged friends.

I hope you've also found a person who sees the extraordinary soul you are. Someone to share your dreams, support your ambitions, and, most importantly, make you laugh until your sides ache. Life is too short not to revel in the joy of genuine, deep connection.

As I read over my mother's words, memories flood back to my 25th birthday, a snapshot of a life intertwined with someone I thought belonged there. I make a face of disgust and a bitter laugh escapes me, a laugh not at my mother's hopeful words, but at the misguided path I once thought was the right one. How naïve I had been to believe I was in the right place at the right time.

How pathetically wrong I was.

Looking back at that version of myself, I see a woman now shaped by the choices she had made. A woman who, instead of embracing the warmth of a newfound commitment, lets fear guide her steps. I know better. I know better than to follow in these footsteps, and the thought that I could have now potentially ruined the one thing that meant to the most to be, fucking kills me.

I pushed Xavier away because I'm a fucking sook, and I think part of me is too embarrassed to confront him, for this sole reason.

With a lump in my throat, I pick up the third letter, uncertainty clinging to me like a shroud. The words on the envelope, *Isla - to finding love*, send a tremor through my body. I drop the letter into my lap, my hand covers my mouth as silent sobs wrack my frame. I'm not sure I can bring myself to read it. An image of my mother looking down on me crosses my mind. She wrote these letters with the hope that I would read them one day. So, I wipe my nose, take a shuddering breath, and tear the envelope open. As I read through the letter, my tears continue to flow, the words a bittersweet embrace.

Isla, my love,

I hope this letter finds you at a time when love has woven its way into the fabric of your life. By now, you may have encountered the person who makes your heart dance and your soul sing. Whether it's a slow burn or a whirlwind, embrace it with all your being.

Love is a journey, my dear, and it comes in unexpected ways. Sometimes, it's found in shared laughter, stolen glances, or a comforting touch. Cherish those moments, for they are the threads that weave the tapestry of a beautiful life.

Remember that love isn't always perfect, and it doesn't have to be.

It's the messy, imperfect moments that make it real. Find someone who sees you at your worst and still chooses to stand by your side. Someone who appreciates your quirks and celebrates your victories.

May your heart find solace in the company of someone who adds joy to your days and comfort to your nights. And if you've already found this love, hold on to it with both hands and a grateful heart.

Also, please remember that your father's love is one that will always be with you. Despite the rifts and challenges, deep down, he loves you with everything. Fathers have a unique way of expressing their love, and despite any misunderstandings, his love for you is undying.

With all my love, always.

Mum

I don't even have it in me to look at the last letter. I let out a strangled cry and a cough, hastily bundling the torn, tear-stained letters under my arm. Closing the drawer with a trembling hand, I stand abruptly and hurry out of my parents' bedroom. Running down the stairs and out the front door, I gasp for air, the weight of the emotions leaving me breathless.

Gasping for air, my lungs constrict, and pain courses through my chest. A wince escapes my lips as I struggle to breathe. Unable to keep the nausea at bay, I stagger towards the nearest bin and vomit, heaving and gagging, my body convulsing with each cough.

Confident that the contents of my stomach have been emptied, I stand up straight, wiping my mouth with the back of my hand. I walk over to my car with careful yet hasty steps, not wanting to upset my stomach further. Getting into the car, I take deep breaths, wiping at the tears that just won't fucking stop.

Driven by a desperate need, I start my car and keep driving, the familiar scenery passing by in a blur. Lost in my thoughts, the roads seem to guide me on their own until, before I know it, I find myself at the doors of the church in Wattle Creek, a place I haven't visited in ages.

I push open the heavy wooden doors, their groans echoing through the mostly empty church. The scent of polished wood and aged hymnals permeates the air as I step into the hallowed space. Sunlight filters through the stained glass, casting vibrant patterns on the worn floorboards. A few elderly individuals occupy some of the pews.

I kneel down on the worn wooden pew, the echoes of my emotions reverberating through the empty church. The cold, musty air envelops me as I close my eyes, seeking solace in the quiet sanctuary.

"I know I haven't been here in a while, but I just—I need you right now." My words come out shaky, and I take a deep breath before continuing.

"God, if you're listening," I whisper in the quietude, "I need your help. My father is in pain, and I don't know how to bear this burden alone. Guide me, give me strength, and bring healing to him." I sigh. "Just give me a sign—anything—to just... let me know that everything will be okay or that things will get better."

My words linger in the air, a plea intertwined with the essence of my struggles. Despite never being a religious person, here I am again, seeking solace in the echoes of prayers. This situation is fucked, and

I'm grappling with uncertainties that have driven me to a place I'd long neglected.

As I kneel in the quiet solitude of the church, lost in my thoughts and prayers, I'm startled by a presence beside me. Looking up, I find Xavier's father standing there, a figure unexpected and surprising in this space. My shock is evident, and questions whirl in my mind. *How did he find me here, of all places?* The air thickens as our eyes meet in the dimly lit church.

"Sorry, I don't mean to be a bother," he apologises, clearing his throat as if searching for the right words. "I saw you come in, and I thought I might offer some company," he adds, his eyes reflecting a genuine concern that surprises me, considering the tensions that usually linger around him. "Would that be alright?"

I hesitate for a moment, the complex history between our fathers flashing in my mind. Despite the past turmoil, I manage a polite nod. "Uh... sure."

Dominic clears his throat, and a hint of formality creeps into his tone. "I'm Dominic Mitchell," he says, extending a hand toward me, "but you can call me Dom if you prefer."

"Okay," I say softly.

"I know you probably don't want to speak to me. I can understand that. Things with your father and I—" He sighs, his voice trailing off, the weight of unresolved issues evident in the air.

He chooses his words carefully, navigating the delicate topic with a sincerity that catches me off guard.

"Isla, I want you to know how deeply sorry I am for what your father's going through. No one deserves to see their loved ones in such pain, and I can't help but feel a certain responsibility for all the turmoil."

Dominic's apology seems genuine, and for a moment, the tension in the air softens. He takes a deep breath, as if gathering the courage to confront the past.

"Over the years, I've let stubbornness and resentment cloud my judgement. I've caused problems, and I know it. But standing here, in this sacred place, I can't help but realise how trivial those issues were compared to the pain you must be going through. I've carried a grudge for far too long, and it's time for me to set things right."

His words hang in the air, heavy with regret and a genuine desire for redemption. I watch him, surprised by the vulnerability he's displaying in this unexpected moment of confession.

Dominic continues, his gaze sincere. "A recent altercation with my son made me realise the gravity of the situation. It opened my eyes to the pain we've both been carrying, and I couldn't ignore it any longer. That's why I'm here, Isla, to apologise sincerely and to offer whatever support I can. Your father... he deserves better, and so do you."

As he speaks, my mind races. *Recent altercation with his son...?* The realisation hits me like a ton of bricks. *Xavier.* I wonder what could have transpired between them, a knot forming in my stomach.

Xavier's father continues, "I want you to know that the issue with the money, it was never really an issue. My stubbornness and resentment got in the way, and for that, I'm truly sorry."

Stunned, I sit there, my breath heavy as I process the weight of his words. Tears rim my eyes as a mixture of emotions floods over me. The apology is unexpected, and the sincerity in his voice catches me off guard. "I appreciate your honesty and apology. It means a lot, especially during a time like this," I manage to say, glancing away for a moment, grappling with the unexpected turn of events.

"Seeing Xavier affected by all this has been a wake-up call for me. I've never seen him like this before, and it made me realise I've let my own stubbornness deprive me of relationships that matter. I don't want the same for him, or for you."

I listen intently, still processing the unexpected conversation. The mention of Xavier adds another layer to the complexity of the situation.

I nod in understanding, still processing the unexpected turn of events. "I appreciate your honesty, Dom. It means more than you know."

He offers a small, genuine smile. "If there's anything I can do, anything at all, just let me know. For Xavier's sake, and for yours."

I hesitate, a timid expression crossing my face. "Uhm, Dom, about Xavier... I never meant to hurt him," I admit, my voice soft. "He's been really caring through all of this, and I'm afraid I might've ruined things. I sound like a broken record, I know, but... it's just so hard to find the courage to talk to him."

Dominic nods understandingly. "Look, I've always had a mutual understandin' with my son. Being the eldest, he's shouldered many responsibilities, some I'm afraid to admit. But one thing I do know is he is incredibly stubborn—I'm afraid he gets that from me," he huffs a laugh. "He's hard-headed, but... he has a big heart. I can see that he cares a'lotta 'bout you. Somethin' I thought I'd never see. So, uh, I'd really like to see you guys work it out."

His words carry a weight of sincerity, and I find myself contemplating the layers of complexity in Xavier's character.

"I hope we can," I respond with a sigh.

The corner of his mouth turns upward. "Knowing my son, you will." He winks and then pats my shoulder. I nod appreciatively, feeling a strange sense of gratitude toward Xavier's father in this unexpected moment.

As Dominic leaves, I'm left alone with my rampant thoughts, running wild in my head. The weight of my assumptions about my dad's resentment lingers. All this time, I believed he harboured a grudge because I left without a trace, without a word. Yet, now, in the wake of Dominic's unexpected apology, I'm forced to reconsider.

My father wasn't always a kind person, especially after my mother's death. Dealing with his grief became too much for a 19-year-old girl to bear. Time, as I've come to realise, is a fickle thing. I don't know how much time I have left with my father, and instead of dwelling on negativity, I need to face things head-on, with a strong heart, just as my mum always advised.

I gaze up at the ceiling of the church, adorned with stained glass windows depicting scenes from the Bible. *Perhaps Dominic Mitchell walking in here was the sign I needed.*

I need to bite the bullet, confront my fears, and reach out to

Xavier. We need to talk, hash out everything that's been going on between us. It's time to mend what's broken, not just with my father, but with the people who still have a place in my life.

Pulling out my phone, I move my fingers over the screen, pulling up my text messages with Xavier. My heart aches at the sight of the last message from him.

> **Xavier:** I'm coming past tonight. Dinner is on me ;)

> **Xavier:** In case that wasn't clear, that means I'm staying over tonight. See you soon, princess.

Just weeks ago, things had finally started to fall into place, and look where I've gotten myself now. I release a long sigh and begin typing out a message. *Is he even going to reply?* Ugh. *Why am I so nervous all of a sudden?* After multiple tries, I manage to type out:

> **Me:** Can I come over? I miss you.

I hit send, my heart pounding in my chest as I wait for a response. The seconds tick by slowly, each one feeling like an eternity. Why am I so nervous? I just need to talk to him, to fix things between us.

As the message shows 'Delivered', a wave of anxiety washes over me, its grip tightening around my chest. *What if he doesn't reply?* The thought alone sends a jolt of embarrassment through me. I feel my heart racing, my palms growing clammy.

Desperate to quell the rising panic, I take a deep breath, trying to steady my nerves. I remind myself that I can handle whatever response comes my way. I close my eyes briefly, focusing on the sensation of my breath entering and leaving my lungs, a grounding technique I learned from a mindfulness app recently. After a moment, I open my eyes, my resolve firm. Fuck this feeling. I can't let fear hold me back.

I'm going there anyway because I need to. I need to make things right.

I need him.

42

Xavier

Bent down in the barn, I'm busy cleaning out Duchess's hooves. Blue's done, and I'm all fucking sweaty. The weather outside today is a bit gloomy, but this grind of hard work makes you break a sweat, without a doubt. I wipe my forehead with the back of my arm, before moving to lift one of her strong legs onto my thigh.

Before I can continue, Blue in his stall starts whinnying loudly, knocking against the stall. That old trick again—he's restless and wants to get out.

"Alright, Blue, you impatient brute. I'll take you out." I mutter, earning a snort from the horse as if he understands every word. I shake my head, smirking. Duchess nudges my shoulder playfully, and I chuckle. Never a dull moment with these two.

"Easy, girl. Just finishing up here." The routine in the barn keeps my mind occupied, providing a momentary escape from the outside world.

As I finish cleaning up her hooves, giving Duchess a quick pat, I lead her back to her stall—but I'm stunted for a moment, as a sensation tingles at the back of my neck at the feeling of a presence from behind. I don't need to turn around to know it's her. I've grown so attuned to her presence that it's become second nature.

My body reacts before my mind fully comprehends, a shudder coursing through me. Slowly, I turn around to face the woman who's become the rhythm to my heartbeat. It's been weeks since I last saw her, and the sight of her now leaves me breathless.

Still gripping Duchess's bridle, the charged air between us is palpable. Our eyes lock, a silent exchange that speaks volumes. She glances down, attempting to conceal a small smile, and I seize the moment to truly take her in. Dressed in those damn perfect blue jeans that cling to her curves, she's a sight that I've longed for. The work boots and the frill-sleeved black t-shirt tucked into her jeans—fuck, I've missed her. My craving for her touch intensifies. When she looks up, our eyes meet, and a blush instantly paints her cheeks a rosy hue. So, we're back to this now, huh?

Isla breaks the silence with a timid, "Hey."

"Hi," I respond, my voice gruffer than I intended, but a smirk plays on my lips.

I notice her voice soften as she continues, "I, uh, sent you a text..." Her words trail off.

I pat the back of my jeans, realising my phone isn't there. It must've been left inside the house. "My phone is inside. Sorry."

"That's... all good," she says, fiddling with the hem of her shirt.

My gaze lingers on her, tracing the lines of her face, the subtle changes that time has brought.

The silence stretches, a chasm of unspoken words and unresolved feelings. As I look at her, I notice a subtle fragility, a frailty that wasn't there the last time we crossed paths. She seems to have lost a bit of weight, and the realisation tugs at my chest. I can't help but wonder about the stress and turmoil she's been through, the toll it's taken on her body.

The ache in my chest deepens, a mix of concern and an unspoken desire to shield her from whatever burdens she carries.

Duchess shifts restlessly, sensing the tension in the air. I release her bridle, my hands now free, but uncertain of where to put them. Isla's eyes meet mine again, and I can see the vulnerability in them, a reflection of my own feelings mirrored back at me.

She begins to speak, her words stumbling and stuttering as she tries to express her remorse. "Xavier, I'm... I'm so sorry," she stammers, a genuine regret in her eyes. "I'm such an idiot for what I did. I was just... scared," her voice falters, the vulnerability palpable in the air.

As she speaks, a heavy silence lingers in the barn. The air is thick with tension, the only sound breaking the quietude is the distant rustling of leaves outside. My gaze remains fixed on her, my eyes betraying a mix of emotions—confusion, hurt, and a lingering affection that refuses to fade away.

Isla continues, her words carrying the weight of her sincerity.

"I never wanted to push you away. I was just overwhelmed with everything – my dad, the accident, and then us." She glances down at her hands, fingers nervously intertwining. "I thought I needed space, but now... now I just realise how much I miss you."

My expression softens, a subtle understanding in my eyes. The ache in my heart responds to her admission, the silent plea for forgiveness. Yet, words remain elusive as emotions swirl within the confined space of the barn.

I take a deep breath, the weight of her words sinking in. "I missed you, too, Isla," I admit, my voice a low murmur. The vulnerability in her eyes resonates with my own internal struggle. The barn seems to close in around us, amplifying the intensity of the moment.

She looks up, her eyes searching mine for a reaction. The distance between us feels palpable, an invisible force that both separates and connects. I want to bridge that gap, to pull her close and assure her that everything will be okay.

"How are... uh, how's things, you know, around here?" she asks softly.

"Same old, same old," I respond, keeping it vague. Opening up feels like prying open a wound, and I'm not sure if I'm ready for that.

I glance toward Blue, the restless stallion in his stall, eager for some action. "I was just about to take Blue for a ride. Wanna... join me?" The invitation hangs in the air, loaded with unspoken emotions and the complexity of our shared history.

Isla takes a moment to contemplate my invitation, her eyes flickering between me and Blue. The silence stretches, echoing with the weight of unspoken words. Finally, she nods, a tentative smile playing on her lips.

"Yeah, I'd like that," she says, her voice softer than I remember. "I've missed this place."

I nod in response, a mix of emotions swirling within me. Taking a deep breath, I lead Blue out of the stall. I insist that Isla ride Duchess, assuring her that she's a lot more placid and easier to handle. As I work on gearing up the horses, the familiar routine brings back memories. The scent of leather, the creaking of saddles, and the soft whickers of the horses create a comforting backdrop.

As I finish saddling Blue, I glance over at Isla, a mix of anticipation and uncertainty in her eyes.

I instruct Isla to come stand next to me, beside Duchess. "Just stand here," I say, gesturing to a spot by the horse's shoulder. "Let her get used to you, and when you're comfortable, give her a gentle pat."

I watch as Isla cautiously approaches, her hand outstretched. Duchess snorts softly but seems at ease.

"That's it, nice and easy," I encourage, appreciating the gentleness in Isla's touch.

A sense of déjà vu washes over me. It feels like an eternity ago when I helped her onto Blue. So much has changed since then, and it's hard to believe how different things are now.

"Nice and easy," I repeat, offering a reassuring smile. "She's a sweetheart once you get to know her."

Isla nods, her hand gentle as she pats Duchess.

"I remember that day you had brought her into the clinic..." her voice trails off. "She was so unsettled. It's nice to see her in a good mood," she says as she continues to pat her neck, just underneath her long white mane.

"Don't be fooled. She can be feisty," I say with a smirk.

"She's beautiful," she remarks, a hint of awe in her voice, looking back at me.

"Yeah, she is," I agree, my eyes locked on Isla. The air seems charged with unspoken emotions. "Now, when you're ready, I'll lift you up, okay?"

She nods again, a subtle blush tinting her cheeks. Following our established routine, I place my hands at her waist, lifting her with practised ease onto Duchess's back. The contact sends a jolt through me, and I try to focus on the task at hand, pushing the memories that threaten to resurface away, for now.

Memories flood my mind. Duchess was my first baby—I bought her as a foal from a farm about ten or so kilometres from here. I recall the day vividly, choosing her among a group of foals. Her brown and white coat made her stand out, and in that moment, I knew she was the one.

As Isla settles onto Duchess, I move towards Blue's stall. I grab Blue, giving him a gentle pat as I secure his saddle and bridle. With everything in place, I swing myself onto his back. The familiar sensation of being astride my horse brings a comforting sense of normalcy, a welcome distraction from the unresolved emotions lingering in the air.

I glance over at Isla, offering a reassuring smile, and I grab hold of Duchess's reins and give a gentle click with my tongue, urging them forward as we head outside.

I turn to Isla and suggest, "We'll take them just a bit further up ahead. There's a nice trail along the edge of the farm."

She simply nods, her response a playful, "Lead the way, cowboy," accompanied by a smirk.

My lips break into a full-blown smile at her remark. I can't help but feel a surge of warmth. It's one of those little things she does that never fails to bring a smile to my face. She's called me 'cowboy' before, and each time, it stirs something in me.

I guide the horses forward, enjoying the banter and the warmth that's slowly settling between us. Isla's blush, however, doesn't escape my notice. It only adds to the joy of the moment.

We've ridden far down the trail, the sun now blazing through the clouds, erasing the earlier gloominess. The hum of cicadas and chirping birds fills the air, creating a serene symphony. This place, with its quiet magnitude, resonates with me, and I love it. A while back, I let go of Duchess's reins, and Isla now clasps them in her hands, a smile gracing her face. Her eyes squint from the sun, and she lifts her hand above them. Without a second thought, I take off my hat and lean over, placing it on her head.

"Oh no, Xav. I don't—" Isla starts protesting.

"I'm used to the sun out here. You need it more than I do," I drawl, a mix of protectiveness and casualness in my tone. As we continue along the path, my gaze keeps drifting towards Isla, and I can't help but wonder when caring for her became such a natural thing. The hat perched slightly too big on her head adds a touch of charm, and it's a sight that makes my heart stir. We're surrounded by the tranquillity of nature, the crunch of gravel beneath the horses' hooves, and the soft rustling of leaves overhead.

The sun casts a warm glow on everything, and in that moment, I realise how much I've missed these shared silences, these stolen glances, and the quiet connection that binds us.

Isla catches me staring, and a blush creeps up her cheeks. Breaking the tranquil silence, she sighs. "We should talk... no, we *need* to talk." Her voice falters, carrying a weight that matches the seriousness of her words.

"Yeah," I respond, my tone serious yet soft. "There's a lot we need to sort out."

The horses plod along the trail, seemingly attuned to the tension between us. As we ride side by side, I steal glances at Isla, uncertainty lingering in the air like an unspoken promise.

Isla's grip on Duchess's reins tightens, her knuckles almost white. There's a hesitant energy between us, as if the words are eager to escape but fear the consequences.

"I'm sorry, Xavier," Isla finally says, repeating her earlier sentiment, breaking the silence. "Fuck, I sound like a broken record. I—I never meant to hurt you."

I glance at her, taking in the sincerity etched across her face. "You did, though," I admit, my voice low. "You hurt me, Isla."

"I know, and I hate myself for it," she confesses, her eyes searching mine for understanding. "But I need you to know it wasn't about you. It was about me, about my fears and insecurities."

Her words hang in the air, and for a moment, I feel a pang of sympathy for her pain. But the frustration and hurt override it.

"Fears and insecurities? What do you mean?" I retort, my voice betraying the mix of anger and hurt. "I thought I had made it clear that I wasn't leaving your side. I never wanted to leave you, but you made it real clear." My voice falters, a surge of vulnerability breaking through.

"How do you expect me to help you, to be there for you when you shut me out?"

Isla's eyes well up with tears, and she takes a deep breath before responding, "I know, Xavier. I messed up. I let my own issues cloud my judgement. I was scared of burdening you with my problems, scared that I would drag you down with me. I thought pushing you away was the best thing for both of us."

My jaw tightens, processing her words. The silence stretches between us, the weight of unspoken emotions settling heavily on our shoulders.

I run a hand through my hair, a mix of frustration and understanding bubbling within me.

"You didn't burden me, Isla. You shutting me out hurt more than anything else. I wanted to be there for you, to help you carry whatever weight you were carrying. But you decided for both of us, and that hurt." My gaze softens, my anger giving way to a deep sense of longing.

I run a hand through my hair, a mix of frustration and sadness settling in. "Isla, you've got to understand that I've seen you at your worst, and I've stood by you. I never saw it as a burden. I wanted to share everything with you—the good and the bad."

I sigh. "Still do."

In my mind, I'm grappling with the realisation that I care for her deeply, love her, so fucking deeply. The depth of my feelings is almost overwhelming, but I know she's not ready to hear those three words. That piece of shit ex-boyfriend did a real number on her, and I want to make things right. I want to assure her that I'm here for her, no matter what.

Isla finally looks up, "Xavier, I want to *try* to fix things between us. I know it won't be easy, but I want to give us a chance."

A wave of relief washes over me. "I want that, too, princess," I respond, a soft smile playing on my lips, "but we have to be honest with each other, communicate better. No more shutting each other out."

She nods, a determined glint in her eyes. The path ahead may be uncertain, but we've taken the first step toward healing.

We share a brief, understanding smile, acknowledging the unspoken agreement to face the challenges ahead together. I clear my throat.

"How's your father?" I ask cautiously, breaking the silence.

Isla's expression softens, a mix of gratitude and concern. "Things have remained the same," she begins, her voice measured. "But they've weaned him off the anaesthesia. The plan is to eventually allow him to regain consciousness. He's stable for now," she adds, exhaling as if lifting a weight off her shoulders.

As she exhales, Isla continues, "Thank you for visiting him, Xav. I know you've been coming in to see him," she says with an empathetic smile.

I freeze, shock coursing through me. How did she find out? My mind races with self-admonishment. *It's a small town, you dickhead,* I chastise myself internally. Obviously, she'd find out sooner or later. My bet is the nurses.

I huff out a laugh. "Guess my undercover skills are pretty shit, hey?"

"Yeah, I guess so. Maybe you need to take a page out of Brad's book, learn a thing or two about being a police officer or an undo," she suggests with a wink.

I laugh at her remark, tipping my head back. She giggles, and I can't help but revel in the sound.

"I fucking missed hearing you laugh," I admit with a grin, and she blushes at my admission.

"So 'Brad' huh, you're on a nickname basis now?" I inquire, with a curious smirk.

She smiles before saying, "I guess we are. He's been really kind. I think I... I look up to him like the brother I never had." Well, that's better than anything else, I guess. But a part of me softens at the thought of her finding some comfort in Bradley. She's a part of me now, just as much as he is.

"Well, Brad's got a knack for being the supportive type," I say with a casual shrug.

"Yeah, he is. But seriously, I appreciate you coming past, Xav," she says, a genuine warmth in her eyes. I just nod.

"Your, uh, your sister came past with Harrison the other day. You can imagine how that went down with Imogen." She laughs, and I smirk. Ah yes, those two bicker like an old married couple, worse than my parents, who are actually married.

I chuckle. "Those two can argue over the colour of the sky. It's a talent, really." I offer her a playful grin, enjoying the light banter.

As we guide our horses to turn around, the afternoon sun casts a warm glow on the landscape. Blue and Duchess, sensing our shift in direction, let out occasional whinnies, creating a symphony of equine sounds. I glance at Isla. "We should start heading back," I suggest, my eyes catching hers briefly before I guide Blue in the opposite direction, leading the way back along the trail.

As we make our way back, the air between us seems to lighten, transforming into a more playful and comfortable atmosphere. I've been trying to break that awkward tension lingering, cracking jokes here and there. Liv calls them 'dad jokes' and I've never understood the term.

Isla's laughter, like a melody, punctuates the quiet hum of the horses' hooves against the trail.

I shoot her a sly grin. "Why did the horse go behind the tree?"

She looks at me, curious. "I don't know, why?"

"Because he wanted to change his jockeys!" I deliver the joke with a smirk, and Isla can't help but chuckle.

She shakes her head, still smiling. "You're an idiot. Where did you even come up with that?"

I wink. "Well, I've got a whole stable full of them."

The banter and laughter continues, Isla shaking her head at me, turning the ride back into a blend of laughter and the gentle sounds accompanied by the thudding of the horses' hooves.

Turning serious, I instruct Isla to squeeze her legs to the saddle. Confused, she asks why, but I cut her off, demonstrating how to hold the reins real tight.

"Hold it like this," I say, showing her the grip. When she questions why, I reply, "When the horse moves, you move with it, like this," and shift my hips back and forth on the saddle.

"Basically, just imagine you're riding my cock," I say casually, with a wink.

Her breath hitches, confusion written all over her beautiful face. I look up at her with a mischievous smirk and say, "Race ya back home."

With that, I click my tongue, nudging Blue, and we take off into a gallop.

Trusting Duchess, an easy horse to ride, I believe she'll make the journey comfortable for Isla. As Isla exclaims, "What, wait!" I turn to look back at her.

Duchess follows suit, galloping off to follow. Isla squeals in a fit of laughter. "Xavier, you arsehole." I see her gripping the reins as instructed, her body moving back and forth.

"Atta girl, that's it." I laugh, turning back to focus on the direction I'm heading.

43

Xavier

I dismount Blue once we reach the stables, swiftly latching his rope onto the post. Turning, I offer a hand to lift Isla off Duchess.

"I can't believe you did that! I could have fallen off and been trampled to death, you ass," she exclaims, slapping me on the shoulder, a full-blown smile on her face. I watch her, a sense of contentment filling my eyes. Isla continues rambling, her eyes sparkling with awe, "But, *wow*! That was amazing! I want to do that again. I want to ride horses all the time, oh my god."

I smirk, teasing, "I have something else you can ride," throwing in a wink. Isla huffs in disbelief, shaking her head, a blush creeping onto her face.

"Must you always be so dirty?" she retorts, a hand on her hip.

"Always," I growl, a playful glint in my eyes. "Especially around you."

She scoffs but can't hide the amused glint in her eyes. "You're incorrigible," she says, crossing her arms.

Closing the distance between us, I shoot her a mischievous grin.

"Well, princess, I can't help it. It's just the way I am," I reply, the playful tone lingering in my voice.

Leaning against the stable door, I drawl, "That's what you *like* about me."

Isla rolls her eyes at my response. "You're lucky you're charming," she retorts, a smile playing on her lips. Closing the distance between us, I shoot her a smirk.

"Charm is just one of my *many* talents," I tease, enjoying the playful banter. She blushes, and I can just imagine exactly what she is thinking about.

She then laughs, a genuine sound that warms my chest. "Modesty is not one of them, though."

"Who needs modesty when you've got all this?" I gesture playfully to myself.

She smirks, her eyes dancing with amusement. "I should've known better than to expect humility from you."

Leaning against the stable door, I chuckle. "Eh, humility is over-rated."

"So you do, huh?"

"I do, what?" She questions.

"Like me?" I tease, closing the distance between us until we're standing inches apart. The air crackles with a different kind of ten-sion—a palpable awareness of each other.

Her lips curve into a small smile. "Hmm, maybe," she replies, her eyes locked onto mine.

I can feel the warmth emanating from her, and my gaze lingers on her lips. The mischievous banter fades into a charged silence. The stable seems to shrink around us as the unspoken tension grows.

In that moment, I'm acutely aware of her presence, the softness of her breath, and the electricity in the air. I fucking hope she feels what I'm feeling.

A part of me wants to close the remaining gap, to bridge the space between us and see where this might lead us again. But hesitation lingers, a reminder of the complexities we're both navigating. I notice a flicker of vulnerability in her eyes. It's subtle, but it's there. I reach out, gently tucking a strand of her hair behind her ear.

"You know," I say, breaking the playful tone with a touch of sincerity, "there's no rush. We can take things at whatever pace you're comfortable with."

In the quiet pause that follows, my thoughts echo with the awareness that despite the progress we've made, the mind blowing sex we'd had—Isla has brought up some walls again.

It's a familiar defence mechanism, and I can't blame her. But I can be a patient man, where it's warranted, of course. And I'll just about wait as long as I have to—a fucking eternity, if needed, for this girl and this girl *alone*, until she is ready to take that next step with me.

Just as I go to mutter something to her, distant barking echoes through the air. I recognize it immediately—it's Buddy, probably coming around to sniff what we're doing. Then it hits me—she doesn't know about Luna. I quickly mutter, "Uh, Isla, there's something I need to tell you."

Before I can get a word out, Buddy and Luna come barreling into the barn, their playful barks filling the space. Isla freezes beside me, her body stiffening. Luna spots her and bounds over, jumping and tagging at Buddy. Isla's eyes widen in pure shock.

"L-Luna, is that you?" she stammers, looking up at me. I can sense the astonishment in her voice.

As she looks at me with pure confusion, Isla utters, "You, it was you." She bends down, patting Luna's back. "You adopted her." Her eyes well up with tears.

I nod gently. "Yeah... I needed another dog around here, you know, with Bud getting old and all. Luna here just fits in so well." I try to sound casual, waiting for her response.

Isla sits there for a moment, her eyes locked on Luna, seemingly at a loss for words. Then, as if a switch flips, she abruptly stands up and throws her arms around me. "Thank you, thank you."

I embrace the sudden hug, my grip tight, and bury my head in the nook between her head and shoulder.

"I thought she'd never find a home. I'm such an idiot, like a complete idiot. It didn't ever occur to me to ask you," she says, her voice catching, eyes glistening with unshed tears.

The moment lingers as she stares into my eyes, close enough that I can feel the warmth of her breath. Slowly, she releases me and moves back down to Luna, who sits with her tail wagging.

"Oh, Luna, girl," Isla murmurs, rubbing underneath her chin, Luna's tongue hanging out with content. "You found your home, beautiful." She looks up at me, eyes still sparkling. "This makes me so happy. Thank you, Xav."

"Thank *you* for bringing her into my life," I say sincerely, my gaze lingering on Isla. Luna seems to sense the gratitude in the air, and she nuzzles against Isla's leg, tail still wagging.

In that moment, I can't help but marvel at how Luna has seamlessly become a part of this little world we're building. It's only been a week or so, but already, she's proven to be a real asset. Isla's presence in my life, along with the addition of Luna, has brought a new kind of warmth to the farm, and I find myself appreciating it more than I can express.

"Why don't you stay for dinner?" I suggest a hopeful tone in my voice. The thought of her leaving again doesn't sit well with me.

"I can whip us up something, and we can... uhm, spend more time together."

She hesitates, uncertainty flickering in her gaze. Not wanting to give her too much time to dwell on it, I quickly add, "No one's home today. Mum and Dad are off to some wedding about an hour away—they've driven up and are staying there for the night. Brad's gone back to Goulburn for another week before he can stay again. Liv won't be home either." I silently make a mental note to shoot Liv a quick text, suggesting she extend her time out. She won't mind—she's always up for some solo adventures. Anything to ensure Isla stays for dinner and we get a chance to catch up.

Fuck, why do I sound so desperate? But then again, that's what she does to me.

Isla hesitates for a moment, uncertainty evident in her gaze, but eventually, she nods. "Yes. I'd like that."

The cosy warmth of my house envelops us as Isla settles comfortably on the kitchen island, a glass of her favourite coke in hand—a little thoughtful gesture on my part.

"What are you in the mood for? I can make anything, so tell me," I offer, glancing over my shoulder. Isla, with a playful smile, rises from her seat, determination in her eyes.

"Why don't I whip something up for you? It's the least I can do, you know, after everything."

I start to protest, "No, don't be silly, I'll cook for—" but she cuts off my words with a determined look. My protest is halted as she cuts in, "Xav, sit. Let me cook."

"Yes ma'am," I concede, taking a seat at the kitchen bench where Isla had just been. The warmth from her recent presence lingers on the seat, a subtle reminder of her proximity.

As Isla takes charge of the kitchen, I observe her with a mix of amusement and appreciation. When she asks where things are, I just point in the general direction, letting her find her way. She moves with a natural grace, effortlessly navigating the space as if she's lived here forever. The clinking of utensils and the sizzling sounds from the stove create a comforting rhythm.

As I watch her, a warmth settles within me, a sense of contentment at the domestic scene unfolding. It feels so normal, so right. In that moment, a vivid image flashes in my mind—Isla in our kitchen, barefoot, her tummy full with our child. The thought halts me in my tracks.

Where did that come from? I had never envisioned the future so vividly before, and it stirs something deep within me, intensifying my love for her in ways I couldn't have imagined.

I shake off the sudden intensity of my thoughts. Fuck, I've got it bad. It is becoming increasingly clear that I need to tell her. My love for Isla is growing, evolving into something profound, and I can't keep it to myself any longer.

"So, what's on the menu, Chef?" I tease, propping my chin on my hands as I lean on the kitchen bench.

Isla shoots me a playful glance over her shoulder. "Well, how about spaghetti bolognese? It's a classic."

I chuckle. "Sounds perfect. But you didn't have to go through all this trouble, you know."

She turns towards me, a twinkle in her eye. "Consider it my thank you for adopting Luna. Besides, I enjoy cooking. I'd never had the urge for it until now."

As she continues to work her culinary magic, I can't help but appreciate the easy banter that has settled between us again. It feels like a comfortable dance, each step bringing us closer. The air is filled with the enticing scent of the simmering sauce, a tangible warmth that extends beyond the kitchen.

Deciding to contribute to the setup, I get up to set the table for the two of us. I place the table mats, arrange the cutlery, and grab glasses. Wanting to add a touch of romance, I even dash upstairs to snag a candle from my sister's room. When Isla shoots me an inquisitive glance, a smile playing on her lips, I wink at her, well aware of the effect it has on her every single time. However, I push these thoughts aside, not wanting to sport a fucking hard-on before dinner even begins.

Before long, Isla sets two steaming pots of bolognese sauce and spaghetti in front of us at the dining table, the aroma inviting.

"Voilà! Bon appétit," she declares, a proud smile on her face. Deciding to extend some hospitality, I offer her a drink, suggesting a beer or something else. Opting for wine, she politely asks if I have any. Knowing Mum keeps a whole heap in the fridge, I pad over and grab a bottle of Brown Brothers moscato, along with a beer for myself. Snagging a wine glass from the cupboard, I bring it all to the table.

"Is moscato okay? Dunno what the difference is, but they all look the same," I quip.

"Moscato is fine," she says with a smile.

As we sit next to each other, preparing to dive into the delicious meal Isla has crafted, I feel a surge of anticipation. However, before things can progress further, I stand abruptly, prompting Isla to inquire, "What, what?"

"Nothing, sorry," I respond with a laugh, not meaning to have startled her, "just going to play some music, to uh... set the mood."

She teases, "First the candle, now music. My, my, what have you done with the grumpy Xavier?"

Smartass. I shoot a teasing glare, shaking my head.

Connecting my phone to the speaker on the kitchen bench, I ask, "What are you in the mood for?"

She purses her lips in thought and then replies with a smile, "Do you want my honest answer or what you want to hear?"

I raise my brow, fully aware she's about to suggest something rock. While I enjoy that, I think something a bit more mellow might be suitable.

"Play whatever you like, I don't mind," she says softly. So, I search for an artist and end up shuffling Morgan Wallen's essentials playlist. 'Cover Me Up' starts playing, instantly filling the room.

"Oh, I love this song."

Well, that settles it. I walk back over, taking my seat beside her.

As Isla scoops a generous portion of spaghetti onto our plates, a portion that satisfies my appetite, I lift my fork, twirling the pasta, and shoot her a grateful look.

"Impressive, Doc. Let's see if it tastes as good as it looks."

She smiles, saying, "I added a little twist to it. It's my mum's recipe—she uses carrots and ground cumin. It used to be my favourite dish ever... apart from her apple pies," she says with a genuine smile. Taking the first bite, the flavours explode on my palate—a perfect blend of savoury and comforting. Isla watches with anticipation, and I can't help but be genuinely impressed.

"Holy shit, this is good," I exclaim. "I think this is my new favourite dish," I say casually, shooting her a wink.

"Oh, bullshit," she laughs. "You're just saying that."

"Nah, I'm being serious. This is fucking amazing. Sorry, but I think you're going to have to cook this for me for the rest of my life," I drawl.

Isla just looks at me, something flickering in her eyes. That had just come out so naturally, I didn't even think about it.

"Oh, am I, huh?" she retorts back. She's flirting. She's flirting back, right? Fuck yes.

"Yeah, you are," I narrow my eyes as the air around us becomes more intense. "You up for the challenge?" I say, leaning in closer, resting on my elbows.

She holds my gaze, a playful glint in her eyes. "Hm, I suppose I can manage that. Cooking for you for the rest of your life, huh?" Her tone is teasing, and the atmosphere between us is charged with a newfound energy.

I match her playfulness. "I'm warning you, it might be a lifetime commitment. Can you handle it?"

I wink, keeping the banter light, but beneath the words, there's a layer of something more significant. It's a dance, a delicate step forward in this evolving connection.

Isla smirks, the corner of her lips curving mischievously. "Challenge accepted, cowboy." The nickname rolls off her tongue with a hint of affection. It's an unspoken agreement, a silent acknowledgment that maybe, just maybe, this could be the beginning of something more.

Two beers down, and Isla's on her second glass of Moscato. We're having a great time, catching up, talking about work, and sharing laughs about Luna and Buddy, who are now comfortably sprawled out at our feet. They were barking at the door earlier, so I let them join us. The background music is playing Chris Stapleton's 'Tennessee Whiskey' now—a pleasant surprise to the playlist. The atmosphere is easygoing, and the air is filled with a subtle charge.

Isla's is now sporting a rosy hue on her cheeks, probably from the Moscato. Me? I'm feeling pretty good, just a light buzz from the beers. The vibe between us has shifted, becoming more intimate. I can't help but gaze at her as the lyrics of the song fill the room.

The atmosphere around us is laced with a mix of nostalgia and something unspoken. Isla's laughter rings through the room, a melodic harmony to the music playing softly. The dogs, Luna and Buddy, lay contentedly at our feet, adding to the domestic scene.

I take a sip of my beer, catching her gaze. "You know, these dogs—" I nod towards the two furry companions, "they really hit it off. Just like us, huh?"

Isla raises an eyebrow, a playful smirk on her lips. "Hit it off? If I recall correctly, it was more like you begging me to go on 'one' date."

I chuckle at this. "And did you say no?" I question, taunting her.

"Well, I reluctantly agreed, and you promised you'd leave me alone," she retorts with a raised brow.

"Ah, hate to break it to you, but I lied," I drawl, leaning in closer, eyes narrowed. "It was never going to be just 'one' date," I say, my voice low, and I can just make out the shiver coursing through her body.

Isla's eyes reflect disbelief, a frown forming on her face as she questions, "Why, Xavier?"

"Why, what?"

Isla's question echoes in my mind. Does she truly not understand why it's her? Why she's the one who consumes my thoughts, day in and day out?

"Why me?"

I feel a surge of frustration and a twinge of hurt. Haven't I made it clear enough? I take a deep breath before responding, "Isla, it's always been you. Since high school, you've been the one invading my thoughts, whether I liked it or not. I was a dumb, arrogant teenager who acted out—an asshole who pushed you away, but the truth is, it's always been you."

She shakes her head, as if she can't comprehend what I'm saying—hearing these words for the first time out loud.

"But... we never spoke to each other," she questions, her voice laced with confusion. "I mean, look at me. I'm not your average size ten girl. I'm not easy on the eyes. I'm not like the girls you used to go for in school."

I lean forward, frustration and urgency in my eyes. "Isla, don't you see? It's never been about some damn size or an idealised version of beauty. Those girls weren't anything more than flings, a fucking act. It's about you. The way you make me feel, the connection we share. You've been the only one on my mind for *years*. Years, Isla."

As my words linger in the air, her breathing falters, her expression serious. I reach out to gently cup her face, my thumb brushing across her cheek. "You're more than enough for me. It's about who you are, not some fucking superficial standard."

Not wanting to waste any more time, I continue, "This—us—I never expected it to become something more, to be honest, but over time, it's changed from attraction, lust, to—"

My words trail off, and she prods further, "To... what, Xavier?"

"To love, Isla," I growl, the words leaving my lips with a weight that hangs in the air. Her breath hitches, and she draws in a breath, the gravity of the moment sinking in. Fuck, there's no going back now. The room is charged, tension swirling between us as our eyes lock, and in that moment, it feels like the world has slowed down.

As Isla sits there stunned, stuttering her words, I can't help but feel a surge of emotions. It's as if time has come to a standstill, and I need her to understand the depth of what I'm saying.

"Isla," I say, my voice low and intense, "I've never been good with words, but this is as clear as I can make it. I care about you more than I've ever cared about anyone. It's not just attraction or some fleeting feeling. It's deeper, something that has grown over the years. I fucking love *you*."

I watch her closely, waiting for her response. The vulnerability in her eyes tugs at something within me, and I find myself holding my breath, hoping she understands.

As the intense desire rages through me, I can't contain it any longer. I push my chair out abruptly, commanding, "Come here," gesturing for her to sit on my lap. There's a moment of hesitation in her eyes, but she stands up and moves to sit on the edge of my thigh.

I grab her roughly, pulling her closer and adjusting her position so she ends up straddling my lap. The air between us crackles with anticipation, and I can't help but revel in the intoxicating proximity.

"Is there any doubt left in your mind?" I murmur. My hands move over her body, tracing the curves and contours as if memorising every inch.

My hands grip her waist, and I grind her body onto my lap, over my now hardening cock.

"Tell me, Isla," I murmur, my lips brushing against her ear, "do you feel it, too? Do you feel what you do to me?" The atmosphere is charged, and a primal desire courses through me as I wait for her response.

Isla looks into my eyes, her gaze reflecting a mix of emotions. "Xavier," she breathes out, her voice a soft melody in the charged air. "I do feel it. It's not just you. There's something here, something I can't deny."

My heart pounds in my chest as her words wash over me. I lean back slightly, capturing her gaze with mine. "Good," I murmur, a satisfied grin playing on my lips. "Because, Isla, what I feel for you... it's beyond words."

I claim her lips, the kiss deepening into a fervent dance of tongues. My hands trail down her back, pulling her closer, melding our bodies together. Isla responds with a whimper, her fingers threading through my hair. The intensity of our connection sparks a fire that consumes us, erasing any lingering doubts or uncertainties, once and for fucking all.

As our lips part momentarily, a heated gaze lingers between us.

"So fucking beautiful," I growl in a low, possessive tone. I capture her mouth again, licking the seam of her lips. She parts her mouth and I dip my tongue into her mouth, a low groan resonating from deep in my chest.

In the electrifying aftermath, my mind races. *Fuck, Xavier, keep it together.* But her taste, her response. It's intoxicating.

I can't help but savour the way she yields to me. Is it the way she looks at me, or the lingering warmth between us? No denying she's got me hooked. I can't shake the possessiveness that surges through me right now.

It's not like me, but with her, it's different. A magnetic pull that defies reason.

It's *everything.*

44

Isla

As the echoes of his growl linger, I can't ignore the undeniable fire simmering between us. His words echo in my mind—Xavier Mitchell loves *me*. It's like a thrilling revelation, a declaration that's both comforting and electrifying. A rush of emotions swirls within me—relief, excitement, a tinge of nervousness. He loves me, and even though I didn't actually say the words back, they're there—doing a happy dance in my head. Love. It's there—a deep, magnetic love and desire for Xavier Mitchell.

As a soft whimper escapes my lips, his kisses trail down my neck, and the grinding intensifies. In that heated moment, he murmurs, "What do you need, baby? Tell me."

I want him—all of him. Sure, I've had him before, experiencing the rough and the tender, but this feels different. His words linger in the air, solidifying any lingering doubts. To hell with 'distractions'—I need him as much as he needs me. It's like air to breathe, and I don't want to let him go. Never again.

"Xav, I need you," I whimper, the urgency evident in my voice. "Like, right now."

A growl rumbles through him, and he utters a satisfied, "Finally."

With that, he rises, lifting me effortlessly. His strength always wows me—corded muscles straining against his t-shirt as he holds me close. We're in motion, heading up the stairs, towards his bedroom. He kicks the door open with a casual ease before giving it another nudge to close.

In his arms, Xavier walks us over to his bed. With a swift yet controlled motion, he drops me onto it. His eyes, once icy blue, now darken with desire, pupils dilated. The atmosphere is charged with an intensity that leaves no room for hesitation or insecurity.

His growl breaks the silence, a command that sends shivers down my spine.

"Clothes. Off." I comply without a second thought, a wave of confidence washing over me. No hesitation, no insecurity present.

"Have I ever told you I love it when you growl at me?" I say, my body trembling with desire as I make a quick haste in taking off my clothes.

In the dimly lit room, his eyes blazing with an unfiltered longing, he releases another low, primal growl that just spills out naturally. It hits the air, a raw echo of desire that somehow makes my heart race and leaves an electric charge in the room.

"Like that?"

"Y-yes," I murmur, "like that. Sounds so sexy. Possessive."

A wicked grin plays on his lips, and he moves closer, the heat radiating between us. "You have no idea what you do to me," he confesses, his hands reaching out to trace the contours of my body.

"But I plan to show you for as long as you'll have me."

Xavier's hands move with a purpose as he discards his clothes, revealing his sculpted body. Fuck, I will never tire of the sight of him naked. His cock rests against his stomach, begging for attention. The dim light highlights the contours of his muscles and the tattoos that stretch across his arm.

As he hovers above me, his lips claim mine once again. "Isla," he breathes between heated kisses. "While I want to take my time with you, savor every dip, curve, and taste of you, I need to fuck you, real bad. Right now."

"Yes," I gasp, my voice barely audible amidst the rising desire. "Please."

His eyes, dark pools of intensity, lock onto mine. "That's what I want to hear," he growls, the hint of a smirk playing on his lips.

"I'm not going to be gentle," he says. I catch my breath, feeling the anticipation rise.

"Don't. Don't be gentle. Just fuck me, Xavier."

He moves down my body, lifting my hips upward, pressing my thighs back and buries his face in my pussy in a split second—licking me from bottom to top, before sucking on my clit.

"Always so wet for me," he murmurs. A few more strokes of his tongue have my toes curling and my back arching for more. I'm already so close and we've barely even started.

Then just as quickly, he releases my clit with a 'pop' and moves to sit in between my thighs, lining his tip to my entrance, lubricating himself with my arousal, that now drips down my inner thighs.

In a single, decisive motion, he plunges deep, and we both release a gasp in response to the overwhelming sensation. He stretches me wide, and I savour the fiery feeling, completely filled by him.

As he moves, his intense gaze remains fixed on the point where our bodies connect, tracing the rhythm of his movements. Awe reflects in his expression, and then his focus returns to me, and I meet his eyes. I raise myself onto my elbows, observing him as he penetrates me with deep, unhurried motions.

"Keep watching, baby," he murmurs. "Watch me fuck this beautiful pussy." His thrusts are relentless now, urging me closer and closer to my orgasm. I can feel my body start to tense from the buildup. I whimper, and he glides his hand up my stomach to grab the space between my collar and jaw. Feeling bold, I guide his hand to my throat, watching as his eyes narrow into intense slits.

"Fuck, you want me to choke you, baby? My girl likes it rough, huh?"

I whimper in agreement. "Fuuckk," he groans, his grip on my neck tightening. I cover his hand with mine, urging him to tighten his hold even more. In that moment, I crave the feeling of being choked, as if I'm starved for oxygen and he's the only one who can bring me back to life.

"Harder, squeeze me tighter," I gasp, the desire evident in my voice.

"Fuck, Isla," he groans. His body is a canvas of corded muscles and tattoos, lids heavy, chest heaving with the intensity of the moment.

He delves deep within, and a soft whimper escapes my lips. "I'm so close," my voice is clipped from the pressure around my throat, "so *close*."

"Yes, come for me. Come all over my cock." His voice is strained with tension, his thrusts now become punishing, hitting me so deep, I can feel my core start to flutter. With one hand tightly gripping my throat, he moves the other to grab hold of my breast.

He pinches my nipple between his forefinger and thumb, and before I know it, I'm exploding into pieces. My eyes roll into the back of my head and a feeling of lightheadedness overwhelms me as I arch my back into his thrusts, crying out to him, his name leaving my lips.

My breathing has become shallow, and Xavier eases his grip on my throat, allowing me to regain control of my breathing. Fuck, this turns me on so much.

My orgasm must spur him on, because I can feel his movements falter slightly, a groan escaping his lips before he hits me with a few more gruelling thrusts.

"Fuck, yes, Isla. This pussy is all mine." He accentuates that last word with a growl that I fucking love.

"You" *Thrust*. "Are." *Thrust*. "Mine." *Thrust*.

Each deliberate thrust carries with it a declaration, punctuating the intimate space between us with the fervent expression of his feelings. With that last deep drive, he slows his pace, spilling his load into me, and drops his head to capture my lips with a debilitating kiss, sucking my bottom lip into his mouth, biting down hard.

I rub my hands up and down his muscular back, before running them down to cup his ass—moving slowly with him as he finishes inside me.

We remain entwined in that moment, time slipping away, with him still inside me, his forearms framing my face. Slowly, he withdraws, sending a shiver through my body. He sits back up, watching intently as his semen drips out of me.

With a swift movement, he slides two long fingers inside me, pressing them in deeply, keeping all the contents of his arousal inside.

Oh, oh my. Why is that so fucking hot?

As he drops back beside me, "God, that was…" his voice trails off as he exhales, lying on his back.

I offer a soft smile, revelling in the connection that lingers between us. "Amazing," I finish his thought, words whispered in the hushed post-climax atmosphere. We both chuckle at this.

"Hm, I feel so sore," I admit, a playful note in my voice.

"Shit, I wasn't too rough, was I?" he immediately sits up, concern in his eyes.

"No, god no. It's a *good* sore," I reassure him, turning to face him and lying on my side.

"Yeah, well, I did just rail the fuck out of you, and we're only just getting started, princess," he teases, a mischievous glint in his eyes.

"Oh my… I may need a minute," I gasp with a breathy laugh, he just smirks.

"Good, because I plan to go again," he declares, moving in to capture my lips with a sensual kiss. "Again," another kiss follows, "and again."

His kisses are intoxicating—I could melt just from the heat of his lips alone.

After multiple orgasms, I lost count somewhere around the third or maybe fourth—heck, who's keeping track? We're sprawled across Xavier's bed, limbs all tangled in his sheets, and our breathing has settled into a slow rhythm. My head nestles comfortably on his chest, and my arm drapes over him, creating a cosy haven of shared warmth.

"So, um, your dad came and spoke to me today," I start, gauging his reaction.

"What?" he blurts. "When?"

"This afternoon, at the church in town. I was just there to clear my head, you know, pray for my dad. And he, well, he saw me walk in, so he joined me. He was... strangely calm—-actually nice."

He frowns, but I continue, "Earlier I had gone to my dad's house."

"Your house, you mean, you used to live there, too, you know," he adds reassuringly. True.

"Yeah. Well, I went there today to tidy up the place for him—and I went into my parents' room, I found..." I falter, swallowing hard. "I found letters. Letters my mum wrote to me."

"Isla," he says softly, his hand rubbing circles on my arm as he turns his head to look at me.

"I—I'm not ready to talk about that just yet," I sigh. "There are still a few more I need to read. But after that I just needed space—clarity—to clear my head."

"Of course. I'm all ears whenever you're ready," he assures me. I appreciate his understanding and respond with a grateful smile.

Changing the subject, I ask about the altercation between him and his dad. "What happened between you and your dad, Xav? He'd mentioned some altercation."

He sighs, and my head moves with his chest. "I was so angry. I lost it at him. I... just needed him to understand."

"Well, I guess whatever you said kind of worked. He apologised for everything—the grudge against my father, about the money." Xavier's reaction is a mix of shock and something else that flits through his eyes—relief, perhaps?

"My dad apologised, huh?" he remarks, almost incredulously.

"Yeah," I confirm, looking up at him.

He processes this for a moment, and I can see the wheels turning in his head. "I can't believe it. I mean, I've been at odds with him about this for weeks, and suddenly, he just says sorry?"

I nod, my fingers tracing patterns on his chest. "It caught me off guard, too."

He chuckles softly. "Yeah, it's a lot to take in. Apologising isn't exactly his strong suit."

"This is a big step. Not just for your father, but for us, too," I say, feeling the weight of the words hanging in the air.

"Yeah, I guess it is," he responds, nuzzling his face in my hair and planting a soft kiss on the top.

A surge of warmth fills me. Despite everything that has happened, there's no other place I'd rather be than in his arms. Here, I feel at home, safe. With Xavier, I can navigate through anything, and with his love, I finally find the space to breathe. No matter what life throws at me, no matter what happens with my dad, I draw strength from the certainty that his love will see me through.

I find comfort in knowing that he'll never leave me.

45

Xavier

It's been a few weeks now since I told Isla I love her. She hasn't uttered those words back to me, but I can feel it in every gesture, every shared glance. Her love emanates in subtle ways that don't necessarily need words.

Isla's actions speak louder than any declaration of love. She's gone out of her way to ease the tension with my father, offering a compassion that only someone who cares deeply could. The soft, lingering kisses planted on my forehead or the sweet pecks she leaves on my cheek—each gesture a silent testament to the depth of her affection.

In the quiet moments while visiting her father in hospital—when we just hold each other, I can sense her love in the softness of her touch, in the way her fingers intertwine with mine. It's in the small gestures, the shared laughter over inside jokes—that make me realise how much she cares.

The past few weeks have been challenging, especially with Isla's father still in a stagnant state. The doctors and nurses remain hopeful, assuring us that he may regain consciousness soon.

In the midst of this uncertainty, Isla's unwavering support and the love that resonates between us become anchors, grounding us in the face of life's unpredictable currents.

The hum of beeping noises fills the room, rhythmic and somewhat unsettling, as we sit by Isla's father's bedside. Imogen breezes in just after my mum leaves, bringing with her a burst of energy and a handful of well-wishing flowers.

"G'day peeps!" Imogen chirps, tossing the flowers into a vase on the bedside table. She glances at the two of us with a mischievous smirk. "'Bout time you two sorted your shit out."

Isla rolls her eyes, and I just chuckle.

"Yeah, she kept waiting long enough," I say, squeezing Isla to my side.

"Stop! You guys are just the cutest. *Ugh*, I went on that date with that guy I told you about the other week."

"Oh, god! How'd it go?"

"Terrible, terrible, terrible," she says, shaking her in disapproval. "Why is it so hard to find a decent guy in this shitty town? Maybe I need to dip my toes in the pool of city men."

"Trust me, they're not any better there. Just ask Claire," Isla says with a laugh.

"Well, I might just know a few around town," I quip, a teasing grin on my face.

"Xavier Mitchell, if you mention his name, I will walk over there and—" Imogen's threat gets cut off with my laugh.

"Woah, take it easy tiger." I shoot her a playful grin. I love how I don't even have to mention Harrison's name for her to know who

I'm referring to.

"Seriously, what's so bad about him? He's a catch, Midge—single, caring, funny," Isla suggests.

"Nah, I would like to find myself a mature man, not a twenty-eight-year-old who acts like a child."

"But that's what makes him so unique," I retort, raising an eyebrow.

"You have to admit, he's incredibly attractive," Isla says, raising her arms in defence, "I mean that in the friendliest way possible, not in any other way," she rambles quickly, and I laugh, pulling her close to kiss the top of her head.

"Yeah, I know, princess. I agree, the fucker knows he's attractive. That's why he is the way he is, because he knows girls will fall for his charm."

"Yeah... *girls*. Not this woman," Imogen retorts, pointing at herself.

"I'm not saying he's *not* attractive—he is *very* attractive—*but* if you ever hear me utter those words to him or anyone else, then I give you permission to slap me silly. Because surely I must be on drugs." She points her finger at Isla and me.

"This is a safe space, and it stays between us," Isla says with a smirk, and we both laugh.

Imogen then glances at the beeping monitor and then back at Isla, changing the subject. "How's he doing today?"

Isla sighs. "No change, Midge. Doctors are hopeful, but it's a waiting game."

"Well, you know where I am if you need anything. Seriously, any-thing," Imogen reassures, moving closer to Isla, to give her shoulder a reassurance squeeze.

"I know. It means a lot," Isla says, her voice filled with gratitude.

Imogen gives us both a lingering look before excusing herself, promising to check in later. As the door closes behind her, Isla lets out a heavy breath.

"This waiting stuff is brutal," she says, leaning into my shoulder.

"Yeah, it is," I agree, wrapping my arm around her. "But we're in this together."

We sit in companionable silence, the beeping of the monitor cre-ating a strange sort of rhythm in the room. Isla breaks the silence, "You know, your mum was sweet to stop by."

I nod. "Yeah, she cares. We all do."

She looks up at me, her eyes reflecting a mix of exhaustion and appreciation. "I'm lucky to have you, Xav."

"Luck's all mine, sweetheart," I reply, pressing a kiss to her fore-head. "We'll get through this, Isla. Together." She nods.

"Together."

I stand beside her father's bed, my arm wrapped around Isla's shoul-ders. She moves to stand closer to him, gripping his hand as she leans down to whisper, "Dad, it's Isla. We're all here with you, waiting for you to wake up. You're not alone, okay? Please, just open your eyes."

An audible gasp leaves her lips suddenly and in an instant, I'm by her side, my concern mirrored in her eyes. "What is it, baby? What happened?"

"He moved, Xav. His hand twitched," she stammers, wide-eyed.

I glance at her father, then back at her, my expression shifting from concern to a mix of disbelief and excitement. "Really?"

Just then, another movement, more pronounced this time. Her dad's hand twitches again, and Isla gasps once more. "Xavier, call the nurses! Now!"

I reach for the call button, pressing it urgently. The room is soon filled with the sound of hurried footsteps as the medical team rushes in.

Isla, still holding onto her father's hand, speaks to him with a trembling voice, "Dad, can you hear me? If you can, squeeze my hand." In an eternity that lasts a moment, her father's hand tightens around hers.

"He's responding! He's waking up!" Isla exclaims, her joy and relief palpable.

The nurses arrive, checking vital signs and assessing her father's condition. Isla continues to talk to him, encouraging him to stay with them. I stand by, offering silent support, marvelling at the unexpected turn of events.

The nurses swarm around her father, assessing his condition and exchanging rapid-fire information. Isla, still gripping his hand, looks at me with a mix of hope and trepidation.

One of the nurses, a friendly face with a calming demeanour, addresses Isla. "Ms. Thompson, we're going to run a few tests to check his responsiveness."

Isla nods, her eyes never leaving her father. "Please, do whatever you need to do. Just help him."

As they conduct the tests, another nurse approaches me, asking, "Are you family?"

"I'm—I'm Isla's—" My words hang in the air, interrupted by Isla, who nods.

"He's my boyfriend. Yes, he's family," she says, her glistening eyes meeting mine. I shoot her a knowing look, surprised that she announced it out loud. *We're boyfriend and girlfriend?* God, I sound like a fucking teen. But despite the awkwardness, my chest warms.

The nurse acknowledges us with a smile, turning her attention back to the medical proceedings. In that moment, standing by Isla's side, I feel a connection that goes beyond labels and titles. Whatever we are, it's real, and it matters.

I stand back, watching the medical team work with a mix of anxiety and hope. Isla, still holding her father's hand, remains a pillar of strength, her gaze unwavering.

After a series of tests, one of the nurses turns to Isla. "He's showing positive signs of responsiveness. We'll continue monitoring him closely."

Isla's eyes well up with tears, a mixture of relief and gratitude. "Thank you, thank you so much."

As the nurses share encouraging words with Isla, another nurse approaches Callum Thompson, the one who seems to be in charge. "Mr. Thompson, can you hear me?"

Her father stirs, and the nurse prompts, "If you can understand me, try to squeeze my fingers. Can you open your eyes?"

Callum Thompson's hand twitches, responding to the nurse's prompt. The room is filled with a collective breath as everyone watches the encouraging signs of his recovery. In a moment of cautious optimism, his eyes flicker open slightly, fluttering and squinting, probably adjusting to the lights overhead.

The nurse continues, "Good, Mr. Thompson. Now, I need you to follow my finger with your eyes. Can you do that for me?"

His eyes track the nurse's finger, and a sense of hope fills the room. The nurses continue their assessment, asking questions, prompting him to regain full consciousness.

Isla, overwhelmed with emotion, turns to me, her eyes reflecting a mixture of joy and disbelief. "Xav, he's waking up. He's really waking up."

I pull her into a reassuring hug, watching as the medical team works tirelessly to bring Callum Thompson back to full consciousness.

The nurse observes Callum's responsiveness, noting the progress. "Good, Mr. Thompson. We're encouraged by your response. I'm going to contact the doctor so we can run some blood tests and schedule another MRI scan for later this afternoon. We want to make sure we have a comprehensive understanding of your condition."

She steps away, grabbing her phone, and dials the doctor. After a brief conversation, she hangs up and addresses us. "The doctor will be here shortly to discuss the next steps. In the meantime, continue to talk to him, keep his consciousness on you."

Isla's eyes are still fixed on her father, a mixture of relief and concern. I place a reassuring hand on her shoulder, and the nurses leave the room, leaving just Isla and me. I watch as Isla approaches her father, tears now falling down her cheeks. My heart breaks at the sight of her crying, but I can't help but feel a glimmer of hope now that her father is showing signs of improvement. I step closer, rubbing comforting circles on her back as she leans over, talking to her father.

"Hey, Dad," Isla whispers, her voice filled with a mix of emotions. "You're doing great. The doctors are going to run some tests to make sure everything is okay. I'm here."

I remain silent, offering a supportive presence. I understand the weight of the moment and the significance of these small steps toward recovery.

As Isla continues to speak to her father, sharing words of encouragement and love, I can't help but marvel at the strength emanating from her. Despite the tears, there's a resilience in her voice—a determination to be the anchor her father needs.

In this intimate moment, I'm feeling a bit out of place. Figuring Isla might want a sec alone with her dad, I pipe up, "I'm just gonna step outside for a moment. Give you a moment. I'll be right here when you're ready."

But Isla grabs my wrist, spinning me around to face her with that determined look in her eyes. "Together," she says, dead serious. Abso-fucking-lutely. We're in this together.

I give a nod, getting that unspoken thing that ties us in this crazy journey.

Several hours have passed, and Isla's father is making progress, regaining approximately 80% of his consciousness. They just did the whole bloods thing and had taken him in for another MRI to check out his brain activity, about an hour ago. Isla had stepped out momentarily to speak with the nurses, leaving just her father and I. Now, Isla's perched on a chair beside his bed, keeping him in the loop about everything.

She speaks of her visit to her mother's grave, sharing an intimate conversation, followed by a visit to the church where she dedicated prayers for his recovery. Though her father remains alert, he chooses a silent response. The medical team speculates that the intubation process might be causing some discomfort, offering Endone—controlled with the touch of a button.

Dr. Anderson makes his return, bringing with him the weight of new insights gleaned from the MRI. He explains, in measured terms, that Isla's father is dealing with atrophy in a region of the brain known as the hippocampus. Essentially, it's a shrinkage, a diminishing of brain matter. His brain activity is registering quite low, which might explain the fluctuations in consciousness and potential lapses in memory or responsiveness.

Isla absorbs the information with a nod, her questions cutting through the medical jargon. "So, what does this mean for his recovery? Can we expect improvement?"

"Recovery might be gradual, and the extent of improvement can vary. We'll continue monitoring his condition closely and adjusting our approach accordingly."

Shortly after this, in a fragile moment, Isla's father stirs, opening his eyes briefly. His gaze, though tired, holds a flicker of recognition. "Isla," he rasps, his voice hoarse and deep, punctuated by laboured breaths. Isla, already overwhelmed, tries to hush him, urging him to rest. But he persists, insisting with a feeble but determined voice that he has something to say.

Beside him, Isla sobs, her tears flowing freely. I stand beside her, witnessing the emotional exchange, offering my silent support. Despite the turmoil in the room, there's a palpable connection—a shared understanding of the weight carried in the words about to be spoken.

Through intermittent breaths, he manages to utter, "Letters."

Isla, choked with emotion, catches her breath and replies, "Dad, I know. I found letters at home. Mum wrote them to me."

Her father, his eyes glistening with unshed tears, tries to absorb the revelation. "Letters," he repeats, his voice barely audible. His trembling hand reaches out to touch her face, and a single tear escapes, sliding down his weathered cheek.

"I'm sorry," he murmurs, his words heavy with emotion.

Isla, overwhelmed, clings to his hand. "Dad, it's okay," she reassures him, her voice quivering. "You don't need to apologise."

As he drifts in and out of consciousness. Beside Isla, I remain a silent witness to the raw, poignant exchange, my heart aching for both of them. Her father turns his gaze and notices me standing beside him. A look of appreciation fills his weathered, hooded eyes. He nods at me, his acknowledgment silent but profound, holding a much deeper meaning that Isla can comprehend. In a raspy whisper, he mutters, "You look after my girl."

I respond, my voice choked with emotion, "Yes, sir."

Turning his attention back to Isla, her father's eyes widen for a split second before he croaks out, "Cheryl, love, that you." Isla releases a sob, her emotions bubbling to the surface. His voice remains hoarse and croaky as he slips in and out of consciousness.

Recalling the doctor's mention of potential memory lapses and confusion, Isla braces herself. "Dad, it's me, Isla," she says gently.

But her father, caught in a momentary lapse, repeats, "Cheryl, love. Love you so much. You 'n Isla." His words emerge in fragmented breaths, a poignant reminder of the challenges they face. Beside Isla, I offer a steady presence, understanding the depth of the moment and the weight of the emotions swirling in the room.

In between swallows and laboured breaths, Isla's father croaks out an apology—the weight of a lifetime's regrets carried in his words. "I'm sorry for everythin'," he manages, his gaze fixed on Isla.

"I see you in 'er face," he whispers, his voice trembling. "I love 'er, even if I never showed it." He's looking at Isla, but in his mind's eye, he sees his late wife.

"Tell 'er I love 'er. Proud of 'er. Hope she goes to that big school, becomes a vet, like ya wanted."

Isla cries, but nods through tears, whispering, "I will, Dad. I will." Leaning down, she places a gentle kiss on his forehead.

Isla chokes on her words, her voice thick with emotion, as she apologises to her father. "I'm sorry, Dad. I'm sorry for everything, for leaving all those years ago."

"No need," he responds weakly. "She did the right thing, Cher. I'm so-sorry."

Isla just nods, softly saying, "It's okay. I forgive you, Dad. I love you." Another silent tear slips out of the corner of her father's eye before he releases a breath and slips back into unconsciousness.

This time, the monitor on the machine starts beeping loudly, numbers escalating on the screen. I'm clueless about medical jargon, watching in growing panic.

"Xav, what's happening?" Isla frantically moves to press the button on the side of the wall labelled 'emergency.' An alarm blares in the room, and instantly, two nurses rush in.

"Shit, he's going into cardiac arrest," one mutters to the other. A third nurse joins them, and they immediately start CPR. Isla, a mess of tears and panic, is sobbing as she tries to explain. I step in to tell the nurse what had happened, recounting the moments leading up to her father's sudden deterioration.

The nurses move with urgency, a symphony of expertise and determination playing out before us. Each compression is a beat, a rhythmic dance attempting to breathe life back into Isla's father. The monitor's harsh beeping punctuates the room. Amidst the controlled chaos, a nurse calmly calls for the defibrillator.

Isla, overwhelmed, seeks solace, burying her face into my chest, her tears silently absorbed by my shirt. I stand there, watching the scene unfold with a focused clarity. The defibrillator is brought forth, and the room briefly hums with charged energy before delivering its decisive shock. Isla's sobs intensify, the gravity of the moment pressing upon her. I, maintaining a steady composure laced with empathy, feel the weight of the situation. As I stand there, I grapple with the magnitude of the situation. I contemplate how this moment would feel if it were my father lying on that bed or if I had experienced the loss of my mother.

Determined to stay composed for Isla, I steel myself to keep it together. Amidst the controlled tumult of emotions, a resolute commitment takes root in my heart. I'll spend the rest of my days proving and showing Isla that she is cherished, surrounded by a new family ready to love and support her through whatever trials life may throw our way.

The room collectively holds its breath as the medical team works their magic, and then, a sigh of relief as they manage to bring Isla's father's weak heart back to life. Isla, still tucked under my arm, goes through the emotional wringer—fear, hope, and everything in between.

But reality isn't all sunshine and rainbows. His heart, although kickstarted, is still on the fragile side. The medical team, a mix of satisfied and concerned expressions, breaks it down for Isla. Tough call, but they had to slide him back on the ventilator, a necessary move to give that struggling heart some much-needed backup.

Isla exhales, a combo of relief and acceptance. The room eases back into a sort of tense calm as the medical crew tweaks the ventilator settings. I tighten my hold around Isla, fully aware that, while this round may be won, the war ain't over.

In my head, thoughts swirl—life's a delicate balance of hoping for the best and facing harsh realities. Yet, a nagging worry lingers, gnawing at the edges of my thoughts. How much more can Isla take? The weight of her struggles weighs heavily on my heart, and I resolve to be her unwavering support.

The path ahead is murky, but side by side, we're gearing up for whatever punches life throws our way.

Together, we'll navigate this storm, one step at a time.

46

Isla

Two days later, after Dad spoke his first words in weeks, he passed away peacefully in his sleep.

Dad's body finally succumbed to the relentless battle, his weakened frame unable to bear the weight any longer. The brain, once the conductor of his every move, quietly gave up its role, refusing to send those crucial signals that kept everything in check. There I stood, at the epicentre of the wreckage left in the wake of his departure.

Xavier, my solid anchor, stuck with me through those crazy hours. His whispered words were like a balm to my battered soul. His warm embrace had been a welcoming refuge when I'd hit the floor—not in a dramatic way, more like a controlled crumple to the cold, unforgiving tile.

His hands, both strong and tender, rubbed and massaged my back, silently promising to bear the weight of my grief alongside me.

As they made the official call on his time of death, it felt like we were in this circle of love. Imogen, Olivia, Amelia, Bradley, Harrison, Michael – the whole gang, all sharing in the pain. Even Xavier's parents were quietly doing the supportive thing. And when my teary eyes met his old man's gaze, it was like opening the floodgates. Tears, the heavy kind, filled with grief, made a grand entrance.

His father offered condolences with a pat on Xavier's back. Then, to my surprise, Xavier's father pulled me into a comforting hug, his hands rubbing circles on my back. In that unexpected embrace, my gaze remained locked on Xavier. His eyes, glistening with unshed tears. A nurse approaches me, a mix of sympathy and professionalism in her eyes.

"I'm so sorry for your loss, Isla," she said softly, placing a comforting hand on my arm. "The hospital will take care of the necessary procedures. They have forwarded the notification to the funeral director, who will lodge it with the NSW Registry of Births, Deaths & Marriages."

I nodded, my emotions still raw but concealed beneath a fragile veneer of composure. She'd informed me that in the coming weeks, Births, Deaths and Marriages would issue a Death Certificate. I could obtain it from them when it was ready. And as for his belongings, like clothing, shoes, and toiletries, I could collect them from the ward—once I was *ready*. Her words hung in the air. Questions swirled in my mind.

Now, presently, as the doctors prepare to wheel my dad away, Xavier, sensing the gravity of the moment, gently instructs everyone to leave the room. Overwhelmed with gratitude for his understanding and support, especially after pushing him away before due to my own fears and distractions, I feel immense love and appreciation in these final moments. With a lingering kiss to my lips, Xavier leaves me alone with my father.

With tears streaming down my face, I lean close to my father's ear, the words tumbling out in a mix of deep love and profound regret. "Dad, I'm so sorry," I choke out, my voice trembling with emotion.

"I wish I had come home sooner, so we could have had more time together. I love you so much, and I'll miss you every day." Each word is heavy with the weight of missed opportunities and unspoken conversations, a lament for the time lost and the moments we'll never share.

The room is filled with the sound of my sobs, the rawness of my grief echoing off the walls. I bury my face in his chest, seeking solace in the familiar scent of him, in the warmth of his presence that still lingers. The reality of his passing crashes over me like a wave, leaving me gasping for breath, clutching desperately to the hand that will never hold mine again.

Memories flood my mind, a torrent of images and emotions that threaten to overwhelm me. I remember the sound of his laughter, the way his eyes crinkled at the corners when he smiled, the warmth of his hugs that made everything feel okay.

With a final, lingering touch, I gently squeeze my father's hand before releasing it, a silent farewell to the man who taught me so much. Turning away, I take a deep, shuddering breath, the first step on a new path without him by my side. Even though I had been gone for so long, even though our relationship had been strained over the years, he still always remained close. In my *head*, in my *heart*, in everything I did—in everything I still continue to do *now*.

He taught me more than words can express, and I'll forever cherish the bond we once had. His presence lingers, a gentle reminder of the love that will always remain in my heart. As I step forward into this new chapter of my life, I carry his memory with me, a guiding light in the darkness of my grief.

Yet, amidst the emotional turmoil, a sense of clarity and peace emerges, knowing that my father is no longer suffering and has finally joined my beautiful mother in heaven. "Look after her for me, would you?" I whisper to my father, my voice filled with a mix of sorrow and acceptance. "I promise I'll be okay."

As I stand there, surrounded by the quiet of the room and the memories of the past, I feel a gentle sense of closure wash over me. The weight of grief still lingers, but there's a glimmer of hope in knowing that my parents are together once more, watching over me from above.

As I speak, I look up and see Xavier standing beside the door—a personal protector. Directed to both my father and my mother listening from above, I whisper, "I found him. I found the one person who makes everything whole, the one person to fill the void that stained my heart over the years."

With one last cry, I sob on my father's chest, allowing the flood of emotions to wash over me.

In these final moments, as tears stream down my face onto my father's chest, a sense of longing fills my chest. The warmth of love lingers, a bittersweet feeling that accompanies the finality of his departure. His apologies and words of love in these last moments become the closure I desperately need to heal my once-broken heart. For years, abuse and disconnection and a failed relationship have left me questioning my worth and whether I am truly loved.

In these fleeting moments, my father's sincere apologies and expressions of love reassure me. The weight lifts, and I find solace in knowing that, despite the past, I am loved. The pain of the years starts to fade, replaced by a newfound understanding that healing is possible, even in the wake of loss.

A wave of warmth fills my chest, a desire, a longing, a need, a love for the man standing just outside those doors. I need to tell him how much I love him—I'm ready. Ready to pour my heart out for the man who has relentlessly been in my mind since before I can remember. Just as he once said, 'it's always been you,' well, it's always been him for me. I'd just been blinded by hate to realise.

Time is fleeting, and I'm determined not to repeat the mistakes I made with my father—neglecting to be there for him, failing to express my love enough. After one final kiss on my father's head, I rush to the door and push it open, where Xavier stands.

"What's—" he begins, a concerned look on his face. Not caring for the audience lingering in the quiet hallway, I throw my hands around his neck and slam my lips to his.

Xavier's strong arms wrap around me tightly, before moving them to grab my ass, effortlessly lifting me into his arms. The world fades away as our lips collide in a deep, passionate kiss. My love pours out in waves, a cascade of emotions that have been held back for too long. We stay like that for a while, just kissing, before a clearing of a throat breaks our little love filled bubble.

As Xavier releases me, words tumble out of my mouth in a rapid, sincere confession.

"I love you, Xavier. I fucking love you so much. I'm so sorry it took me this long to say these words, but they're here now, and they're everything. My love for you is so overwhelming, I ache for you. I can't thank you enough for the strength and support you've given me over these past weeks, these months. I want you to know that I am yours."

In that vulnerable moment, surrounded by audible gasps from the group behind me and a collective "aww" likely from Xavier's mother, I lay my feelings bare, letting the weight of my emotions speak for themselves. Xavier's response is a soft affirmation, his voice carrying a sense of finality.

"Isla, I've known it's always been there. I'm yours too," he says, relief etched across his beautiful, rugged features.

"It's always been you. I'm fucking ruined for anyone else. I'm yours for as long as you'll have me. You're it for me." he says, sincerity colouring his every word.

"Forever, we have forever."

47

Xavier

In the quiet aftermath of the funeral, the gathering of sombre faces moves towards Isla. The small service, surrounded by close loved ones, as per Isla's request—our friends Imogen, **Amelia**, Harrison, Michael, Claire *and* my family, are all here, offering their unwavering support and love, yet now, it's time to say the final goodbyes. Isla stands strong, her eyes a mix of sorrow and gratitude. I can feel the weight of her grief, the heaviness of loss, as each person shares their condolences for her father. The priest, a figure of solemn reassurance, guides the process.

The cemetery, adorned with flowers—daisies and wildflowers, Isla's choice, becomes the final resting place for her father, laid to rest beside her mother. The simplicity of the service aligns with Isla's wishes; no wake, just a space for shared remembrances and silent reflection.

Isla, with a graceful nod, steps forward as the priest calls upon her to share a few words. The space around us settles into respectful silence, and with one reassuring squeeze from my hand, she walks up beside her father's grave.

She takes a deep breath, her eyes fixed on the earth that now envelops her father. Her voice, a mix of vulnerability and strength, carries over the gathering.

"Thank you all for being here today," Isla begins, gratitude threaded through her words. "Your presence means more than I can express. My dad... he was a man of few words but he had a heart full of love." She takes a moment, looking out over us, and a wistful smile graces her lips.

"He had this way of making even the smallest moments feel significant. From teaching me how to ride a bike to how to shoot a gun, and sharing quiet Sunday afternoons with Mum and I, his love was always there. With age, although we had grown apart, I take comfort in knowing that his love for me was always there, and mine too."

As a gentle breeze rustles through the air, she continues, "And as we say our goodbyes, let's remember those happy moments, the laughter, the wisdom that he imparted. Those moments are our shared treasures, the legacy he leaves behind. Dad, you've reunited with Mum now, and I find absolute comfort in that. Your love lives on in each of us, and as we bid you farewell, we carry your memory in our hearts."

With those final words, Isla steps back, and the priest offers a consoling nod. As she returns to stand beside me, there's an unexpected shift in the atmosphere when my father steps forward, seeking the priest's permission to share his thoughts.

"I know I'm the last person you'd expect to see up 'ere," he confesses, his tone carrying a mixture of regret and sincerity. "But I just wanted to voice my thoughts. Things... uh, didn't end too well with Callum and me. He'd been an old comrade of mine for years, and I let one damn incident blind me with resentment 'nd grudges. I'm embarrassed to admit that it took me years to finally succumb to my actions. My son, uh, opened my eyes to everythin'."

His gaze shifts to Isla, and his sincerity is evident. "Isla, I've said it before, but I'mma say it now. I'm sorry for the distress I caused, not only you, but your father. Deep down, he was a good man, a troubled man, but he had'a good heart. I hope he is up there now, forgivin' my actions, but I know he's probably shakin' his head and cursin' like a madman," he chuckles. "Rest easy bud."

As my father steps back, the weight of his apology lingers in the air, leaving a complex mix of emotions in its wake.

My father turns to look at me, and in the exchange, there's a silent understanding that transcends the spoken words. His nod carries a depth of acknowledgment, love, and relief. In his eyes, I find a connection that speaks volumes, and for a brief moment, the weight of our recent rifts feels a bit lighter.

As the priest announces the conclusion of the service, everyone begins to approach Isla, offering hugs, kisses, and heartfelt condolences. I watch her, noting her calm and composed demeanour, yet I can't shake the underlying nervousness. Beneath her serene exterior, I know there's a storm of emotions, and I long to know how I can help her weather it.

Despite my nerves, I find comfort in the outpouring of love and support surrounding Isla. She is not alone in her grief; she is embraced by my friends and family, who have become her own. For now, that knowledge brings me a sense of peace, knowing that she is cared for and supported, and I wouldn't have it any other way.

"Hey, I'm going to drop my parents off and then meet you at your place later, okay?" I say to Isla, a gentle smile on my face as I reassure her.

Isla nods. "Take your time. I'll be waiting," she says, her voice filled with warmth and appreciation. She places a tender kiss on my lips, and with a nod, we part ways momentarily.

As I guide my parents to my ute, they take their seats, with my mother in the front. As I drive away, she places a comforting hand on my thigh and says, "Proud of you, Xavier. You've grown up to become such an amazing man, and your father and I are proud."

"Thanks, Ma," I reply, stealing a glance at my father in the rearview mirror. He nods at me, and a swell of emotions fills my chest as we navigate through the quiet streets back home. My mother's next words catch me off guard, "She's going to need you now, the most. Be patient with her, dear."

Her words resonate deeply within me, and I vow silently to be there for Isla, to support her through whatever comes next.

As I pull up to Isla's apartment, the quiet neighbourhood wraps around me. She had texted earlier to let me know her door was unlocked, so I park my ute and make my way up. The shower's faint sound reaches my ears as I kick off my boots and enter her apartment, closing the door behind me.

In Isla's room, my eyes catch the scattered letters on her bed. These must be the ones she had mentioned. Picking up one with an envelope marked 'Isla—21 years old,' I feel a mix of curiosity and hesitation. Another envelope reads 'Isla—25 years old,' and another 'Isla—to finding love' and then there's one intriguingly titled 'To the one who stole my daughter's heart.' I furrow my brows and decide to open the latter, unfolding the paper within.

Before I have a chance to read the words, I catch the faint sound of Isla's crying coming from the bathroom. Worry fills me, and I drop the letter onto the bed and rush in to find her on the floor of the shower, her knees bunched up, head buried in them, as the water cascades down her back.

Without any hesitation, I open the shower door and step inside, under the water. Isla looks up, her eyes, puffy and glassy, staring at me. Fuck. How long has she been here like this?

I pull her into my arms, and we sit together on the shower floor, the water pouring over us. Isla's tears mix with the water, creating a heartbreaking sight. "He's really gone. He's gone, Xav—" she sobs.

I reach out and pull her into a hug, letting the water from the shower drench us both, not giving a fuck that I am now completely soaked. "I know, sweetheart, I know. It's okay. Let it out, baby."

I can feel her pain, her grief, as if it were my own. My heart breaks for her, for the loss she's experiencing. All I want to do is take away her pain, but I know I can't. All I can do is be here for her, to support her, to hold her as she grieves. And so, I hold her tighter, letting her cry, knowing that sometimes, that's all we can do.

"I love you," I murmur over and over again, my words a soft reassurance. I pepper kisses on her head, her forehead, and her cheeks, each one carrying the weight of my love and support while she sobs into my shoulder. I reach up, grabbing her shampoo bottle.

"I'm going to wash you, okay, baby?" She manages a soft nod while taking a big breath in. Gently, I lift her up from the ground, her tears mixing with the cascading water. I start to lather up her hair, my fingers working through the strands, massaging her scalp as the suds form.

The water washes away the soap, and I grab her sponge and body wash. With careful hands, I start cleaning her body, making sure to cover every inch. The tension in her body begins to ease as I massage the soap into her skin, offering comfort through the simple act of caring for her. Together, we share this intimate moment, where words are unnecessary, and the healing power of touch speaks volumes.

Once her body has been thoroughly cleaned, she turns to look at me. Wrapping her hands around my neck, she grabs onto my now wet hair and says, "I love you so much."

"Me too, baby," I reply, capturing her mouth with mine.

As she deepens our kiss, murmuring a soft, "I need you, Xav," I respond, "I'm here, baby. Forever." I step out of the shower, discarding my now-drenched clothes, leaving a trail of wet footprints on her tiled floor.

Once I've discarded my clothes, I pick her up—our mouths now entwined together—and carry her into her bedroom. With one arm holding Isla, I grab the letters on her bed and place them on her bedside table before dropping Isla gently onto her bed. I take a towel and dry her body down, moving the towel gently, caressing her body. Her tears have ceased, replaced by an occasional sniffle. As she runs her hands through my hair, I close my eyes, savouring the sensation.

"No, I *need* you, now," she croons.

As she speaks, her voice is husky, her nose stuffy from crying. She's in a vulnerable state, and I can't help but feel torn. I don't want to take advantage of her, but at the same time, I want to help. Is this what she needs? Because, fuck, I'll do anything for this woman.

Our mouths still locked in a passionate kiss, I find myself on top of her, the intensity of the moment filling the room with a palpable heat. Breaking our kiss, Isla moves with a purpose, pushing me gently to the side. She positions herself to straddle me, hovering just above my groyne—her hands finding support on my chest.

Isla's kisses trail a heated path along my face, down my jaw, and along my neck. A low groan escapes my lips as her hips grind against my dick, and I respond by gripping the sides of her hips.

"God, Isla," I breathe out, my voice a mixture of desire and need. I'm consumed by the intensity of our connection, my hands tightening on her hips. "Wait, are you sure? We don't have to do anything, baby. Tell me you want this."

"Yes, baby, I need *you*," she whimpers. "I want this."

Baby? It's the first time I've heard her call me that, and I want to hear it every day for the rest of my life.

"I'm all yours," I say, nudging her hips upward to grab hold of my dick. I nudge it at her entrance and I'm instantly welcomed with her wet arousal. *Always so wet for me.*

I place my tip against her folds, rubbing it up and down, before guiding her hips back down to sit on me. We both groan out at the contact, and Isla moves above in a slow, tortuous rhythm, but in this instant, it's perfect. There will be plenty of time for hurried, intense sex.

I savour the moment, the deliberate slow pace allowing us to be fully present with each other. The world outside ceases to exist. Right now, it's about intimacy, it's about the two of us, joined together as one, as Isla overcomes her waves of grief and loss, relishing in the feeling of my love for her.

Our breathing entwines, her whimpers and moans blending with mine as she rides me, bringing her to the brink of her orgasm.

And when she cries out, my name escaping her lips, burying her face in my neck, I follow suit not long after, releasing my load deep inside her, where it belongs. I run my hands up and down her back as she trembles, coming down from her orgasm. And while laying on top of me, we sit like that for a while, until her body becomes limp and she rolls gently to my side.

I move quickly to grab a towel from her bathroom. As I wipe between her legs and clean her up, I hear Isla let out a soft sigh, a sign that she's reaching the brink of sleep. Laying back down beside her, I wrap her up in my arms, creating a cocoon of warmth and comfort.

"Isla," I whisper, my voice a gentle murmur.

"Mmm?" she responds, her voice sleepy and content as she rests her head on my chest.

"You okay, love?" I ask.

"Mhmm, more than okay." I continue to pepper gentle kisses on her head, tracing comforting circles along her spine with my fingertips.

"Thank you, Xav. For everything," she sighs. "I love you so much."

I tighten my embrace, planting a soft kiss on her forehead. "Always, baby. I love you more. Rest now. I've got you."

As Isla's breaths ease into a steady rhythm, the room settles into a cosy quiet—only the soft sounds of our breathing present in the room. As I lie here, enveloped in the afterglow of our post-orgasmic haze, my mind drifts back to the day Isla re-entered my life. It was a twist of fate, an unexpected turn that brought her back into my world. If Duchess hadn't fallen ill that day, leading me to the clinic and into her presence, our paths might not have crossed again. Perhaps, someday, in the vague future, but not *then*.

In that rushed, hectic moment, she became everything. Since that day, Isla has been a constant presence in my thoughts, a force that refuses to be ignored. She recreated the chaos she stirred in my high school days, but this time, it was different—more profound, more intense. Isla effortlessly upended my world at a time when I least expected it, and now, lying here, I can't help but marvel at the unpredictable beauty of our journey.

She came back into my life, sweeping me off my feet in a way I never expected—a dance of fate, a *lassoed love* that roped us together against all odds. And she's mine now.

Forever.

Epilogue

Xavier

Two Months Later

Christmas Eve has arrived, casting its enchantment over our 'annual' dinner, though this year it bears a bittersweet tinge. Around the table, the familiar faces of Bradley, Harrison, Michael, Isla, Imogen, Olivia, Amelia, and Mum and Dad sparkle with festive joy. Claire, Isla's urban-dwelling best friend, is the lone absentee, entangled in work commitments. Our gathering is animated with lively chatter, punctuated by the comforting presence of Buddy and Luna, nestled by our sides.

Amidst the festive air, my thoughts drift back to the recent loss of Isla's father, recalling the profound impact it had on her. In the weeks following the funeral, Isla was consumed by inconsolable grief, withdrawing from the world and even shunning my comfort at times, which shattered my heart. She endured days where she refused food and company, convinced she couldn't bear the pain. Through it all, I remained a steadfast pillar of support, unwavering in my devotion to her. I witnessed her struggle, her good days, and the moments when she felt utterly defeated.

I knew that unless one has experienced a loss like Isla's, they couldn't truly comprehend the depth of her sorrow. The mere thought of her father brought waves of emotion crashing over her, rendering her unable to visit her childhood home. But I never pushed her, understanding that healing takes its own time. And slowly, with our unwavering support, Isla began to emerge from the shadow of grief, stronger and more resilient than ever before.

Even amidst her own grief, Isla helped organize Bradley's birthday celebration at home, marking that old fucker's twenty-ninth birthday. We decided to avoid going out anywhere, considering what had happened the last time. Phew!

Olivia has been planning this since back in September. She's gone all out this year, with decorations on every part of the house, both inside and out. Our tree is decked out in ornaments and fairy lights. Isla and I helped her with this, although it was more like we were forced to do it, much to our initial dismay. Surprisingly, we ended up having fun.

The house feels warm and inviting, filled with the scent of Christmas spices and the sound of laughter. As we sit around the table, sharing stories and enjoying each other's company, I can't help but feel grateful for these moments of togetherness.

Harrison chuckles, "Remember that time Michael tried to cook Christmas dinner and set the kitchen on fire?"

Michael rolls his eyes. "It was one small fire, and I learned my lesson. Besides, I'm much better at telling stories than cooking."

Olivia and Imogen giggle, their faces glowing with mirth. "I still can't believe you thought salt was sugar," Olivia teases.

I smile as I recall this memory; it was around three years ago, when the boys had come for dinner and tried to help mum out with the cooking. It ended up being more of a disaster than a help, but we all had a good laugh about it afterward.

Mum chimes in, "Yes, that was quite the adventure. But we managed to salvage the dinner in the end, didn't we?"

Dad adds, "And it made for a memorable Christmas, that's for sure." His response catches me off guard. He's really stepping up, especially with Isla, and it fills me with joy. Isla hasn't just changed my world; she's brought so much warmth and happiness to everyone here, and I couldn't be more grateful. I'm so proud of her.

Isla squeezes my hand under the table, and I'm flooded with warmth and affection for her and everyone else gathered around. This is the essence of Christmas—being together, sharing stories, and crafting memories that will endure for years to come.

After dinner, we settled into the cosy living room—the excitement of Secret Santa filling the air. Outside, the cicadas were singing their evening song, while Olivia's phone pumped out Christmas tunes from the kitchen speaker. We'd all gathered—me and Isla on the recliner,

Harrison and Michael lounging on the couch, and Imogen giving Harrison the evil eye for something he said. That guy's mouth has a mind of its own, no filter whatsoever.

Olivia couldn't contain her enthusiasm and tore into her gift first, revealing a limited edition series of her favourite books.

"Oh, I saw them and I had to get them for you, Liv," Mum had confessed, earning a playful scolding from Olivia.

"Mum, you're not supposed to say who you got the present for, ugh!"

The rest of us eagerly followed suit, unwrapping our gifts with a mix of curiosity and anticipation. Bradley ended up with Michael, Harrison got me, and Liv got Bradley. Imogen, well, much to her dismay, got Harrison. With her trademark smirk and a glare pointed towards Harrison, we all watched him open his gift—unwrapping a Comedy 101 book, which left everyone in stitches.

Amelia's gift to Imogen and Isla's thoughtful present for Mum were both hits, eliciting smiles and laughter all around—Isla surprised everyone by getting Mum a limited edition cookbook she had found online.

Then there was my gift—luck had it that I got Isla. From the moment her name popped up on the spinny wheel thing, I knew exactly what I was going to get her.

Meanwhile, Dad didn't want to participate in Secret Santa, so he sat aside, watching us all open our gifts with an amused face. Mum didn't want him left out, so she surprised him with a gift—a branded t-shirt with his favourite TV show 'Yellowstone' on it.

Now, as we sit in the aftermath of opening up presents, Liv turns to Isla and says, "Well, what did you get, girl?"

Isla looks around before saying, "Uh—"

I cut her off, "Hold on, wait," and jump up to run upstairs to my room. Little Henry, the Italian greyhound from Isla's clinic, has been resting there in his fluffy bed. Katy had dropped him off this afternoon with all his essentials. I had even ordered a new collar from the local pet shop to match Luna and Buddy's, personalised with his name and a message on the back.

As I return to the living room, I carry the carefully wrapped gift in hand—well, it's more like just a blanket draped over little Henry. Thank goodness the little fella is quiet.

As Isla catches sight of Henry resting in my arms, shock etches across her face. "Henry? Is that Henry? My Henry?" she sputters out, her voice filled with disbelief. I can't help but smile at her reaction.

"Surprise," I say, my tone filled with warmth. "I thought our family needed a new little addition, so I signed some paperwork and he's now yours, well, ours. He's already made the best of friends with Old Bud and Lu."

A collective 'awww' escapes from the women in the room as Isla launches herself at me, giving me a tight hug. "Thank you, thank you, thank you," she exclaims, her voice choked with emotion.

"He has a permanent home now!"

As Henry now rests in her arms, Isla starts nuzzling him, introducing him to everyone, while also mentioning his dysplasia. "This is the best Christmas gift ever. Honestly, Xav," she says, her eyes sparkling with joy. Little does she know that this wasn't the actual gift I had planned to give her.

Amelia, who has now moved closer to the girls, stands next to Isla, pointing out Henry's collar. "Oh look, it's personalised! How cute!" she exclaims.

"Xav, this is perfect," she murmurs.

"Look at the back of it," I say, and as Isla does, engrossed in reading the two words I had engraved on the back, I drop down to one knee.

As I read the words engraved on the back—*Marry me?*—my heart skips a beat.

My eyes widen in surprise, and I look up to see Xavier, down on one knee, a small velvet box in his hand, open to reveal a beautiful ring—a gold platinum band holds a brilliant diamond, surrounded by smaller ones that, together, form a delicate, sparkling flower. The sight takes my breath away, and I find myself frozen in surprise and awe. Tears well up in my eyes as I realise what is happening.

"Xavier," I breathe, my voice filled with emotion. As I process what is happening in front of me, with everyone still standing around us, audible gasps fill the air.

I hear Harrison call out, 'Holy fuck!' and a chorus of 'awwws' coming from Olivia and Imogen. The moment is surreal, like a scene from a dream. I adjust Henry in my arms. In that unexpected moment, surrounded by gasps, Xavier locks eyes with me.

"Isla Thompson, you're everything I ever wished for, if not more," he declares, the sincerity in his voice ringing through the silent air.

As Xavier speaks, his words are like a floodgate opening, washing over me with a mix of emotions. "Xav, I—" I gasp.

My breath catches in my throat as I try to find the words to respond, but Xavier continues, cutting off my attempts.

"Two months ago, I stood by your side while you dealt with the impossible," he reveals, and my heart skips a beat. "Two months ago, when your dad woke from his coma, he shared a few words with me."

"W-what? When?" I gasp, trying to process this new information.

"After they brought your father in from his MRI, he was awake. You had stepped outside to talk with the nurse," Xavier explains gently.

"I spoke to him. Told him I wanted to marry you. He spoke only for a second, Isla, nodding his head. He'd said, '*You have my blessing, son,*' and—" Xavier's voice falters, tears welling up in his eyes. I'm stunned. This man, usually so composed and serious, is tearing up in front of my eyes, and my heart aches for him, yearning for him.

I choke out a sob. "Xav, oh my god."

He continues, his voice filled with love and admiration, "Isla, you are the strongest person I know. You inspire not just me, but everyone around you, every single day. You are everything I dreamed of, if not more. I just knew, from all those years ago, and it's something I can't explain."

He had asked my father for his blessing. The realisation hits me like a tidal wave, memories flooding back of my father's last words to Xavier that day.

"I know we didn't get off to a good start back in school," he confesses, his voice brimming with sincerity.

"And I know we haven't been together for that long, and that we still have so many things to learn about each other, but I couldn't give a damn. We have forever—the rest of our lives to spend learning about each other. Please give me that second chance to prove to you that I am no longer that young, immature prick from high school."

This earns a snort from the boys, and a smack, followed by an 'ow' from Harrison, but I don't bother to turn back and look. My gaze is locked on Xavier's, his tear-filled eyes boring into mine. Love pours from him, emanating an aura that is so magnetic. His words echo in my heart, reassuring me that our journey is just beginning.

"I love you. Marry me, Isla. Because there is nothing I want more in this world than to spend the rest of my life with you. Please, say you'll be my wife." His words hang in the air, and I'm overwhelmed with love and gratitude, my heart overflowing with emotion.

As tears stream down my face, I feel Imogen's presence from behind me. She places a hand on my shoulder, and I take her hand in mine, placing it atop of hers.

"Yes," I manage to say through a choked whisper, tears streaming down my face.

"Of course, yes. A *thousand* times, *yes*." A radiant smile breaks across his face, and he slides the ring onto my finger. The fit is perfect. He looks into my eyes, a depth of emotion reflected in his gaze.

Harrison whoops from behind us, and the girls giggle, followed by loud whistles. We both turn to look at our friends—our family—and spot Xavier's father with his thumb and forefinger in his mouth, whistling loudly. Xavier's mother, Grace, stands by his side, wiping tears from her eyes.

With a chuckle, Xavier suddenly scoops me up into his arms and twirls me around before kissing me senseless. His lips are warm and tender against mine, conveying all the love and passion he holds for me. It's a kiss filled with promises of a future together, of endless love and unwavering support. I melt into him, wrapping my arms around his neck, lost in the moment and the overwhelming emotions coursing through me.

And just like that, the boy from my high school days—surrounded by those jerks, with his dark chocolate hair and icy blue eyes—who lingered in my mind for *years*, is finally *mine*. Forever.

Seated on the lounge, I relax with my legs draped over Xavier's lap while he traces circles on them softly. We'd all changed into our matching Christmas PJs not long ago, courtesy of Imogen. Trust her to come up with that kind of festive cheer.

While everyone is engrossed in 'Home Alone' playing on the TV, Xavier taps me on my thigh, drawing my attention away from the movie. With a playful wink, he nods towards the stairs. I raise my eyebrows in playful anticipation, smirking back at him. God, I need him right now. He takes that as his cue, standing up and announcing, "Righto, I'm heading upstairs. I'm knackered."

Glancing at my phone, I see it's only 8:54 pm. I shake my head, smiling. What an idiot. Way to make it obvious.

"But it's only 9, you old fart," Olivia chimes in, checking her own phone. Sweet girl. Sometimes, she can be so naïve. My cheeks flush even harder.

"Oh, he's not going to sleep, little one," Harrison blurts out with a snort.

"Ew," Olivia makes a disgusted face, fake gagging. "Thanks a lot, Harrison."

"Yeah, like we needed that mental image," Michael adds with a wink.

"Boy, you gotta watch that mouth of yours," Xavier's dad throws in, and we all burst out laughing.

The girls dissolve into giggles, and Xavier rolls his eyes in mock exasperation.

"Right, goodnight. Merry Christmas Eve," he salutes, before pulling me up from the couch and leading me upstairs. In a hurry, I wave to everyone, and Imogen just winks at me.

As he pulls me upstairs, Xavier rushes me into his room. Before I can even take a moment to compose myself, he's on me, his lips on my jaw, peppering me with open-mouthed kisses. I respond eagerly, tangling my fingers in his hair and pulling him closer. Xavier's touch sends a wave of tingling sensation through my body, stirring every nerve.

With a soft moan, I surrender to him, my body melting into his. As he continues to shower me with kisses, Xavier whispers to me, "Fuck, I love you. I've been waiting for this all fucking night." *Me, fucking, too.*

His words send a chill racing down my back, and I pull him closer. Our lips meet, his tongue exploring mine, eliciting a deep, primal moan from deep within me. I let him guide me to his bed, our bodies moving as one. I push him to sit at the edge of the bed, and I start to peel off my clothes—starting with my shirt, leaving my chest bare for him, instantly. I watch as his eyes darken, as I move onto my shorts, shimmying them down my thighs, leaving in just my pink lace g-string. I sway my hips slightly, letting my hands trail down my chest, thighs before hooking into the waistband of my underwear.

"Don't tease me, Isla," he growls. "Take them off. Show that perfect pussy of yours."

This newfound confidence of mine is in full swing, and I have no one to blame but Xavier. In a good way, of course. He's made me realise that my body, with all its rolls, dips, curves, and cellulite, is beautiful just the way it is. And knowing that Xavier loves me exactly as I am is enough for me.

I do as he says, pulling my underwear down my thighs, revealing to him my glistening pussy. I can feel the wetness pooling between my thighs. This is what he does to me, without any doubt.

"God, Isla," he murmurs, breathless. "You're fucking perfection." He leans back on one arm, stretching out his thighs, adjusting to his growing bulge. He palms his erection through his shorts, probably trying to reduce the ache, and I watch him with pure satisfaction.

"Take your cock out," I urge, and his eyes widen a fraction—no doubt surprised at my boldness. *Not gonna lie, I am too.*

"Yes, ma'am," he drawls, before sliding his shorts down his thighs, revealing his hardened cock, glistening at the tip with his pre cum. He grabs hold of it, pumping it once, twice, and I salivate at the mouth.

"You like watching me play with my cock, huh?" I nod.

"Play with those perfect titties of yours while you watch, baby," he says in a low murmur, and I do as I'm told. I lift my hands to gently caress my boobs. His eyes are glued to me—his hand still pumping that monstrous cock of his.

He emits a low groan, pumping harder now and in the moment, I let my hands drift lower, to rub my now sensitive clit. "Oh, fuck." He groans.

"Slip a finger inside. Show me how wet my girl is for me." *Oh boy.* Just when I thought I couldn't be any more turned on, I am now. I slip a finger inside and it glides easily through my folds. So slippery—fuck, I'm so wet.

"Such a good girl," he breathes. "So good at listening. Now add in another." And I do, moving them both in and out slowly. A growl erupts deep from his chest.

"Show me, baby. Bring those fingers here." Slipping my now saturated fingers out, I move closer to him, pressing my body against his. With a teasing smile, I place my fingers into his mouth.

He moans softly at the taste, murmuring, "So sweet. Perfect." Xavier grabs the back of my neck, pulling me closer, and our lips meet in a hungry, passionate kiss.

He murmurs against my mouth, "Taste yourself," before guiding my hand to his cock. "Feel what you do to me," he whispers, his voice husky with desire. "This is all yours."

"Mine." I moan against his mouth.

"Damn fucking right, baby. Forever."

He trails kisses down my jawline, trailing further onto my neck, before sucking onto the sensitive skin there, no doubt leaving a mark. Fuck it. I'm too aroused right now to care about a hickey.

"I'm a patient man, but when it comes to you, I'm a goner." *Oh my.*

"I need to fuck you." He growls. "No, I need to fuck my *fiancé.*"

Bloody hell, it seems now I'm impatient too. I waste no time, seizing his cock with a firm grip, a low moan escaping my lips. He groans in response, his desire mirroring mine. I love hearing the word, fiancé slip from his lips. And to think that soon, I'll be his *wife.* I give him a few pumps and he meets each movement with a thrust of his hips.

His breath swirls against my skin. "You have no idea how much I need you, Isla."

I tilt my head against his, my hand moving to cup the back of his head, holding him tightly to me. "I need you, too," I whisper.

Abruptly, he stands, his cock leaving my grip as he grabs a fistful of my hair—tilting my head to look up at him. "Get on the bed. Now," he commands. "Spread those legs for me."

"Anything for you, cowboy," I murmur with a smirk, before hopping on the bed and doing as I'm told. He swiftly sheds the rest of his clothing before joining me on the bed, hovering above me. I lift my thighs, wrapping them around his midsection.

"I love you so much," he whispers.

"Say it again?" I urge, craving the reassurance.

"I fucking love you, Isla Mitchell," he declares with a smirk. His words wash over me like a warm embrace. "And I'll say it again, and again, and never get tired of it."

My heart swells at the mention of his last name—*Isla Mitchell*. It sounds like music to my ears, resonating with a sense of belonging and love. At this moment, I realise he's not just giving me his last name. He's giving me a home. A new family of our own.

His mouth finds mine, soft and gentle, as he lines himself up and slowly pushes into me. Our lips part, gasping against each other, as we hold eye contact, and the sensation is incredible. He maintains a slow, steady rhythm, our bodies moving in sync. Then he shifts, leaning up on his elbows to gain better leverage. His pace quickens, and he uses more force.

He circles his hand around the base of my throat, completely lost in the moment. He pounds into me, almost punishing, my tits bouncing with every intentional thrust.

Xavier continues his relentless movements, grinding and rolling. Everything feels heightened, and I feel my eyes roll back into my head from the pleasure. He fits inside me like a glove, gliding against my walls in the most incredible way.

He tightens his grip on my throat, and I whimper with need. Leaning down, he takes one of my nipples in my mouth. Fuck, fuck, I'm getting close, and I know he is too, because his breathing quickens.

"You feel so good," I cry out—I can feel my body begin to quiver and shake.

"Fuck, Isla. I'm not going to last long," he groans before pulling out and flipping me around so I'm on my stomach, lying flat. He grabs a pillow from beside him and slides it underneath my stomach, so my ass is propped up in the air. *Oh. This is new.* It's like doggy-style but *different.*

A sharp crack echoes in the room as he slaps my ass cheek, sending a sudden jolt of pain through me—but fuck, it feels good. He repeats the action on the other cheek, this time with even more intensity.

"I fucking love this ass." He lets out a loud, deep groan, then grabs a handful of my ass, giving it a playful shake so it jiggles in his palm. I laugh softly, the sound mingling with his own.

Then, with a fistful of my hair, he positions himself behind and plunges in deep. *Oh. My. Fucking. God.* This position is just... he seats himself so deep—I swear I can feel him in my stomach. I cry out in pure ecstasy.

"Jesus Christ," he groans, but doesn't move. I need the friction, like right *now*.

"Xav?" I whisper, my voice barely audible.

"Yeah, baby?" he responds, his voice strained.

"I need you to fuck me hard, right now. Please." He chuckles at my admission. This is not a laughing matter now—this is serious. I rock back onto him, craving his touch, urging him to move.

"Fuck, but you just feel—" he begins, but I cut him off.

"Now, Xavier!" I whimper, desperation evident in my voice as I yearn for release.

With a deep growl, he seizes the front of my throat, lifting my head and exerting a gentle pressure that sets my nerves ablaze. The amusement between us shifts into something more primal.

"Then beg for me," he demands, desire dripping from his words. "Tell me how much you need my cock, Isla." A whimper escapes my lips as I respond to his dominance, my body arching off the mattress, craving more of him.

"Please, Xavier," I plead, unable to hold back. "I need you to fuck me." And with that, he pulls back out thrusts in deep, again. His thrusts are hard. Punishing. The base of my spine is buzzing, ready to come.

"Oh my... fuck," I murmur. "Right there. Don't stop, Xav. Please, don't stop."

"Come, baby. Come all over me."

He doesn't stop. The sound of his skin slapping onto mine fills the room as he continues the same unrelenting pace. Finally, I fall apart, my body succumbing to the waves of orgasmic bliss, every muscle tensing and releasing in uncontrollable spasms.

He leans forward, capturing my lips in a searing kiss as he thrusts into me, his movements becoming more urgent. I can feel my pussy pulsating around him, and with a loud groan, he finds release, his climax echoing mine.

"I love you," he murmurs between heavy breaths, his arms enveloping me in a comforting embrace, his lips brushing against mine.

"I love you, too." I manage to whisper back, my voice barely audible as we both bask in the aftermath of our shared ecstasy. We linger in silence for a few precious moments, savouring the intimacy of our connection as we gradually come down from our highs.

As he gently pulls out from me and pads quietly into his ensuite to grab a towel, I feel his hot cum drip onto my thigh as I shift to my side.

Turning the lights off, he comes back to me, cleaning me up with tender care before discarding the towel on the floor. Moving up onto the bed, he pulls the covers over us both.

Xavier's body envelops mine, his warmth instantly surrounding me. I sigh in pure relaxation, feeling completely at peace in his arms.

"Do you think we were too loud?" I ask, anxiety kicking in. *Fuck, I hope we weren't.*

"Who cares?" he responds, a mischievous glint in his eyes.

I shoot him a playful glare. "Well, if anyone complains, I'm blaming you. You're the one who can't keep quiet."

He chuckles, pulling me closer. "Hey, it's not my fault you're so irresistible."

I roll my eyes, unable to suppress a giggle. "Right, blame it on me."

He chuckles back, nuzzling his face into my hair, his warmth enveloping me.

As I lay there, enveloped in Xavier's embrace, a contented smile plays on my lips as I reflect on the events of the evening. From the warmth of our Christmas Eve dinner to the joy of exchanging gifts, every moment had been perfect. But the highlight, the one that still feels like a dream, was his proposal. It's a moment I'll cherish forever, a beautiful beginning to our journey together.

I lift my hand up, admiring the ring he gave me. It glistens under the moonlight streaming through his large windows. The shape, in the form of a flower, catches my eye.

"It's beautiful," I murmur, turning to him. "How did you choose this one?" He smiles, gently tracing his finger along the band.

"I'll admit, Brad helped me out a bit. We looked at so many, but when I saw this one, I knew it was the one for you. Your love for daisies inspired me, and I wanted it to reflect that."

I gaze at the ring, feeling overwhelmed with emotion. It's more than just a piece of jewellery; It's unique, just like our love. Perfect.

Xavier's touch is gentle as he lifts my hand to his lips, kissing the finger where the ring sits. It's a simple gesture, but it speaks volumes of his love and devotion.

Feeling tired but content, I yawn softly as Xavier wraps his arms around me, his warmth comforting.

"Sleep, my love," he whispers softly, his words like a soothing melody. "I love you," he adds, pressing a tender kiss to my forehead.

In my sleepy haze, I mumble, "Mmm... love you." And with a heart full of gratitude for the love and joy in my life, I drift off to sleep.

Extended Epilogue

Xavier

FEBRUARY

In the months following Christmas, Isla had summoned the courage to sell her apartment, marking a significant milestone in our journey together. With her official move back into her family home, following her dad's passing, I joined her by officially moving in not long after.

Amidst managing the family farm, I devoted my spare time to renovating the house, tackling projects like fixing old foundations, fencing, and refurbishing the shed out back. I enlisted the help of Bradley, Harrison, and Michael to redo the pavements out front and replace all the timber flooring. Though there were still major remodelling tasks on the horizon, we were in no rush. After all, we had forever.

Now, I stand at the altar, my heart racing as I take in the sight before me. The makeshift arch, lovingly crafted by Olivia and Amelia, frames our intimate gathering perfectly. Isla and I agreed on a small, intimate wedding, surrounded by only our closest family and friends. The guests, a mix of neighbours, Harrison and Michael's family, Imogen's parents, Claire, Isla's work friends, Molly and Katy with her husband, and a few of Bradley's work friends, create a warm and familiar atmosphere.

Beside me stands Bradley, Harrison, and Michael, the three men I've chosen to stand by my side on this momentous day. The thought of it all being real, of it being our wedding day, feels surreal to me. As Imogen, Claire, and Olivia walk down the aisle to join us, the celebrant instructs everyone to stand.

Tennessee Whiskey, a rendition by another artist, fills the air, its soulful melody wrapping around me. A tingling sensation spreads throughout my body, amplifying the significance of this moment.

I recall the boys' bets from this morning, their doubts about whether I'd cry during the ceremony. I had been adamant then, but as I watch Isla walk down the aisle with my father by her side, the sight of two of my most respected people together, hand in hand, overwhelms me. Just the sight of her knocks the breath out of my lungs. My eyes start to well up as the lyrics of the song filter through my mind.

But you rescued me from reachin' for the bottom and brought me back from being too far gone. The words resonate deeply with me, reflecting our journey and the profound impact Isla has had on my life. She is my rock, my guiding light, my love.

You're as smooth as Tennessee whiskey,
you're as sweet as strawberry wine,

you're as warm as a glass of brandy, and honey,

I stay stoned on your love all the time.

As I reminisce on our time together, every moment, every laugh, every tear, floods my mind, bringing all my emotions to the surface. In this instant, watching Isla walk towards me, I know with absolute certainty that I am exactly where I am meant to be.

As I wipe at my eyes, trying to compose myself, I hear Harrison's voice next to me, teasing, "Looks like the boys won their bets, eh?" Michael snorts, and I can't help but chuckle through my tears.

Bradley, always the supportive one, pats me on the back, resting his hand on my shoulder. Their presence, their support, grounds me in this moment of overwhelming emotion.

I steal a glance back at Isla, her eyes now locked on mine, a mixture of love and happiness shining through her tears. Seeing her, so beautiful and radiant, walking towards me, fills me with a sense of awe and gratitude. I never imagined I could be so lucky, so blessed, to have her in my life.

She's wearing a figure-hugging lace dress, accentuating the curves that I love *and* worship, with a long trail at the back. Her veil rests over her head, and over her shoulders her hair falls in loose waves. In her hands, she carries a bouquet of daisies and wildflowers, her mum's once favourite, and now hers. She looks like a vision, a dream come true, and I can't believe she's about to become my *wife*.

As she finally reaches me, I clear my throat, trying to compose myself. My father steps forward, lifting her veil over her head and planting a gentle kiss on her cheek. From where I'm standing, I can see Isla's eyes, blurred with unshed tears.

My father whispers something into her ear, and they both smile softly, sharing a moment that I know will stay with us forever. He then turns her to face me, and as our eyes meet, I feel a rush of emotion unlike anything I've ever experienced. This is it, the moment I've been waiting for, the moment when I promise myself to Isla, for all eternity.

Isla turns to face me, and I grab hold of her hands, looking into each other's eyes. I whisper out, "Hi," and she replies with the same, "Hi."

We share a smile, a moment of quiet connection, before turning to face the celebrant. The celebrant begins his speech, his voice gentle yet firm, filling the air with warmth.

"Dear friends and family, we are gathered here today to celebrate the union of Xavier and Isla in marriage. Today is a celebration of love, of commitment, and of two souls joining together as one.

"As Xavier and Isla stand before us, they do so with hearts full of love and devotion. They have chosen to take this step together, to embark on a journey of love and partnership, promising to support each other through all the joys and challenges that life may bring. As they exchange their vows and rings, let us all bear witness to the love that they share, and let us all offer our support and encouragement as they begin this new chapter in their lives together."

The celebrant pauses, then adds, "Xavier and Isla have decided to share their own personal vows with each other. Isla, would you please go first?"

As Isla's shaky yet feminine voice fills the air with her vows, I feel my heart swell with emotion. Her words are like music to my ears, each one resonating deeply within me.

"Xavier, from the moment I met you, I knew there was something special about you. You have shown me what it means to be truly loved, cherished, and supported. You are my rock, my best friend, and my soulmate. I promise to stand by your side, to support you, and to love you unconditionally, for all the days of my life."

She pauses, as if reflecting on the twists and turns that brought us together. "If it weren't for the clinic shutting down, looking for new management, our paths probably wouldn't have crossed again. Fate most definitely brought us back together, although not on great terms to start off with," she adds with a chuckle, earning laughter from our friends and me.

"The day you stormed back into my life, with that damn cowboy hat, permanent scowl, 'n all, will be one that I'll never forget." She looks up at me with a smile, and suddenly, it's like I can't breathe.

She continues, her voice quivering with emotion, "We've come a long way since high school, and for years after, you'd intruded on my thoughts. Never in my life did I think I'd be standing here today. Yet here we are." She takes a deep breath.

"I know my parents are looking down on me, proud of everything that I have achieved, and proud of the man that I have found. Mum would have absolutely adored you, and I know for a fact that my fath—" She pauses, her voice cracking. I urge her to continue, saying, "It's okay, baby."

"My f-father would have taken you in as his own. He gave you his blessing, and that's all I need to know that he loved you. You've been by my side through the worst of things, and I appreciate you in ways words can't describe. But I look forward to showing you, for the rest of our lives. Love you, cowboy."

Her words bring a smile to my lips. Her mention of high school brings back a flood of memories, reminding me of how far we've come together. I squeeze her hands gently, inhaling a shaky breath while mouthing the words *I love you* back to her.

As Isla finishes her vows, whistles break out from the crowd, and I notice the girls behind her wiping at their eyes. Tears slip from my own eyes, and I blink them away, but Isla reaches up to wipe them for me. A small laugh ripples through the crowd, and I hear Harrison behind me mutter, "Sappy fuck," earning a smirk from me.

The celebrant acknowledges Isla's words with a nod before turning to face me. "Xavier, it's now your turn to share your vows with Isla," he says, urging me to continue. As I stand before our loved ones, I inhale and exhale, feeling a surge of emotions.

Clearing my throat, I begin, "Shit. How do I beat that?" I say with a laugh, and the crowd follows suit. I clear my throat.

"A while ago, I stumbled upon some letters, including this one," I explain, holding up the letter from Isla's mother. "And, unashamedly, I took it," I admit with a sheepish grin, glancing up at Isla. Her reaction is a small gasp.

"Sorry, babe," I apologise, prompting a huff of laughter from Isla. She whispers back, "Omg, I hadn't even checked to see if it was still there," shaking her head with embarrassment.

I take a deep breath, my eyes shining with emotion. "But in all seriousness, this letter, it means the world to me, and I can only imagine what it means for Isla. These letters... they are a testament to the love and support that Cheryl, Isla's mother, has for her, and I promise to cherish and protect that love for as long as I live."

I blow out a nervous breath and begin.

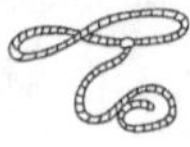

Oh. My. God.

As I stand before Xavier, watching him hold the letter in his hands—a letter from my mother that I have in fact, not yet read—a wave of nervousness washes over me. My body shakes with anxiety, my heart racing as I wonder what the letter says. I had tucked it away, intending to read it when the time felt right, but now, faced with Xavier holding it out to me, the time has come sooner than I expected.

How did he find it? How did he remember? These thoughts race through my mind, mingling with a sense of gratitude for his thoughtfulness. It's just like him to surprise me in the most thoughtful ways, to remember even the smallest details. As I take a deep breath, I look up to the sky, imagining my mum and dad looking down on me from heaven.

"*Hi, Mum. Hi, Dad,*" I whisper in my head. "*Look at me now, huh? I love you both so much. Thank you.*"

The words bring me a sense of peace, a connection to them at this moment. I look up at Xavier, and he gives me a reassuring smile. With a gentle squeeze of my hand, he signals that everything will be okay. I take a deep breath, trying to calm my nerves, as he begins to read the words that my mother wrote. I hold on to his hand tightly, seeking comfort in his presence as I wait anxiously to hear her voice, her words, through him.

To the one who stole our daughter's heart,

I write to you with a heart overflowing with love and gratitude. Though we have never met, I know you through the love you share with my daughter, Isla. You have become a part of our family in a way that I could never have imagined, and for that, I am truly grateful.

Isla has always been a special soul, full of kindness, compassion, and love. From the moment she was born, she has brought joy and light into our lives. And now, seeing her with you, I see a happiness and a light in her that shines even brighter.

I know that loving someone means opening your heart to joy and to pain, to laughter and to tears. I know that it means being there for each other through thick and thin, through the good times and the bad. And I want you to know that I am grateful to you for being there for my daughter in ways that I could not.

Isla, with her composed demeanour and strength, often hides the depth of her emotions. But underneath that composed exterior lies a heart of gold, capable of experiencing love in its purest form. Please guard her heart with your life, and in turn, she'll do the same for you. As you embark on this journey together, I want you to know that you have our blessing, from both Callum and I.

I may no longer be with you in the physical world, but my spirit is with you always, watching over you, guiding you, and cheering you on. We both love Isla and you with all of our hearts.

Take care of each other, cherish every moment, and never forget the love that brought you together. And know that wherever life may take you, my love will always be with you, a guiding light in the darkness, a warm embrace in times of need.

With all my love,

Cheryl Thompson.

As Xavier finishes reading the letter, tears stream down my face uncontrollably. I'm a crying mess, my sobs echoing around us—I don't give a fuck if people can hear me. Xavier pulls me into a tight hug, his arms warm and comforting around me. He places kisses on my head and whispers in my ear, "You are so loved; they love you so much. They're always with you."

He gently pulls away from me, his hands cupping my face as he wipes away my tears. The celebrant, still holding the microphone near us, looks on with empathy. Xavier reaches for the microphone, his voice steady and strong as he continues.

"Cheryl, Callum. Thank you," he says, his voice filled with emotion. "Thank you for your words, your love, and your blessings. Isla means the world to me, and I promise to cherish her, to love her with all my heart, and to always be there for her." He looks into my eyes, his gaze unwavering.

"I love *you*, Isla," he says, his voice filled with sincerity. "And I always will." I lean into his touch, feeling his love and the love of my parents surrounding me. In that moment, I know that no matter what challenges life may bring, as long as we have each other, we can face anything together.

The celebrant takes this moment to continue. "As they exchange their vows and rings, let us all bear witness to the love that we share, and let us all offer our support and encouragement as we begin this new chapter in our lives together," the celebrant's words resonate around us, a solemn promise of love and commitment.

Bradley approaches us, a box in his hands, and from it, we each take a ring—symbols of our love and promises made. As we slide the rings onto each other's fingers, a wave of emotion washes over me, knowing that these simple bands represent a lifetime of love and devotion.

"Xavier, do you take Isla to be your lawfully wedded wife, to have and to hold, from this day forward, for better or for worse, for richer or for poorer, in sickness and in health, to love and to cherish, until death do you part?"

"I do," Xavier's voice is strong, filled with conviction and love, tears streaming down his face.

"And Isla, do you take Xavier to be your lawfully wedded husband, to have and to hold, from this day forward, for better or for worse, for richer or for poorer, in sickness and in health, to love and to cherish, until death do you part?"

"I do," my voice is steady, sure, my own tears spilling down my cheeks.

"By the power vested in me, I now pronounce you husband and wife. You may now k—"

Before the celebrant can even finish his words, Xavier grabs me by my face—his touch gentle yet firm—and kisses me passionately. He bends me backward as he leans over me, our lips meeting in a moment of pure love and connection. The crowd erupts into cheers and loud whistles, the sound echoing around us. Right now, I am complete, *whole*.

Despite all the turmoil, heartbreak, and loss, surrounded by our loved ones, I can feel my parents with me, their presence a comforting embrace, their love enveloping us like a protective shield. And here, in Xavier's arms, cocooned in the warmth of his love, despite everything, I have found what I never thought I'd be able to find.

Home.

The End

Acknowledgments

Where to even begin? Taking the leap to begin my writing journey for Lassoed Love was monumental. If you had asked me this time last year if I'd be a published author, I would have laughed. It took some time to muster the courage to embark on this dream of mine, one that had lingered for so long.

Last year, I set out on an unforgettable adventure across Europe with my best friend, Georgia. Amidst the breathtaking landscapes and soul-stirring moments, I found clarity and inspiration. It was during those travels that I began to truly believe in the possibilities ahead.

And now, the reality of being a published author is beyond surreal. The journey from dream to reality has been filled with challenges and triumphs, but every step has been worth it. It most certainly wouldn't have been possible without the incredible support of so many amazing souls.

Michelle, where do I even start? Your alpha reading skills are seriously next level. Our brainstorming sessions? Total magic. We laughed, we had our 'awww' moments, and your knack for reading my words aloud? Priceless. Thank you for breathing life into this story alongside me.

To my partner, Thomas. Thank you for putting up with my long hours of writing, for patiently answering my endless stream of random questions, and for your constant support and love. You're a true champion. Love you, always.

To my best, bestest friend Georgia, and her amazing Mumma, Christine, your unwavering support and love means the world to me. I am so blessed to have you both in my life.

To my thirst trap girls, Tia and Samantha, who became the most unintentional best of friends, your comments and voice messages have lit up my days more times than I can count. Who knew that Instagram could lead to such genuine friendships?

And to my amazing booksta girlies, Brittany, Kristina, Ayla, and Mel, you all have been my cheerleaders, my sounding boards, and my sanity savers. Your encouragement and unwavering support have meant the world to me. Brittany, you're a superhero in disguise, guiding me through the trenches of publishing with your advice, wisdom and kindness.

This book holds a piece of my soul, a piece of my heart, and I hope it finds a special place in yours, too. May you connect with these characters, laugh with them, cry with them, and feel every ounce of emotion poured into these pages.

Thank you all for being a part of this incredible journey. Here's to many more adventures together.

With all my love and gratitude,

XO Elle

About the Author

Elle Mariah is a teacher turned aspiring debut Romance Author from Australia.

Growing up, her ambition was also to be able to inspire others and educate young individuals on the beauty of art and literature. For the past four years, she has successfully been able to do just that, educating young minds on the world of Creative Arts through Painting, Photography, Graphic Design and more! Recently she has embarked on this journey to put pen to paper and pursue her dream of becoming an author, where she could still continue to inspire others, although this time, through fictional worlds and characters.

Elle Mariah enjoys writing heartfelt, swoon-worthy, raw romance about extremely relatable characters with snarky humour on their journey to their happily ever afters.

Instagram: @ellemariahauthor
Website: www.authorellemariah.com